ALEXANDER

Pharaoh of Egypt

Sharon Janet Hague

Printed in the United States of America. Published by Kenton House, 2025.

ISBN: 9781991196910

Other books by the same author
Moses and Akhenaten: A Child's Tale
The Tutankhamen Friendship
The Queen Who Became King

For my grandfather

Main Characters

Macedonian Royal family
Alexander of Epirus – brother of Olympias
Alexander – son of Philip and Olympias
Arrhidaeus – Philip's son with Philinna of Larissa
Cleopatra – daughter of Philip and Olympias
Olympias – Queen of Macedonia
Philip – King of Macedonia

Philip's men
Aeropus – commander at Chaeronea, later exiled by Philip
Amyntas – son of Andromenes, brother of Polemon
Andromenes – general, father of Amyntas and Polemon
Antigonus – a commander of the Silver Shields
Antipater – general, father of Cassander
Attalus – general, son-in-law of Philip
Cleitus (the Black) – senior Macedonian officer
Demetrius – fleet admiral
Parmenion – senior general, father of Philotas and Nicanor
Polemon – Macedonian officer, son of Andromenes

Alexander's men
Cassander – general, son of Antipater, King of Macedonia after Alexander
Coenus – general, son-in-law of Parmenion
Craterus – general
Hephaestion – general, cousin of Alexander
Heraclites – cavalry officer
Meleager – cavalry officer
Nearchus – fleet admiral

Nicanor – son of Parmenion
Leonnatus – general, royal from the house of Lyncestis
Perdiccas – general, regent of the empire after Alexander
Philotas – son of Parmenion
Ptolemy – half-brother to Alexander
Seleucus – general, later creator of the Seleucid empire
Sopolis – cavalry officer, aristocrat

Friends of royals
Airlia – friend of Queen Olympias
Helen – friend of Cassander
Polymarchus – Helen's son

Mentors of Alexander
Aristotle – tutor at Mieza, philosopher
Lanike – nanny, sister of Cleitus
Leonidas – tutor, relative of Queen Olympias
Lysimachus – tutor, friend of King Philip

Greeks
Alcimachus – Greek nobleman, friend of Philip
Chares – Athenian general, fleet commander
Cressida – wife of Demosthenes
Demosthenes – Athenian statesman
Diomedes – Greek soldier at Chaeronea
Ephialtes – commander at Halicarnassus
Isocrates – a spy
Lysicles – Greek commander at Chaeronea
Memnon of Rhodes – Greek commander in the service of the Persians
Nikomache – mistress of Chares
Phoenix – instigator of Theban revolt
Prothytes – instigator of Theban revolt
Theagnes – leader of the Theban Sacred Band at Chaeronea

Themistocles – a Greek in service to Persia
Thrasybulus – commander at Halicarnassus
Timotheus – friend of Chares

Persians
Arsames – satrap of Cilicia
Artabazos – ambassador
Artaphernes – admiral
Arsites – satrap of Hellespontine Phrygia
Barsine – daughter of Artabazos, girlfriend of Alexander
Boas – a satrap
Mithridates – son-in-law of King Darius
Omares – leader of Greeks at Granicus
Orontobates – satrap of Caria
Pharnabazus – a satrap
Rheomethres – a nobleman
Rhoesaces – a nobleman
Spithridates – satrap of Lydia and Ionia
Tiribazus – a satrap

Rulers
Abdalonymos – King of Sidon
Ada – Queen of Caria
Azimilcus – King of Tyre
Batis – Governor of Gaza
Darius – King of Persia
Hegistratus – Governor of Miletus

Timeline

356 BC – Alexander's birth (20 July)

343 BC – Aristotle hired as Alexander's tutor

336 BC – Philip's assassination

334 BC – Conquest of Miletus

334 BC – Siege of Halicarnassus

333 BC – Battle of Issus

332 BC – Siege of Tyre

332 BC – Siege of Gaza

332 BC – Conquest of Egypt

Glossary

Greek gods
Apollo – god of the sun, and music
Ares – god of war
Athena – goddess of war
Demeter – goddess of the harvest
Hades – god of the underworld
Hera – Queen of the gods, Zeus' wife
Poseidon – god of the sea
Zeus – King of the gods, Hera's husband

Heroes, mythological figures
Achilles – Greek hero in the Trojan War, son of King Peleus and Thetis
Heracles – son of Zeus and Alcmene, famed for his labours under King Eurystheus
Peleus – King of Phythia, father of Achilles
Phoenix – adviser to King Peleus, teacher of Achilles
Thetis – mother of Achilles

Places
Mount Haemus – mountain in Thrace
Mount Olympus – home of the Greek gods
Mount Parnassus – location of the Temple of Apollo in Greece
Temple of Apollo, Delphi – sanctuary dedicated to Apollo on Mount Parnassus
Troy – city in Asia Minor (modern Hisarlik in Turkey) known as *Ilios* to the Greeks and *Ilium* to the Romans

Organisations
Amphictyonic League – ancient religious and political organisation of tribes, which predated the *poleis* (Greek city state). Members were forbidden to destroy the cities of other members.
Hellenic League – (see League of Corinth)
League of Corinth – federation of Greek states created under King Philip, (see Hellenic League)
Thessalian League – confederation of Thessalian tribes

Famous Greeks
Aeschylus (525 – 456 BC) – playwright
Aristotle (384 – 322 BC) – philosopher
Demosthenes (384 – 322 BC) – orator and statesman
Euripides (480 – 406 BC) – playwright
Homer (8th century BC) – poet credited with writing the *Iliad*
Pindar (518 – 438 BC) – poet whose work included the *Victory Odes*
Plato (427 – 348 BC) – philosopher
Polyidus – torsion catapult designer

Other terms
Centaur – mythical creature, half man and half horse
Chiton – robe fastened at the shoulder
Mole – large structure, used as a breakwater, pier, or a causeway separating two bodies of water.
Nestor's Cup – breakfast with ingredients of flour and egg.
Peace of Philocrates – peace treaty established in 346 BC, ending the decade-long War of Amphipolis between Macedonia and Athens. The main negotiator of the treaty was the Athenian politician, Philocrates.
Philippic – a tirade against a politician, originating from Demosthenes' speeches against King Philip.
Sacred Band of Thebes – group of three hundred elite warriors of the Theban army.
Trojan War – war fought between the Greeks and Trojans at Troy.

Literature

Iliad – poem about the Trojan War, attributed to Homer

Iphigenia at Aulis – play by Euripides

Medea – play by Euripides

Odyssey – poem about King Odysseus' voyage home after the Trojan War, attributed to Homer.

Troops

Agrianians – light infantry archers

Companion cavalry – used in battle charges, (Greek, *hetaroi*)

Foot Companions – wielders of the pike or *sarissa,* (Greek, *pezhetairoi*)

Greek allied cavalry – light cavalry, skirmishers used for scouting, (Greek, *prodromoi*)

Hypaspists – squires, shield bearers

Thessalian cavalry – elite cavalry

Contents

INTRODUCTION

1.

"Alexander! Alexander! Alexander!"

Cheering Egyptians threw flowers and perfumed water at the conquering army. Golden-haired, riding his black charger emblazoned with a white star on its forehead, King Alexander drove the crowds into a frenzy.

Acrobats tumbled merrily down the city roads, narrowly missing horses. Soldiers marched at a slow pace to avoid incidents. Drummers beat a tattoo as they cornered the last street and made their way into the town square.

The bearded and jovial half-brother of Alexander, General Ptolemy, rode with his Silver Shields. Composed of experienced veterans, the unit once fought for Alexander's father, King Philip. Even now, their eyes searched the house rooftops for concealed assassins.

Laughing heartily, Ptolemy accepted garlands, hugged women, and blessed babies. Behind him rode General Seleucus with Perdiccas, one of the king's favourites.

Peering from under his heavy hooded eyes, Seleucus was looking forward to a bath and lunch.

"You would think Ptolemy was Pharaoh," he said.

"The Egyptians love him," Perdiccas replied. "I wouldn't be surprised if he received this country as a satrapy one day."

"And you, Perdie?"

"I follow wherever Alexander goes."

"Then you would be wise to embrace Memphis. We're staying for several months."

Up ahead, more of Alexander's generals rode in the procession. At twenty-three, Lord Cassander was ruddy faced, with plump cheeks and an innocent expression which belied his sharp wit. He turned to his friend, Leonnatus, who was riding next to him.

"I may as well sheath my sword, Leo. It's of no use here."

"It's time to enjoy the parade."

Shrugging, Cassander pulled out a bag of shelled macadamia nuts. Popping several into his mouth, he offered the bag to his friend.

"It's better than Gaza," he said with his mouth full.

Grey-haired General Parmenion accompanied his sons, Philotas and Nicanor.

"Have you ever seen such a welcome?" he asked in wonder. "We're gods!"

"If only they had greeted us like this in Tyre, Father," said Philotas.

"Hear, hear," added Nicanor.

Cleitus, saviour of Alexander at the Battle of Granicus, ambled past on his horse. Sporting a red cape and polished cuirass, he drew up alongside Andromenes and his son, Philemon. All three were veterans who had served under King Philip, and they had much in common.

After a while, Cassander's adopted son, Polymarchus, joined him. Astride his white pony, the lad's face was flushed with joy. Cassander offered him some fruit from his satchel.

Leonnatus tipped his hat. "Enjoying the parade, young man?"

"It's the best day of my life!"

"There will be another when Alexander is crowned."

"But he's already King."

"Not of Egypt, yet."

"He'll be *Pharaoh*," said Cassander, biting into a pear.

"That's right, Cassie," said Leonnatus. "*Pharaoh* means *Great House*."

The child laughed.

"*Great House*?" he exclaimed. "That's silly!"

As they chatted, Ptolemy's eyes swept over the fine monuments which lined the boulevards. A decade older than Alexander's

Young Companions, he led the regiment of the Silver Shields. Once the late King Philip's elite fighters, the men were technically retired.

"Despite winning battles when it gets too tough for the young men," he muttered.

Patting his horse's neck, Ptolemy took a deep breath and composed himself. Chosen partly because of his resemblance to Macedonia's late king, it was important to appear in good spirits, especially in front of the old guard.

In the town square, Alexander's army halted to receive the adulation of the Egyptians. After a time, the young leader departed with his friends for the palace. His army continued to celebrate with drinking and feasting in the streets.

At the palace, high gates swung open to receive the conqueror, before quickly closing on the street revelry. The Macedonians followed servants along pathways through the vast gardens, until they reached the apartments which had been prepared for them.

A weary, but excited Alexander dismounted his great war-horse, Bucephalus. With his dearest friend and cousin Hephaestion, he climbed the stairs to the royal chambers. Furnished in wood and gold, with sumptuous trappings, the ceramic tile floors were polished so they shone. Painted walls depicted wildlife and strange animal-headed gods.

Alexander's oddly coloured eyes, one blue as the Egyptian skies and the other, black as night, swept the room.

"This is grander than our home," he said.

Sitting on a wooden chair inlaid with gold and semi-precious stones, he leant forward to inspect a footstool. Its designs were of Egypt's enemies, bound and standing on tiptoe. Unable to set a single foot in the Two Lands, they remained forever Pharaoh's subjects. With satisfaction, Egypt's new ruler rested his own feet on the stool.

Stewards poured wine. A royal taster sampled snacks before they were served to the group.

"I want to visit Siwa, Hephaestion," said Alexander.

"Why?"

"It has an oracle."

"Ours is at Delphi."

"Egypt has one far more ancient. Besides, to secure my legitimacy as Pharaoh, I must visit the place."

"I'll arrange it. Be prepared, he'll have questions, cousin."

"I have a question for him. If he's a true oracle, he will know the answer."

"And, if not?"

A darkness passed through Alexander's eyes. "He will know. My destiny depends on it."

***

PART I

2.

It was dawn. Palace shutters were firmly closed. Gold and pink flecked the skies. A chubby, blond-haired child stomped along the corridor.

"Nanny Lanike, I want to sing Mummy my new song."

"Where's your harp, Alexander?"

"On my bed."

The woman's eyes swept over him. "You need a bath."

"There's no time."

"At least put on a clean chiton."

Lanike led her charge to his bedroom and picked out his clothes for the day. Next, she led him to a gold basin. A silver pitcher and linen towels were stacked neatly next to it.

She poured warm water from the pitcher into the basin. Taking a towel, she soaked it and swiftly rubbed the boy's face and arms.

The prince slipped his robe over his head. His nanny adjusted the garment so it hung correctly. She shod his feet with a pair of sandals. Ready for the day, Alexander picked up his lyre and accompanied Lanike to his mother's apartments.

***

It was morning. Servants opened curtains. Maids set out fresh pomegranate juice. A silver bowl filled with fruits of the season sat on a table next to the bed.

Queen Olympias pushed back silk sheets and propped herself against the bedhead with a pillow. Half asleep, she drank the juice and picked at the fruit, wondering what the day would bring.

Yawning, she recalled that her husband, King Philip, was going into battle again. He would return with new wives. On their arrival at court, Olympias would delegate spies to garner intelligence reports. Politics, she reflected, was an unrelenting fact of life.

Rustling curtains and the thumping of small feet announced the arrival of her son. He was dressed for the day in a white chiton embroidered with a red border, denoting his status as a prince of Macedonia. In one hand, he clutched a lyre.

"What do you have there, Alex?"

"My harp, Mummy." Hopping onto the bed, he kissed her. His short legs dangled over the silk quilt. "I want to sing you a song. We learned it in music class."

"Let's hear it."

The queen straightened her posture and folded her hands on her lap. Strumming his musical instrument, Alexander closed his eyes and sang. Gold hair framed his small face. Ruddy cheeks glowed.

At the end of his song, he opened his eyes.

"Did you like it?"

Scooping her son into her arms, Olympias kissed both his cheeks. Then, she sent him outside and readied herself for the day, before joining him for breakfast on the patio.

While he ate, Alexander watched the birds, which twittered amongst the branches of the trees and bushes and occasionally flitted to the ground to retrieve the morsels he threw for them. Soon enough, it was time for school.

***

3.

A local Athenian lawyer paced the shore, getting as close to the stormy sea as possible. Waves crashed onto the rocks. Wind billowed through his robes.

"A-Ath-th-enn-en-ia-ia-ians,   M-m-mag-g-i-istrates, hear me!"

Despite the bad weather, Chares was walking with his friend, Timotheus. An ambitious man, it was the goal of Chares to be a general one day, and perhaps even command the Athenian fleet.

He caught sight of a lone figure on the shore. Berating the waves violently with his fists and shouting, the man seemed possessed.

"What on earth is that madman doing?" Chares asked.

"That's Demosthenes."

"Is his name supposed to mean something?"

"He's famous."

"But why does he have beef with Poseidon?"

"He lost his parents."

"Did his family drown?"

"His parents died here, in Athens."

"I am sorry for his loss – and his madness."

"Demosthenes is not mad. He's practicing."

"By ranting?"

"Speaking."

Chares stared hard at Timotheus. "He's yelling at the wind."

"It strengthens his voice for speeches. After the death of his parents, Demosthenes' appointed guardians stole his inheritance. He took them to court and won back his fortune with his oratory. Now, Demosthenes is one of the wealthiest men in Athens."

"I must make his acquaintance."

Chares quickened his step. Timotheus kept up with him. As they neared the orator, the latter took out a handful of marbles from his billowing robe and stuffed them into his mouth. Oblivious to anyone else's presence, he tried to talk.

Chares halted. "Another time, perhaps."

***

King Philip and his generals were in the Great Hall, planning for war. Tall and bearded, the king had one eye. He had lost the other at the siege of Methone when he was twenty-eight. His right lid was surgically stitched down over the empty cavity. However, his remaining eye burned with fire.

The men stood around a vast oak table strewn with maps. Ewers of wine rested on side tables. Everyone was drinking, while Philip paced up and down. They were in the middle of exchanging views in the frank manner of Macedonian warriors. No title was used to address the king. Considered to be the first among equals, a Macedonian monarch was treated on the same level as his senior staff.

The army's foremost general, Parmenion, stabbed a map with one thick forefinger. "Your plan is to conquer Greece, Philip!"

"I must exert tact. Athens has Thermopylae."

Cleitus, a senior Macedonian officer, scratched his short black beard. "Despite the ravings of Demosthenes, Athens is not Greece."

The king turned one bright eye on the speaker. "Athens is important and must be treated with respect. Don't forget, I am leader of the Thessalian League."

A general, by the name of Amyntas, sipped his wine. "Thessaly is not all of Greece, either."

His father, Andromenes cleared his throat "Take no notice, Philip. My son is young."

"But I agree with him," said General Aeropus. "You appear to be going in the opposite direction of your goal, Philip."

11

"Hear, hear," agreed another of Andromenes' sons, Polemon.

The king ceased pacing. He glowered.

"I claimed Perrhaebia and Magnesia," he rumbled. "In doing so, I expanded into Pagasae. My aim is to unify this region. Only then can we march into Persia."

Parmenion moved towards the king, his massive physique drawing all eyes. "Don't forget Philip, Thebes is also the heart of resistance in Greece."

"What are you implying?"

"I'm not implying anything. As your liege, I'm telling you the unvarnished truth."

"Greece will be unified, but I prefer diplomacy."

"With a sting in its tail," chuckled Cleitus.

"True," said Aeropus. "You built an army while in peaceful negotiations."

"It gave us time," said Philip.

"Now we have the best military force in the world," Parmenion added.

Attalus, an important general from lower Macedonia, raised his cup. "To mighty Philip's rule."

The assembled men raised their goblets.

"To Philip!" they roared.

***

It was evening. Demosthenes placed his marbles in a wooden drawer. Looking at his face in a mirror, he saw a batch of new lines across his forehead. His cheeks, freshly scoured by the sea air, shone in ruddy health above his close-trimmed beard.

A serving boy brought wine, figs and goat cheese. The master of the house ate and drank, after which he went to his study and sat at his desk.

He applied himself to writing a speech on the subject of Philip. The King of Macedonia, who wanted to be the tyrant of all Greece, required a strong hand to stop him. And Demosthenes was just the man.

A stuttering orphan with no rights, he had transformed himself into both an orator and barrister, who won back his inheritance from corrupt guardians appointed to him. Now that he had his independence, he was in the position to turn more than Poseidon's seas back.

He would change politics forever.

***

4.

At bedtime Alexander was tucked in between fresh sheets. His mother sat next to him.

"If I were a god, I would live on Mount Olympus at Zeus' right hand," the boy said.

Light fingers smoothed his brow.

"Where is Zeus' wife, Hera, seated?" asked Olympias.

"Next to him, on his left."

"Not on his right?"

"That's for someone else."

Hair, soft as silk, fell over Alexander's face. It was time to say goodnight. His mother kissed his smooth brow. After Olympias had left his chamber, the child closed his eyes and continued with his fantasy.

"Apollo and Heracles dine with Zeus, and my ancestor, Achilles."

A smile travelled across his chubby cheeks. He opened his eyes. Achilles! The hero of Troy, the valiant warrior, the king whose name would last for all time. A man who was a god. And yet …

"I'll beat him! I'll be on Zeus' right."

Alexander's eyes fluttered as he fell into a deep sleep.

***

While his son slumbered, King Philip schemed. He had done well for a man who was not expected to rule.

Death to his opponents – some of whom were family – mixed with luck, secured his sovereignty of Macedonia as a young man. His ascension to the throne, however, met with no interest from his neighbours. Hardly worth ruling, Macedonia was a weak nation.

Without resources, the cunning Philip had resorted to pen and parchment. Thousands of letters, over many years, secured his position as chief negotiator of peace in Greece, Illyria and Thrace.

As he wrote, the king also developed a professional army. Now, no one could compete with Macedonia on the field of battle. He was the gadfly of Greece, the despot of Macedonia, who riled Demosthenes to new heights of oratory. In fact, Philip reflected, he greatly enjoyed himself.

A sentry put his head around the door. "Generals Parmenion and Attalus, to see you."

Waiting servants were galvanised into action. They offered refreshments to the visitors. A fire in a hearth was fanned until it blazed.

Parmenion accepted a cup of wine from a royal steward. "We need to keep up with our campaign in the hill country, Philip."

"It goes without saying," Attalus agreed.

"We must attack west and north," Parmenion continued.

"And in the opposite direction of Greece," added the king, walking around the room with measured steps. "Although there is one exception to our campaign."

Picking up a handful of almonds, Parmenion crunched them between powerful jaws. "Olynthus."

"Precisely."

"We should give it a wide berth," Attalus said.

"I want the city onside," Philip declared. "At least until the others have fallen into our hands."

He continued pacing as they discussed the future of Greece.

*****

With Alexander tucked up in bed, Olympias left her quarters for the greater palace. Male voices drifted up a hallway. She heard Parmenion's deep baritone, interwoven with Attalus' fawning.

Shivering, the queen pulled her robe tighter around her head and shoulders. Walking in the opposite direction, she gave Philip's apartment a wide berth.

At the end of the corridor lay the garden. Olympias hastened her step. Suddenly, a man's silhouette appeared in front of her. "Lysimachus of Acarnania?"

"Greetings, noble Queen."

"Are you on your way to see my husband?"

"I have an appointment with the great Peleus himself."

"My husband's name is King Philip, and he has company."

"What can I say? I am a romantic when it comes to history. I'm always early for appointments. By the way, how is little Achilles?"

"Alexander grows by the day."

"Soon, he'll be a mighty warrior, storming the gates of Troy."

Olympias' mouth curved slightly. "With Peleus urging him on, no doubt."

"Do you know Phoenix was the teacher of Achilles?"

"My husband tells me you refer to yourself as such. He says you want the job of tutoring my son."

"I'm on my way to see about the position. I trust this meets with your approval?"

"My approval is not required. You do know Phoenix was not the father of Achilles, only his caretaker?"

"Your knowledge of history is impressive, my lady."

"I trust it is a fact you will remember. My son Alexander's real father is Zeus, King of the gods."

Before Lysimachus could reply, Olympias hastened away, down the garden path.

***

It was the ninth hour of the evening. King Philip dismissed his generals. The door of the hall was opened to ventilate his audience chamber. Yawning, he stretched his arms high above his head.

A few yards away from Philip, his guards chatted together. Outside in the garden, the night watchman's stick tapped up and down the pathways. Philip joined the guards, striking up an easy conversation, peppered with jokes and gossip.

The sound of rustling in the garden outside the corridor was followed by a tread. Immediately, the king swivelled round. "Ah, Lysimachus!"

"I'm not too early?"

"You're just in time." Leaving the guards, Philip beckoned his visitor inside. "I need an opinion. My generals were debating on the correct way to unify Greece. What are your thoughts?"

"Mine?"

"You're a fine soldier, as I recall."

"I'm a teacher these days."

Philip's left eye gleamed. "So you are."

"But if you must know, I would follow your orders."

"You don't have thoughts of your own?"

"My sovereign understands the Greeks. You even lived in Thebes."

"As a hostage, when I was fourteen."

"But you saw how soldiers, like those in the Theban Sacred Band, were trained, did you not?"

Philip smiled. "I did."

"And you created a professional fighting army for Macedonia."

"The best."

"It was based on what you saw in Thebes, was it not?"

"It was."

"Macedonia was a second-rate power. Now, thanks to you, we will conquer all of Greece. No one has your insight or experience. Therefore, I say if the father of the new Achilles wishes to give an order, let him."

Philip raised his goblet. "I'll drink to that. By the way, what do you teach?"

"Literature, philosophy, mathematics, and botany."

"You will instruct my son and his friends. Zeus knows, those boys need help."

***

5.

Cassander was in Prince Alexander's class. It was night, and the child was engaged in homework by the light of a study lamp.

Taking a deep breath, he opened a scroll. "Not the *Iliad* again!"

He removed his hand so that the parchment rolled up. At that moment, his mother entered the room.

"Are you doing your homework, Cassie?"

"Yes, Ma."

"I brought milk and sweets."

"Put them down. I need to concentrate. And close the door."

With his mother gone, the boy scoffed her sweet pastries, and sculled the milk. Satisfied, he blew out the lamp and went to bed.

***

Leonnatus pored over his *Iliad*. He wrote out tracts of ancient Greek phrases. Towards midnight, his lamp flickered. He put down his pen and unfurled his fingers.

At six, the boy knew how to handle a lamp. Getting up from his seat, he searched for oil. Finding a ceramic jug, he unstopped it, and poured its liquid into the bronze receptacle on his desk. Trimming a new wick, he let it float in the oil and lit it. The lamp sparked into life.

Pleased with himself, he returned to his text.

***

Having finished his mathematics homework, Perdiccas chucked a soft ball from one hand to the other. Its leather cover felt strange. He looked down and turned the ball over. The name of Leonnatus was scratched on its exterior.

Making a mental note to return the ball to its owner, he looked at his homework scroll. Sitting down, he opened it, and was pleasantly surprised.

He knew this passage of the *Iliad*. Alexander often sang it. Once, when Perdiccas asked him about its meaning, the prince had given him an expository lesson, worthy of a great tutor.

Dipping his brush in ink, the boy scribbled down explanations of the phrases with ease.

***

It was a new day. A blue sky arched above Athens. Most of its citizens were in the town square. Hundreds were getting ready to listen to Demosthenes' historic speech.

Stalls, which opened early, were already doing business. Traders from Crete, eager to cash in, set themselves up on the fringes of the gathering. They laid out their wares on dyed fabric.

Blue, red, and green scarves contrasted with jewellery of silver and gold inlaid with semi-precious stones. Bracelets, necklaces and rings gleamed in the strong morning sun. Pottery jars, painted with lively sea creatures, were displayed next to rugs and tapestries. Embroidered bodices favoured by Cretan women, lay next to polished bronze knives and cups of gold.

It was now past the ninth hour of the day. Demosthenes gargled with water and spat into a silver cup. He was ready. People left the shopkeepers' wares. Attentive, they stood in silence, awaiting the latest offering from one of the great orators of the age.

"The issue with the King of Macedonia, and against those of his supporters with us in Athens, is that he violates the terms set out in the Peace of Philocrates."

Murmurs ran through the crowd. Spectators inched forward.

***

It was breakfast time in Chares' home. He ate bread and honey, occasionally sipping a cup of milk flavoured with spices. His children munched cheese and bread, while his wife dined on thick yoghurt and gazed out the window. It was a quiet but congenial atmosphere.

Suddenly, a thunderous banging on the front door reverberated through the house. A manservant answered. Chares heard a gruff voice, and the sound of running feet. Grasping his sword, which stood propped against a corner of the hearth, he waited.

A breathless Timotheus erupted into the breakfast room. "Demosthenes is speaking in the town square!"

Chares put down his sword. "The man who rages at the sea?"

"The very same."

"What's that to me?"

"He's addressing Athens on the subject of King Philip. The entire population is out there, listening."

Chares did not wait to put on his cloak. Rushing from the house, he hurried with his friend to the square.

***

In mid peroration, Demosthenes caught sight of two men running. He turned his eyes upwards. "Athenians, there is no need to despair," he said.

Chares shoved several men away. "What's he saying?"

"Your affairs are in this evil mess," Demosthenes continued, "because you, men of Athens, utterly fail to do your duty."

Chares gave Timotheus a look. "I thought he was supposed to be railing against King Philip, not us."

Several men glared at them. "Ssh!" they hissed.

"Be quiet," whispered Timotheus. "Listen."

Folding his arms, Chares turned his gaze on the orator.

21

"Some of you have been told, others know and remember, how formidable the Spartans were –"

Chares shook his head. "He's talking about the Spartans? That was years ago."

A fat town councillor waved his fist. "Get those two out of here!"

A burly soldier was about to oblige when he recognised Chares. Immediately, he saluted.

"Sir, what may I do for you?" he asked.

"Get us up to the front – now."

Demosthenes' voice projected across the gathering. "I remind you of this, Athenians, because I want you to know that no danger can assail you while you are on your guard."

The soldier made a way through the congestion to a space in front of the speaker. Chares stood on tiptoe. Timotheus helped him up onto a nearby stone seat so he could see.

Now, Chares could both see and hear. The sun ascended further into the sky. It was close to the tenth hour of the day.

"Athenians, if any here thinks Philip is too formidable, he is right. Yet he must consider that we too, men of Athens, once held Pydna, Potidaea, and Methone."

It was going to be a long speech.

***

6.

A messenger dismounted from his exhausted horse in the royal courtyard at Pella. Standing on her balcony, Olympias was enjoying a brief spell of sunshine in a day of rain squalls. A butterfly beat its wings as it brushed her arm.

Requesting an audience with the king, the sweating rider was escorted into the presence of Philip. Roars of rage exploded across the palace grounds. A thunderclap from the heavens signalled more rain.

On Olympias' balcony, the butterfly beat its wings and soared upwards into the ivy. With a shudder, she returned indoors.

***

A breeze wafted through the crowd, rippling the speaker's robe.

"And you too, men of Athens, if you are willing ... you will consent to become your own masters, and if each man will cease to expect that, while he does nothing himself, his neighbour will do everything for him, then, God willing, you will recover your own, you will restore what has been frittered away, and you will turn the tables upon Philip."

Timotheus put his mouth to Chares' ear. "One thing I'll say for Demosthenes, he isn't afraid."

"I've noticed he has no bodyguards."

Now, the orator lifted one arm to the sky. The crowd moved forward.

"Do not believe that his present power is fixed and unchangeable like that of a god. No, men of Athens; he is a mark for the hatred and fear and envy even of those who now seem devoted to him. ... When, Athenians, will you take the necessary action? What are you waiting for?"

Timotheus, who had missed breakfast, was feeling peckish. He ducked under a soldier's arm and hurried to the nearest shop. Like everyone else in the square, the proprietor was listening to the speech.

Clearing his throat, Timotheus leaned across the counter. "A loaf of bread with a waterskin. How much?"

Without answering, the shopkeeper put the provender in a basket. He added a jar and two cups.

"What's that?" Timotheus asked.

"Beer."

"I don't need beer."

"Don't worry, it's on the house – with the food."

"Why?"

The shopkeeper raised his brows. "I serve a friend of the great Chares. Now, let me listen to our speaker. Today Demosthenes will take his place in history."

Timotheus did not argue. He took the basket and returned to his place in the crowd. Chares grasped his arm.

"Thank Zeus, you're back! Demosthenes is about to outline the battle strategy against Philip."

Placing the basket on the ground, Timotheus took the jar and poured out two cups of cool liquid. He handed one to his companion.

Demosthenes turned his shoulders directly towards them. "First then, men of Athens, I propose to equip fifty war galleys. Next, you must make up your minds to embark and sail in them yourselves, if necessary. Further, I recommend the provision of transports and other vessels, sufficient for the conveyance of half our cavalry."

Chares choked. Timotheus patted his friend's back. "It's an orator's technique. Demosthenes appears to be personally addressing you, but he can't see for the sun."

"I don't care about his speech technique," Chares gasped. "It's his ideas!"

Demosthenes now faced the other side of the crowd. His voice rang out as clear as a bell.

"In addition to this, Athenians, I propose that you should get ready a corps to carry on a continuous war of annoyance against Philip."

Chares wiped his mouth and took another sip of beer. "A war of annoyance? Is that what he calls outright confrontation with Macedonia?"

"It will give you a chance to lead our fleet," Timotheus said.

"Taking on Philip will be akin to a gadfly attacking a bull – a very angry one at that."

Demosthenes took a breath. The crowd did so as well. He continued: "Not an imposing army – on paper – of ten or twenty thousand mercenaries! It shall be a real Athenian contingent, and whether you appoint one general or more, whether it is this man or that or the other, him it shall strictly follow and obey. I also urge you to provide for its maintenance."

Chares bent his head towards Timotheus. "How are we going to afford this?"

"It's only an idea, although Demosthenes probably knows what our city coffers hold. Be prepared – your dream of being a fleet commander is not far away."

Chares sat down on a broken marble step. "I'm going to faint."

***

7.

Parmenion's family was at lunch on a warm afternoon. During dessert, a royal messenger was admitted to the patio. He approached the general and his wife, who were both eating watermelon. The messenger handed over a letter and departed. Taking a deep breath, Parmenion broke the seal.

His wife put down her slice of watermelon. "What is it, dear?"

"A royal summons."

Most of the children continued chatting. They were accustomed to their father being summoned by the palace. One of them, however, was watching Parmenion.

"Papa, am I allowed to come?"

"Not this time, Philotas."

Parmenion's daughters finished their fruit and went into the house to put their own children to bed for an afternoon nap. Meanwhile, their brothers and husbands moved to the garden, where they drank wine under the hibiscus bushes. With a sigh, Philotas joined them.

The general's wife leaned forward. "Is it an invitation to attend a war council, dearest?"

"The letter does not say."

"Do you think someone died?"

"All I know is Philip needs me. I'll leave in the morning."

Parmenion kissed his wife on the cheek and went upstairs to wash in preparation for the evening's activities. For her part, the lady of the house wrapped her stole about her and joined their family in the garden.

***

Descending from the podium, Demosthenes was aware of his raging thirst. He hailed a water boy, who immediately ran to him. The child dipped a wooden cup into his pail and handed it to the speaker.

Quaffing the cool liquid, Demosthenes handed the cup back. "Nothing sweeter than Athenian water," he declared.

A slim bronzed man stood before him. "My name is Chares."

"I've heard of you."

"You made a great speech."

"Then, I've failed. Words mean nothing unless there is action. I exhorted Athens to prevent the wolf in our hills from attacking our fold. Athens must do something now, before it's too late."

"I am a general who intends to be Admiral of the Athenian fleet one day. I will lead us against Philip."

"You'd better have your wits about you. King Philip intends to crush us." Demosthenes' eyes followed the water boy.

"I hope we have the opportunity to speak again," said Chares.

Inclining his head, he left the orator and walked back to Timotheus. After a few steps, he turned his head round to see Demosthenes catch up to the boy. Draining cup after cup of his water, he afterwards pressed a few coins into the lad's hand. Judging by the child's expression, it was a generous recompense.

***

Olympias reflected that the entire palace could hear her husband.

"That man is a lunatic!" Philip roared from his office.

Parmenion rubbed his brow. He was beginning to suffer from a headache. "It's only a speech. You know what he's like. Demosthenes needs an enemy. It gives him publicity."

"He's Athenian after all," Aeropus added.

Philip turned his one good eye on his generals. "Have you nothing worthwhile to say? After all that I pay you? Your lands and holdings are more than mine."

"Our sovereign is most generous," Attalus replied.

Philip did not answer. Instead, he sat down. No one said anything.

"This is not simply a rant," the disgruntled king explained, after a while. "Messengers came to me yesterday. Demosthenes has a war plan."

"What is it?" Parmenion asked.

"A naval fleet of fifty galleys bearing two thousand Greeks. Attached to the infantry will be two hundred cavalry, with cavalry transports provided. There are also mercenaries."

"Is that all?"

"Ten fast-sailing war ships."

"Anything else?"

"I have a transcript of the speech. You will all receive a copy." Philip rose. "Demosthenes is more than an orator. He intends to fight on the battlefield."

The generals glanced at each other. Nervous tension pervaded the atmosphere. Parmenion scratched his whiskers.

"That could mean motivated troops," he said.

"Precisely!"

Philip threw his cloak around him and stormed out of the meeting.

***

<h1 style="text-align:center">8.</h1>

On a fine spring morning, King Philip arrived at the door of Queen Olympias' apartment. His wife was combing her long golden hair. When her locks caught the sun they glinted red. She hummed a pretty song. He remembered the tune from the days of their courtship.

"I'd forgotten how young you are."

"Why are you here?"

"Is that any way to greet your husband?"

"I haven't seen you in a year."

Has it been that long? Philip regarded his feet, and then remembered. "It's about the boy."

"You mean our *son*, Alexander."

"I'm appointing Lysimachus as his tutor."

"And you want my approval?"

"I want you to tell me if you think he's suitable."

Olympias put the brush down. Winding a gold filagree around her hair, she bound it in place.

"This is the same Lysimachus who calls you *Phoenix* and Alexander *Achilles*?" she asked.

"He's a learned man and the right choice."

"He behaves like a common flatterer."

"Then propose a solution, my dear."

"I will approve Lysimachus on condition that I also recommend a teacher."

"Who do you have in mind?"

"Leonidas."

"Your cousin? I don't want my boy mollycoddled! Alexander gets enough of that from you."

"Leonidas is a disciplinarian. He won't be soft on our son. Speak to him about his teaching methods, if you wish."

Philip mulled over her words. Finally, he looked her in the eye.

"A teacher from both parents sounds fair," he said.

Without further ado, he departed. Olympias walked to the enormous window overlooking the garden. She hummed a tune. Bees buzzed lazily in the heat, carrying great gobs of pollen from flower to flower. Gardeners dug trenches for compost and watered the latest additions to Philip's shrubs.

For a warrior, he was more botanically minded than most. As his wife, the garden was a perfect haven to be enjoyed. Olympias continued humming.

***

In his office, Philip waited. After a turn of the sun dial, a sentry banged his spear on the ground. "Pausanias of the royal bodyguard to see the King of Macedonia!"

A tall man, in a long robe, entered and bowed. He waited for his sovereign to speak.

"My son is to have two teachers. I want you to check the credentials of one, Leonidas. He teaches in a school, close to the palace."

A puzzled expression crossed the man's face. "Leonidas is Queen Olympias' cousin."

"He is."

"But why would Prince Arrhidaeus require one of her kinsmen for his education?"

"I'm talking about Alexander."

"With respect, Olympias is your fourth wife."

"And Queen because of Alexander's birth. You weren't at the wedding, as I recall."

"I didn't approve of her. I still don't."

"Why would you? She's a dangerous woman."

"Arrhidaeus is your first born with another, and may I say, more compliant wife."

"He's also retarded. I need potential successors who aren't idiots." Philip handed his bodyguard a piece of parchment. "Leonidas' school is a block away from the palace. Find out what sort of man he is and how he trains his pupils."

Pausanias bowed and slipped away. Philip poured a drink and sat at his desk. He still had to devise a battle strategy against the Illyrians.

***

9.

It was a new term in a new school. Alexander entered his classroom and took a seat at the front. His companions were awaiting the arrival of their teacher. Most of them were on the floor, playing knucklebones.

Cassander threw the prince a look of contempt. "You're late, Alex."

"It's *Prince* to you, Cassie." Alexander looked about. "Where's Lysimachus?"

Hephaestion chuckled. "The teacher is later than you, cousin."

Squatting on the floor with the others, he rolled the bones. Alexander stayed in his seat. He squinted at the sun dial outside. "It's already eight."

"Don't worry about it, Alex," said Hephaestion. "Come, have a game with us. It'll pass the time."

"I want to be prepared for the new term. I must say, this isn't a good start."

Cassander threw a handful of knucklebones.

"Maybe Baldy slept in," he snickered.

Perdiccas picked up the pieces. "Don't be an idiot, Cassie. The new teacher has hair."

"Stop name calling, Perdie. We all know you're illegitimate."

"And you're a troublemaker. There's a reason why our last teacher retired."

"Is that – er – an insinuation?"

Cassander chuckled at his use of a big word. Rolling his eyes, Perdiccas threw the bones.

A lanky youth, carrying a scroll, entered the class. Over a decade older than the children, everyone recognised him as Alexander's half-brother, Ptolemy.

"Lysimachus is with the headmaster," he said. "He asks you to take out your copies of the *Iliad*. You are reading about Hector."

Alexander straightened his posture and pulled out a scroll.

"Are you taking the class, Ptolemy?" he asked.

"I'm here to supervise. The headmaster is having a word with Lysimachus. Apparently, your last teacher had to leave."

"Not on my account," Alexander said. "I've read the *Iliad* nine times."

Cassander snorted. "Alexander committed it to memory in the first week."

Ptolemy fixed his attention on the child. Seated on the floor with his companions among the knucklebones, he looked like their ringleader.

"Thank you for your input, Cassander. Who knows, one day you too, might memorise it? For now, take your seat."

The boy turned bright crimson. Alexander opened his scroll.

"It's a wonderful story," he enthused. "Every time you read it, there is something new to discover."

"Agreed," Ptolemy said. "Now, everyone get back to your seats before your teacher arrives. He's better than the last one. You will all like him."

Reluctantly, Cassander pulled out his text. Perdiccas packed away the knucklebones and rummaged around in his satchel for his scroll of the famous poem. Hephaestion took a seat next to Alexander. He put a protective arm around his cousin's waist.

"Alex sings passages of the *Iliad* on his lyre," he announced with pride.

"I've heard him," said Ptolemy.

Alexander noticed the older boy held a worn scroll.

"Is that yours, brother?" he asked.

"It's mine. I take it with me everywhere."

"You must like it a lot."

"It has much to teach."

While the brothers talked, Perdiccas found his text. Wiping off smears of egg and flour from the Nestor's Cup he had eaten for breakfast, he started to read. Cassander pored over his copy, occasionally giving a rebellious yawn. Leonnatus was fascinated with the verse, pausing to sigh with inexpressible joy at passages which resonated with his heart.

Ptolemy found it easy to supervise the boys as they read to themselves. Absorbing the poetry of brave deeds from bygone heroes, they were transported to another world.

At last, Lysimachus arrived. His hair was carefully combed, and he was carrying an assortment of scrolls. "You may go back to your horse-riding class, Ptolemy."

Cassander pulled a face. "Meanwhile, we're all stuck here with Homer."

"Be quiet," said Perdiccas. "Ptolemy is older than us. He has different things to learn."

"Besides, he knows the *Iliad* by heart," Lysimachus said.

An evil smile curved the upper ends of Cassander's mouth. "So does Alexander."

"I gather you don't."

The boys tittered. Cassander turned the colour of a ripe plum.

"I told you to keep quiet," whispered Perdiccas. "Now, he's embarrassed you."

Lysimachus picked up a scroll.

"There's no shame in speaking," he said. "However, we are here to study, not tear our betters down. I shall read the first page of Hector's demise. Listen to the rhythm of the poetry. Then, you are all to copy an exercise I set."

***

10.

A new harpist caught Attalus' eye. Every time the Macedonian war machine penetrated new territories, the house help improved. Other generals milled about, accepting wine from the stewards and hot pastries from scantily clad serving girls.

Known for his self-discipline, Parmenion averted his eyes from the women. Aeropus gawked shamelessly. In a corner, Cleitus chatted to one-eyed Antigonus and General Antipater. General Andromenes kept his eye on his sons Amyntas and Poleman.

At his large oak table, Philip hunched over a map.

"We attack Olynthus," he declared.

Aeropus, accepted a savoury from one of the serving girls. "Athens is a friend to that city."

"And blocked by Euboea," Philip countered. "There's a revolt there. No Athenian troops will be sent to Olynthus."

Parmenion nodded. "We should make a start."

"I agree," said General Andromenes. His sons, who stood next to him, made appropriate noises.

"Aren't your brothers there, Philip?" asked Aeropus.

The king's left eye flickered. "Half-brothers."

"They are a threat to the Macedonian throne," Attalus pointed out.

"But they are your blood," Aeropus protested.

"Bad blood," Cleitus laughed, moving closer to the table. "You executed the eldest, Archelaus, a few years before Alexander was born, isn't that right?"

Philip drew his brows together. "He opposed me."

"You have an agreement with Olynthus, Philip," Antipater pointed out.

Antigonus, scratched his shaggy beard. His single eye roved the map.

"An agreement is only as good as its practice," he growled.

"My friend speaks the truth," said Philip. "Which is why, at the opportune moment, that city will be razed to the ground."

***

Behind the classroom, Cassander flopped down in the cool green grass. His schoolmates joined him, taking their seats on rocks and under trees. Unpacking their satchels, they snacked on pieces of fruit.

Leonnatus threw a red leather ball into the air and played catch for a few minutes. Cassander finished a bunch of grapes, arose and joined him in the game. Perdiccas was next. The boys talked as they played.

"By Zeus, that man bores me, Leo!"

"You just don't like school, Cassie."

"You can be a swot like Alex, but one day I'll be a great warrior."

Perdiccas caught the ball and threw it hard. "I like our teacher."

"Bah!" retorted Cassander. "He's a self-righteous prig."

Seated on a rock, a short distance away, Alexander finished his apple in swift bites.

"What's wrong with being virtuous, Cassander?" he asked.

"Nothing, if you're a prude, Alex."

Hephaestion balled his fist. "One day I'll knock your block off, Cassie."

"Why, Heph bristles like a bride!" laughed Cassander.

Alexander started on another apple.

"Shut up, Cassie," he snapped. "Hephaestion is supporting me as a companion and soulmate."

With a grunt, Cassander threw the ball hard at Perdiccas, smashing the catcher's fingers in the process. He then retrieved it and sat, throwing it from one hand to the other.

Perdiccas waved his hand about. "Ow! You'll need a soulmate when I recover, Cassie. I'm going to box your ears!"

"My soulmate will be my wife. Men are good for nothing except as protection on the field of battle."

Perdiccas wrested the ball back from Cassander. "And the only thing women are good for is bearing children."

Alexander finished his second apple. "Hephaestion and I are cousins. Good friends are more important than wives. Now, let's get back to class."

Groaning, Cassander joined the boys as they trooped back inside for the afternoon session. Perdiccas poked him in the back to hurry him along. Leonnatus took back his ball. Throwing it in the air, he fitted in a few more catches before the afternoon classes.

Hephaestion stayed with Alexander, who walked with rapid footsteps.

"No school tomorrow, Alex. Any plans for your day off?"

"There's a horse sale at the royal stables. You can come if you like. Father's going to buy me one."

"Wonderful! We can ride the hills together."

Alexander beamed. "I'm going to get the best horse for that!"

***

11.

A cloak of stars fell over Pella. Roast wild boar was served to Macedonia's military elite. King Philip presided over the feast. Women danced, while young men served wine to the boisterous crowd.

Parmenion was asking questions. "What about Thessaly, Philip?"

"I don't move into that country without permission."

"Larissa asked for help with Pherae before you met Queen Olympias. Thessaly is at war with us."

"I have been Archon of the League since having children with my wife. I want to concentrate our military might in the north."

"You're missing a great opportunity."

"Are you at the horse market tomorrow, Parmenion?" asked Philip, changing the subject.

"Why? Do you need me to haggle the price of one?"
Several generals within earshot, laughed.

"You know your horses, Parmenion. Besides, there is a visiting Thessalian owner. It is rumoured he has a magnificent black colt. They say it is already seventeen hands."

Philip upended his cup. He looked over the rim. From his left eye, he regarded his senior general's dumbstruck expression with amusement.

"If that's true, I might buy a horse myself," said Parmenion when he had recovered.

"And me," boomed Attalus. "After our sovereign has had his pick."

"I'll have to watch this," said Aeropus.

"My son, Alexander will be there," Philip added. "With Olympias."

Aeropus grimaced. "Bah! That boy is always hanging onto his mother's skirts."

Cleitus ripped the wing off a pheasant. Crunching through its burnt skin, he savoured the tender meat, which slid easily down his throat.

"My sister was Alexander's nanny," he said.

Aeropus looked at him. "What does that mean?"

"My family personally cares for the prince."

"Are you threatening me?"

"I love Prince Alexander." Cleitus rinsed his fingers in a gold bowl of water. "To the death."

Parmenion accepted a dessert plate from a servant. "Sounds as though you are the boy's caretaker now, Cleitus."

"I am Philip's man."

The king slapped Cleitus on the back, while the latter wiped his hands with a napkin. "Spoken like a loyal Macedonian officer! Come to the horse market tomorrow."

***

Alexander twisted his head this way and that. Horses were paraded around the grassy arena. Shouts from onlookers mixed with men haggling. Stallions pulled on their ropes, tossing their manes in the morning sun.

Philip drank uncut wine from a gold goblet. Occasionally, he spat oaths and laughed loudly at the bidding prices. Veterans eyed their next battle stallions, being careful to allow the King of Macedonia first pick. When he bought one, Philip waved to a man with a large bag filled with gold who paid up. An accountant recorded all the purchases.

Morning gave way to afternoon. Hephaestion finally appeared. Alexander turned away from the horses. "Where were you?"

"My sister's getting married, Alex. I forgot."

"You forgot your sister's wedding?"

"No, but I was supposed to help this morning. She wanted me to stack presents with her friends. It must have slipped my mind."

"You should never forget your sister, Hephaestion."

"You have only one, Alex. I have six. They boss me about. It's a relief to get away." Servants moved through the throng with food and drink. "Hey, it's time for lunch!"

Snatching a piece of chicken from a servant, Hephaestion devoured it. Alexander hung over the wooden railing, desperately looking for the right horse.

And then, there he was. A magnificent black colt, with a white star on his forehead. Bucking and neighing, the steed strained against his owner's rope as he was led around the arena.

Alexander nudged his cousin. "What do you think?"

"That's not a colt," Hephaestion choked. "It's a monster!"

"I'm going to buy him."

"With what?"

"Father said he would buy me a horse."

"Take it from me, Alex, that thing was made for giants. It'll trample you underfoot sooner than let you ride it."

Philip moved forward in his seat. Setting down his goblet, he beckoned to the colt's owner. "How much do you want for him?"

"Thirteen talents, Your Majesty."

Frowning, the king picked up his goblet. Parmenion leaned over his shoulder.

"A fair price for a magnificent beast, Philip. You should add him to the royal stables."

"Very well. Let's see how he rides."

One of the squires moved forward. Neighing, the colt bucked his head. His owner pulled on the rope to make him kneel, but the frightened animal whinnied and reared on his hind legs.

Desperate to please his king, the squire grasped the black mane. However, the colt tossed his head, and pawed the ground. Falling back, the embarrassed man retreated with horsehair in his hands.

"Why do I pay for these mother's boys?" Philip roared. "Get another rider!"

Parmenion motioned to one of his officers. At twenty-nine, the man was a hardened warrior. Barking to the owner to pull on the rope, he attempted to mount. Kicking out his back legs, the young horse made the task impossible. Three more men attempted to ride the fiery steed, with the same results.

Suddenly, a black-bearded cavalry officer leapt over the main railing to enter the arena.

"Ah good," Philip said. "Cleitus should do it." But the creature bucked with loud neighs, and would not be mounted. "Forget it! He can't be tamed."

Pulling on the colt's tether, his owner made a desperate plea. "You will never find a better warhorse, Your Majesty."

"Stop wasting my time, you Thessalonian oaf! Away with that infernal monster."

Alexander ducked under the railing and ran into the open space.

"Let me try, Father." He turned to the colt's owner. "Please sir, let go of the rope."

The man shook his head.

"Do what my son asks." Philip craned his neck round to Parmenion. "This, I want to see."

"Is that wise? Even the owner sees danger."

"Alexander has to learn."

"That beast could kill a man, Philip. Your son is only a child."

An odd light glinted in the king's eye. Taking a deep draught of wine, he watched the wild animal paw the ground, its distinctive white star bobbing on his angry forehead. Neighing, the colt bared his teeth at Alexander.

Undeterred, the prince took the halter and turned the steed gently around. Immediately, there was quiet. Standing on tiptoe, the boy rubbed his shoulder, and spoke soothing words in a low voice.

Then, swift as lightning, the prince vaulted onto his back. He urged the colt a few paces forward, careful to steer him away from his shadow. No longer able to see the frightening dark blotch on the ground, the animal moved forward. His rider was as light as a feather, and he enjoyed the pleasant whispering in his ear.

After putting him through his paces, Alexander dismounted. Rubbing the black muzzle, he looked directly at his father.

"This is my horse. I'm going to call him Bucephalus."

Hugging his new friend, Alexander scratched the silky black bristles. The colt responded by snuffling affectionately in his ear.

Philip was on his feet. He motioned his man with the money bag to pay the owner in gold ducats. Alexander ran to his father's side. Philip took his son's head in his hands and kissed the top of his golden head. Then, seizing the boy's shoulders, he kissed both his cheeks.

"Find yourself another kingdom, my son. Macedonia is too small for you!"

***

12.

Strumming his lyre, Alexander waited for Hephaestion under a tree, next to their classroom. So far, the new school year was going well.

His older half-brother, Ptolemy passed by, carrying a staff. Noticing the boys, he gave a cheery wave.

"All the best, Prince!" he called out in a deep baritone.

Alexander waved back and continued strumming. Suddenly, Hephaestion appeared out of nowhere and skidded to a halt. He was out of breath. "Sorry I'm late, Alex. My sister's engaged."

"That's your excuse for everything. How many times can your sister get engaged? Beware of lies, Heph. Once you start, you can't stop, and then you'll be a lawyer in no time."

"I'm telling you the truth."

"You must have a lot of sisters."

"Six – you know that. Here's a wedding invitation."

Hephaestion thrust out his hand. In it lay a gold token. Alexander's brows rose.

"It must be an expensive wedding."

"Daughters *are* expensive."

"Are you telling more fibs?"

"Their dowries cost a fortune for their parents. You should know that."

"I hadn't thought about it." Running his fingers across the strings of his lyre, Alexander began humming a hymn to beauty. He stopped. "When I'm old, I'd love to be surrounded by pretty daughters."

"Then, you'd better inherit the throne. You'll have to be as rich as your father if you want daughters. At the moment he's still buying you horses."

"And he will after Olynthus."

"He was there last week. My father told me."

"True. And?"

"You must know we razed it to the ground."

An amber flicker passed through Alexander's eyes. Smoothing down his rumpled chiton, Hephaestion started climbing the stairs to their class.

"Wait, Heph! I composed a tune."

"Leonidas is here."

"Don't worry, he's one of Mummy's kinsmen."

"He also beats boys for no reason."

Hephaestion grabbed his cousin's lyre and ran up the stairs. Incensed, the prince pursued him. They were seated in class just in time.

Cedar doors flew open. Leonidas appeared, and Alexander's heart sank. The man's pitiless visage was unexpected. No wonder Ptolemy had wished him the best.

"Who here knows the *Iliad*?"

The voice was dry and scratchy. Alexander looked about, but no one answered.

"We all do, sir."

"It's well that you address me with respect, because you've broken the first rule, Prince."

"You asked a question of us. I answered on everyone's behalf."

Whispers travelled through the class.

"So, a leader of men, are we? A sacker of cities like his father?"

At the back, Cassander snickered. Alexander's ears reddened.

"I answered your question, sir."

"We all know the *Iliad* by heart," Hephaestion interrupted.

"But I don't know your name."

"Heph-Hephaestion, s-sir."

The teacher fixed his attention on Alexander. "And you?"

"Since you addressed me by my title, you must know I am Alexander."

***

"Day not going well?"

From the school steps, Alexander looked up at Ptolemy. His eyes were filled with tears. "I was expelled from class for answering a question."

Sitting next to him on the cold stone, his brother patted his back. "Leonidas is picking on you because you're our future king."

"That's treason, Ptolemy. Father will choose the strongest for his heir. At the moment, that's you."

"I'll be an old man by the time he dies. You, on the other hand will be just the right age. Come, it's cold out here. Let's get you inside."

Alexander shook his head vigorously. "I have to stay here for the whole day."

Taking his younger brother by the hand, Ptolemy jerked him to his feet. He propelled the snivelling child indoors, back to his class.

"I've returned your pupil, Leonidas," he announced at the door.

"Alexander is to stay outside until he learns his manners."

"It's cold."

"He needs to buck up. Macedonians are tough warriors."

"My brother is a *child*. See he stays inside, or I shall report you to King Philip. He's back from Olynthus. A stunning victory, by the way, which means a pay increase for you."

Without waiting for a reply, Ptolemy left. Ignoring his royal student, Leonidas continued with the lesson.

***

45

13.

It was nightfall. Ptolemy and his bodyguards made their way to the palace's main gate. Sentries waved them through. Filling his lungs with jasmine laden air, the young man strolled towards the royal quarters. The gardens were pleasant to walk. Soldiers, specially trained for night duty, guarded pathways which were lit by torches.

Eventually, Ptolemy and his men reached the king's apartments. Armoured guards, bearing spears, halted the party. There was a wait until the newcomers' identities were checked. Inside, King Philip was asked whether he expected visitors. Finally, Ptolemy left his bodyguards and went inside, alone.

Arms outstretched, Philip walked towards him. "My favourite son!" The two embraced.

Servants brought wine, grapes, and cheese. The pair reclined on fleece-covered couches to eat and drink.

"Father, what is your wish?"

"I need you with me in battle."

"I'm honoured."

"It's necessary."

Philip drained his goblet. Ptolemy noticed a hard look in his eye and stayed alert. A roasted pheasant arrived. Stuffed with nuts and spices, its mouth-watering aroma filled the room.

"Give me the order and I shall obey."

"Good! Now, I want to talk about a different subject – Alexander."

Ptolemy fixed his attention on Philip. With their curled locks and full beards, the pair were mirror images. "I'm listening."

"Your brother needs discipline."

"Yesterday, Alexander was freezing outside Leonidas' classroom. Sickness would put him out of school for an entire term. I know how much you value your second son."

46

Choking on his wine, Philip coughed for several moments. At last, the fit subsided. "It is a thorn in my side that my eldest cannot be King."

"Prince Arridhaeus could be, if you wished."

"That simpleton should have been exposed on Mount Olympus at birth."

Deciding the roast pheasant was of particular interest, Ptolemy dug in. Breaking off a leg, he devoured the tender meat. Wiping his hands on his kilt in his best warrior manner, he burped to show his satisfaction with the meal.

"While I care for Alexander, I care for Macedonia more," he said.

"Do not hide your love for your half-brother," Philip said. "Lagus may take credit for your siring, but we all know he's your stepfather. Unfortunately, Alexander is also a mother's boy. I would never have hired one of Queen Olympias's relatives, if he was going to mollycoddle that child. I spoke to Leonidas. He is a fair man. I don't want your interference."

Ptolemy lifted his cup. "To toughening up the brat!"

Manly laughter filled the room as the pair drank their fill.

***

It was noon on the second day of school. Leonidas put down his textbook. "Now, I have a treat for you all."

Eagerly, the children craned their heads forward. With a kind smile, their teacher picked up his staff and led them outside.

Perdiccas nudged Cassander. "He must have a picnic planned."

"Wonderful! I'm starved."

When they were all outside, Leonidas pointed his staff towards the main road leading into the school. "March down that road, boys. At its end, start climbing the first hill. I expect you back at six."

Cassander's mouth fell open. "In the evening?"

"Do you have questions?" Leonidas asked.

Shaking his head, the boy retreated into the group. The children began walking.

"This is outrageous!" Cassander hissed to Perdiccas. "I'm getting lunch at my house. You're welcome to join me."

"Pipe down. Wait till we're out of earshot."

"Don't think I won't know if you're slacking," Leonidas called out from the school steps. "Instructors are watching you!"

Leonnatus waited until they were out of their teacher's sight before speaking. "This must be illegal."

Head down, Alexander started to speak rapidly. "Friends, we have to figure out a way to complete the task."

"Tell us before we all faint," Cassander puffed.

"Ptolemy informed me about this exercise last year. Six men are stationed along the way. You'll recognise them from their beards. None of them will see what we're doing until we're up close."

Hephaestion drew up alongside Alexander. "What's your plan, cousin?"

"Space out. I'll lead."

Cassander wiped his sweaty face on the back of his hand. "Why should you lead?"

"So no one has any suspicions."

"He's right," Hephaestion said. "Alexander always leads."

They passed a man with black hair and a moustache, who was relaxing in the shade of an olive tree. Spotting the school insignia on his chiton, Alexander recognised him as one of Leonidas' spies.

"My plan is we all take turns exchanging places," he suggested, "so we all get something to eat."

"I don't follow," said Hephaestion.

"There's a nut stall under an ancient oak tree. We're coming up to it, soon."

Cassander belched loudly behind them. "Are you suggesting we steal from some poor farmer?"

"I'm suggesting Cassie, that you take a bag of nuts from old Xanthius under the tree, in exchange for gold." Alexander slipped Hephaestion's wedding token into his hand.

"Hey, that's my invitation!" his cousin protested.

"We'll come back later, and exchange it for a ducat," Alexander replied, before fixing his attention on Cassander. "Get a bag of nuts, Cassie. Eat a handful. Then, give Perdie the bag, and overtake him to shield him from spies. Keep doing that until everyone has something to eat. If we take turns, we'll have energy to scale the hill."

"But we can't survive on a bag of nuts!" Leonnatus wailed.

Alexander was irritated. "Oranges grow on the hills, Leo. Pick some."

Cassander snorted. "I don't know about Leo, but oranges aren't going to fill *my* stomach."

"They're also figs in the valley, Cassie," Alexander said. "Must I paint you a picture?"

Hephaestion suddenly brightened. "I know the route. It goes around a mountain. There's food there. Lots of fruit trees, and fish in the streams."

"That's right," Alexander said. "But this is a test. We must grab food on the run. We can't stop. Everyone must be back by the sixth hour of the evening, otherwise we'll be punished."

Hephaestion turned his head. "Why six?"

"Leonidas' wife will have supper ready. She throws the pots about if he doesn't eat her food while it's hot."

The boys giggled. Deciding Alexander's plan had a chance, they spaced out. Hephaestion stayed directly behind his cousin. Their classmates fell in behind them.

Cassander allowed Perdiccas in front, while he took the rear, and kept his eye out for the nut stall.

***

14.

Panting, the boys drew up before the classroom. It was dusk. Leonidas was waiting.

"You're on time," he said in a disappointed tone.

Alexander bit his lip. No one said anything. Glancing at the golden sun setting over the hills, Leonidas shouldered his satchel, and walked down the same road he had made the children march six hours ago.

The prince's eyes followed the man until he was out of sight. Then, he sank to the ground. His calves were so sore, he did not know whether he could get up. The others followed suit. Cassander spat. Perdiccas looked as though he was about to burst into tears.

Before he could do so, Alexander clapped him on the back.

"Great teamwork, everyone!" he declared, beaming at his colleagues.

Leonnatus leaned on a tree, catching his breath. "My question is, what next?"

"What do you mean, Leo?"

"It's not over, Alex. That man's plotting to torture us in the future."

"Leonidas is training us. He's our *teacher*."

"I agree with Leo," Cassander said.

Hephaestion pursed his lips. "You would."

"Trials are to toughen us up, not to punish us," Alexander said.

Cassander laughed. "Says you, who was expelled on the first day!"

"I've learned." Alexander rose. "Come, let's all go home. There's roast boar tonight, Hephaestion. In time, we'll all hunt one and be men."

Heartened at the thought of dinner, the boys rose, dusted themselves off and dispersed to their homes. Hephaestion accompanied Alexander to the palace, where they washed before dinner.

***

Ptolemy walked home from the Royal Riding School. His horse was in the school stables eating vegetables and hay. Autumn leaves crunched pleasantly underfoot. An orange sky was discernible through the tree tops.

It was several days since his meeting with King Philip. His latest invitation to the Dionysius feast was confirmation of royal favour.

Up ahead, he recognised the figure of a middle-aged man walking with a determined step. "Greetings, Leonidas!"

"Where are you going so fast, Prince Ptolemy?"

"Home to dress for the Dionysius feast. You're invited."

"I don't attend debauches."

"Lots of tasty food at the palace."

"I prefer to fast. Did King Philip speak to you about his son?"

Ptolemy stopped and forced a smile. His dazzling teeth glinted in the last rays of the dying day. "Did our illustrious monarch tell you I'm to be at his side on his next campaign? Remember, you're invited to dinner."

Clenching his fists, Ptolemy hurried off. At the gate to his home, he took the shortest garden path to the main door. In the hallway, he waved off the servant who was waiting with a traditional footbath.

A woman walked down a long marble staircase into the hall. Her slim figure was encased in a pleated gown of white linen. On her head she wore a thin diadem of gold. Around her throat hung a gold necklace with the Argead star picked out in emeralds.

"You're late, Ptolemy."

"We still have time before the feast, Thais. I was held up by Alexander's teacher, Leonidas. Awful man!"

"Isn't he Olympias' uncle?"

"And a harsh taskmaster. I must bathe."

"I asked the boys to heat the water."

"You're a wonderful woman."

Giving his lady a swift peck on her cheek, Ptolemy strode towards the bathroom. Pouring herself a cup of wine, Thais waited. A while later, the master of the house reappeared, clad in a plain bathrobe.

"What are you going to wear, dearest?" Thais asked.

"I hadn't given it any thought."

"Perhaps the outfit I laid out on your bed will please you."

Ptolemy went to his room and picked up a turquoise robe. A wine-coloured cape and gilded leather sandals were also set out. Tossing the garment over his head, he found it fitted perfectly. He draped the cape around his shoulders and tied on the sandals.

***

15.

By the time Ptolemy and Thais arrived at the banquet, King Philip was already carousing. Dressed as Dionysus, god of wine, his head was wreathed in a gold diadem of ivy leaves.

The couple joined the senior generals. Parmenion beckoned to a waiter, who served them wine. "I believe you are accompanying us on the winter campaign."

Ptolemy took a cup. "That's what I hear."

Thais slipped away, leaving the men to talk.

"You were brave to bring her," Parmenion remarked.

"She's a courtesan, used to men."

"And a friend?"

"One day I shall marry her."

"Friends make the best wives. However, men have been known to lose lovers at celebrations which honour the god of wine."

"I shall not lose her at this or any other feast."

Cleitus joined the pair.

"Young Ptolemy is already mixing in the circles of the great," he said cheerfully, as he swiped a wine cup from a passing servant.

"He's campaigning with us this year," said Parmenion.

"Which division?"

"Silver Shields," Ptolemy replied.

Cleitus was impressed. "Philip's crack unit – you must be good."

"I think it's because he wants to keep an eye on me," Ptolemy smiled.

"Not necessarily," Parmenion said. "Philip always plans for the future."

"Agreed." Cleitus finished his drink. "Where's Thais?"

Ptolemy nodded towards a table where a group of women were congregated. "With the other ladies."

Parmenion cleared his throat. "She is with our young friend, Cleitus."

"Exclusively?"

"Thais belongs to Ptolemy," said Parmenion. "Make it known."

The senior military officer selected a pork canape from a plate of delicacies offered by a serving girl.

"I shall." He clapped Ptolemy on the back "Well done, lad!"

With that, Cleitus disappeared into the crowd of diners.

***

It was nearly the end of term. Their race was over. Bodies aching, ears ringing, the boys collapsed on grassy mounds surrounding the chapel.

Only Alexander was squatting on his haunches, having finished the race long ago. Several yards away from the group, he cut slices of dried meat for his dog, Perdias.

Hephaestion lay on his back, gulping air and staring at the sky. Cassander wheezed as he joined the others. His thoughts were on lunch. He was hungry and his stomach gave out sounds that alarmed the other runners.

Staggering up to Hephaestion, Leonnatus fell down in the grass, panting. "How many more sprints, Heph?"

"Only one, according to Alexander."

"Thank Zeus! We've been running since sunrise." He turned his head to a puffing Perdiccas who joined them. "How are you, Perdie?"

Perdiccas sprawled on the grass next to them. "Exhausted! No matter how much I tried, Alex still won everything."

"Maybe you need breakfast. It gives extra speed."

"I'm so hungry I could eat an entire boar."

The pair laughed. Leonnatus sat up and took a ball from his satchel. They started throwing it back and forth between them.

Cassander propped himself up on his elbows. "The squirt cheated, as usual."

"Alexander's *fast*," Hephaestion replied.

"Your legs are longer than his. When we're all boarding next term, he won't be able to cheat so easily. Leonidas will be all over him."

"Leonidas will watch everyone, Cassie. If you must know, I lack Alexander's power on the last stretch."

Making himself comfortable in the warm grass, Hephaestion reflected that it was against protocol to outdo a prince, especially one who might be their future king.

***

16.

It was the boys' second term as boarders. Leonidas opened the chest. With his stick, he prodded the bedding packed inside. Alexander hovered about, while Hephaestion rubbed his hands like a worried accountant.

"Empty it, Alexander!"

"He can't lift the chest, sir," Hephaestion pointed out.

Perdiccas peered round the door. "Everything alright? I heard shouting."

Leonidas glared at him. "Get out! You're next. People think you're disciplined because you don't eat breakfast, however, I know all about your sweet tooth."

The boy retreated behind the door. Meantime, Alexander struggled, but could not lift the chest with his bedding. Deciding on a new tactic, he tipped it over with his foot.

Quilts spilled onto the floor. He scrabbled at the back of the box, trying to pull out everything. Leonidas kept prodding the contents with his stick. Eventually, he was satisfied. Alexander attempted to tidy up, but received a smart whack on his wrists.

"Leave it. Get to class."

The prince did not need to be told twice. He scurried out the door and promptly bumped into Perdiccas. "Out of my way!"

"Slow down, Alex. We can go to class together."

But, pushing past his friend, the prince hurried away as fast as his short legs would carry him.

Freshly bathed and scented, with his study scrolls tucked under his arm, Cassander sidled up to Perdiccas.

"Alex is keen to get to class," he observed.

"It's not his love of academia, Cassie."

Leonidas loped past, his brows contracted in wrath. Cassander's mouth upturned. "I must say, I like our teacher more and more each term!"

"Cassie, you need to stop with the taunts. One day you might find yourself in a war with Alex."

"Which I'll win."

Shaking his head, Perdiccas pulled out his ball of leather and twine and started tossing it between his hands. Cassander hurried to class. It was going to be a good day.

***

It was the fourth week of term. After his riding lesson, Alexander went to his room. Picking up his study scrolls, he grabbed a pear and made his way to class. Crunching his snack, the prince ambled down the tree-lined paths. It was spring. Leafy branches joined together, to form a canopy overhead.

After a few minutes, Alexander spotted Lysimachus. The man was strolling ahead of him. Occasionally, he stopped and studied a plant or flower. The boy caught up to him and they walked together.

"These lanes on the way to school are most interesting, my prince. They contain plants rarely seen, except at King Philip's palace."

"He collects them during his campaigns."

Lysimachus took his eyes off a particularly large and fragrant water lily. "Is there something on your mind?"

"I hate Leonidas!"

"He's your teacher – and your beloved mother's cousin."

"I was thinking of speaking with my mother."

"Queen Olympias chose Leonidas."

"I don't believe you."

"King Philip told me your parents came to an arrangement. Each selected a tutor for you."

"It must be the only time my parents agreed on anything."

"Not so. You're in this world because of them." With great gentleness, Lysimachus put one hand on the prince's arm. "Your mother selected Leonidas, knowing he would teach you discipline. She believes you will lead Macedonia one day as its warrior king."

"And yet my father, the current monarch, chose you, a much kinder man."

"Interesting, is it not?"

The two proceeded down the path to the school. At the main door, Alexander went into class. Lysimachus waited for his assistant to arrive. Eventually, Ptolemy appeared laden down with scrolls.

"Do you have Homer's *Odyssey,* lad?"

"I do, sir. Each boy has a scroll with their exercises for this term, with some of the more interesting plants for their botany class."

"Ah, good! These young men need to be ready for next year's tutor."

"Who is he, sir?"

"I don't know, but it is rumoured King Philip is searching Greece for the greatest teacher of our age."

"So long as it's not Demosthenes."

Lysimachus chuckled. "Have you heard his latest speech?"

"Who hasn't? Another tirade against our king is going to dig the orator's grave, especially if we conquer Greece."

"Mark my words, one day King Philip will have his head on a stick."

Climbing the stairs, the pair went into school to set up the day's classes.

***

58

17.

Hephaestion and Alexander were enjoying a much-needed day off, swimming in a pond, while their horses grazed nearby. Afterwards, the boys retired to sit on the temple steps of Artemis, goddess of wisdom and war. The sun was already dipping in the sky.

"What a wonderful day we've had, cousin!" said Hephaestion.

Alexander furrowed his brow. "Did you know my mother chose Leonidas?"

"That's surprising."

"Lysimachus thinks there was a reason behind my parents' choices."

"I'm listening."

"Mother is preparing me to be a warrior king. Father doesn't want me to rule."

"Lysimachus surely didn't say that."

"After our conversation, it's my view. Leonidas is supposed to discipline me. It makes sense for a future king and warrior."

Hephaestion wrinkled his nose. "If you think being thrashed for no reason is discipline."

"I was going to speak to my mother about it, but Lysimachus doesn't think it's a good idea."

Hephaestion selected two oranges from his lunch pack. He gave one to Alexander. The latter peeled it swiftly with his fingers.

"Alex, your mother is Queen. Don't cross her. You are still free to hate Leonidas."

Alexander ate his orange in swift bites. "Naturally, I will have to exact revenge one day."

"Give the order, and I'll despatch him for you!"

Alexander accepted a handkerchief, which Hephaestion supplied out of his well-stocked snack pack. He wiped his hands on the scented linen.

"I appreciate your loyalty. Isn't it interesting Father chose the mild-mannered botanist?"

"Lysimachus was a soldier. He'll follow you into battle. He told us on a class hike."

"Now I've heard it all."

Hephaestion finished his orange and wiped his fingers on the grass.

"Your parents chose your tutors together, Alex. One was for the discipline –after all, there may be no fruit in a war. The other is your Dad's man, ready to follow you to the ends of the earth."

"If there's no fruit in wartime, it'll be because Leonidas has confiscated it! Lysimachus, on the other hand, can join my army any day."

Hephaestion burped to indicate he had eaten. Their horses whinnied and shook their manes in the setting sun.

"It's dusk, Alex. Let's ride home."

***

Demosthenes rubbed his jaw. It was four years since a powerful citizen named Meidias had punched him in the face. Four years since he had retaliated with a lawsuit which included his famous judicial speech entitled *Against Meidias*.

It was a rousing address, describing how society suffered as a whole when it was undermined by the evil and the rich. Democracy, it was argued, suffered because the rule of law perished under such men as Meidias, who were allowed to dictate the terms by which others lived.

As the most famous orator of his time, Demosthenes expected to win his charge of aggravated assault against his wealthier opponent. However, the end of the feud between the men was shrouded in mystery. Rumour had it that the complainant was bribed to drop charges against his attacker. The public would never know the truth. But Demosthenes' jaw still hurt when the weather changed.

It was late. Outside the window, lilac clouds tinged with pink, hung in the sky. Demosthenes stretched his arms above his head. A serving boy entered his office.

"Is it eight, already?"

"You asked me to remind you of the *Second Philippic* – in case you were distracted, sir."

"How did you know I was distracted?"

The boy blushed. "Intuition, sir."

"There's a bonus in this month's wages. Take a horse from my stable for yourself."

As his overjoyed servant left, Demosthenes reflected the *Second Philippic* was both easier, and more difficult, than the first. Easy because he knew how. Difficult, because he had to keep the audience amused with his latest speech. Even harder to ensure Athens committed itself to war against Philip.

Bending his head, the statesman picked up his stylus and began to write.

***

18.

Alexander rolled out of bed and hit his head. His teacher was standing above him with a stick and a piece of fruit.

"What do we have here?"

"A p-pomegranate, s-sir?"

"Are you not sure what it is?"

"I-I c-can't s-see. I've just woken up."

"It's *fruit*. Get up!"

Alexander tried to rise. A cane whipped a stinging rebuke across his chest and shoulders. Still half asleep, the boy desperately tried to focus.

Leonidas shook the pomegranate in his face. Pushing it into his own leather satchel, which was strapped around his shoulder, he opened all of Alexander's chests. Their contents spilled over the wooden floorboards. Bowls, cups, paintings, clothes, bedding, and rugs were prodded by the relentless teacher.

"Wh-what are y-you d-doing, sir?"

"Inspecting. You overslept. Join the others in the hall. You're all on a morning march."

"But it's dark."

Before he had time to realise, Alexander felt another sting across his shoulders. A commotion in the corridor distracted the irate man. Two boys were fighting. Distracted by the ruckus, Leonidas left.

Quick as lightning, Alexander dressed for the march. Pulling on a warm fleece vest, he dropped a clean chiton over his head and laced on strong walking sandals. He packed a hat to protect his face from the burning midday sun.

Slinging a bag across his shoulders, he cocked his head sideways to listen. Leonidas' voice drifted up the corridor. Alexander heard footsteps, but judged correctly that they belonged to a class-mate.

He rummaged under his mattress for figs, which he stashed there for emergencies. Cramming a handful into his mouth, he washed them down with water from his bedside table.

Cassander's head appeared around the lintel. "What are you doing, Alex?"

"Getting ready."

"We're waiting. Hurry up – and leave the bag."

Ignoring Cassander, the prince pushed passed him. Their fellow students were lined up in the hallway in front of Leonidas who stood at the main door. Suddenly, it swung open. A cold breeze blew in, and the children's skin raised in goosebumps. A stocky youth stood in the doorway.

Leonidas scowled. "What can I do for you, Prince Ptolemy?"

"I had a meeting with Father this morning."

"I thought King Philip made my duties clear to you."

"He sent me to supervise this march."

"The boys take care of themselves. It breeds independence and toughness."

"Not today."

"Why?"

"Bears."

A baffled expression crossed Leonidas' face. Before he had time to think, Ptolemy crammed a piece of parchment, stamped with the royal seal, into his hands. Ushering the boys into the cold air with his jolly manner, he accompanied them out of the school and along the dark road.

Hephaestion caught up with his cousin. "My heartfelt thanks, Alex."

"I didn't do anything."

"Ptolemy's your half-brother, isn't he?"

"I didn't talk to him about this."

The boys puffed along. Ptolemy passed out pastries. Alexander took a bite, but Perdiccas fell back. His teeth chattered uncontrollably.

"What's the matter, Perdie?" Alexander asked.

"I'm freezing."

Immediately, the prince stopped at the side of the road. A sliver of moon hung overhead. He stripped and handed Perdiccas the fleece vest.

"Put it on underneath your chiton."

"But you'll get cold, Alex."

"I'll build up heat with running."

Leaving his classmate at the side of the road, Alexander picked up the pace and reached the head of the column.

"Morning brother!" Ptolemy boomed. "I wondered how long it would take you to catch up."

"Did you really speak to Father?"

Smiling into his beard, Ptolemy made no reply. Sunrise gleamed above the mountains as the group ran together at a comfortable pace.

***

Alexander stood in Lysimachus' doorway. His cheeks were red with fury. "I don't know how to deal with that man!"

His teacher looked up from a scroll he was reading. "I take it you mean Leonidas."

Alexander sat down in an available chair. "I refuse to be taught by a cruel idiot."

"This reminds me of your ancestor, Achilles and his dealings with Agamemnon."

"Can't you, for once, lay off the ancient Greek literary references? I need a solution."

"Agamemnon was forced to give back Achilles what he had stolen."

"What are you suggesting?"

"Leonidas cannot legally confiscate your possessions. They belong to the Crown, and you are King Philip's son."

"In theory, but fruit only lasts for a short while. He ate it all!"

"I'm sincerely sorry, but there is nothing I can do."

"Can't you speak to my parents?"

"And interfere? I'd lose my job."

"My mother is a fox. She pretends to love me, while saddling me with this tyrant."

"Her Majesty is trying to protect you."

"By appointing an abusive teacher? All I can say, is she charges high rent for nine months in the womb."

"King Philip was not going to allow your mother to have any say in your education. Now, she has input. Leonidas meets with her every week."

"I don't believe it."

"It's the only way she can receive updates on your progress. Your mother wants you to fulfil your potential. She desires that you be outstanding in everything you do."

"I didn't know that."

"Queen Olympias had to choose a tough instructor, otherwise King Philip would never have allowed him to teach you, let alone report to her. Don't be offended by the man. He greatly admires Leonidas of Thermopylae."

"I'm not Spartan."

"Sparta produces the best soldiers."

"I'm Macedonian. My father will rule Greece, which will include Sparta."

"Leonidas' methods will give you an edge."

"I disagree."

"Have it your way, but study the *Iliad*, my son. It has lessons for you. My personal view is that you will one day surpass Achilles, whom you so admire."

Alexander heaved a breath. "I will not forget your kindness Lysimachus, but as the gods hear me, I will avenge myself on that evil man one day."

With his characteristically swift stride, the boy left his tutor's apartment.

*****

19.

Philip stared out his window. Below, in the courtyard, a Macedonian intelligence officer dismounted his horse. As a nation with a strong desire to conquer its neighbours, the country needed spies to keep it informed about the Greek states. A meeting was scheduled for the afternoon. In the meantime, the man was led away to his quarters to rest.

The king returned to his correspondence. Settling in with a pile of tablets, papyri and parchment, he read in a long uninterrupted stint. Towards noon, he heard clattering on the cobblestones outside his window. Alexander's teachers descended from a carriage in the courtyard. A smile traced itself under Philip's beard. He stacked his documents neatly to one side.

Standing up, he stretched and swung his arms to loosen stiff muscles. Beckoning to his chief attendant, he issued his orders. Servants entered the office. Chairs were arranged for the royal interview. Food and wine were set on side tables.

Meanwhile, royal sentries pulled out a screen from one corner of the office, and erected it around their sovereign's work area. Covered in paintings of birds and the palace gardens, it blocked off prying eyes. All this was executed swiftly and in total silence.

When the tutors entered the royal office, they were greeted warmly and set at ease. Relaxing after their trip, the men gave Philip the report he wanted to hear.

***

After their first interview, Alexander's teachers headed towards the Queen's apartments. As they traversed the maze of corridors, Leonidas reflected that Olympias' youthful figure was probably due to the endless walking necessary to reach her accommodation.

After the corridors were the stairs. Rivulets ran down Lysimachus' face.

"Hold on!" he gasped, clutching a banister.

Leonidas waited patiently for him on the second floor. He noticed potted palms and creeping jasmine vines cascading down a wall.

"This is right up your alley," he chuckled, nodding towards the plants.

"My sole interest at this point is water," Lysimachus gasped, reaching his colleague.

Finally, they arrived outside an oak door. Two guards surveyed the bedraggled pair with suspicion. Leonidas arranged his robe in a style befitting a respected mentor.

"Prince Alexander's teachers for Queen Olympias," he snapped. "Announce us."

"Wait here." The first guard disappeared. After a short interval he returned. "Her Majesty is waiting for you."

"He sounds surprised," Lysimachus remarked.

Queen Olympias welcomed the men into her living room. With his eyes, Lysimachus indicated the nearest jug of water. He was rewarded with an efficient steward who poured him a cup.

Olympias waved towards two chairs. "I trust you both had a pleasant journey."

Leonidas glanced with disdain at his colleague.

"The carriage was small," he replied.

Ignoring this sleight about his weight, Lysimachus gulped back water.

"I hear my son excelled at school this year," Olympias said brightly.

"The boy is still soft," replied Leonidas, "although he shows promise at sports."

A steward offered Lysimachus a serviette. He wiped his lips.

"Alexander is first among equals," he countered.

Olympias laughed. "That is a title reserved for my husband!"

"True," Leonidas agreed. "Your words are a little short of treason, Lysimachus."

"I beg to differ," was the bold reply. "The prince was first in mathematics, botany, and gymnastics."

"Let's not forget literature," Leonidas added drily. "He keeps a copy of Homer's *Iliad* under his pillow."

"That's nothing new," the queen said.

Lysimachus continued to praise his student. "The prince is gifted, which is why King Philip is hiring an outstanding scholar for Alexander's further studies."

"Do not forget Alexander has classmates," Leonidas pointed out. "Cassander was first in his class this year."

Olympias gave Leonidas her full attention. "General Antipater's son?"

"And unlike Alexander, he is unspoiled with rich food."

"I find that hard to believe," Lysimachus said. "With his weight, I would say he consumes more than the odd pomegranate at night."

Leonidas flushed beetroot red.

"I have noticed Cassander is pudgy," Olympias said. "However, I believe you conduct night raids, Leonidas."

"It's part of the discipline. Alexander is all muscle now."

"And the others?"

"They exhibited self-control from the beginning."

"Rubbish!" snorted Lysimachus. "You've been picking on the prince from his first school term."

"It is my duty to ensure he is fit for his future office. I am his kinsman."

"And mine," said Olympias quickly. "Thank you, gentlemen. Now, I must talk to my husband."

After Alexander's teachers departed, his mother walked onto her balcony. It was evening. Jasmine, oleander, and hibiscus nodded

in the gentle breeze. While her maidservants lit lamps and burned incense in her rooms, Olympias filled her lungs with the fragrant night
air. She reflected that her son was a genius and the only prince eligible
to be Philip's successor.

Her brows knotted. Being married to an older man was not all
she had hoped it would be. True, the most powerful warrior in Macedonia had given her a son worthy of his kingdom. Still, it was her
preference to think Alexander was descended from Zeus, King of the
gods. Shivering, she drew her shawl about her. After dinner, she
would chat with Philip.

***

20.

Late in the evening, dinner ended in the great banqueting hall of Pella. Philip descended from his dais, where he had feasted with his courtiers. The men trooped down a passageway to a living room, where they could talk and drink into the night.

Seeing his royal consort, the king hung back, allowing the others to go ahead. "This is a pleasant surprise."

"I intend to return to my apartment, before your drinking bout begins."

"As I recall, your Dionysian rites differ little from my evenings."

Ignoring the barb, his wife pushed on. "We both know Alexander's next term is important. Have you given any thought to which school he will attend?"

"Mieza."

Olympias swallowed. "That is far."

Philip's face flickered in the lamplight. "One day he will be at my side in Persia. It's time you were accustomed to his absences from your side."

The King of Macedonia was gone before his wife had time to recover, or ask any more questions.

***

It was the end of term. A water clock marked time in one corner. Alexander calculated he did not have long to give an account of himself.

Lysimachus viewed his student for a few moments. Thrusting his jaw out, he paced the room slowly, deep in thought.

"You are to be thirteen soon, Alexander. Your father is searching for the right tutor. He wants my advice."

"Someone to develop my strengths?"

"In a few years, your father will consider you a man."

"He already does."

"Your first hunt defines maturity. Battle confirms it. But, I also want you to develop in other areas, so that you can live a meaningful life."

"Which means I must have a tutor who excels in every subject."

"I have someone in mind. By the way, when you go on campaign in the future, I should like you to send me some botanical specimens."

"It would be an honour."

"You need to be ready, Alexander. Your father aims to be ruler of Greece and Asia."

"I wouldn't know anything about Father's ambitions."

"You've been asking Persian ambassadors the distances to their empire since boyhood!"

"I was ten. It was childish curiosity."

"It was the mark of someone planning to follow in his father's footsteps. Or create his own."

"Are you finished, sir?"

"Your final school report is with King Philip. It has been a privilege to be your teacher."

***

Alexander wandered outside. Hephaestion was putting his stallion through his paces. On seeing the prince, he leapt off his horse.

"Everything alright, cousin? You were in there for a long time."

"Lysimachus complimented my academic performance."

"Perdiccas was offered the choice of a caning by Leonidas, or an extra term."

"And you?"

"I passed."

"We need to celebrate. I'll get Bucephalus."

***

The boys rode until sunset. Jogging on their steeds, they crossed hills bathed in gold. Hephaestion pointed.

"Is that snow on the mountains?" he asked.

Alexander shaded his eyes against the glare of the melting sun. "Spring is late this year."

"It's also the season in which your father rides out to battle."

"To subjugate Greece."

"You're not going to fight, are you Alex?"

"I would have told you."

With a faint knot in his brows, the prince urged Bucephalus forward. Hephaestion followed, keeping pace. After the ride, the boys took their horses back to their stalls.

Alexander personally checked Bucephalus' food and water. He waited for Hephaestion to do the same for his steed. A sharp smell of horse dung followed them downwind as they walked to the dining hall.

Evening stars filled the skies. Turning a corner at a garden wall, they meandered through the paths filled with jasmine. Macedonian royal guards lined the route.

"I wish you hadn't mentioned him, Hephaestion."

"Who?"

"Father! Why talk about him on a perfect ride?"

"I thought he chose you to campaign with him this season."

"Why on earth would you think that?"

"It's common knowledge."

"I'm disappointed in you, Hephaestion. I thought you were better than a gossiping palace maid."

"Ptolemy told me."

Alexander halted. "Ptolemy?"

"Now, do you understand? I wasn't trying to spoil your ride. I thought you had good news."

"Maybe there's more to celebrate than I thought."

The boys turned indoors.

***

21.

King Philip was toasting his guests from his throne. A diadem of finely worked gold encircled his head, and he wore a purple robe embroidered with the Argead star.

He rose when Alexander and Hephaestion entered the dining hall. Approaching his son on unsteady feet, he embraced him. Alexander tried not to gag on wine fumes. Hephaestion was similarly hugged by the king. Afterwards, Philip wobbled back to his seat.

At the base of the throne, Macedonian courtiers were ranged on dining couches. Hephaestion and Alexander took theirs with the young males.

Cassander looked at Hephaestion, who was next to him. "What's on the menu? I'm starving."

"Sheep's eyes and cold water."

"Don't be rude. You might reflect badly on Alexander. Can't you see, our prince is busy buttering up his father for his future kingship?"

Hephaestion clenched his fists. "Another comment like that, and I swear by Zeus I'll box your ears, in front of everyone."

"Relax, Alexander's soulmate. I mean no harm. I only have one concern. How afraid is Alexander that he might *not* be Macedonia's next king?"

"Shut up, Cassie! That's treason."

"I only ask because we will all become great lords one day, not just you."

Cassander turned his attention away from Hephaestion to the fresh cheese and warm bread at his elbow. Alexander glared at him.

On his throne, Philip stroked his beard. His one eye darted back and forth across the youngsters. Many did not know his faculties functioned whether he was drunk, or sober.

***

It was the tenth hour of the morning. Clad in a long robe, a middle-aged man with a beard was admitted to the throne room.

Philip descended the steps of the dais on which he sat. "Aristotle!"

"Your Majesty summoned me."

"As a Macedonian, surely you know we do not address the monarch with titles as they do in other countries. You have been called back to your native home."

"My home is in Stageira."

"So it is."

"How may I help, Your Highness?"

"I want you to tutor my son."

"Which one, sire?"

Philip felt a twinge. "Alexander."

"And the terms?"

"Gold and a villa." There was an awkward silence. Outside, birds chirped in the early morning. "I would also be willing to rebuild your hometown."

"There are no people there since Your Highness razed it to the ground."

"That can be addressed."

"New people are not the answer. I shall be waiting in the visitors' quarters, should you need me."

Before Philip knew what was happening, the philosopher was gone.

***

Later in the morning, the Macedonian generals gathered in the outer conference room. Their king had already finished one carafe of wine and was on the second.

Parmenion cleared his throat. "Give him what he wants."

"Since when does a king bow to a philosopher?" slurred Philip. "Aristotle should be crawling before me. Instead, the rascal sits in my guest quarters, refusing to speak to his host!"

General Amyntas spoke up. "Do you want Aristotle? If not, get Alexander another tutor."

"He makes good point," said Andromenes.

Philip upended his goblet.

"More wine!" he shouted to the servants. He faced his generals. "Aristotle is the greatest philosopher in Greece. I want the best for my son."

"Then, repopulate his hometown by freeing its citizens whom you have enslaved," said Parmenion.

Philip stared at him. "And bankrupt the economy?"

Cleitus joined in. "I agree with Parmenion. There are plenty of slaves. There is only one Aristotle."

Philip slammed down his goblet. His eyes were as clear as if he was drinking water. "Cleitus is right! Aristotle's hometown is liberated by royal decree. And now, that our sons have a teacher, we need to go to war."

***

22.

With Aristotle contracted to teach in Macedonia, King Philip was free to break the news to his heir apparent. Several weeks after the philosopher's arrival, Alexander was summoned by his father to an audience chamber in the main palace.

It was a cold morning and the king had wrapped his robe around his knees. An old war wound was throbbing in the winter temperature. At thirteen, Alexander was still shorter than boys of his age.

I wonder if he'll grow, Philip thought. Aloud he said: "I hear you keep a copy of the *Iliad* under your pillow at night."

"Achilles is my ancestor, Father."

"On your mother's side. Your illustrious ancestor on *my* side is Heracles. Heroic blood runs in your veins. And, as the head of the household, it is my responsibility to ensure your development is worthy of such lineage."

"I'm listening, Father."

"Aristotle will train you, and your comrades, in the groves of Mieza." Philip rose. His right leg needed to stretch.

"I will excel in my studies, Father."

"I hope so. Zeus knows I'm spending a fortune on your education. Your new teacher is a sharp man. He had the gall to bargain with me."

Philip's mouth upturned behind his beard. His son did not respond. Instead, he stood to attention, waiting to be dismissed. Slightly irritated, his father waved him away, and hobbled out of the room.

After the interview, Alexander took his dog, Perdias for a walk. Snow drifted over the mountains. The prince was so excited, he could scarcely breathe. With his canine friend trotting at his heels in the cold morning air, he made his way along a path to the hills which surrounded the palace.

Below, lay a stunning view of green and gold fields. Climbing as far as he would allow his companion to go, Alexander gazed up at the expanse of sky above them. His one blue eye reflected it, while the other remained as black as night.

"I shall learn all the mysteries of philosophy and kingship," he whispered.

His dog barked. They played fetch in the hills until the midday sun melted the snow, and it was time for lunch. Perdias sat on his hindquarters, awaiting his next instruction. Alexander broke a stick over his thigh to signal the end of playtime.

Patting his golden dog on the head, he whistled, and they started down the hill to the palace.

***

Two weeks later, Hephaestion was visiting his cousin's quarters. They were in an uproar. He stood in a whirl of busy servants, trying to avoid being struck by moving furniture.

"Do you think I'm taking too many things, Hephaestion?"

"This is nothing compared to my house. Mother thinks I'll die of cold at Mieza. I've never seen so many fleeces packed."

"My scrolls are in cases. I don't want them damaged. Aristotle might think I don't care for learning."

"Don't worry, we have Ptolemy to protect everything."

"Is he part of security?"

"I thought you knew."

"It's good of him to look after us, don't you think?"

Hephaestion shook his head and laughed. "He's *enrolled*, Alexander."

"In Mieza? But Ptolemy's old."

"Your father doesn't want anyone to miss out on Aristotle's teaching."

"Wonderful! All my friends will be at Mieza."

"And with no night raids."

Pointing to his bedding, Alexander directed his packing team. "Take the most comfortable quilts. And a hundred crates of fruit!"

***

Thin, balding, and dressed in a long robe, Aristotle waited for roll call. His students' names were engraved on a clay tablet.

Excited youngsters piled into his stone classroom. Two of them were playing catch. One boy, with a nasty grin on his face, made sarcastic remarks. Another handsome and tanned, was having a tug of war with a much smaller, fair-headed child over a lyre.

Despite his size, the blond boy was perfectly proportioned, with the muscles of a highly trained athlete. He wrested his lyre from the taller boy with ease. Aristotle was about to say something, but the pair hugged and took their places with the others at his feet.

When everyone was settled, the teacher put aside his clay tablet. "You're all here, I see."

Perdiccas looked about. "Aren't you going to take a roll call, sir?"

"I can count."

"There are hardly any of us," muttered Cassander. "What's to count?"

Ignoring the comment, their mentor focussed his attention on the prince. "Your tutors tell me you're a mathematician, Alexander."

"I enjoy the subject, sir."

Aristotle picked up a scroll. "Then we shall start."

Taking his pupils through their first lesson, the new teacher made his students calculate several equations. Afterwards, he gave the answers, effortlessly, with explanations, and without referring to his text.

"That's enough," he said after an hour. "Let us begin the school day."

He headed out of the classroom door to the groves. The students exchanged looks. Picking up their wax tablets and writing equipment, they followed.

Outside, Alexander slipped off his sandals. The grass, which was thick with daffodils, felt good underfoot.

Seating himself on a rock, the teacher lifted up his walking staff. "Make yourselves comfortable, gentleman. Prince Alexander, you may sit at my feet." The boy reddened. "Are you embarrassed?"

"Equality is encouraged at court, sir," said Cassander.

"What does that mean?" asked Aristotle.

"None of us is considered higher than another."

"Alexander's father is King, Cassander. Yours is a general. Therefore, it would seem, there is hierarchy in the court of Macedonia."

Cassander's face purpled with rage.

"What Cassie means is that Alexander is one of us, sir," Perdiccas said quickly. "We are the Young Companions."

"And what does that mean?"

The prince cleared his throat. "Friends for life, sir."

"You don't have to address me formally, Alexander. We are all equal, according to your friends."

"But you are our tutor."

"And you will be our sovereign, one day."

"Not necessarily," Cassander blurted.

"I would say it's logical your friend here will be overlord of you, Cassander," Aristotle averred. "In which case, I am singling him out."

"That's not fair! I'm brighter than him."

"There can only be one monarch."

"I prefer to be seen as equal to the others," said Alexander.

Cassander bristled. "*Seen*? So, you secretly think yourself above us, while pretending to be equal?"

"That's not what I meant."

"None of us are his equal," Hephaestion interrupted.

"Greasing the wheel again, are we, cousin of King Philip's brat?" Cassander's tone was fierce. "While I received first prize at our last school, I don't recall Alexander getting more than canings for eating forbidden fruit in his rooms."

Aristotle's beard twitched.

"It is right and proper that Alexander's cousin defend him," he said. "Do you have an issue with that, Cassander?"

"No," the boy lied.

"Good. You may call me *sir*. All of you, except the prince." Aristotle fixed stern eyes on Alexander. "Being singled out does not mean favour. I expect you to do twice the reading of your classmates. You are to be the fastest, most courageous, most studious of all. That includes obtaining a first. And I expect you to lead. In leadership you are to demonstrate empathy, patience, and endurance."

Cassander's face assumed an innocent expression. "And what if Alexander doesn't perform?"

"His progress reports go to King Philip. Our prince knows the consequence of failing to come up to expectations."

"A drubbing?" Cassander looked hopeful.

"Replacement as heir apparent."

Alexander decided to speak. "Aristotle is right," he said. "My father expects the worthiest successor to inherit."

"So long as you don't mind the pressure," Cassander sneered.

"I've had you on my back for thirteen years."

Laughter drifted through the grove. Rising, Aristotle paced slowly among the daffodils and began his philosophy lecture.

***

23.

Scribbling by the lantern, the prince copied out his favourite verses from the *Iliad*. Between exercises, school, and study there was no time for homework. The only thing for it was to stay up at night.

Hephaestion groaned and rolled over to face the wall. Leonnatus watched the corridor. The penalty for not abiding by the lights-out rule was harsh.

When Alexander wrote, he had total concentration. The *Iliad* transported him to another world. Completely oblivious to everything, he found he learned his lessons in a new way by the act of writing. Everything was more tangible, more real, somehow. Of course, he already knew the poem by heart.

"I wish I was Achilles, Hephaestion."

"Sleep Alex, otherwise, you won't grow."

"I'll always be short, but I *will* be like Achilles one day."

"You're still growing. Who cares about Achilles? He's dead."

"How dare you? He's my ancestor!"

"You will be far greater than him."

The prince stuck his stylus thoughtfully between his wide-gapped teeth. "You may yet have wisdom, Hephaestion."

Looking out the window, Alexander watched the stars overhead. Hanging close to the earth, he felt he could reach out and pluck one from its canopy of the sky. Meantime, the exhausted Leonnatus fell asleep at his post.

Bunching his pillow under his head, Hephaestion turned on his side. "Go to sleep, Alex."

***

The dead frog lay pinned back on a board. Using a slender bronze stick, Aristotle pointed out its innards. Gagging, one of the smaller boys ran out of the class. Cassander laughed loudly and was silenced by a look from the teacher.

Alexander peered at the entrails. "It's strange how all animals have the same insides."

"Even humans," Aristotle said. "Look at the frog's lungs and heart, so like ours."

"I don't have webbed feet," said the prince.

"Or gills," added Hephaestion.

"Many creatures have different bodily systems to us," Aristotle pointed out. "However, you will find most living beings share the same organs."

Alexander looked up from the dissection table at his teacher. "I wonder if there are components of the body so small we can't see them," he said.

"I've often thought blood might have various unseen elements. However, we are not here to speculate."

The morning was spent studying a variety of creatures, while Aristotle explained the function of the circulatory systems and muscle structure.

During the morning break, the boys sat under the trees. Alexander removed himself to a boulder to be alone. Hephaestion joined him.

"You've really taken to the dissection class, Alex."

"It's fascinating. I wonder if there are bodily components, or even elements within us, as Aristotle suggests, which are invisible to the naked eye."

"You two mentioned it in class. It's an interesting thought."

"I want to find out. When I'm King, I shall build a place of learning."

"Are you going to expand Mieza?"

"Egypt has the most ancient culture. When I conquer it, I will build a world centre there, and fill it with philosophers and scientists. Men will design new systems to see into other worlds."

"If you say so cousin, it will be done."

Cassander's impertinent face loomed around a tree trunk. He held a ball in his hand. "What, in Zeus' name, are you talking about?"

Perdiccas ran up, out of breath. "Give me my ball back!"

"Have it," said Cassander, throwing it to him. "I would much rather listen to our classmate. Come everyone, Alexander has turned a new corner in lunacy!"

The other boys crowded round. Alexander's face was thunder. "Mind your manners, Cassander, or I'll thump you."

"Let's all bow before our future monarch. Alex said he is going to create a world centre for scientists and philosophers."

Leonnatus whistled. "That's thinking on a grand scale."

"It's a wonderful idea," said Hephaestion.

"They'll make devices that find unseen animals," said Cassander. "Without respiratory systems, no doubt. I wonder if Arridhaeus is the only fool in the family."

Alexander's right hand clenched into a fist.

"Don't!" Hephaestion's lips barely moved. "You'll lose face with Aristotle when he hears about it."

"Time for a wrestling match," Alexander announced, grabbing Leonnatus and toppling him.

Without hesitation, Cassander tossed Perdiccas. Missing the grass, the latter caught his head on a boulder. Blood gushed over the stone. Leonnatus got up and ran over. Tearing the sleeve off his chiton, he wrapped it round the boy's head. Hephaestion hurried to his side.

"Fetch a doctor, Heph!" Leonnatus shouted.

Alexander jumped up and slammed Cassander's face into the mud. His cousin ran into the school building. Aristotle was at a bench with two assistants, who were sterilising and packing medical equipment.

"Sir," Hephaestion said, trying to catch his breath, "one of the boys has fallen and gashed his head."

The teacher took only moments to be at Perdiccas' side. His assistants arrived soon after, with salves and bandages. Puffing from the exertion, they laid out their instruments and medicines.

"He'll be alright, it's not serious," said Aristotle. "Perdiccas, how did this happen?"

"I fell."

"Were you boys fighting?"

Cassander pointed his index finger. "Alexander wanted to wrestle."

"Is this true, Prince?" Aristotle asked.

Alexander's face flushed. Hephaestion straightened his back and looked their teacher in the eye. "Cassie threw Perdie."

"It was Alexander's idea!" Cassander shrieked.

"But you injured our friend," Hephaestion said.

"You need to improve your skills, Cassie," Leonnatus joined in. "Your clumsiness could kill someone."

Aristotle motioned to his assistants. "Get Perdiccas to sick bay. Everyone leave, except Alexander." The teacher waited until the boys had gone, and there was only birdsong in the grove. He locked eyes with his student. "I expect the highest conduct from you."

"I didn't break Perdiccas' head open."

"You pushed Cassander in the mud."

"How did you know that?"

"Logic. You were standing next to an angry, mud-encrusted boy."

"I didn't want a fight. I wanted to be alone. Then, Hephaestion joined me."

"And everyone else. That's because you are a leader, Alexander. It's going to happen more as you grow up. The wrestling match was instigated by you. It was a dangerous idea."

"Cassander is always stirring up trouble."

"Don't you think I see that? But you are a prince, directly in line to the throne. More is expected from you."

"I'll do better next time."

"I hope so. I file monthly reports on your progress to King Philip. You're dismissed."

The forlorn child ascended the stairs to class. One of the teaching assistants joined Aristotle.

"Why aren't you punishing Cassander?" he asked. "I have a mind to cane the brat myself."

"Because, young man, General Antipater only expects his son to be educated. King Philip pays me to train his successor."

"In Macedonia, the crown goes to the strongest. Nobody can predict the identity of the next king. It's treason to do so."

"Perhaps, but I know what our sovereign wants. His eldest son, Prince Arridhaeus has the mind of a child. He cannot inherit."

"It is rumoured Queen Olympias poisoned him, which affected his mind."

Aristotle stared at his assistant, who blushed. The older man's face softened.

"Don't worry," he said. "Today's incident involving Alexander won't enter the monthly report."

"You have a kind heart."

"I don't wish to be seen as a bad teacher."

"It's not your fault there was a fight at lunch."

"If the boys' parents, including King Philip, hear about this, they will blame me for losing control of my charges. I'll lose my post."

"You will if General Antipater hears. I heard Cassander received a first in herbology."

"He did."

"That boy never studies. Why don't you set him extra homework?"

Aristotle put his hand on his assistant's shoulder. "It's cold. Let's go inside."

***

24.

It was school holidays and Philip's court was bustling with activity. Macedonian nobles took their seats directly below his throne. A group of Persians were located further away in another section, while Alexander and his mother sat with the royal wives.

As they prepared for the morning session, King Philip beckoned to his son. Olympias gave the boy a kiss and sent him across to his father.

Philip bent his head. "Alex, have you met Artabazos?"

"The general sitting with the Persians?"

"You've spotted him already. Good work!"

"I haven't met him."

Leaning to his right, Philip whispered to a councillor. Soon, the Persian general and his daughter were at the foot of his throne.

"Normally, they prostrate themselves before royalty, but I'm not the Persian monarch yet."

Alexander was intrigued. "Why would they do that?"

"Full prostration is the way Persians bow before their sovereign. This is Artabazos and his daughter, Barsine." Philip faced the pair. "Meet my son, Prince Alexander."

The boy stared. In front of the throne, next to her father, stood the most beautiful girl he had ever seen. Artabazos chatted with Philip for some time, before retiring to his seat with Barsine.

For her part, the girl sat next to her father, the epitome of perfection. Alexander noticed her black hair was caught back with gold filagree, similar in design to bands worn by Cretan women, but much more ornate.

The boy waited until the morning session was over. Nobles gathered outside. Philip conversed with his generals. Olympias departed to her quarters with her lady-in-waiting.

Searching for the beautiful girl, Alexander finally spotted her being served refreshments on the main porch. People were milling about, eating snacks and sipping wine.

"Lady Barsine?"

"You may drop the title."

"As you wish. My friends call me Alex."

"Alexander is more appropriate for a prince. Are you eating? The fish pastries are very good."

The boy's hands were sweating. "N-no. I was g-going for a w-walk."

Barsine put her plate on a nearby table. "I shall come with you."

Under the pillared porch, they made their way past statues and flower beds. A cool breeze ruffled Alexander's thick locks.

"Your hair's like gold," Barsine said.

"I'm blond – with a hint of red." Alexander bit his lip.

"Like fire."

"You have lovely hair. Black, like my horse."

Barsine was amused. "I've never been compared to a horse before."

"There has never been one like mine. His name is Bucephalus."

"Ox-head?"

"He has a white star on his forehead – like the holy Apis bulls of Egypt."

"Oh – I think I see."

"He will be famous for all time. I'll show you to him. He has curls like yours."

Alexander wanted to stretch out his hand to touch the beautiful girl's hair, however, he restrained the impulse.

While the youngsters talked, Philip's generals congregated in a nearby pavilion. Fresh fruit and nuts filled gold bowls which were set out on tables.

Parmenion put his head close to the king. "Your son has taken a shine to the Persian lass."

"He's learning their customs," was the terse reply.

Cleitus chewed a handful of nuts. "I would watch those two. We don't want Graeco-Persians at court."

"Why not?" asked Philip.

"It'll be the end of civilisation."

"I wed women from one end of my kingdom to the other. It's good for diplomatic ties. Good for business, too."

"This is different."

"Let them be. They're only children."

While the elders conversed, Hephaestion looked about. Catching sight of Alexander, he ran up to him. The latter frowned.

"Not now, Heph."

Barsine welcomed the newcomer with a smile. "Who is your friend, Alexander?"

"Nobody. He was just leaving."

"So handsome! He must be your brother."

"Not if he has a black eye," muttered Alexander.

"Lady Barsine, I am the prince's cousin, Hephaestion. I'm on my way to see my father."

Noticing his cousin's frown was still in evidence, he hurried off. Barsine fixed Alexander with eyes of stone. "Are you always so rude to your family?"

"Guests come first. Let me show you the gardens."

From a distance, Parmenion continued to observe the pair. "He appears to be running off with her, Philip."

"It's just a garden walk. Now, if you will excuse me, I have a kingdom to administrate."

Downing a cup of wine, Philip retired with his bodyguards to the royal offices. Despite the delightful numbing effects of alcohol, it was not enough to dull the aggravation caused by his military staff.

***

In the palace grounds, the children enjoyed their walk.

"It's a beautiful garden, Alexander," Barsine observed.

"Trees are imported from all over Greece. My father intends to conquer the Greek states one day."

"Dad told me."

"After that, we will start a war of revenge against Persia."

Barsine's lips twitched. "It's a good thing my father is an enemy of King Artaxerxes."

"I am also here to learn Persian customs."

"To understand the empire which will be yours one day?"

Her words floated across the garden's flower bed where a bee hummed in the daffodils. In the corner of his eye, Alexander caught sight of Cleitus. Standing by a statue, nonchalantly eating an apple, the latter was clearly spying on the pair.

"Let's talk about something else."

Putting his hand in Barsine's, Alexander quickly led them down a tree-lined path.

***

25.

Demosthenes pulled out several scrolls from the cupboard above his desk. Unrolling one, he spread it across the polished cedar. After studying it for some time, he referred to another. Tabulated figures were checked and re-checked. He rolled up the first two scrolls. Afterwards, he turned his mind to those which contained maps.

Later, he requested a snack from the kitchen. While he waited, the philosopher stretched and walked about his study. Going to the window, he noticed the sea crashing on the rocky beach.

Eventually, the food arrived. Slices of octopus on a bed of dandelion greens, drizzled with olive oil, were placed on a gold side table by a servant. Next, the man poured out a cup of white wine, which had been made on the estate.

Demosthenes recalled the man's name was Temocles and, while he was of age, the statesman had never seen him with his family.

"Your service is excellent," he said. "I apologise for keeping you from your family at this time of night. Do you have to travel far?"

"My wife lives in the servants' quarters with me."

"Do you have children?"

"Two sir. Both girls."

"How long have you served me?"

"Since childhood." The man swallowed. "I was with – er – your guardians when you were growing up."

"I remember, now." Demosthenes finished his food. "It's summer. Why don't you visit my estate in the hills with your family? Your wife might return pregnant with a son. In the meantime, consider yourself promoted to Chief Steward."

Not knowing what to say, Temocles collected the plates, and left quickly before his master could change his mind.

Demosthenes returned to the scrolls on the table. Satisfied, he shelved them. Going to the window, he watched the shoreline where crests of waves gleamed white against the dark sky. A saucer-sized moon hung above him. The statesman's lips moved as he recited his speech. Eventually, he blew out the lamp and retired to his bedroom.

He now had enough resources to support a war against the King of Macedonia.

***

Philip rolled up a papyrus missive. Next week, the ambassador of Egypt was expected at the palace. The king did not mind administration work. The problem was the interruptions.

Now, Cleitus was at his door. "Philip, you need to take this relationship between Alexander and Barsine seriously."

"I introduced them. Are you questioning my judgment?"

"Supervision must be arranged."

"Alexander isn't interested in women. If he was, you would have a new public holiday."

"He kissed her, Philip! They're even holding hands in public."

"This *is* good news."

"It's dangerous."

"I'll deal with it, Cleitus. For now, that will be all."

After the senior officer left, Philip called for uncut red wine. A servant filled his goblet. Taking a few sips, the king set it aside. He pulled out his battle plans from the surrounding shelves, including the maps of Greece and Persia.

Olympias was at the door. "May I come in?"

"You are always welcome. I was thinking about our son."

"And Barsine?"

"Word gets around fast."

"I'm worried."

"You should be overjoyed. You're always complaining about Alexander's lack of interest in girls."

Ignoring the comment, Olympias pressed on. "Is Aristotle still his teacher?"

"According to our son's tuition invoice."

"Aristotle preaches the superiority of Greek culture. Meanwhile, Alex is running around with a Persian. I'm sure Barsine is a witch. Our boy's besotted."

"He isn't going to marry her."

"Courtship is in the air. I want to know what you intend to do about it."

"There's no courtship, dearest. Alexander will be back in Mieza next week. It's good for him to talk to a few girls."

"It all depends on the sort."

"Barsine's father is a general, here at my invitation. I introduced Alexander to her. Naturally, when the time comes, our son will marry a Macedonian – or Epirite. You may choose."

Mollified, Olympias excused herself. With a sigh of relief, Philip drained his goblet and returned to his battle plans.

***

26.

Barsine sat still while a female attendant combed her hair. Tangling easily, the girl's locks required grooming twice a day. When she had finished, the attendant massaged olive oil into Barsine's scalp and pinned her hair up.

Neither of them spoke. Many a noblewoman had her jewellery poached by such attendants. It always started discreetly. A gold pin here, a tiny piece of carnelian there. Not enough to complain about. Easily replaced. Until eventually, the filched pieces attained an amount commensurate with the daring of the thief, who was now a confidante of the noblewoman.

Perpetrators of household theft were never caught. A new employee was always blamed. A maid who desperately needed her job would be banished, or a slave beaten and turned to the kitchens to haul water until her back broke. Barsine preferred to keep things simple – and keep her jewellery.

After the woman left, she went to her window. Opening the shutters, she gazed out at the vast palace. Its marble edifice glowed in the light of the moon. Barsine reflected on how her father brought his family here from Persia.

The girl had never trusted this foreign land. Her father said they were settling in Macedonia rather than Greece, which was the traditional enemy of Persia. But the country felt like Greece. Its sculpture and architecture were the same. Artabazos tried to placate his daughter, by telling her King Philip hated all Greeks.

Still, Philip aspired to be one of them. He proactively sought and hired Aristotle for the tuition of his son. As Barsine's father pointed out, the philosopher was Macedonian by birth. However, he was hailed as a Greek.

Aristotle's teachings were pure propaganda, lauding the greatness of Greece and its master race, while relegating Barsine's people to the rank of pond scum. And his fame was growing. Even though he was not yet at Plato's level, he was widely considered to be Greece's most eminent living philosopher.

To her, there was no difference between Greeks and Macedonians. They were both coarse by comparison to the ways of her countrymen.

And they all hated Persia.

***

For the remainder of the school holidays, Alexander met Barsine in the garden every day. One evening, during a walk back to the palace, they stopped outside a door.

"Is this your chamber, Alex?"

"I share it with Hephaestion."

"Where is he?"

"At a poetry competition. It finishes at midnight."

Alexander pushed the door open. Barsine stepped inside.

***

Perdiccas settled down to sleep. With a royal hunt in the morning, he wanted to prove himself a man alongside the king and other hunters. A hard bed in the vestibule was just the thing to prepare himself.

Suddenly, a guard outside banged his staff on the ground. The front door swung open, and the man poked his head in. "Friend to see you, sir."

"Now?"

"In future, please let us know if you are planning to have overnight visitors."

"But, I have no plans to entertain."

"King Philip's orders, sir," the guard continued. "The place is crawling with Persians."

Hephaestion was standing in the vestibule with his bedding. "Is it alright if I stay the night, Perdie?"

"Er – of course."

Satisfied, there was no danger, the guard closed the door and returned to his post. Avoiding a nearby couch in the living room, Hephaestion arranged his bedclothes on the floor.

Perdiccas saw the boy's face was the colour of wax. "Did you have a fight with Alexander?"

"He has a guest." Hephaestion tucked himself under the blankets. "I'll be quiet. I know about your hunt tomorrow."

Perdiccas swung his legs out of bed. "You can't lie on the ground."

"But, I might fall off your couch."

"There is the Athena suite. Come, I'll show you."

Before the visitor could say anything, Perdiccas whipped back his bedclothes, and dumped them on the couch. He took the boy up a short corridor. At the end, he pushed open a door.

Hephaestion uttered a gasp. Inside, was the most enormous bedchamber he had ever seen. Sumptuous wall hangings kept out the drafts. Gold stands held burning braziers to keep the room warm. At the end, a bed the size of a dormitory at Mieza Groves, peeked out from behind ornate screens.

"It's huge!"

"This is Athena's master bedroom." Perdiccas winked. "The one in which she waits for Ares."

"But why don't you sleep here?"

"Not before a hunt."

Two Persian attendants welcomed the boys to the couches by a fire. They brought food and wine. Hephaestion's eyes widened.

"What a feast!" he exclaimed.

"After you've eaten, we can play draughts."

Colour returned to Hephaestion's cheeks. "I should like that very much."

***

27.

It was the tenth hour of the day. Perdiccas ran his index finger around the neck of his vest. Everyone was dressed for the royal hunt. Alexander and Hephaestion were chatting in low voices. The older guard, including Parmenion and Antipater, ordered their beaters to encircle a group of thickets.

A few yards away on his horse, the king was stabbing at the underbrush.

"I see droppings," he announced.

"A mother and her piglets were spotted here last week," said Parmenion.

Perdiccas gripped his reins. Below his horse's hooves, bushes rustled. Suddenly, a wild boar shot out of a thicket. Alexander's javelin was already in mid-flight. Perdiccas' horse reared as a boar's tusk missed its shins. Grasping his steed's reins tightly, the boy tried desperately to control its bucking. Meanwhile, the frightened boar fled downhill, and out of view.

"Get that pig!" Philip roared.

Alexander and Hephaestion disappeared down the hill, followed by the rest of the party. Perdiccas' horse returned to earth. Patting one of its flanks, he urged it on.

Descending into a valley, he saw the first javelin hit the boar. It was Alexander's. Instead of being felled, the animal swivelled round to face the men. Lowering his head, he pawed the ground. Ivory tusks caught the sunlight.

It was then that Perdiccas noticed the animal was fully grown. Those fangs were over a cubit long, he thought. Tilting his head, he noticed the beast was aiming directly for Philip. Parmenion immediately shielded his king.

In a reflex action, Perdiccas kicked his horse's sides. Swooping across the beaters' main flank, he struck the boar squarely in its left side.

General Antipater waved to Cassander. "Get over here, son!"

But Cassander and Leonnatus were engaged in their own tussle.

"Cassie, I'm a hunter and should be in front."

"Out of the way, Leo, it's mine!"

On impulse, Leonnatus ran his friend through the thigh with his spear. Screaming, Cassander fell forward over his horse's mane. Realising he needed his weapon for the boar, Leonnatus jerked it back. His friend's thigh spurted blood.

"Be grateful I spared your horse."

Racing away, Leonnatus closed in on the boar. Several bodyguards galloped to Cassander's side. A horrified Antipater dithered. Torn between protecting his king, and rushing to his child's aid, he rapidly assessed the situation. Seeing his son taken away on a stretcher, Antipater chose to back up the senior command around Philip.

There was no need. The boar was being repeatedly stabbed by youngsters, who wanted to become men with the privilege of reclining on a banquet couch. Squeals and roars of the dying animal rang through the fields. Echoing in nearby glades, the sounds terrified local wildlife. Birds flew away. Thudding miniature hooves signalled that the piglets were near. Fleeing with their mother, they escaped into a wood.

When it was safe, several of the senior officers abandoned their positions around Philip to rein in the youths, who were in danger of destroying the carcass altogether.

***

Olympias stepped onto her balcony. It was midday and there was a commotion in the palace grounds. Several other royal women were on their balconies, craning their necks to find the source of the noise.

She spotted Hephaestion and Perdiccas in the courtyard, assisting Alexander with a huge dead boar. Its bristles were black, thick and spiky. Cassander was limping, and his thigh was bound. Leonnatus, who was normally at his side, seemed to be avoiding him.

In the courtyard, a sweaty Parmenion drank deeply from a waterskin. Philip wiped his brow and dismounted. He was immediately surrounded by pages. Royal bodyguards hovered nearby. Pausanias undid his body armour.

Olympias shaded her eyes and took in the scene. Behind her, the apartment door opened. Her sentry announced a visitor.

A woman entered and put her basket on an oak table. "Are we spinning today?"

"My husband is back, Airlia."

"Lion hunt?"

"Boar. Alexander's."

Airlia stepped onto the balcony. Her sharp eyes spotted the hunters. Philip's bodyguard, Pausanias was locked in conversation with him.

"Pausanias is close to Philip," she remarked.

"I'm aware of that."

"A royal bodyguard?"

"From Orestis."

Airlia permitted herself a smile. "So you've already conducted a background check, my dear."

"I wouldn't be Queen if I didn't keep up with the latest news."

Olympias turned indoors. She picked up her spindle from a corner and took a basket of dyed wool to the oak table.

"Alexander was on the hunt," said Airlia.

"Which means the King of Macedonia publicly acknowledged his successor to be a man today."

Olympias selected a piece of sheep's wool from her own basket. Airlia joined her. Together the women began to spin.

***

28.

Barsine yawned. It was the fifth time she had heard the story. Alexander stopped.

"Are you bored?" he asked.

"I would like our afternoon walk, my sweetheart."

Brightening, the prince took his girlfriend's hand. Late afternoon was always Barsine's favourite time of day. Gold light picked out the leaves of hibiscus bushes and jasmine plants. They strolled through paths lined with statues of Philip's victories over his enemies. The air was balmy at this time of year. Finally, they came to the edge of the gardens where wild roses and honeysuckle grew.

In the royal quarters, the king's men spotted the couple before anyone else.

"I warned you, Philip," said Parmenion.

"They're children taking the air. What's wrong with that?"

"It's obvious they're lovers," said Aeropus.

"Alexander killed a boar today, which makes him a man," Philip pointed out. "It's about time."

Parmenion's brows drew together. "Have you considered what Artabazos might do when he finds out his daughter is having an affair out of wedlock?"

"Are you suggesting a wedding?" Philip asked.

To his amusement, rumbles broke out among the infuriated generals. Things grew heated. Finally, Cleitus decided to calm everyone with a few words.

"Why worry?" he said in an attempt to mollify the more aggressive speakers. "Alexander is due back at Mieza in a few days."

As Philip's men debated the pros and cons of intermarriage, Barsine and Alexander reached the garden's edge. White walls, covered in ivy, reared above them.

Turning around, the prince squinted in the last gold rays of the setting sun. He heard coarse men's laughter from his father's quarters. It floated across the gardens.

"Come Barsine, let's return to the palace. I have a gift for you."

"So long as it's not another copy of the *Iliad*."

"Don't worry, you'll like it."

Alexander took the opportunity to kiss her under the tall trees which covered their route all the way back to the main palace.

*****

At the entrance to the prince's apartments, the couple noticed Hephaestion. Shouldering a backpack, he was ready to depart.

"Please don't leave on our account," implored Barsine.

"On the contrary," Alexander encouraged. "Hurry along."

"Why are you so rude to your cousin?" asked Barsine. She smiled at Hephaestion. "Where are you going, with all your belongings?"

The boy blushed. "Perdiccas is putting me up."

"You're lucky," said Barsine. "He's in the Athena apartment."

"Why is that significant?" asked Alexander.

"It is the most sumptuously appointed apartment in the palace," Barsine replied.

"More so than my father's?"

"Far more," said Hephaestion. "So I believe," he added, blushing again.

"It has its own kitchen, which never closes," explained Barsine.

Hephaestion adjusted the pack on his shoulder. "I'll be on my way."

Hurrying down the passage, he vanished around a corner.

"I am told that your cousin is your closest companion," said Barsine, as Alexander escorted her inside. "And still, you sent him away."

"I'll make it up to him. After all, Hephaestion is the only person who loves me for myself."

"What about your parents?"

"Aristotle is more of a father to me than my own. I keep out of my mother's way. She is a witch."

"Be careful of how you speak about your mother. The gods hear everything."

"They agree with me. Mother is a high priestess of Dionysius, in other words, a real-life witch."

Alexander walked over to a table and picked up a cedar box. Barsine opened the lid. Inside, was a necklace of pure gold. Wondering at it, she slowly took it out of the box. Intricately worked, it bore filigrees of leaves and acorns.

"It's breathtaking."

"That's because it's for the most beautiful girl in the world."

Barsine kissed Alexander's cheek.

***

Perdiccas rose to greet his visitor. "Back again, Hephaestion!"

"Alexander is with Barsine."

"It's good to have your company." Perdiccas relieved his friend of his backpack. "Why didn't you use a servant to carry your things?"

"I'm Macedonian."

"Fair enough. Did you enjoy the hunt?"

"I was proud of Alex."

"We all brought down the boar."

"My cousin's was the first spear."

"Don't forget, our sovereign was also pleased with you."

"And you, Perdiccas. He said you placed your horse's needs above your own glory. And your spear in the animal's left flank saved his life."

"I didn't expect a fully grown boar with cubit-long tusks, especially after Parmenion said there was only a mother and piglets about."

"At least they're safe," Hephaestion said.

Perdiccas digested the words. Sensitivity was not considered to be a virtue in Macedonia.

"Like a drink?" he asked.

***

29.

Leonnatus barged into the room where Cassander was waiting. A worn leather ball flew above him. Lurching forward, he caught it.

"Ninety-six!"

He took out two more balls and threw all three into the air. Cassander put out one leg to trip up the intrepid juggler. As he did so, his injured thigh went into spasm.

"Ow, the pain! For goodness' sakes, Leo, can't you let the juggling alone for a moment?"

"I've just broken our record. Is your leg alright?"

"You've beaten me again." Cassander rubbed his thigh. "Like at that boar hunt. Was it really necessary to put your spear into my leg?"

"It was an accident."

"Liar! You can't stand me winning. By the way, where are the others, Leo?"

"They're not coming."

"We can't have a drinking party with only two of us. Where are they?"

Leonnatus fell into a chair. He ticked off his fingers. "Let's see – Alexander's with Barsine. That means Perdiccas is putting Hephaestion up at the Athena apartment. Meanwhile, Parmenion and Cleitus are taking the air, no doubt attempting to spy on the lovers –"

Cassander's eyes grew large. "Alexander's with Barsine?"

"They're having an affair of the heart."

"Since when?"

"Since we got here."

"This is the first I've heard of it."

"You must walk around with your eyes shut, Cassie. The entire palace knows. Anyway, I think we should pay a visit to the Athena apartment."

"I'd rather visit Alexander's."

"We can swing by his rooms and ask him if he wants to come to the party."

"You're on!"

***

The boys hurried down the corridor. Making their way past the sentries, they cut across the gardens to approach Alexander's apartment from the rear. At last they reached an older part of the palace. The yellow paint was a faded lemon. Cornices bloomed with green mould.

Shading his eyes, Leonnatus craned his head back. "Drapes are closed, Cassie."

"So?"

"Alex will be angry if we disturb him. You know what he's like."

It was too late. Cassander was already banging on the door. A sentry who had been snoozing in the sun, abruptly pulled himself off the garden bench and hurried over. "Hey! You can't just knock on the prince's door."

"We're his friends. Prince Alexander is due at a function."

The sentry looked up at the first floor. Purple curtains were drawn across the window. "He's sleeping."

"He most certainly is not," Cassander said.

Upstairs, the curtains flicked back. A tousled fair head appeared. Leonnatus threw his ball upwards. On a reflex, Alexander caught it.

"We're off to a party, Alex – at the Athena apartment."

"Wait!"

Cassander turned to the sentry. "Imagine if you had stopped the prince from attending an important function."

"I'm paid to protect his privacy."

"You're not doing a very good job, sleeping in the hibiscus bushes."

"I was on the guards' bench."

Leonnatus snorted. "Sitting or sleeping?"

Cassander joined him in mocking laughter. The man's face reddened. Alexander appeared at the door. Clad in a blue chiton, his hair was combed, and he sported a gold necklace and bracelets.

"Which way is the fastest route?" he asked the guard.

"Across the pond," the man replied.

Barsine appeared. She stood behind Alexander in a blue robe and gold jewellery, which was almost identical to his in design. Cassander let out a slow whistle. Leonnatus dug him in the ribs.

"This is Lady Barsine," said Alexander. "She's coming with us."

"To a drinking party?" Cassander asked.

"Do you have a problem with my girlfriend?"

"I only wonder if it is appropriate to allow a member of the fair sex to attend a man's drinking party."

"We're not men, Cassie. We're students on holiday."

"We killed a boar. That makes us men."

"I don't recall you doing anything except getting speared." Alexander took Barsine's hand. "We're going out to dinner at the Athena, where you my friend, *might* be allowed to recline on a couch with us."

The group strolled in the direction of the pond. Grinding his teeth in fury, Cassander resisted the urge to toss his friend off the bridge.

***

Perdiccas was perplexed. "I hadn't planned a party."

Shifting their feet in awkward silence, the youngsters stood at his door. Hephaestion appeared at his roommate's elbow.

"We're glad you're here," he said cheerily. "Follow our prince down the corridor." As Alexander and the guests trooped past, Hephaestion restrained Perdiccas. "Alex's girlfriend is the Persian ambassador's daughter. Tell the cooks to add more courses to our dinner. We don't want anyone drunk. I'll keep an eye on Cassie."

Perdiccas hurried to catch up with his guests, who were waiting by the door to the main suite. When he flung it open, the reaction was gratifying. The prince tilted his head back to observe the gilded ceiling cornices.

"The rumours are true," he said. "This is bigger than Father's apartment."

"It takes after the royal palace in Persepolis," Barsine said.

Alexander's ears pricked up. "In size?"

"It's a replica, down to the Persian attendants. I shall be staying quite a long time."

Barsine gave a tinkling laugh as she swung Alexander's hand. Cassander's eyes bulged.

Leonnatus tugged at his sleeve. "Let's grab a couch, Cassie. I need a drink."

***

Philip looked about the banqueting hall. "Where are the Young Companions?"

"It's their last night," Aeropus reminded him.

"They're late. No one is to be later than the king."

"Your son killed a boar, Philip," Cleitus explained. "The youngsters are celebrating."

"Where?"

"Er – in the apartments."

"There are thousands of apartments in my palace. Which ones, Cleitus?"

"I can't say."

"You can't, or you won't? I brought those whipper-snappers on a royal hunt today. They're supposed to be at dinner."

Artabazos shifted anxiously on his couch. "My daughter isn't here, either."

"You're right, Ambassador. Where are they, Cleitus?"

Pausanias who was behind the king, leaned over and whispered in his ear. Philip threw the hem of his robe over his right shoulder.

"Come, Artabazos. We're going to a party."

"But it is customary to dine here, Your Majesty. And your son must come to you, not the other way around."

Philip's one eye twinkled. "It's important we check on how the future King of Macedonia entertains."

***

At the Athena apartment there was a queue. A hundred guests were in attendance. Musicians played flutes. Persian dancers spun around the room.

Ignoring the rumblings from Artabazos, Philip waited to be announced.

"Half my harem is here, Cleitus," he whispered.

"If I were you, my focus would be on the Persian ambassador. His imminent eruption threatens to be worse than any on Mount Aetna."

Spotting the king waiting patiently, Leonnatus fell off his couch. Cassander, who was merrily waving a full wine cup, froze.

Hephaestion, however, was on his feet. "Welcome distinguished guests! It was good of you to respond to the invitation."

Philip exchanged a look with the Persian ambassador.

"I don't recall us being invited," he whispered.

"We weren't."

Hephaestion gestured towards the eating area. "Your dining couches await."

Accepting the one indicated, Philip reclined against a cushion, an expression of good humour on his face. Grumbling, the senior members of the Macedonian court took their places. Meanwhile, Perdiccas hurried to Alexander. The latter, who was talking to the butler, was prodded from behind.

"You'd better have a good reason for poking me in the ribs, Perdiccas."

"Your father and Artabazos are here."

"Why didn't you announce him?"

With swift strides, Alexander went to greet his father. Philip lounged against a cushion, eating grapes. "I expected you at the hall this evening, son."

"I meant to be there."

The king eyed a dancing girl. "This is much better. Next time, invite me."

"That lady is from your harem."

"This is the first time I've noticed her." Philip finished the bunch of grapes. "You and Barsine are together, I see."

Alexander flushed. "She's my girlfriend."

"It's not surprising. She is beautiful. Do you plan to return to Mieza next term?"

"Do I have a choice?"

"You always have a choice."

"I am Aristotle's pupil. You have invested in me, Father. It's my duty to study."

Philip picked up a wine cup. His one eye flicked across the room to the ambassador. "Barsine's father disagrees with your liaison. However, I think it is a good thing."

"It is more than a liaison."

"That's excellent news, Alex. It's important to consider that the conquest of Persia will mean a new world."

"You will be at the helm of our army, which will right the wrongs done to Greece."

A wicked smile crossed Philip's face. "We're not Greek."

"You will subdue the Greek states and make Macedonia and Greece one nation."

"And what happens when our lands amalgamate with Persia, Alexander?"

"We shall be part of an empire."

"An empire won by the sword."

"Your sword, Father."

"You say that now, but you're already sleeping with the enemy."

Alexander clenched his fists. "I love Barsine."

Philip leaned forward and patted his son's knee. "The way to seal conquests is by marriage. I've done it all my life. Even your mother is Epirite. I approve of Barsine, and will take care of the ambassador." Philip sat back. "Now, let's get drunk together."

***

30.

Alexander's face was ruddy in the torchlight as he and his friends negotiated the gardens on the way back to their rooms. Their bodyguards followed, a few steps behind. Dew covered the grass. Above, the moon was high in the heavens.

Leonnatus took deep breaths of the evening air. It was warm and fragrant, with the scent of damp jasmine.

"What a wonderful party!" he said.

"Right up until Artabazos' abduction of Barsine," Cassander snickered.

"She had to leave with her father," Alexander explained.

"Barsine was tired," Leonnatus said. "Women are weaker than men. You, of all people should know that, Cassie."

"Why? I know nothing of girls."

"But you prefer women to men, don't you?"

"To any of you, it's true."

"Women aren't weaker than men, Leo," said Alexander. "They're different, that's all."

Leonnatus tossed his ball to Cassander, who caught it.

"We mustn't forget, they are dangerous," the latter said, in a matter-of-fact tone.

"More so than men," Alexander muttered.

"Has she a very great hold on your heart?" In the flickering light, Cassander looked serious, even compassionate.

"I wasn't thinking of Barsine," Alexander replied.

"Your mother, then?"

The prince nodded. Cassander's face wobbled as it slid into the darkness. He threw the ball back to Leonnatus. The boys refrained from comment. When it came to Queen Olympias, there were some things better left unsaid.

***

It was the early hours of the morning. Perdiccas' apartment was emptied of the evening's visitors. Servants cleaned up. Hephaestion sat in a corner, reading. While raking embers in the marble fireplace, Perdiccas glanced at his studious friend.

"What have you there?" he asked.

"Homework. We're back at Mieza next week."

"Are you reading the *Iliad*?"

"Biology, for dissection class."

"I thought we'd finished studying the topic."

"This is different. Next term, we'll learn how an animal's body works. Did you know that blood is pumped around through something called circulation?"

"Is this knowledge necessary? The gods give life."

"True, but bodies in all living beings have various functions which are worth studying." Rising from his corner, Hephaestion walked to the fireplace and showed Perdiccas his scroll. "See this diagram? It's a frog."

Still glassy-eyed from the evening's wine, Perdiccas peered at the drawing. "It looks like nothing I've ever seen."

He hiccupped. Hephaestion placed his scroll on a side table. Gently removing the bronze poker from his friend's hand, he steered him away from the fireplace.

"Time for bed, Perdie."

***

It was a chilly morning as the Young Companions left for another term at school. King Philip was asleep with his dancing concubine from the night before. Barsine and Alexander took leave of one another in the garden, where they had spent so much of their time during the school holidays.

112

At the palace, Olympias kissed her son goodbye. Shedding copious tears, she watched until the cavalcade of horses and carriages heading to Mieza was completely out of sight.

Cassander rode in silence most of the way. Leonnatus made do with attempting to throw a ball in the air while mounted on horseback. A few times, he lurched forward. Eventually, his stallion tired of his unsteady rider, and on a catch which threatened to spin out of control, stood stock still.

"Watch out, Leo!" Perdiccas called from behind.

Leonnatus tumbled forward. A vice-like grip seized the neck of his chiton and pulled him back before he fell off his surly steed.

"Cassie, I owe you my life," Leonnatus gasped.

"Don't make promises you can't keep."

"You're finally talking. I thought you were in a bad mood."

"I was quietly enjoying the scenery until you spoiled my view."

"I assumed you were quiet because you didn't want to go back to school."

"That, too. By the way, did you know we have to dissect frogs this summer?"

***

Dusk rolled across the groves of Mieza. Alexander inhaled the air. The smell of wood fires and pine trees greeted the returning students.

Servants assisted with the luggage. Bodyguards headed for the kitchens to warm themselves up with bowls of hot chicken broth. Meantime, the boys went to their rooms, where bread and stew awaited.

Cassander and Perdiccas joined Leonnatus in his quarters. The boys sat at a cedar table and attacked their meal with gusto.

"This is delicious," said Perdiccas.

Tearing his bread, Leonnatus wrapped it around a piece of stew. "I'm hungrier than I thought. Mind you, we were riding all day."

Slurping his gravy, Cassander finished first. He pushed his chair back. "I'm still ravenous." Leaving the room, he went to the kitchen. Servants looked up from their dinner. A look of contempt crossed his face. "Aren't you supposed to be unpacking?"

One of the cooks smiled at the youngster. "May I get you something, Cassander?"

"Stew – and dessert. I like honey cakes."

"I'll have them sent to your room."

Cassander hesitated. "Do you have wine?"

Several of the diners tried not to smile.

"I'll have a jug sent up."

"I have company," the youth explained.

"Go back and entertain your friends, Lord Cassander. Your luggage will be up shortly."

***

31.

Aristotle was patient. Red-cheeked boys, fresh from their holiday, chattered like birds. Leonnatus had four oranges in the air, while Cassander's sarcastic remarks floated across the noisy classroom. Only Alexander was facing the front. Seated next to him, Hephaestion was studying a diagram in his scroll.

When the sun dial pointed to the eighth hour of the morning, Aristotle stepped forward. "Does anyone know what we are studying this term?"

"Biology, sir," said Hephaestion.

Alexander looked surprised. "I thought it was the ninth book of the *Iliad*."

"You are both right," their teacher said. "We are inside this morning for roll call."

"Which he never takes," Cassander said, sticking out one arm to disrupt Leonnatus' juggling.

Aristotle faced the boy with a genial expression. "You're as sharp as ever, Cassander, but I've already counted. Now, boys, through the door behind me, your first biology lesson awaits. Don't worry, Alexander, this afternoon we shall study your favourite poem in the groves." He spread out his arms. "Welcome back to Mieza!"

Filled with wrath at losing his stride in juggling, Leonnatus cuffed Cassander across his scalp. Then, stuffing his oranges in his satchel, he joined the others.

***

The class did not go as expected. While Hephaestion and Alexander were excited, many of the boys recoiled at the dead sheep's eyes placed in front of them. Frog innards followed. Students fainted, or ran outside to vomit.

Cassander and Leonnatus found the glutinous eyeballs of interest, and started playing catch. Pelting other boys with frogs' legs also seemed like a good idea to them. As a consequence, Aristotle spent the morning alternately shouting and calling for first aid.

After lunch, which Cassander scoffed, and many bypassed, afternoon classes were transferred to the groves. There they listened, enthralled by the most beautiful poem in the world, Homer's *Iliad*.

Brave deeds of heroes from long ago, recounted in Aristotle's clear voice, rang out through the trees under a bright blue sky. Eyes contemplating the space before them, the boys dreamed of a world filled with the clank of shields and advancing armies.

At the end of the afternoon, Aristotle rolled up his copy of the *Iliad*. "My assistants will hand out your homework in a few moments. Your task is to write an argument on a subject which I have set." He fixed his eyes on Alexander. "You are expected to argue."

"When do we start?"

"For you, tomorrow."

"I'll be ready."

"A good argument should contain logic, ethics, and emotion. I shall be your opponent."

Leaving the boys to digest this information, Aristotle made his way back inside the school. At the right time, his assistants came out of the main doors to distribute scrolls to the students.

"We each have a different exercise," said Cassander, looking over his colleagues' shoulders.

"It's so that we can't cheat," said Leonnatus. "Not that Alexander has much time."

The boys laughed.

"Don't worry, Alex," whispered Hephaestion. "You'll be great."

"What are you talking about? I've never argued in my life. Now I'm up against the best. I'll be humiliated, and Father will hear of it."

Perdiccas rose from the moss-covered boulder on which he had been resting during the afternoon. Dissection of frog innards had not agreed with his own. He walked up to Alexander on unsteady feet.

"Aristotle has given you a great honour. I'll be rooting for you." He turned a delicate shade of green. "Now, I have to go to my room."

"We'll cheer you on, Alexander," Leonnatus added. "Wait, Perdie! I'll help you."

He took his classmate's arm. They walked slowly to the students' quarters, with Perdiccas making frequent stops at the flower beds.

"I don't have any time," Alexander wailed.

"That's what you get for opening your big mouth," retorted Cassander.

Evading Hephaestion's left jab, he trotted after Leonnatus and Perdiccas, ensuring he kept his distance from their sick comrade.

***

It was the second hour of the morning. Mindful of the harsh lights-out rule, Alexander placed Leonnatus on watch in the corridor while he studied. After midnight, Leonnatus closed his eyes. His head dropped onto his chest. He snoozed.

Meanwhile, Alexander wrote into the new day. Aristotle's exercise of pitching a raw youth against his experience seemed unfair at first, however, after several drafts, the prince knew he would win. Why would the distinguished philosopher make it so easy?

Perturbed, the royal student finally blew out his lamp. Above him, through his window, a pall of stars glinted over the cold grass. Mieza, so inviting by day, was freezing at night. The boy felt no cold or fear. It was trained out of him a long time ago.

"Goodnight, Barsine," he whispered into the darkness.

A warmth enveloped him. Instantly, he fell asleep. In the corridor, Leonnatus woke with a start. There was no light under Alexander's door. Relieved, the exhausted child abandoned his post and made his way down the empty corridor to bed.

***

117

32.

The verbal duel lasted all morning. Alexander's impassioned rhetoric moved the boys, who cheered him on. Aristotle spoke carefully, allowing his argument to make the impression, rather than using emotive delivery to sway his audience. Pacing himself, he made statements in a clear, concise manner.

Two assistants scribbled furiously on their wax tablets as they allocated points to each orator. Eventually, after much consultation with each other, the scribes declared Alexander the winner.

At midday, the class broke for lunch. The boys ate in the groves. Some wrestled. Perdiccas sat by himself, practicing his juggling with several multi-coloured balls. Eating a cold pheasant sandwich, Hephaestion looked on.

The last to leave class, Alexander packed his oratory exercise in his satchel. He took out several plums and a lamb shank. Picking up a wine flask he went to join the others.

Aristotle put his hand on his pupil's arm. "Stay."

The boy swallowed. "What is it, sir?"

"Do you know Euripides?"

"*To Greece I give this body of mine. Slay it in sacrifice and conquer Troy.*"

"Excellent! Learn all his works by heart. It will stand you in good stead."

"Is that all?"

"Today you earned the merit of Philosopher."

"In the line of Plutarch and Socrates? You honour me."

"Alexander, you will become much more than a king, or a philosopher, but you will be both. Now, go and join your friends. You can all have another hour for lunch."

Elated, Alexander joined Hephaestion. "Was Aristotle impressed, Alex?"

"He congratulated me. And I thought he would be offended."

"You're supposed to argue in philosophy. You've won your first debate, cousin. I'm proud of you."

The prince was about to say something, but hesitated. A few yards away, Leonnatus threw Perdiccas a ball. The latter caught it and threw it in the air. He added two, then three more as he juggled. It was the first time he had done it. The Companions roared encouragement.

"Let's go for a run," Alexander suggested to Hephaestion. "You must be tired of this circus by now."

***

Demosthenes paused in the middle of his speech before the Athenian assembly. Known as the *Third Philippic*, everyone knew it was his attempt to ignite Greece with hostility against Macedonia. The streets were packed with people, who were being fed a running commentary from those inside. As he scratched his bearded chin, the lines on the speaker's brow deepened.

Taking a breath, he continued with his denunciation of King Philip. Using reason, he pointed out the danger of keeping peace with an outsider, who ravaged their cities.

"… But if anyone mistakes for peace an arrangement which will enable Philip, when he has seized everything else, to march upon us, he has taken leave of his senses, and the peace that he talks of is one that you observe towards Philip, but not Philip towards you."

Scribes took notes. An artist sketched the scene. General Chares, who was seated in a prominent position in the hall, listened intently.

Timotheus entered, and spotting his friend, he went to his side. "People say this is his best speech, Chares. Demosthenes has been rehearsing by the sea for weeks."

"I heard him on an evening walk. It was powerful. I am not sure the Greek states will change, but even if they don't, our statesman has predicted their future with chilling precision."

At the front, Demosthenes paused to consult his notes. Timotheus leaned towards Chares' ear. "It *is* good to see you after so long, General. How is your family?"

"Fine. I also have a mistress, these days."

"Ah well – you have been married for some time."

"Two years. It was arranged. She bore me a son, so the marriage has not been a total loss."

"A son is a blessing. My congratulations to you."

"I heard you also have children."

"Three boys and a girl."

"No mistresses, yet?" Chares jested.

Timotheus paused before replying. "I have never known another woman. My wife and I fell in love when we were young."

Demosthenes cleared his throat, to indicate he was ready. Chares fixed sad eyes on the front. The speech rolled on.

"I pass over Olynthus and Methone and Apollonia and the two and thirty cities in or near Thrace, all of which Philip has destroyed so ruthlessly that a traveller would find it hard to say whether they had ever been inhabited."

Rumbles filled the assembly. Demosthenes may have made elaborate speeches, but they always carried truth and packed a punch. The audience listened on.

***

33.

King Philip smashed his fist on the oak table. "Athens provokes us once again!"

"We need to do something," said Parmenion. "This has been going on for years."

"I already have a battlefield in mind on which the fate of Greece could be determined."

"And yet you focus on Asia."

"Which is the first step to Persia."

Parmenion rubbed his brow. "How can we advance on Asia without the Greeks?"

"I'm with Parmenion," Aeropus interrupted. "We need to conquer Greece first."

"Agreed," Attalus and Andromenes chimed in.

"The Greek city states hold us back," said Philip. "I've spent decades negotiating with those people. Backstabbers all! Did you know Demosthenes delivered his *Third Philippic* last week? He blames me for breaking the peace."

Parmenion mulled over his friend's words. "Athens has only a statesman making speeches," he said at last. "You Philip, are a mighty king. I say let's march on Asia while the Greeks listen to speeches."

***

It was the end of school. Servants' shouts filled the student quarters as men packed the boys' possessions in chests and loaded them on horse-drawn carts.

Hephaestion ran to Alexander's room. "We're in the same carriage, cousin!"

"I'm riding home."

"How? Every horse is hitched to our luggage train."

"Bucephalus arrived from Pella last night."

Hephaestion looked through the window and started. "He's grown!"

"And ready to take his master home," Alexander grinned.

Shaking his head, Hephaestion left to finish his packing. Cassander put his head round the door. "All ready, Prince Slowpoke?"

"Be warned Cassie, your insolence will cost you a drubbing."

"Face facts, Alex, the tortoises in Micza's groves are faster than you. I'm packed and waiting. Next to Aristotle, in case you're thinking of doing me mischief."

He was gone before Alexander could react. The prince stuck a dagger into his waistband and picked up his worn copy of the *Iliad*. As he was about to depart, he found his way blocked by Aristotle who held out a book.

"I already have the *Iliad*, sir."

"This one is annotated. You might find my thoughts of interest."

He was gone before Alexander could thank him. Checking his room a final time, the prince headed for the foyer. Aristotle was there to see everyone off. His fellow students were crammed into the small space, talking in excited tones. While Leonnatus wound new twine over his favourite ball, Perdiccas chatted to Cassander. Hephaestion was nowhere to be seen.

"Your lover is with your horse, Alex," Cassander grinned.

Tempted to hit his smile sideways, the prince only ground his teeth. Aristotle was standing in front of the prince.

"I had a wonderful term, sir," Alexander said politely. "Thank you for your copy of my favourite book. I'll treasure it."

"It's been a pleasure teaching you. Your cousin is with Bucephalus. He's a big horse. Doubtless, you plan to take him into battle one day."

"That's my intention."

"You and Hephaestion should ride him back to Pella. It would save you both being cooped up with Cassander on the journey home."

"An excellent suggestion, sir."

"Remember your destiny, my son. Don't give into rage, especially with those jealous of you. At least, not until you're King. And stop calling me *sir*."

Aristotle continued with the job of wishing the other students farewell. The prince made his way to the courtyard where Bucephalus was tethered.

Hephaestion stroked the black mane of the gigantic steed. "See, how he lets me pat him!"

Alexander wrapped his arms around his horse's neck. Bucephalus nuzzled his owner's ear and shook his head in greeting. "Aristotle suggested we ride together, Heph."

Vaulting onto his horse's back, the prince stretched out his hand. Hephaestion grasped it and leapt up to sit behind him. They clopped over to join their fellow students. Slowly, the party headed home towards Pella.

***

PART II

34.

It was late afternoon in the royal gardens. A messenger approached Parmenion, who arose from the warmth of his wooden bench and followed the man. Together they climbed marble stairs which led to the king's apartments.

At the door, guards clad in the distinctive regalia of Epirus, waited. Parmenion's arrival was announced, and a footman ushered him into King Philip's presence. In the middle of the room, a fire crackled in its hearth. Occasionally, a slave stirred the embers with a bronze poker to keep the flames alive.

The king stood next to a table on which lay several maps. Bent over them, he feverishly pushed one away in favour of another.

Parmenion rubbed the bridge of his nose. "You have Epirites guarding your door."

"It keeps Olympias happy."

"But, is that wise?"

"We share a son. I doubt her bodyguards will assassinate me."

"You have every map on Asia, in front of you. Are we going into battle?"

"I'm taking Perinthus."

"Difficult place."

"Illyria is tougher."

"We've defeated the Illyrians in battle."

"That's why you're here, Parmenion. I need your advice as a senior member of my military staff."

"There are three problems with Perinthus. First, the town is built into a hillside."

"Which is natural protection. Next?"

"It faces the sea of Marmara."

"We have a navy."

"But, cliffs protect the coast."

"What else?"

"Athenians."

Philip was surprised. "We'll beat the Athenians."

"Not when directly assisted by the Achaemenid Empire. Athens will ensure Persian supplies get into Perinthus by way of their navy."

The king rolled up a map of Asia and pointed it at Parmenion. "My aim is to conquer the Greeks."

"You shall, Philip. In Greece."

"I have a battlefield in mind."

"But you won't tell us where."

"You never know who could be listening."

Parmenion's brow crinkled. "You could test Asia at Perinthus. It wouldn't matter if we lost."

"I don't intend to lose."

Maps on the desk fluttered in a draft. Parmenion guessed that some were from the old library. "I hope you know those maps are out of date."

"Not the one in my hand."

"When do we go?"

"After I crown Alexander."

***

It was a spring morning. Birds sang enthusiastically under the palace eaves. Clad in a red robe, embroidered with gold, Alexander waited.

Philip was enthroned at one end of the audience hall, with his generals before him. Behind these senior military men sat the prince's friends. Queen Olympias was in a separate section with her lady-in-waiting.

127

Cassander was already jeering at Alexander. "Look at our philosopher, decked out like a bride." He swivelled about. "Speaking of whom, where is Hephaestion?"

Leonnatus wriggled into his seat to make himself more comfortable. "Don't be rude, Cassie. Hephaestion is Alexander's other half. It is fitting for civilised men, and I'm proud to know them both."

"As am I," added Perdiccas.

Hephaestion entered the hall, and took his place at the end of the row. Ptolemy followed, in the company of Philip's senior officers. They sat in front, with the generals.

Cassander took out a peach from his pocket. "My, my! Have any of you noticed how much Ptolemy resembles our sovereign?"

Leonnatus scowled. "You're not going to eat that, are you?"

"Why, yes Leo, I'm hungry."

Cassander opened his mouth. Leonnatus swiped the peach from his hand. "I'm not having you splatter juice over my coronation robes."

"Give it back!"

"Shut up, Cassie!" Perdiccas hissed. "Stop provoking him, Leo."

From his throne, Philip focussed his attention in the direction of Alexander's friends. Cassander gazed at the front, the picture of innocence, while Leonnatus and Perdiccas assumed stony expressions.

Satisfied there was a respectful silence, Philip beckoned his son to approach the throne. Alexander obeyed.

His father rose to face the assembly. "Courtiers, generals, and illustrious Queen, as you are all aware, I am embarking on our glorious Asian campaign."

Spontaneous cheering broke out from the audience. Cassander swung his shoulders towards Leonnatus. "Give me back my peach!"

"Can't."

"Can't or shan't? I'm warning you."

"Ptolemy's got it."

Cassander looked about. He saw the fruit held up by a smirking Ptolemy.

"You're welcome to get it," Leonnatus said.

Shuddering, Cassander sat back. "Not likely. That man has hams for fists." He turned to view the proceedings.

Philip still held the floor. "Fellow Macedonians, you will be delighted to know I have appointed my son, Alexander as regent in my absence."

Philip's generals made sounds of approval. The Young Companions, apart from Cassander, cheered. As soon as the ceremony was over, the latter bowled across the hall to Ptolemy.

"You have something of mine."

"What?"

"A delicious peach, which I should have been snacking on, instead of you, during that boring ceremony."

"I don't know what you're talking about."

Standing up, Ptolemy wrapped his cloak about him, and joined the military personnel in congratulating Alexander.

Pursing his lips with fury, Cassander looked about. Then, he spotted it. A large brown pit on the seat Ptolemy had vacated. Eyes flashing, Cassander's pupils dilated from green to black.

***

35.

Filling his lungs with ozone laden air, Philip viewed the peninsula. Connecting it to the land, was an isthmus. His eyes swept upwards, while his ship ploughed through choppy water.

Perched on a hill, was a city that was terraced and heavily fortified. The king's heart beat fast. He noticed a sweep of cliffs which protected the coastline. Parmenion was correct. Naval attack was out of the question.

Straightening the buckle around his waist, Philip's face was set. Now in his forties, his body was muscular and carried no excess fat. The creator of a professional army, he was still one of its fittest members. Wind whistled through his thick hair. It was time to moor the Macedonian fleet.

Once ashore, the generals inspected their troops. Andromenes and his sons, Amyntas and Polemon drilled their men. Parmenion donned his helmet. Flexing his muscles to limber up, he checked his sword blade for sharpness.

Cleitus walked over to him. "This is going to be a siege operation, Parmenion. I thought you advised Philip not to come."

"He didn't listen."

"Storming the walls will take months, even with siege engines. And, look at those terraces – the moment we take ground, the enemy will shift up to the next tier."

"Ensure the blade of your sword is sharp, Cleitus. We'll be in hand-to-hand combat today."

Satisfied with the condition of his own blade, Parmenion sheathed his sword. Mounting his horse, he moved to the front of his unit.

***

Dawn broke across Pella. The new regent was awake and working in the king's office. Acquainting himself with the layout, he quickly located the royal correspondence, battle plans, and library.

At the seventh hour of the day, Philip's elderly secretary, Thersites entered the room. Surprised to see the young man at work, he waited while Alexander leafed through maps and documents.

"Does my father keep a record of his duties?"

"King Philip *remembers* everything."

Alexander fixed the secretary with a stern look. "That's not very helpful."

Thersites blinked. "I could make a list for you."

"I expect it on my desk after lunch."

"But –"

Alexander was already outside the office, striding towards the hall where the military council waited.

***

Gathered before the walls of Perinthus, the Macedonian foot soldiers were ready. A red sun rose above the hills, splashing the battlements with bloody rays.

Attalus drilled his men. Andromenes watched the sunrise while his son, Polemon started on a Nestor's Cup for breakfast. Amyntas picked his teeth. Parmenion and Philip chatted to pass time. Eventually, their siege engines rolled over the rocky ground.

Cleitus watched their progress. "They're new."

Philip puffed out his chest. "Torsion catapults. I commissioned the famous designer, Polyidus."

Parmenion was visibly impressed. "They're an improvement on the flexible bow."

"And they fire large missiles."

"An appropriate siege engine for this city," Cleitus remarked.

"The walls are huge," Andromenes added.

"So long as their aim is true," Parmenion said. "It is not always the way of catapults."

The king scratched his chin. His beard prickled, whether from heat or aggravation, it was hard to tell.

"My catapults destroy walls," he growled.

***

It was the eighth hour of the morning. Alexander joined senior members of his father's military staff, as well as his own Young Companions. Antipater stood on his right. Dressed in ceremonial robes, the veteran general cut an imposing figure.

Perdiccas was late. He joined Leonnatus and the young members of the military council.

"Shove along, Leo," he said, taking the last seat in a row. "Look at the way these old men are dressed! Are we going into battle?"

"King Philip is at Perinthus."

"And losing," muttered Cassander behind them.

Alexander's ears pricked up.

"Did someone say something?" he asked.

Antipater cast his steely gaze across the assembly. "I hear my son."

Leonnatus rose quickly from his seat.

"I wanted to offer my services to fight the Thracians," he announced.

"As do we all," Perdiccas agreed.

Legs apart, General Antipater placed his hand on his sword. His voice was clear. "Welcome, valiant young warriors. While King Philip is leading his victorious army through foreign lands, his regent has summoned us here due to Thracian insubordination."

He gestured to several officers. They carried two bronze stands to the front. Between them, they pinned a cured sheepskin on which was drawn a map.

Alexander unsheathed his sword and pointed. "We have been attacked by the Maedi. This map of raided territory also shows the route they took back to their home. Tomorrow morning I will lead a campaign against them. Are there any questions?"

Cassander burped. "Not from me."

Perdiccas glared at him. "Shush, Cassie!"

"Do I hear my son, again?" Antipater asked.

To his friends' dismay, Cassander rose. His plump shaven cheeks were ruddy. Pudgy fingers gleamed from their latest manicure. He grasped his gold belt, and placed his legs apart, in imitation of his father.

"I speak for all the Young Companions when I say we will follow Alexander to the ends of the earth."

Cheers broke out. Antipater beamed. Even Alexander was delighted. Seleucus moved into a space behind the speaker.

He tapped him on the shoulder. "You're full of surprises."

"My father is King. It is my duty to back him."

"I wouldn't say that in Alexander's earshot."

"Alex is as deaf as a post. But you are right, Seleucus. I am full of surprises. One day I might even be *your* king."

The light touch on his shoulder turned into a clawlike grip. Gasping, Cassander tried not to show fear. As people continued to cheer Alexander, the hand relaxed and Seleucus melted into the background.

Breathing again, the portly teen regained his composure. Leonnatus hugged him. Cassander realised his legs were shaking. He smiled up at the bearded bronze god with muscular arms.

"You know, Leo, even though my disposition tends towards fair maidens, I would be glad to call you my Hephaestion."

"And despite your round cheeks and wide girth, I shall be your partner until death. This, I promise."

"We should exchange rings but I'm afraid I like mine too much."

No one heard the jesters. Pella had a new king.

***

<h1 style="text-align:center">36.</h1>

Hacking upwards at the enemy with his fellow Macedonians, Cleitus advanced onto another terrace. Calves straining, he pushed himself to climb. Once on top of the new terrace, he swapped his sword from his right to his left hand and continued. Fighting in the afternoon, under the merciless sun was the worst time.

Below him, King Philip removed his iron helmet. His hair was wet. He pushed it back, off his forehead. Up ahead, his soldiers fought relentlessly, but slowly and surely, they fell back.

Parmenion, who was next to the king, dabbed his brow. Weary with the lack of progress, they made their way down the terraces to the plain where their tents were pitched.

"We're retreating at the same time every afternoon, Philip."

"Your perspicacity never fails to amaze me."

"Men require training to push through fatigue."

"How do you propose we achieve that, Parmenion? We're in the middle of a war."

"You've done it before. Our men are the crack troops of Greece, thanks to you, but now, even they are tired."

"What I would like to know, is why my foremost general failed to tell me the city was terraced?"

"It should be on your map."

"My map is outdated!"

Storming down the terraces, Philip dumped his helmet on the ground outside his tent. It rolled in the mud. A page ran to pick it up. Carrying it down the side of the royal tent, he took it to where cloths and gold water basins sat on oak trestles. Picking up a cloth, the boy dipped it in a bowl of water, wrung it out and began to remove the filth.

Emptying a drizzle of olive oil from a vial, he took a polishing cloth of soft calf hide, and worked it into the iron. At last, when he was satisfied, the page went into the tent to place it on a shelf where it sat until it was needed again.

Meanwhile, Parmenion continued down the terraces at an even pace. Cleitus joined him. His upper arm was bruised, and his forehead was bleeding.

Parmenion offered him his waterskin. "You need the hospital tent."

"They're only scratches." Cleitus guzzled from the waterskin. Handing it back, he sat down. "My sword arm is tired from striking upwards. All the soldiers are feeling it."

"I was telling Philip."

"Those terraces soar a hundred and sixty feet. We could be here forever."

All afternoon, Macedonian soldiers battered the walls of the city, to no avail. At midday, a bloodied Parmenion retreated to their encampment. Outside his tent, Philip was emptying a goatskin of water over his face to wash off battle grime.

"Our attack isn't working," said Parmenion. "It's time to reassess our strategy."

"I disagree."

"What progress have we made?"

"My scouts say there is a breach in the wall."

"If that's the case, we need to get there before reinforcements arrive from Byzantium, Philip. Don't forget, General Chares is also in charge of the Athenian grain ships."

"I'm well aware of that."

"Do you know he's arriving today with another month's supplies?"

An attendant offered the king a towel. He dried his face. "Let's check the breach, shall we?"

***

Throwing a dark cloak over her red linen dress, Olympias made her way down a private corridor to Antipater's office. Guards admitted her into a room which smelled of rosewater and incense.

An attendant ushered her to a seat. Cushioned with fleece, it was made of ebony, inlaid with gold, and covered in bright patterns of stars and ducks. In many ways, it resembled a throne.

The senior general bowed. Olympias unfastened her cloak and handed it to the attendant, who took it away. She noticed her host's reaction to her dress with sly pleasure. He looked away and gestured towards the seat.

"I see you saved the best chair for me," she purred.

"It's an Egyptian import," he said blandly.

Olympias lowered herself onto the fleece cushion. Wine from Epirus was poured by a steward, who then left.

"We are alone now, my Queen." The general's face was impassive.

"I'll come to the point. Alexander should remain in Pella. He is the regent. I don't want him fighting in Maedia."

"Neither do I."

"Then we are agreed, General."

"Alexander is going."

"Why?"

"He pulled rank on me."

"Surely, you can stop it."

Antipater looked at his guest directly. "I know you think I should go in his stead."

"You are the experienced warrior."

"Alexander wants to do this with his friends."

"Send his friends! Make your son the leader. Only do not let mine go to the front."

"My lady," Antipater said softly, "you express the wish of mothers since time began. It cannot be done."

Olympias' stomach knotted. "I am *Queen*."

"Philip is King, and he agreed to allow his son to fight in Maedia."

"How is that possible? My husband is overseas. Any communication between the palace and Asia takes weeks."

"The revolt in Maedia has been brewing since last year. Alexander requested his father's permission before the mighty Philip left home."

"So, my boy planned ahead. I always thought Alexander was straightforward."

"May I be permitted to share an insight?"

"If you must."

"Your son knows he has to fight to prove his worth," said Antipater. "So does mine. Let them."

A shadow passed across his face. Olympias placed her hand on his arm. "Forgive me. I know, you too, are a parent."

"There is nothing to forgive, Your Highness. Even as a veteran, I find it hard to let little Cassie go."

***

37.

Sitting upright on his horse, Philip wondered if it was a figment of his imagination. A crack before him extended over several courses of stone. And it was still moving.

"Attack!" he roared.

Infantry rushed in. Moving past a siege engine, they battered a section of unprotected wall. A cracking reverberated above the noise of battle. With Parmenion in tow, Cleitus made his way towards the section of collapsing wall. King Philip urged his horse to the front of his army.

A block gave way in the middle of a stone course. More toppled inwards. With a savage cry, the Macedonians rushed inside the city. In moments, Cleitus' head and shoulders were covered in limestone mortar. Wiping his eyes, he saw Parmenion standing still in the thick of battle. Taking several men, he hurried to the general's side.

"Why aren't you fighting, Parmenion? Are you hurt?"

"Look up."

An intact wall of rock soared fifty feet high in front of them. Shorter than the outer wall, it had escaped their sights.

Cleitus dropped his sword arm. "There's another wall."

"And thicker than the first."

"Maybe we can use more men."

"We can't get through this, Cleitus. I have to tell Philip."

***

It was the dead of night when Alexander's men left Pella. Cassander jogged along on a stallion, which had just been broken. He was behind everyone, including the pages.

After a while, Leonnatus dropped back. "How are you faring, Cassie?"

"As well as I did on our boar hunt."

"You have a new horse. Don't worry, he'll soon be accustomed to being ridden."

"Tell that to my buttocks."

"You should be excited. This will be our first battle under Alexander."

"And hopefully, our last."

"Don't you care for glory, Cassie?"

"I care for sleep."

Leonnatus stayed with him. After a while, Cassander's stallion started to imitate his, and picked up pace. By dawn, they were at the front, a short way behind Alexander.

***

At Perinthus, millions of stars were visible in the night sky. Inside Philip's tent, where his military council were gathered, the mood was gloomy. Dark wine glinted in the men's goblets. Outside, a lamb rotated slowly on its spit.

"We've been laying siege to this place for weeks," said Cleitus. "The citizens show no signs of giving up."

"Our enemies are fat," said Polemon. "That's what happens when a city receives aid from its allies, and we can't do anything about it."

"I agree," said Amyntas.

Philip's stony face caught the firelight. "Looking on the bright side, are we?"

"I ask pardon," said Andromenes quickly. "My sons are young."

"They should have stayed in Pella with mine." Philip's single eye glinted. "It's safe."

Muscular young male servants walked out of the tent with empty platters. Through the opening, Polemon saw men take down the lamb. It was charred on the outside, which meant the skin would be crisp and the meat tender. As they carved it into pieces, the aroma wafted across the diners. His mouth watered. At seventeen he was hungry all the time.

"Let's continue discussing our strategy," said Attalus.

"I agree," chimed in Cleitus, making way for the men returning with platters, piled high with mutton.

Philip selected a lamb shank. "I trust we are all decided." He chewed the meat. It slid off the bone. A servant rushed forward to pick up the pieces.

Parmenion bunched forward. His compact figure was still encased in his battle-stained armour. "It's no use Philip. With his grain fleet, Chares of Athens provides food and reinforcements to the city, courtesy of Persia. We can't win in this situation."

Philip waited patiently for the servant to get him more meat. "Very well, let's withdraw."

Rumbles of surprise filled the tent.

"What do you have in mind?" Parmenion asked.

The king's plate was piled with succulent portions of meat. He buried his teeth into a new lamb shank before it could go anywhere. "Byzantium. We leave tomorrow."

"What about the siege?" asked Andromenes.

"Half the army will stay here."

Picking up a cup of wine Philip downed it. Having supped, he rose and left the tent. It was time to pack.

***

On board his grain flagship, Chares took a light breakfast of fruit and honey water. At the seventh hour of the morning, his chief officer reported to his cabin.

140

"We need to get to Hieron by late morning," Chares said.

"The whole fleet, sir?"

"Perinthus needs grain."

"We're ready."

The general dabbed his lips with a linen napkin and rose to go on deck. Breathing in the fresh air, he marvelled at the blue of the sea. Ahead of him was the Macedonian army. Commanded by the one-eyed Philip, its soldiers were arrayed outside the walls of a fortress, which he was required to supply with food and weaponry.

A shudder rippled through his muscles. While it was unlikely Athens would suffer harm from a man, who was only slightly above the barbaric Illyrians and Thracians, Chares did not wish to confront Philip.

There was a reason Macedonia now had the best fighting force in Greece. Rigorous training methods meant that the country's troops had built up their stamina which surpassed that of other soldiers. While Perinthus might prove a challenge, it was only a matter of time before King Philip became Captain General of all Greece.

And the Greeks knew it.

***

38.

Cassander dismounted. It was the third night of travel, and they were in a meadow. A river flowed past in the moonlight. Alexander's page was already feeding Bucephalus. Leaping off his stallion, Leonnatus excused himself from Cassander's side and joined Perdiccas, who was tethering his horse to a tree. The youths conferred in whispers for a few moments. Next, they approached Cassander.

"How are you, brother?" asked Perdiccas. "Horse broken?"

"As much as my hindquarters."

"We have been in the saddle a long time."

"What do you want, Perdie?"

"The Maedi are half a mile away. I thought you should know." Having delivered the news, Perdiccas walked over to Alexander and Hephaestion.

Cassander chewed his nether lip. "Is he declaring his alliance, Leo?"

"It's going to be a lengthy raid. Alexander has several villages in mind."

"Is that why I'm suddenly Perdie's brother?"

"Alexander wants to make sure we're unified, Cassie."

"That's funny, as a Young Companion I assumed I was part of the pack."

"Alexander is King."

Cassander gave a snort of laughter. "He's *acting* for King Philip."

"That's right."

"Who will return."

"He might not."

"You sound hopeful, Leo."

"Don't put words in my mouth."

"My monarch had better return. I'm not serving under a sixteen-year-old."

Cassander's page brought a food pail. His horse immediately buried his head in the provender.

"Maybe Perdiccas knows how you feel about serving our new leader, Cassie."

"Perdie knows nothing. However, I have noticed he's licking Alexander's backside the way my horse is taking to his provisions."

"Our friend knows Alexander's time has come."

"My father is General Antipater, the man who is really in charge of Macedonia while Philip is away. That should be more than enough to qualify me as both a brother and a Young Companion. Now, let me water my horse in peace."

Picking up the empty pail, Cassander walked down to the river, with his page hurrying in his footsteps.

***

Under Greek command, two hundred and thirty ships descended on Hieron. Situated off the Asiatic coast, close to the mouth of the Sea of Marmara, the island was a loading zone for Athenian grain ships.

It was fortunate for Asian coastal cities, which were guaranteed provisions in times of war. Well-stocked forts were unlikely to fall to invaders, even to thuggish Macedonians led by the toughest military leader in the region.

After midday, Chares finished a satisfactory lunch ashore, with an elegant woman who was dressed in silk and brocade.

"You seem thoughtful, dearest," she remarked.

Chares picked his teeth with a fishbone. "I must report Philip's attack on Perinthus to the Persian satraps, Nikomache."

"But you're loading grain."

"There are over two hundred ships. Emptying the holds will take time."

"Aren't you supposed to protect the vessels?"

"They're in one harbour at the moment. My men will watch over them."

Nikomache selected a honey cake. "In that case, nothing stands in your way, my lord."

Chares set his toothpick on the dining table. "The Persian king's favour might gift me with land."

"Then we could be wed."

"I am married. So are you."

"I was jesting."

"Let me be clear about our relationship."

"If you must."

"It is limited to this place and time, and only when I'm away from Athens. Personally, I never want to be married again."

Chares left the room. Nikomache finished her cake at a leisurely pace. Afterwards, she washed it down with a glass of local white wine.

"Neither do I."

***

<h1 align="center">39.</h1>

It was still dark when Alexander attacked the village. Screams rang out in the frosty air. Flames crackled into the black night sky as houses were torched.

Men were killed in their beds. Women and children were captured, to be sold into slavery. Smoke and condensation rose into the freezing air, making it difficult for anyone to see.

Taking advantage of the ensuing confusion, many citizens fled to the safety of the surrounding hills. Others, not so lucky, were cut down.

Towards the fourth hour of morning, in a bloodied and exhausted state, Cassander looked for a place to rest. His horse had bolted long ago. Up ahead, Alexander was still screaming orders.

Feeling faint, Cassander sat on the step of an empty house. It was good to be out of the fray. While he understood the need to put down the rebellion and plunder tin for Macedonia's coffers, it seemed that much of the killing was senseless.

A group of infantry, carrying firebrands interrupted his musing.

"Out of the way, sir," one of them said curtly. "We're going to torch this house."

"Bugger off!"

"King's orders, sir."

"My *father* is King at present. Haven't you done enough damage?"

"There are people inside."

"I killed them all," Cassander lied. "Now leave me."

The men ran to the next group of huts. Suddenly, Cassander was aware of a presence behind him. Unsheathing his sword, he leapt to his feet and swung around. A boy was standing at the door lintel. A woman with untidy hair, grabbed her child's arm.

"You have a choice," Cassander said gruffly. "Be burned by the Macedonians, or come with me."

"Who are you, sir?" asked the woman.

"Son of Macedonia's rightful monarch."

"Can I pack first?"

"Take your time."

Cassander resumed his post on the step.

***

A full moon was high in the night sky when Chares was announced in the hall. Several Persian satraps had finished dinner. Listening to musicians over dessert, they were drinking from vessels of glass and gold.

One of them beckoned the visitor. "Welcome, General of Athens!"

"I am pleased to be finally here, Pharnabazus."

"We heard you were arriving this afternoon," another said.

"I started late, Tiribazus."

"It seems you were not a target for Philip's soldiers," a third snickered. "Perhaps your mistress detained you."

Chares stared into the man's eyes. "You know how it is. You too, are Greek, Themistocles."

"Nicely put," another satrap commented. "Themistocles has four wives, and ten concubines, not to mention several wine stewards."

"You're drunk, Boas!" Themistocles snapped.

Pharnabazus raised his eyebrows. "What can we do for you, General? Or is it Admiral?"

"It's what I, General of Athens can do for you."

"Ah, yes – King Philip. He is raiding nearby towns."

"That upstart's not worth bothering about," snarled Themistocles. "He's not even Greek."

146

"Maybe not," Chares replied, "but Macedonia boasts the hardest army in the world."

The satraps laughed.

"Perhaps, dear Chares, you would care to rephrase your statement," Pharnabazus suggested.

"King Philip created a professional army. His men are paid, which means they are motivated. No one is able to withstand a Macedonian onslaught."

"What about the Greeks?" asked Boas.

"I'm Athenian," Chares replied.

Pharnabazus, wrapped his gold embroidered cloak about him, and stepped off the dais.

"I hear your townsmen enjoy listening to philosophers," he smiled gently.

Jeering filled the hall. Chares waited for the commotion to subside. "You invited me to give you a report. King Philip is attacking Perinthus and Byzantium at the same time. He plans to take Selymbria. It is worth your attention because these sieges are a prelude to his conquest of Persia."

"Impossible!" Boas exclaimed, waving his drinking horn at a servant for a refill. "Although, the news is that Philip won at Selymbria and Perinthus."

"That's not what I heard," said Tiribazus.

"He hasn't finished fighting, yet," Themistocles growled. "Our Athenian general here, may have a point."

"Indeed he has," Pharnabazus said, placing one hand on Chares' shoulder. "Come, there is a private dining room next door. You must be hungry after your journey. The mutton is excellent."

***

40.

Reaching Byzantium under the cover of darkness, King Philip allowed his troops some much-needed rest. In the morning, the men prepared for the day. Andromenes and his sons shared a Nestor's Cup outside their tents. The mixture of egg, flour and condiments was the preferred breakfast of a Macedonian warrior, providing hours of energy.

Dressed for battle, Parmenion tested his weapons. First, a page offered him a spear. Twirling and twisting the weapon, he checked its haft and point.

Outside his own tent, Cleitus' pages dressed their master with his body armour. They gave him a choice of weapons. Adjusting his greaves, Cleitus reflected that his legs were the only parts of his body which were not injured.

Spotting Parmenion, he called out to him: "It looks as if we're on yet another Asian campaign!"

"What did you think was going to happen? Have you ever known Philip to withdraw?"

Leaving his sons to get dressed, Andromenes joined Parmenion.

"Even my young Poleman could see Perinthus was a complete loss," he remarked.

Banging the haft of the spear against the ground, to ensure it did not shatter, Parmenion inspected the tip. "Our king hasn't withdrawn, Andromenes."

"With any luck both cities will fall," said Cleitus.

Parmenion grunted his agreement. "I strongly suggest Poleman keeps quiet until he has attained our rank."

"Why should I stop my son?" asked Andromenes. "He's going to be a veteran in a few years."

"That's what you think."

"What's that supposed to mean?"

"Even my son must attain rank through merit. Getting on the king's nerves isn't the way to do it." Parmenion shoved the spear back into his page's hand. "Fetch me another. This tip is blunt."

***

An exhausted Cassander reflected his hair had grown. In the weeks of Alexander's campaign against the Maedi, it no longer had condition. Lank brown strands hung down his cheeks.

"Sweat sodden as usual," he muttered.

"Hush, Cassie," said Leonnatus. "Alexander is talking."

"Alexander is always talking."

Inside the royal tent, out of the heavy rain, Cassander was so tired, he could barely hold his head up. A page brought him spiced wine. He slurped a few mouthfuls.

"Warmest congratulations to you all," Alexander said. "Especially, the mighty Cassander, who personally took slaves on the field of battle."

"Our distinguished friend was informed a house was empty," added Perdiccas. "Still, he searched it, and found those filthy Thracian rats cowering inside."

Alexander beamed. "Nothing escapes a great warrior. Come, receive your reward."

Leonnatus nudged Cassander in the ribs. The latter rose and made his way to the front. Due to his page's ministrations, he was able to walk. Alexander presented him with a heavy gold plate. Cassander beckoned to his officers, who took it away. Then, he resumed his seat at the back of the gathering. Others went up to receive their rewards.

Slowly, without thinking, Cassander fell asleep.

***

Battering Byzantium was harder than Perinthus. In the third week of the Macedonian siege, Philip lay on the royal couch in his tent, a cloth over his forehead. Stewards filled wine cups, while boys handed around an assortment of fruits, nuts and sweets.

A full moon ascended the dark skies over the camp. Peering under his compress, Philip could see its bright orb through the entrance flap, which hung open to let in a breeze. If only it would let out the sound of Macedonia's senior military personnel, who were still arguing!

While Attalus and Andromenes gormandised snacks, Cleitus gave his view as a man in the field. "The torsion catapults are working."

Parmenion heaved an impatient breath. "What's the use of lobbing missiles over walls that won't fall?"

"We could use infantry to scale the walls at night," Andromenes suggested between bites of dried seaweed and fish. "Once inside the city, we'll be unstoppable."

"Andromenes is right," interjected Attalus. "Macedonians excel in street battles."

Despite his throbbing headache, Philip half rose from his couch.

"We can't climb the walls," boomed Parmenion. "It's why we' re using siege engines!"

With a sigh, the king collapsed back onto his pillow.

"I still think we should fight," said Cleitus.

Parmenion emptied a goblet of uncut wine. "Why bother? This is worse than Perinthus."

"Cleitus has a point," said Andromenes. "Byzantium receives reinforcements and supplies from Chios, Kos, and Rhodes."

Attalus crunched a handful of almonds. "Not to mention, Persia."

"Stop!" Philip handed his head cloth to a page. "We need to negotiate."

"With the Athenians?" asked Parmenion.

"Who else?"

Rising, Philip gestured to a servant for his outer robe. A youth ran to collect it from the back of the tent. Slipping his arms through its sleeves, the king tied the garment around his waist.

Attalus dusted his hands of almond skins. "I gather we are dismissed."

Philip chuckled. "You're free to go to dinner, although I fear you've spoiled your appetite."

"What will you do, my sovereign?" asked Parmenion.

"Chat with Admiral Demetrius. We still had a fleet, last time I checked."

"It's not operational," Andromenes said.

The king fixed him with his one eye. "It will be."

***

41.

In Asia it was the second hour of the morning. Philip paced the floor of his tent while he conversed with the Macedonian admiral.

"Did you know, Demetrius, that Chares wanted to be in charge of the Athenian navy ever since he was a page?"

"I thought he wanted to be a general."

"He did, but Chares is a greedy man. Now he's master of the Athenian fleet, which includes these grain ships. He even thinks he's on par with Demosthenes."

"I don't follow."

"Those two are conspirators. The garrulous statesman wants me dead, and the other has ensured I cannot gain a foothold in Asia."

"Perhaps we should destroy the grain ships."

"Is that your view?"

Uncomfortable with the question, Demetrius shifted from one foot to the other. "Is it not yours, mighty sovereign?"

"Absolutely! Chares is reporting my Asian presence to the Persian satraps. It gives us an opportunity. We need to attack the Athenian grain ships at dawn."

"But that's only three hours away."

"Closer to four. It will give you time."

Demetrius found himself outside the royal tent, with only flickering torches to guide him back to his own.

***

It was a new day. Waiting for his spy's report, Admiral Demetrius was gazing at the sea from his hilltop post. Watching the white breakers crashing on the rocky shore, he thought of home.

Wistfully chewing his nether lip, he reflected that he was trapped in Asia Minor fighting in a war could go on for years. His wife would marry another, his children would grow up without their father – it was like one of Euripides' plays. If only he could remember which one!

Finally, he spotted the intelligence officer. A lightly built man climbed the steep path to the lookout. He showed no signs of exertion. Such men made perfect spies. Fit and wiry, he would have blended in anywhere.

At the top of the hill, he saluted his superior. "The enemy has two hundred and thirty cargo ships, sir."

"How many are not Athenian?"

"I don't understand the question."

As Demetrius was about to explain, King Philip appeared at the bottom of the hill with his regiment. He dismounted and climbed the same path the spy had scaled, but at a faster pace.

When he reached the top, he was barely puffing. "Ready to seize the grain ships, Admiral?"

"Ready, sire."

"Breakfast?"

"With respect, it's best I start now."

"May Poseidon be with you." Turning abruptly, Philip made his way down the hill, back to his men. After a few steps, he halted and turned back. "This is like one of Euripides' plays, is it not?"

Chuckling into his thick black beard, the king made his way back to his men. In a few moments, they were on their way.

Demetrius faced his officer. "Find out how many cargo ships carrying grain belong to Chios, Rhodes, and anywhere else in Greece which is not Athens. Do you understand?"

"Yes, sir. It's *Alcestis*, sir."

"Pardon?"

"*Alcestis* is the play to which our sovereign referred."

"The one in which a blameless wife gives up her life for her idiotic husband?"

"Even so. But Alcestis' children will be raised by another woman, to their detriment, and all because of his inability to accept the will of the gods."

"I remember, now. The play is about greed and cowardice."

"We must be men, sir."

The officer executed a short bow and departed. Shaking his head, Demetrius fastened the buckle around his waist. His armour was light, but designed to keep him protected. He beckoned to a page who brought him an iron helmet.

"If I die, my children will be brought up by another man," he grumbled. "However, I am no coward. That numskull was referring to the wrong play."

"Perhaps you are thinking about *Iphigenia at Aulis*, sir?" his page ventured.

"Which is about a fleet that can't set sail!"

"Sorry, sir – just trying to help."

To cover his embarrassment, the boy stooped to check the ties on his master's greaves. He polished the gold pattern on the front of the leg armour. When he finished, he rose and stepped back.

"We have enough problems without remembering stories of fathers sacrificing their virgin daughters," said Demetrius.

Muttering to himself, the Macedonian admiral trudged down the hill to board his ship. It was half an hour before dawn.

***

A red sun struck the horizon. Philip's troops attacked Greek units which protected Athenian cargo ships. With the sun at their backs, the Macedonians created heavy casualties on an enemy blinded by the morning light.

While fighting raged at the ships, all was quiet in the administration quarter. Removed from the harbour, neat whitewashed buildings faced several tree-lined streets. Men breakfasted on cheese and bread, chased down with wine, or goat's milk as they awaited the grain which would be dispersed to the Persians and their allies.

Towards the tenth hour, armed Macedonians broke into the complex, and reached the cargo superintendent's area. Unannounced, they entered his office. There, they presented the man with a clay tablet on which was inscribed a message. Keeping his composure, the Athenian managed a haughty glance at his unwelcome visitors.

He read the message, before handing the tablet back to the Macedonian officer. "I have heard of King Philip, but who is Demetrius?"

An imposing figure pushed past his officer to stand before the superintendent. "Admiral of the Macedonian navy. I am commandeering your grain fleet."

"On whose authority?"

"That of King Philip of Macedonia."

"He's not my superior."

"But, he's mine."

The cargo superintendent was amazed. "Do you really expect me to hand over the Athenian grain fleet without a fight?"

"You've already surrendered."

"Since when?"

"Since your men became prisoners."

Demetrius' eyes indicated the view behind the superintendent. The latter turned to see his comrades through the window being lined up by rowdy Macedonian officers. Across the docks, hands on their heads, bound in fetters, they were led away.

***

42.

After the day's work, Demetrius regarded himself in a bronze mirror. His beard was trimmed and his hair combed into place with olive oil. Over his ceremonial armour, he wore a red cape.

Taking an attendant to bear his arms, he crossed the ditch which separated his enclosure from that of his king. Outside the royal tent, his attendant handed over his master's weapons to the guards.

Philip greeted his fleet admiral with warmth. "Well done! You seized the grain ships as I commanded."

"I only carried out your orders."

"And with excellence." A wine steward poured out two cups from a custom-made jar with a gold seal. "By the way, how many ships are not Athenian?"

Demetrius was ready for the question. "Fifty." Sipping his wine, he realised it was from a region close to his village in Macedonia.

"Send them back to their islands, Admiral. Dismantle the rest. I need more siege engines."

Demetrius choked. "*All* the ships?"

"Every single one."

"There are over a hundred and fifty."

"Correct."

"But what will happen to the grain?"

Philip turned a bright blue eye on his guest. "I'm selling it to a buyer for seven hundred talents. Should cover war costs, don't you think?"

"The ships will be dismantled as ordered."

"Excellent! Everything needs to be done with the utmost speed," Philip added.

***

Pharnabazus was in dismay. Against all protocol, a Greek messenger was in his office. How the man had managed to bypass his guards was a mystery, but he would deal with them later.

For now, getting anything out of his guest was proving to be enough of a challenge. The man was in front of Chares, breathing so hard he was in imminent danger of bursting.

"Have a seat," the satrap offered.

A servant pushed forward a chair with silk pillows. Another brought water. The man sat down and drank.

"I have a message for the General," he croaked.

"Take your time," Chares said. "It can't be that urgent," he smiled at Pharnabazus. "Unless our grain ships have been burned by Macedonians."

This statement had the effect of turning the messenger crimson. He drank more water. As the pit of Chares' stomach stirred, Pharnabazus raised his arm to prevent him from speaking.

Finally, the messenger was able to breathe. He rose from his seat to address Chares. "Mighty One of Athens, as you have rightly guessed, King Philip of Macedonia has attacked the grain fleet. Shall I give details?"

"Stop!" ordered Pharnabazus. He turned to Chares. "You need to leave."

***

Twenty dejected captains stood before an infuriated Chares. Stomping about the audience chamber, his rant set new levels by the office water clock. One unfortunate seaman calculated they had been there for a full hour.

"That Macedonian cur has destroyed my fleet! Why did no one put up a fight?"

"We tried, sir," a captain said.

"The ships were in *one* harbour. A child could have guarded them."

"King Philip has an army," another pointed out.

"We have an army. We *had* a navy."

"No one expected the attack, sir."

"Everyone in Asia knows King Philip is here," said Chares. "Soldiers guard the ships because Perinthus and Byzantium need grain to withstand his siege operations."

"It was morning, sir," one brave captain ventured. "The Macedonians chose the time of day when there was sunstrike."

Breathing hard, Chares eyeballed the man for several moments. Another decided to assist his endangered colleague. "Sir, we *do* have a navy."

"Are you contradicting me?"

"We still have warships."

The first captain picked up the cue.

"That's right," he said. "What action should we take, sir?"

There was a long pause. Embers in Chares' eyes sparked. Finally, he spoke.

"Attack."

***

43.

Philip scratched his head. It was afternoon. Warm gold spilled over the tent trappings. Servants arranged furniture for the evening's feast.

The king was thinking of wearing a fine green robe, embroidered with miniature gold rosettes, or perhaps his ceremonial armour, after he solved his most recent problem.

"Our fleet is blockaded, you say?" he asked the quaking admiral.

Demetrius swallowed. "It is."

"By Chares?"

"He returned in the dead of night with warships. No one expected it. We can't get home."

Philip looked at his nails. Unlike some of his officers, his were in splendid shape. "I'll have to do something about it."

"Do you have any orders for me?"

"Take the night off."

The admiral did not need to be told twice. He left so rapidly, he bumped into Cleitus on his way out. Mumbling his apologies, Demetrius increased his pace as he hurried away.

For his part, the senior officer took no offense. He entered Philip's tent in a relaxed frame of mind. Looking around for a maid on the staff, to whom he had lately taken a shine, he was disappointed to see only men serving wine and sweets. Accepting a saucer of figs and walnuts, laced with honey, he sat down.

"When do we sail home, Philip?"

"As soon as I get rid of Chares."

"I thought that Athenian was with his Persian satraps."

"Chares returned to attack our men and blockade the fleet."

"That means we can't get home. What are you going to do?"

"Write a letter."

Cleitus was stunned. "A letter?"

"After tonight's banquet. Do you know a good manicurist? Mine was killed at Perinthus."

***

A sumptuous banquet extended deep into the night. Squires hung around in case they were needed, while the younger pages went to bed. Women lingered at the corners of the royal tent. Some cozied up to the men, who were still drinking wine on their dining couches.

Philip put his thumbs behind the straps of his ceremonial armour. Displaying glossy manicured fingernails, he puffed out his chest. "Tonight we celebrate Macedonia's victory. The entire Athenian grain fleet has been converted into the best siege machines in Greece!"

Diners cheered. General Attalus kissed a voluptuous maiden next to him.

"Have you ever heard of a fleet turned into kindling?" he laughed.

Parmenion shook his head in exasperation. "Philip, we're not getting anywhere, even with siege engines."

"Trust Parmenion to dampen our spirits," said Andromenes from one corner.

"Agreed," chimed in Attalus. "This is a dinner party. Have some wine, Parmenion. Choose a girl."

A gust of wind rustled sumptuous hangings. Shields clattered where they hung on hooks. The king's eye trailed to an open tent flap. It was raining outside. Water drops glimmered on wet grass under soft moonlight. In Macedonia, during this time of year, there was also wet grass, hills, and thickets for boar.

He shook off his thoughts. "No matter, Parmenion. We're going to Scythia."

"What's in Scythia?" Cleitus asked, disengaging himself from his latest girlfriend.

"Plunder. The country is rich in horses and slaves."

Parmenion threw up his arms. "You do realise Chares is blockading our fleet? We can't get home, Philip!"

"We will."

"With what?"

"My mind."

***

After dinner, the king set to work. Scribbling by his lamp, on a wax tablet with a bronze stylus, he drafted a letter. In the early hours of the morning, he inscribed the final copy on a papyrus scroll.

Summoning a messenger, he gave the man his instructions, before dismissing him. It was the second hour of the morning. Only raucous laughter from the servants' quarters, broke the still night air. Philip opened a tent flap and looked up to the heavens.

"Oh Selene, my deepest gratitude for giving me time," he whispered to the moon goddess above.

Returning inside, he selected a scroll from his shelf of literature, and began reading Euripides' *Iphigenia at Aulis*. The story of Agamemnon's becalmed fleet whispered across the centuries.

"I, too, feel becalmed," he chuckled.

A male attendant poured warm milk, flavoured with nutmeg, into a cup. He gave it to Philip who continued to read. Next, he prepared his master's bed with fresh sheets and blankets, placing an extra fleece over the covers.

Eventually, Philip finished reading and dismissed his servant. He slipped into the warmth of the blankets. His muscles relaxed and sleep descended.

***

44.

Two messengers erupted into General Chares' office. Flushed with success, they barely concealed their delight.

"I hear you intercepted an enemy letter on its way to Macedonia," the general said.

"We did, sir." One of them nudged the other. "At least, Menelaus did."

A thin man with a pinched face, stepped forward. As office secretary, he was a stickler for protocol. He stretched out a wizened hand. "Give it to me."

Menelaus handed him the letter. After briefly inspecting it, the secretary gave it to his master, who opened it.

"It's addressed to Antipater," Chares noted with surprise.

"Shall I bring in the military advisers, sir?" asked his secretary, as he waved away the messengers.

"A good idea."

Chares frowned as he re-read the contents of the letter. After a time, his advisers arrived.

"Can you be sure it's for Antipater, sir?" a senior officer asked.

"This was on its way to Macedonia," Chares replied. "General Antipater is in charge while King Philip is out here."

"Prince Alexander is acting in his father's place," an adviser countered.

"The boy is sixteen. This message is addressed to Philip's right-hand man, the real ruler of Macedonia at present. For that reason, I think it's genuine."

"Agreed," a senior officer said. "The prince is clearly under Antipater's guidance."

"Makes perfect sense," a lieutenant added.

"Apparently, there is a revolt in Thrace," Chares announced. "The letter reveals King Philip is summoning Antipater to meet him there. We leave tomorrow morning."

***

It was a clear, grey dawn. In shock, Demetrius stared over the Macedonian fleet at the expanse of calm water where there had been a blockade. The Sea of Marmara was empty of Greek ships.

"We're the only ones here," said his chief officer.

"I can see that. What happened?"

"No one knows, sir. Perhaps Chares was asked to return to Greece."

Demetrius galvanised into action. "The fleet moves out, *now*. We're joining Philip."

The officer hurried away to relay orders. By the tenth hour of the morning, the Macedonians were sailing to pick up their troops.

***

By early afternoon, the Macedonian fleet was anchored in a cove, with the army preparing to board. Soldiers packed their kit. Tents were dismantled, and horses were blinkered in preparation for the sea voyage.

A bewildered Demetrius stood before his smug king. "And Chares believed you?"

"I'm not called Philip the Fox for nothing."

"But, it's obviously a ploy!"

"Not to Chares. He believes he's important. That's why he runs here and there, trying to be indispensable to both Persians and Greeks."

"The Persians are going to think he's the silliest man alive."

"People believe what they want."

"And we head back to Pella tomorrow?"

"By way of Scythia. I'd like to win one battle out of this lot."

After his interview, Demetrius boarded his ship where he ate a lunch of vegetables and fish, washed down with white wine from his own vineyard in Macedonia.

It took the remainder of the day for the Macedonian army to board with their possessions, horses, and siege engines. Philip spent the better half of the afternoon with two female slaves he had captured from Perinthus. They were, he reflected, the closest he had come to any type of conquest on his Asian campaign.

In the evening, he strolled the deck of his ship. Breathing in the ozone laden sea air, he thought of home.

I wonder how my son is doing?

***

45.

In the frosty dawn, Alexander stood to address the shivering Thracians of Maedia. A woebegone mass of snivelling children, and terrified women, stood in the grass below him. Local men hung their heads in shame. Many were bandaged and sporting bruises and cuts.

Only Cassander's captives were washed, fed and rested. For his part, he stood nearby, guarding them with his men, who had strict instructions not to hurt them.

"Maedia, you are now defeated," Alexander stated. "Your women and children are slaves. The men who are still alive, will work in the mines which now belong to Macedonia. I declare this city be named Alexandropolis for all eternity." He turned to Perdiccas. "I'm returning to Pella. Stay here and watch over them."

Cassander leaned over to Leonnatus. "That's what Perdie gets for shamelessly greasing the royal backside."

"Do shut up, Cassie!"

"Be grateful it wasn't you."

"What's that supposed to mean?"

"I have noticed you spend less time with me, and more with Alexander's cohorts. No offense taken, but following a tyrant might not be in your best interests."

"Who else do you intend to follow, Cassie? Alexander's our leader. I, for one, am glad to be going home."

Mounting his stallion, Leonnatus joined the other Young Companions. Whistling to himself as they rode away from Maedia, Cassander reflected he had acquired several families for his housework. He would give them a holiday on his estate, which was certain to produce more farmers for his fields.

He noticed the young Thracian boy whom he had saved, riding alongside him. "Your name is Polymarchus, isn't it?"

"Yes, kind sir."

"How would you like it if I paid for your schooling next term?"

"Mother will be pleased."

"Stay with my guards. You'll be safe. I'm going to the front."

Tipping his hat, Cassander left the boy. There was no doubt. He would have a household of loyal employees in Macedonia to match his land holdings.

***

Dismounting Bucephalus in the main courtyard of the King's residence at Pella, Alexander gave his reins to a waiting squire. Antipater embraced him.

"Your first victory, and you bring us back slaves and tin! Wait till your father hears about this."

"Is there any news of him?"

"He's on his way home. Chares blockaded the fleet, but our king managed to trick him with a letter."

"Father isn't called Philip the Fox for nothing."

Antipater wrapped his arms around Alexander's shoulders. "Come, I've prepared a feast."

Together, they walked in the direction of the main banqueting hall.

***

Pouring down the hillsides, the Macedonians were on the shepherds before the morning sun hit the mountain peaks. Animals scattered, herdsmen fell.

At their hamlets, Scythian warriors formed rings to protect their families. It was no use. They were hacked down to the man.

By the day's end, King Philip had captured twenty thousand women and children.

166

***

Back in Pella, after several nights of feasting, Cassander found he was losing at draughts. Leonnatus was removing his pieces with increasing glee. Eventually, Cassander yawned and stretched.

"Do we have any Mycenaean wine, Leo?"

"Not unless you visited the city yourself."

"We should have some."

"This is not the time of Agamemnon, Cassie."

"Tell that to our new Achilles."

"Stop making fun of Alexander. Mycenae does not export wine as it once did."

"Alexander's fixation with the *Iliad* makes me believe he knows Agamemnon. I distinctly saw Mycenaean wine in Pella."

A sputter of laughter preceded Leonnatus swiping another piece. Cassander pushed his chair back.

"Where are you going, Cassie?

"Being slaughtered by you is not my idea of recreation."

"We can start anew." Leonnatus rearranged the board. "See, I put all your pieces back."

Cassander clapped his hands. "Wine!"

A child emerged from the corner of one room and poured a drink for his master. Leonnatus studied the lad. "He's a bit young for service, isn't he?"

"The boy's name is Polymarchus. He offered to be my steward."

"Why?"

"I'm paying for his schooling next season."

"Doubtless, with profits from your booty." Leonnatus removed a piece from the board. "My goodness, I'm winning again!"

"Strange, since your only opponent is yourself."

Leonnatus looked up from the gaming board at the boy. "Isn't he part of that family you rescued?"

"I don't know what you mean."

"His mother's one of your new slaves, sitting in the far corner."

Cassander flushed with irritation. "I gave Helen her freedom. And I pay her. She's a servant, not a slave."

"Who would freely want to stay with you?"

Cassander drained his drink and stared hard at the board. "Helen and Polymarchus. Now, where were we?"

❉ ❉ ❉

46.

Pushed and prodded, thousands of shackled prisoners shuffled through a gorge. By noon they were out of the confined space and moving across a flat plain.

Cleitus had his eye on several young women. They tried to avoid his gaze. An exhausted Andromenes pretended he was in deep thought, so that no one spoke to him. Parmenion kept his eyes on the road and stayed close to his king.

After several miles, the army turned into a wood. Philip pricked up his ears. "Do you hear that, Parmenion?"

"Only the footsteps of prisoners."

"Order them to stop."

The army halted. Philip's good eye flicked to the left and right. The woods were silent. They marched on.

***

Lights from Pella's royal banqueting hall fell across dark empty gardens as the sounds of merrymaking filled the palace.

"Antipater's outdone himself," Cassander said, stripping meat from the bone of a lamb shank and sucking out the marrow with gusto.

Leonnatus toyed with his vegetables. "Alexander is in a good mood."

"And boasting about his tin raid to Antipater."

"We're all richer because of it, Cassie."

Perdiccas belched. "You have fifty new slaves for your estate now, haven't you, Lord Cassander?"

"Two hundred and fifty *servants*, not slaves. I pay them."

"What you do with your spoils of war is up to you," said Perdiccas, "but be a little grateful. Alexander is the source of your good fortune."

"My lands are inherited from my father, who is standing in for Philip. My good fortune is due to Zeus and my wits."

In a far corner, Seleucus chuckled. Perdiccas turned towards him, but he quickly averted his head.

Swivelling back to Cassander, Perdiccas bunched his shoulders forward. "Alexander is the regent and our next king – if he isn't already."

"What are you implying, Perdie?" asked Leonnatus.

"Philip is fighting abroad."

"And will return with great riches." Leonnatus raised his goblet in the lamplight. "To Alexander, and his father, King Philip's safe return!"

Instantly, the toast was taken up. Ptolemy roared and waved his goblet about, while Seleucus gave an approving nod and sipped his cup.

From a few couches away, Alexander and Antipater continued to talk. A harpist struck up a lively tune. Girls appeared. More musicians joined in, and the banquet hall grew noisy with revelry.

"You really need to be more careful, Cassie," Leonnatus said.

Cassander shrugged and reached for a cake. "Where is the real King of Macedonia, I wonder?"

***

Philip looked across his army. The wooded landscape was breathing. He tapped his adjutant on the shoulder.

"Tell the infantry to get into formation."

The man relayed instructions to the first commander, who in turn, sent messengers to the next. Sarissas at the ready, the phalanx fell out.

Cleitus watched with interest. Checking the surrounding woods, he saw nothing. He leaned over to Parmenion, who was riding next to him.

"What is our king worried about?" he asked.

"A sound. He hears something."

"But, we're nearly home."

Suddenly, they heard it. A visceral, bloodcurdling cry.

"Bandits!" Philip roared.

Out of the woods, wild men clad in animal skins, ran out. Brandishing clubs and pointed sticks, they fell on the Macedonians. Parmenion pulled up his frightened horse.

"Triballi!" he yelled.

Cleitus, unsheathed his sword. "Who?"

"Wild men from the Danube. Shield yourself!"

"They look Thracian."

"They are – tribesmen. Guard our spoils!"

Parmenion urged his horse to the head of the cavalry. Meanwhile, launching themselves at their enemy, the wild Thracians destroyed anything in their sight, with no regard for the rules of warfare.

Cleitus found himself hacking below his saddle. Attacking headlong at the Macedonians, the brigands destroyed part of the infantry, even charging into the sarissa-wielding troops.

Leading from the front of his army as usual, Philip gave orders to get his men back into formation.

"Surround the prisoners!" he bellowed.

A nervous infantryman close to him, hastily whirled to the side. His sharp sarissa point gored the king's thigh. Philip's roar was heard by the entire army.

Cleitus waved his sword, trying to capture Parmenion's attention. "Philip's wounded."

"Our leader has been attacked, sir," echoed Parmenion's adjutant.

"Go to his aid!" the general commanded the men nearest to him.

Meanwhile, the fifteen-foot-long spear continued to crunch through Philip's thigh and his horse's ribs. With a grunt, he fell on top of his neighing steed. Blood gushed from his leg. Trying to right himself, the dying horse only tore more of his rider's ligaments. Raising his head momentarily, the King of Macedonia blacked out.

***

47.

At Pella, a messenger ran through the main palace courtyard. Alexander was in his apartments with Hephaestion.

"What's the news?" the regent asked.

"It's about your father."

A cold hand twisted Alexander's stomach. "How is he?"

"Injured."

"Is he here?"

"In the next town. I ran to let you know."

"You did the right thing. See to it this man is rewarded, Hephaestion."

Throwing his cloak about him, Alexander left the room. His cousin ordered a welcome drink for the exhausted messenger. Afterwards, the man was despatched to the visitors' quarters with a pouch of gold ducats.

Downstairs, in the main courtyard, Alexander met Antipater. "Where are the palace doctors, General?"

"In their surgeries, I expect. Why?"

Exhaling an impatient breath, Alexander gestured towards the nearest servant. "The King's doctors – now!"

***

Waiting for his father proved to be longer than anticipated. A servant brought juice and dates. Doctors took their seats around the perimeter of the courtyard. Several of them discussed potions.

Alexander joined them. Due to Aristotle's medical training, he held an easy conversation with the physicians about plant remedies. It helped pass the time and took his mind off the worry of his father's condition. In the meantime, his bodyguards lounged by the pillars, chatting.

Scouts were sent from the palace. They all came back with the same news. Philip's army was on the move and he was alive. Towards late afternoon, there was a rumbling of approaching troops on the King's Highway.

The regent rose to receive his father at the main entrance. Hephaestion joined him. Eventually, men appeared with a stretcher. Covered with a blanket, Philip was barely conscious. Compassion, mixed with anger, filled Alexander's heart.

"Surgeons now!" he ordered. "Everyone else stand back."

Two royal physicians moved forward. They knelt on either side of the injured man and worked swiftly to assess the nature of the wound.

Senior generals filed into the courtyard. Many bore cuts and bruises, which were immediately patched up. Andromenes was gaunt. His eyes were ringed with purple. His son, Polemon was thinner than usual. Alexander noticed he stayed close to his father. Amyntas was nowhere to be seen.

One-eyed Antigonus trudged in and dumped himself on a stone bench. He brooded for a bit and picked at a scab on his knee. Slaves appeared, serving drinks and food. Grabbing a cup of fruit juice, Antigonus downed it in one gulp. Afterwards, he went back to brooding. Of the senior war staff, Alexander reflected that Parmenion alone, looked spruce.

To the prince's relief, Cleitus finally appeared, his legs swathed in bandages. A doctor ran to his side. Swiftly unwrapping the bandages, he applied a poultice of herbs.

Hephaestion put his lips to his cousin's ear. "Do you think it might be a good idea to greet your father?"

"My duty is to stand here."

"A bit pointless, don't you think?"

Alexander moved to his father's side and took one bloodless hand. The doctors continued to work. Philip was finally stabilised.

His eyelids fluttered and he awoke. "I'm thirsty."

A physician trickled water between the king's lips. Philip felt the cool liquid run into his parched throat. Feeling better, he laid his head back on the stretcher's pillow. His one seeing eye locked onto his son. Then, he was taken inside.

***

48.

Reunited with his family in Pella, Andromenes ate dinner in the comfort of his home. Men reclined on couches. Younger males, who had yet to prove themselves at a hunt, took their meal while seated on chairs. Apart from Andromenes' wife and mother, the women were in the kitchen.

As usual, the family was discussing Macedonian politics, which included its king. Polemon was holding the floor. "He lost every battle, Father. We're only back in Pella by the grace of the gods."

"Philip is a great man" Andromenes responded. "Without him, Macedonia would have no power. Now, everyone is afraid of us."

"Including the Triballians?"

"An unfortunate turn of luck."

"Like Perinthus and Byzantium."

"That's enough, son," his mother chided gently.

"Why? None of us can say anything unless it agrees with Macedonian policy. In Athens there is a democracy. Here, we are ruled by a tyrant."

"Philip is your king," Andromenes said. "You have a job and food in your mouth because of it. Be grateful."

On hearing this piece of advice, Polemon swung his legs off the couch. An attendant brought him his cloak. Embracing his mother, he kissed his father on the cheek, before disappearing into the night.

Andromenes beckoned to a security guard. "Take two men and follow him. Make sure he's safe. If he seeks an audience with Philip, prevent it."

"Speaking of our king, how is he?" his wife asked.

"By all accounts, flirting with his nurses."

"He is a character."

Andromenes leaned over to his wife and kissed her cheek. "That's one way of putting it, my dear."

***

Two weeks later, in the great audience hall, King Philip was strong enough to stand. He embraced his son. "You've grown. At sixteen, you are a man."

"Father looks well, too."

The king's one eye roved over his son's physique. "I'm fighting on the plain of Chaeronea in Boetia. It's a decisive battle. Greece will be ours. I wish to include you in my next campaign."

"I am honoured."

"I want you to lead the main cavalry charge."

"Your faith in my abilities moves me."

"You proved yourself at Maedia. I'm placing you between Antipater and Parmenion. By the way, Aristotle tells me you are doing well in your studies."

"I earned the merit of Philosopher."

Philip's beard twitched. "You must be a skilled speaker. And you have no feelings about combatting your fellow orator, Demosthenes?"

"That Athenian is pitted against the House of Philip to which I am loyal!"

The king placed a hand on his son's shoulder. "I was jesting. Stop being so serious all the time. I will call for you in a few days." His brow creased slightly as he watched his son leave the great audience hall.

For his part, Alexander strode out. He rounded a corner. Suddenly, he punched the wall. Hephaestion appeared out of nowhere and ran to his side.

"What's the matter, Alex?"

"It's Father."

"Did he tell you about his plans for Boetia?"

"How did you know?"

"Everyone's talking about how Aristotle is going to defeat Demosthenes."

"That's one way of putting it."

Walking rapidly, Alexander left the main building. Hephaestion followed. Trotting down the steps they headed for the garden.

"Why are you so angry, Alex?"

"Father's always diminishing me."

"Has he invited any other son to fight by his side?"

Alexander stopped. Squaring his shoulders, he faced his cousin. "Apart from me, there is only my retarded half-brother, Arridhaeus."

"You have cousins who could inherit the throne."

"What are you saying?"

"Have you ever thought King Philip chose you because you're exceptional?"

"Father is placing me between Antipater and Parmenion."

"That's because you're young."

"I'm capable of winning a battle on my own."

"This war decides who rules Greece, Alexander."

"I'll be in charge of my own unit, although it will be impossible to lead with two nannies by my side."

"Philip wants you there."

"But, he doesn't trust me!"

"He can't afford to lose this battle, or you, Alex. Otherwise, all Greece is lost, together with his heir."

"Meantime, those greybeards, Antipater and Parmenion will reap the glory, not me."

"Antipater and Parmenion are protecting us all. Have you thought of the trouble Cassie, Leo and Perdie might get into otherwise? Don't worry, you'll be covered in glory."

They stepped outside. Alexander thought for a while. His blond hair glinted red as it caught the sun. "You're right, Hephaestion. I *will* be covered in glory."

***

At her palace apartment, Olympias opened her arms. "There he is, my future king!"

Alexander hugged his mother. "I was only the country's regent for a short while."

"You're far too modest. You did a wonderful job – better than Philip."

"We captured a few villages and their tin mines."

"Tin makes bronze for weapons. I hope Philip rewards you."

A cloud passed over Alexander's face. "He's injured, Mother."

"But happy to see you?"

"A spear went through his thigh."

"No doubt he despatched his enemy."

"It wasn't an enemy, it was a Macedonian soldier. Someone misjudged the distance of his sarissa, and it went clear through Father's thigh. It even killed the horse under him."

Olympias suppressed the beginning of a smile. "Was the man crucified by royal decree?"

"Father showed him mercy."

"That's more than he's done for you. You look worn out."

"Father gave me a taste of kingship. Now, he wants me at Chaeronea."

***

PART III

49.

Leaving Pella, the Macedonian army travelled down the length of Greece. Mountains and rivers merged into one another. After several weeks, Philip recognised the plain of Chaeronea. It was late afternoon when they arrived.

Turning to his favourite bodyguard, he indicated a flat green spot near a group of trees. "We pitch our tent here, Pausanias."

Seeing Philip set up camp, Parmenion's units halted. The general dismounted his stallion. In his sixties, his body was hard as iron. Yawning, he flexed his muscles. His squire poured wine into a cup.

"You will get a bonus this month," the general said. "Now, go and set up my tent with the others."

In the meantime, General Antipater sought out Alexander and his companions. "Pitch your camp near the river, Prince."

"Why?"

"You're fighting on that side tomorrow, with me."

Alexander frowned. "And the mighty Parmenion, no less."

"Do you have a problem with our company, Alexander?"

"Only with glory snatchers."

"You distinguished yourself at Maedia, and you will at Chaeronea."

Antipater turned on his heel. Huffily, the prince indicated the site of an oak tree to his squires. He waited with Hephaestion, while their tent was set up.

Cassander sat on the riverbank, fishing and telling jokes. Settled next to Ptolemy, he found the latter laughed in all the right places. Alexander looked on. Eventually, Ptolemy excused himself to join the senior officers.

After the older general left, Leonnatus and Perdiccas ran down to the riverbank to juggle. Leonnatus won, with more balls in the air for longer periods. Afterwards, Perdiccas picked up a fish and playfully slapped Cassander. Bellowing with rage, the latter rose and thrashed them both with his rod.

"You were right, Hephaestion," Alexander said. "Parmenion and Antipater are going to be babysitters tomorrow."

When the tent was pitched, Alexander and his cousin went inside. They removed their cloaks and armour. Sitting down with a spiced bowl of uncut wine, they played draughts as the sun went down.

***

When the moon rose, Alexander and Hephaestion packed up their board game. Together, they ate a light meal. Afterwards, Hephaestion retired to bed with a scroll of Euripides' plays. Meanwhile, Alexander donned an embroidered tunic and went out.

Followed by his bodyguards, he made his way to King Philip's tent. Torches lit the way. Men's voices floated across the night air. Climbing a grassy incline, the young prince saw several generals leave the tent. Parmenion and Cleitus acknowledged him, but Attalus walked past in silence.

When he reached the top of the incline, Alexander was admitted inside. Lamplight flickered across sumptuous hangings. Oak tables were set with bowls of local wine.

Philip's manner was genial. He held out a cup to his son, after which he picked up his gold goblet. Studded with emeralds and rubies, and displaying the Argead star on both sides, it was one he always took with him on campaign.

"Tomorrow, my son, I fight the greatest battle of my career."

"You will win, Father."

"This victory will seal the conquest of Greece."

"Do you know how the Greeks intend to fight?"

183

"I've some idea of the enemy's strategy, Alex. You can tell by their choice of terrain. With the mountains on one side, and rivers on the other, they think to keep us contained. However, it's important to see how the enemy positions its troops tomorrow."

"Who am I to lead?"

"Your cavalry. I've allocated a Thessalian contingent to you as well."

"How many men?"

"With your cavalry, there should be over two thousand."

"What am I to do?"

With a cunning grimace, Philip set aside his goblet.

***

Next morning, in the cold of dawn, the warring armies rumbled onto the plain of Chaeronea. Philip was seated astride a white stallion. Beside him was Alexander, on his great warhorse Bucephalus.

While they waited, the king studied his son. "You've grown, Alex."

"I am honoured you notice, Father."

"I rather suspect it's the size of your horse."

The prince bit his lip. It was true he was short. Still, there was time to gain height. He stroked the black curly mane of his outsize steed and took a deep breath. There was time for a lot of things. Noticing his son's ire, King Philip smirked.

Movement on the opposite side of the battlefield sparked Macedonian interest. Studying the Greeks and Thebans, Philip saw them positioning their armies on a slant. With the mountains to the south, and Kephisos River to the north, they were completely protected.

Immediately, Philip mirrored the enemy formation. A thousand Macedonian archers, javelin men, and peltasts took the far right. Six thousand infantry men, armed with three-metre spears, stood alongside them. These hypaspists and pikemen resembled Greek hoplites. Unlike the Greeks, they wore light armour. Some wore none.

In the centre, the Macedonian king stationed his phalanx. Serried ranks of twenty thousand men wielded sarissas. A group of pikemen stood on their left.

"Son, I'm taking the right," said Philip. "You will be stationed next to the selected men on the far left. The archers will protect you by the river. Wait for my signal."

Kicking Bucephalus' flanks gently with his heels, Alexander left his father, and took his great warhorse towards the river. Leading his five hundred-strong Companion cavalry to the Kephisos riverbank, he waited. A Thessalian contingent joined Alexander as Philip had promised. Cretan archers and peltasts took their positions on the prince's left.

Cassander pulled a face. "How is that supposed to help? We're directly facing Theagnes and his Theban Sacred Band."

"Are you afraid?" asked Alexander.

"Of fighting three hundred sissies? No, I'm concerned for you, Alexander. Look at your father's left. There must be ten thousand enemies. Philip will reap the glory of your first major battle."

"Father is an experienced warrior. He is expected to confront the bulk of the enemy. But this is my debut at a great battle. And yours."

Hephaestion cantered up on a black stallion. "You might be surprised who we are fighting today, Cassie."

"Privy to innermost battle secrets are we, Heph? It's like school all over again."

Leonnatus galloped up. "Shut up, Cassie! Even the Cretans can hear you."

With a scornful glance, Cassander turned his horse to join the cavalry. Alexander scrutinised the Greek army. On the far right, by the mountains, were ten thousand heavily armed Athenian hoplites. In the centre, was a slightly smaller group, which included mercenaries chosen for their fighting skills.

An army of Thebans, rivalling the Macedonian phalanx in numbers, was arrayed opposite Philip's centre. Elite fighters, they were protected by the legendary Theban Sacred Band. Made up of one hundred and fifty pairs of fighting men, the Band would fight to the death to protect one another.

Alexander swivelled round on Bucephalus to face Hephaestion. "The weakest Greek division is on Father's right."

"How do you know?"

"We went over the battle plans last night. I recognise the group from his description. They may number ten thousand, but this is their first battle."

"Which means we have the bulk of the enemy army," Leonnatus groaned. "Philip left us with the elite Theban army *and* the Sacred Band."

"Theagnes heads a suicide squad," Cassander said from behind. "Just what we need at our first major engagement."

Alexander pulled down his helmet. "It won't be our last. Take your positions, men. We're about to start."

Leonnatus moved to the back of the cavalry. Alexander went over the battle formation in his head. Both armies numbered approximately thirty thousand troops. Both were now in strategic positions with protected flanks.

On his left was the river, on the right were the mountains. Thousands of troops waited. It was quiet, apart from the clank of shields and movement of horses.

Hours passed. On the right, behind his picked men, Philip could hear cicadas in the grass. Parmenion and Cleitus exchanged small talk as they walked their restless horses behind a phalanx of bristling spears. Rows of men, armed with sarissas formed an impenetrable wall while they waited in silence.

A shield winked in the sun. Philip shaded his eyes. Emblazoned in gold lettering, were the words *Good Fortune* written on its protective covering.

"Our friend Demosthenes is on the battlefield," he observed.

"I'll let you take him down," Parmenion said.

Philip adjusted his helmet. "I'm counting on you to keep him safe, General."

"Thousands of men are about to clash. He'll be lucky to survive the first charge."

"Make sure Demosthenes leaves the battlefield alive. That's an order."

Philip nudged his horse in the belly. Together they took a position closer to the left, and in plain sight of the enemy forces. Shaking his head, Parmenion joined Cleitus. They were behind the largest group of infantry gathered under Macedonian leadership. Still, nothing happened.

Looking up at the sky, Philip correctly judged the approach of mid-morning. Grasping his shield firmly, he rode forward to check the lines. In the distance, Athenians glimpsed a flash of his insignia. They responded by beating their shields.

On the far left, Alexander calmed Bucephalus' skittish response to the noise. Bending down, he whispered in his steed's ear before resuming his upright pose.

At sixteen, the prince's blond hair rippled down to his shoulders from under his plumed helmet. His locks glinted with red highlights in the morning sun. Head bent to one side, he had one blue eye on the sky above, while the other, dark as night, was on the enemy formation ahead.

Philip gestured towards a squire.

"Tell Alexander to watch for a moment of crisis," he ordered.

The man galloped away to relay the message. King Philip decided to slowly advance.

Meanwhile, in the Athenian ranks, the anxious commander, Lysicles scratched his beard. His adjutant was already panicked.

"Why did they put us here, sir? None of us have seen a battle, and we're facing King Philip."

"Don't worry, Prince Alexander is up against our elite troops. By evening we will have wiped out Macedonia's army, together with its future heir."

Unconvinced, the adjutant faced the oncoming enemy. In the meantime, Alexander received Philip's message. He informed the Companion cavalry to await his signal.

As Philip's men drew closer, the adjutant bit his nails.

"The enemy soldiers are not wearing armour, sir," he pointed out to Lysicles. "That will give them an advantage by making them swifter than us on the battlefield."

Suddenly, at a prearranged signal, arrows flew from King Philip's special missiles' force. A lethal shower of javelins followed. Lifting up their shields, most of the Greeks withstood the onslaught. Still, there was no mass movement forward.

An anxious Cleitus drew up alongside his monarch. "It's no use, Philip. You've tried everything. They're not attacking."

"In that case, we have no choice."

Philip lifted his sword above his head. A roar rose from his army. He cast his single sharp eye across the serried troops before him. Impervious to the noise, they stood like blocks of marble. At fifty metres away, there was only one thing to do. Uttering a full battle cry, Philip charged. In a single avalanche, his troops were on the Greeks.

To the surprise of the Macedonians, the opposing ranks did not give way. Heavily armed Athenians lashed out. Bronze cut bone. Men fell. Helmets rolled in the dust. Macedonians were decapitated. Others were run through with swords and spears.

From the river, Alexander watched. Hephaestion shifted uncomfortably on his horse.

"The Greeks are holding, Alex. We're suffering losses."

"I have to wait for Father's signal."

Across from Alexander, General Chares of the central Greek elite unit, was observing the battle with one of his most experienced officers.

"It's been two hours, Diomedes. They're still fighting on our left."

"King Philip failed to penetrate our ranks, sir."

"He will. Send word to Theagnes. The Sacred Band could be what we need to stave off King Philip."

Suddenly, part of the Macedonian army in front of them, moved slowly forward. Directed by Alexander, it effectively prevented the elite core of the Greek army from going anywhere.

Diomedes swallowed. "Is that order still valid, sir?"

"Stay where you are!"

Unable to assist their inexperienced colleagues, the elite part of the Greek army was at a standstill. Several hours into the battle, their left flank by the mountains remained in formation.

It was now late morning. Earth and grass ran with blood, but the Greek soldiers refused to give way. Shading his eyes, Alexander spotted his father in hand-to-hand combat. Surrounded by his bodyguard, Philip cut a swathe of bloodied flesh around them.

Hephaestion urged his horse closer to Alexander. "Are you worried about your father?"

"I'm waiting for his signal."

"We're all waiting!" Cassander shouted. He adjusted his broad-brimmed hat and whistled a tune.

Irritated, Alexander turned on his horse to glare at him. "Why is Cassie not wearing a helmet?"

Hephaestion shrugged. "He was."

Inhaling a breath to curb his temper, Alexander turned back and focussed on the battle. The sun rose higher. Sweat poured down Bucephalus' flanks. Tired and thirsty, the Athenians began to wilt under the searing August sun. But instead of taking the opportunity to attack his tired enemy, Philip and his men began to retreat.

"By Apollo, what are we doing?" Cassander screamed. "We were winning!"

"Shut up, Cassie!" Perdiccas and Leonnatus chorused.

Alexander refused to react and watched closely. Not believing their luck, the inexperienced Athenian divisions gave chase. The enemy coalition of Greek states was now torn between joining with the Athenians, or staying with the Thebans.

Deciding to halve its forces, two divisions of hoplites broke away from the main Greek army to join the reckless Athenians, who were in pursuit of the Macedonian monarch. Beating off the Athenians, made it difficult for Philip's men to retreat in dignity.

Alexander rose on his horse. His gilded leather armguard flashed in the sunlight as he raised one arm to motion the army forward. Cassander ceased his commentary. In one lithe move, he exchanged his sun hat for his helmet and tightened his horse's reins. His father, General Antipater, steadied his grey stallion. A battle-hardened steed, it was tired of waiting. On Alexander's command, the Macedonian lines moved closer to Philip.

Meanwhile, the gap in the enemy ranks widened. In its attempt to assist the Athenian advance, half the coalition phalanx was now separated from the rest of the Greeks.

Suddenly, Philip wheeled his horse round, and galloped with his men towards the safety of his own army. The Athenians could hardly believe their luck. Breaking formation, they pursued him.

It was the turn of Parmenion and Cleitus to move their phalanx of long-speared infantry across the plain in a solid block, successfully cutting off the Athenians from their main army. Then, they lowered their spears.

The two armies clashed. Macedonians demolished line after line of Athenian infantry and cavalry. Dust rose in clouds, obscuring men's vision and adding chaos to the battlefield.

Cassander was at Leonnatus' right, watching the carnage. "Sad, really."

"Can you really not control yourself, Cassie?"

"Admit it, Leo, Athenians are gullible. And the way things are, we might be joining them in the underworld tonight."

"Are you afraid?"

"On the contrary, dear friend, I'm here to comfort and assist you."

Before Leonnatus could answer, a high-pitched war cry floated across a wind which blew up from the river.

"Charge!"

In diamond formation, Alexander galloped with his cavalry through a gap in the enemy lines. Signalling to the main part of the Macedonian army to move forward, he led his companions round the back of the enemy phalanx and to the other side.

Dust flew into Leonnatus' eyes as he found himself charging through a haze with Cassander. The army moved as one behind their leader. It dawned on Leonnatus that they were making history by following the youngest royal military commander to lead a major battle.

While Philip fought both the inexperienced Athenians, and half of the breakaway enemy phalanx, Alexander crushed the elite core of the Greek enemy in a horseshoe-like embrace. Within minutes, the Theban phalanx disintegrated. Dropping his shield, Demosthenes fled.

Fighting valiantly, Cassander lay about him with his sword. Mowing down the elite core of the enemy appealed to his general sense of well-being. During a pause in fighting, he looked up. On the periphery of the intense combat, a block of soldiers remained unmoved. Leonnatus was still close by.

Pointing a bloodied sword, Cassander called out to him. "What, by Zeus' beard, is that?"

"Sacred Band. Theagnes won't budge."

Fighting intensified. Finally, most of the elite corps were slain or fled the battlefield. The Macedonians now turned their attention to the remaining troops.

Isolated by the river, the Theban Sacred Band remained obdurate. Cassander gave a wicked grin. As the Macedonians encircled them, the three hundred men fought bravely and were slaughtered to the man.

***

50.

King Philip ordered the enemy bodies to rot in the sun. After several hours, he joined Alexander's regiment by the river. Most of the men were resting upwind from the stench. Some bathed in the water. Others, completely exhausted, were sleeping under trees.

Philip drew near to an ancient oak where his son had pitched camp. On seeing the bodies of the Sacred Band of Thebes, he burst into tears.

Cassander clapped his hands in glee. "Alexander's in trouble, now!"

Leonnatus was tired. His blood-spattered armour weighed heavily on him. "Whatever for, Cassie?"

"Philip lived in Thebes."

"As a hostage, when he was young."

"Our king learned everything about creating a first-rate army from Thebes. He revered the Sacred Band."

"Do you think he knew some of those men, Cassie?"

"Their fathers. These men are too young, but King Philip thought the Band had the best soldiers in Greece."

"Not now. They're all dead."

Leonnatus walked away. Reaching his tent, he collapsed inside the entrance. Two pages hurried forward to lift him up. Taking their master to his bath, they washed the crusted blood and grime away. A doctor visited him and patched up his wounds.

Wiping his eyes, Philip called to his officers. Three hundred corpses from the Sacred Band were cleared away from the plain. Men went into the woods to cut down trees.

Chopping up the wood into smaller logs, they stacked them to make a platform. On it, bodies were laid out in rows. Logs were positioned around them. Smaller chunks of wood were placed between the men.

A royal priest was summoned from Philip's camp. He prayed, then poured oil and water on the ground. Olive oil was also poured over the dead men. Goats were brought. More prayers were said. Incense was lit, and the animals were sacrificed.

During late afternoon, Cassander joined the growing crowd at the funeral pyre. Several goat carcasses were hauled onto the platform and placed with the bodies. Others were taken away to be skinned and turned into a sacred meal. Twenty men with torches stood around the perimeter of the wood pile.

Taking a torch handed to him by his officer in charge, the king stepped forward. "Nearly thirty years ago, I Philip of Macedonia was privileged to watch the Sacred Band train. No finer soldiers existed. Today, I stand before these sons of Thebes. I knew their fathers. On the field of Chaeronea, where Macedonia and Greece unite, we commemorate their sacrifice."

Philip lit the edge of the wooden logs nearest to him. He handed it back to his officer. The man hid his surprise and stayed to attention as the flames fanned out. Other soldiers, who were stationed around the pyre, followed suit. However, unlike Philip, they threw their torches onto the logs, as was the custom. Corpses ignited as sheets of orange and yellow shot into the skies.

The Macedonian king turned and walked away to keep a safe distance between himself and the fire's heat. It was then Cassander saw that his one eye was teary and red-rimmed. When he found a safe position, Philip stood before the pyre, his back to the crowd. From his heaving shoulders, it was clear he was sobbing.

Seleucus walked up to Cassander. "King Philip has always been a consummate showman."

Startled from his reverie, Cassander's head shot up. "Those tears are real. He knew their fathers."

"As he did the Athenians, who were slaughtered today."

"Demosthenes is alive."

"He's dead."

Cassander shook his head. "Our king ordered General Parmenion to keep him alive."

"Since when?"

"I heard Parmenion talking to my father about it. King Philip ordered that Demosthenes be protected."

"I forgot you were privy to the conversations of our high and mighty. But then, your father is almost King."

Before Cassander could reply, Seleucus melted into the evening shadows. Ptolemy was on his left. "You're right, Cassie. Philip's tears for the Sacred Band are real."

"And they are dead to the last man. We have Alexander to thank for that."

"You enjoyed killing them, too."

Cassander's eyes followed the flames as they ascended the evening sky. He watched Philip, who did not move from his spot until the bodies were ashes.

Finally, his voice cracking with emotion, the victor of Chaeronea addressed the crowd: "I, King Philip, order a memorial to be built to the bravery of the Sacred Band. It will be in the form of a stone lion to commemorate the young lions who gave their lives for their country."

Turning, the man who was now in many ways King of Greece, left his position and walked through the gathering. His face was chalk. His knees wobbled.

"You're right, Ptolemy," said Cassander, as evening shadows lengthened across the plain. "I enjoyed killing, but this afternoon I grew up."

Leaving the older general, Cassander made his way back to his tent by the river. Alexander was nowhere to be seen.

***

Night fell and a full moon rose. Carousing from Philip's post-battle drinking party filled the valley. During the celebrations, his veterans Parmenion, Attalus, and Cleitus locked horns.

"You must be joking, Cleitus," rumbled Parmenion. "How could Alexander think he won?"

"It's a fact. Alexander saved the day at the Battle of Chaeronea. Our bards are already singing the song."

Attalus munched a handful of almonds. "Pshaw! It was carefully orchestrated by our mighty Philip here."

"Alexander is a man and a warrior," Cleitus declared. "It might be wise for us all to remember that."

Rolling his eyes, Philip took a two-handled goblet. His good eye flicked from his senior Macedonian officer to Parmenion. The latter took the bait.

"Don't tell me, dear Cleitus, that our puppy actually thinks the mighty Philip turned and ran?"

"What would you think if you were sixteen, Parmenion?"

"I would know my place."

"What's that supposed to mean? Remember, I'm loyal to the house of Philip."

Attalus arched one brow. "Are you?"

Philip put his goblet down. He wiped his mouth with the back of his hand and belched. "Listen up! Alexander is not responsible for songs sung by rabble. I staged the retreat. He was to attack the weak point. My son followed my orders, like the rest of you."

"Victory has gone to his head," Parmenion asserted.

"My son is entitled to feel pride. He's a brilliant commander."

"He could be dangerous," said Attalus.

"Rubbish! An idealist, perhaps. He's an intellectual who knows Euripides and Sophocles by heart, but dangerous? Only to our enemies!"

"I am with you," said Cleitus. "Alexander is a great fighter and scholar."

"He's also a dreamer," Philip slurred. "And listening to that mother of his doesn't help."

Attalus drank a cup of uncut wine. "She's a Molossian. What do you expect?"

Opening his one eye wide, Philip blinked. He fixed Attalus with a stony stare. Waving his goblet at an attendant for more wine, he waited until it was poured. His commanders fidgeted, wondering if their friend had gone too far.

He sipped his drink. His lips curved. "She's a pure wolf-bred – I won't say what – but I agree."

Roaring with laughter, the men quickly moved to a new topic. As the moon rose higher into the evening sky, the generals went outside. While they drank and talked, attendants started their work arranging dining couches into one section.

Furniture, which included oak tables from Macedonia, and gold braziers for incense, were set in intervals around the couches. The royal tent was widened, and new hangings placed on the canvas walls. Carpets were rolled out and cushions set in corners for diners who wished to relax after the main meal.

Roasted goats from the sacrifice were carried into the tent on spits, where they were placed a distance away from the dining couches. Geese, stuffed with herbs and chestnuts, sat by the entrance. Boar and pheasant were positioned on trestles outside the perimeter of Philip's tent.

The aroma of meat wafted over the camp, signalling the hungry guests to ready themselves. It was an hour before the main feast.

***

51.

In his own quarters, Alexander nursed his wine cup. His friends were garrulous. Faces flushed, eyes shining after their first major victory, they were eager to outdo each other in boasts.

Alexander sought out Perdiccas. "Did my father commend me?"

"No."

"But, he spoke to you after the battle."

"I was wounded. He asked after my health."

"He didn't even acknowledge me."

"Your father is grieving. He buried the Sacred Band."

"I can smell barbecued goat from here." Alexander turned to his friends. "Does anyone know whether we are invited to the victory party?"

"In an hour," Hephaestion replied. "Cleitus told me they expect us. Your father is proud of you, cousin."

"As he should be." A spark of doubt flickered in Alexander's eyes.

***

Ptolemy chewed a twig to clean his teeth. He spat into a bowl. Rinsing his mouth, he dried his face with a towel.

A swim in the fast-flowing river, after the bodies were cleared away and burned, had done him a world of good. Now it was time to celebrate. He was in the mood for a party. With Greek women.

***

Revelry in the royal tent at Chaeronea continued until the early hours of the morning. As Hephaestion predicted, the younger military commanders were invited to join.

Alexander pointed out bitterly, that they were included only with the rank and file of Philip's army. His complaints, however, did not overshadow the toasts made in his father's honour.

"To Philip, King of Macedonia!"

"To a great victory!"

"To our chief!"

Undeterred by the lack of recognition for their mighty deeds in battle, Ptolemy and Seleucus danced with anyone who was willing. Their joy was infectious, and even Cassander abandoned his role of court wit, and joined them.

Kicking up their heels and stamping, they led the crowd outside and around the tent. Unable to dance with his injured leg, Philip sang along, content to stand by the gilded oak pole at the tent entrance.

By midnight, Alexander was smouldering. Excusing himself, he rose to leave. Hephaestion pulled him back. "Where are you going, good cousin?"

"To bed."

"We leave when your father leaves."

"He's drunk."

"He's the unofficial King of Greece."

"Which means he's *not* King."

"Your father is too smart to call himself that. Now, have another round."

"I've had enough."

"I'm dancing. I suggest you join me."

Passing by Philip, Hephaestion bobbed his head in acknowledgement. Grumbling, Alexander followed. His father clapped them on their backs as they passed him.

"Go with Dionysius, sons of Macedonia! May he bless and protect you on this most wonderful of nights."

Alexander reflected that his cousin had saved his reputation in the eyes of the hard drinking Philip. To his father, one was only a real man if he could fight in war and make merry at feasts to celebrate his great deeds afterwards. Someone like Ptolemy, in fact. A cold shiver ran down the prince's spine.

Accepting a garland from a page, Alexander put it on his head and joined the throng as they danced around a bonfire. He noticed Ptolemy was hugging two women.

I wonder how Thais would feel? Shaking off the thought, Alexander made sure his father could see him dancing, drinking, talking to women, and laughing with the others.

***

After the party, Philip washed his face. Cold water stung his eyes into wakefulness. He glanced at his reflection in a bronze mirror. The night's festivities had taken their toll. Wiping his hands on a linen towel, the king called for wine and went to his desk. Scanning the contents of his latest letter, he reviewed it for clarity.

Towards midnight, he summoned Parmenion and a messenger. When they entered the royal tent, Philip rose and held out a sealed package to the man.

"This letter is to reach Athens next week," he said.

The man bowed and left. Parmenion remained.

"Why are you sending a messenger to Athens, Philip? I should go with him. He won't survive."

"I requested Demosthenes deliver the funeral oration for Athens. You are my witness."

***

52.

Back at Pella, the festivities continued. During the day, Alexander exchanged letters with Aristotle and studied. His teacher was becoming more famous. Perhaps, one day he would eclipse Plato. Hephaestion said he would be content if their mentor drowned out Demosthenes.

One afternoon, while Alexander memorised Euripides, a manservant appeared. Irritated, the prince looked up from his work. "Can't you see I'm studying?"

"Your mother is here."

Without waiting, Olympias swept in. Kissing her son, she accepted a chair from the servants. They poured wine from Epirus for her and served fruit on gold platters, together with dates imported from Egypt.

"You're well-appointed here, Alex."

"Father takes care of me, especially since Chaeronea."

"He's marrying General Attalus' niece in a few days."

"I'm sorry for you, Mother."

"You don't understand. They will have children."

"Who will be adults in twenty years' time. I'll have a dynasty by then."

"You sound sure of yourself. As sure as you were at Chaeronea."

"What's that supposed to mean?"

"You're so certain you won."

"I *did* win."

"Positioned between Parmenion and Antipater? You were set up. Philip put you in the right place at the right time."

"Bards are singing songs about me, not them."

"Your father bears you a grudge for this."

"What are you talking about? He loves me all the more."

"Mark my words, he'll be rid of you by summer's end."

"Mother, you need to leave now."

"Philip's decree states openly that I was unfaithful to him."

Alexander froze. "I didn't know."

Olympias made to leave. At the door, she looked over her shoulder. "Your sister, Cleopatra will also be married."

"I shall be at the wedding."

"It's an opportunity, Alexander."

In a swirl of soft draperies and perfume, she was gone. Hephaestion appeared.

"Are you ready for tonight's banquet, Alex?"

"I was planning to study for another hour, but everyone keeps interrupting me."

"You need to get dressed. It's a special evening."

"Not least because Father has a new bride."

"Your father always had an eye for women."

"Thank Zeus, he only has one. Imagine if he still had two!"

****

In Athens, Demosthenes warmed up his throat. It was a fine day, and the sky was as blue as the sea. His attendant gave him a cup, holding a concoction of herbs for his tonsils.

A fresh breeze blew across the gathering. Hundreds of army officers and soldiers, together with politicians and shopkeepers, were gathered in solemn silence.

Demosthenes stepped onto the podium. "After the State decreed that those who rest in this tomb, having acquitted themselves as brave men in the war, should have a public funeral, and appointed me to the duty of delivering over them the customary speech, I began immediately to study how they might receive their due tribute of praise ...”

People craned their heads towards the speaker. On a wooden bench, in the strong morning sun, Philip's messenger dozed.

***

Lord Cassander whiled away the afternoon, playing a lute, and gawking at one of his slave girls. Towards evening, the sentries announced the arrival of Perdiccas and Leonnatus.

Cassander waved them away. “I can't come to dinner, yet. I'm still waiting for the manicurist.”

“We'll go on ahead, Cassie,” Perdiccas said. “Don't be late.”

Reaching into his cloak, Perdiccas pulled out a ball. Tossing it to Leonnatus, the two played catch as they strolled down the road leading to the palace.

“Do you think he's really waiting to get his nails done?” asked Leonnatus.

“Cassie's fastidious about his appearance.”

“That girl was pretty.”

“She's only a slave. Daughters of aristocrats dine with us tonight. Cassie wants a wife before we go to Persia.”

The boys entered the palace courtyard and made their way down a long corridor to the banqueting hall.

“Are we going to Persia?”

“I hope so, Leo.”

“So does Alex, but I've noticed King Philip only refers to himself when it comes to war against the Achaemenid empire.”

“Kings always talk about themselves. Generals are self-obsessed. With Philip, we have both.”

“I would be careful not to express your thoughts aloud, Perdie. His spies could be in the next corridor.”

***

53.

Demosthenes paused for effect. He regarded the citizens of his beloved town. The audience had grown. Even women were present. Heads covered, sheltering in the eaves of surrounding buildings, they hid behind the men, or their grown children. All of Athens had turned out for the funeral oration.

It dawned on Demosthenes that no matter what he said, or how it was presented, his speech would make history. King Philip had cleverly honoured him as the orator of the age.

He licked his lips and took a breath. Philip's messenger woke with a start and caught his eye. All Athenians straightened their posture. Demosthenes' powerful voice wafted over their heads, clear even to the women huddled under the eaves.

"The nobility of birth of these men has been acknowledged from time immemorial by all mankind. ... For alone of all mankind they settled the very land from which they were born and handed it down to their descendants ... these men are citizens of their native land by right of legitimate birth."

It was warm. Cicadas sang in the grass. With a happy sigh, Philip's messenger resumed his slumbers.

***

Walking down the main corridor which led to the banqueting hall, Hephaestion tried to keep up with Alexander. His cousin's nervous, quick gait was more pronounced than usual.

"Slow down, Alex. We don't have to be there for another hour."

"Do you know about the decree? Father declared my mother was unfaithful to him."

"Which disinherits you."

"Yesterday they were singing about the hero of Chaeronea. Now, I'm illegitimate."

"King Philip may have mood swings, however, he has no choice but to select you as his successor. You played the principal role in our victory at Chaeronea. It gave us Greece."

"Bah! Father palmed the victory off to me as a compensation prize. While I was filled with pride, he was planning to give my throne to another, and declare me a bastard!"

"Don't let your father see you angry."

"I'm going to challenge him at the banquet."

"That's a bad idea, cousin. You don't know how deep this plot runs. There could be others."

"My father acts alone."

"What about Attalus? His niece is to be your father's chief wife."

Leonnatus and Perdiccas joined them in the dinner queue. The latter tossed Hephaestion the ball. He caught it with ease and threw it over his head to Leonnatus, who joyfully tossed it in the air.

Drawing a vexed breath, Alexander stepped into the hall.

***

Politicians whispered as they critiqued Demosthenes. He ignored them. His keen eyes saw bereaved women, who were grateful to hear honour paid to their lost husbands, fathers, and sons.

And so he continued. His clear voice increased in its volume. Athenian soldiers, who had fought on the plain of Chaeronea, wilted halfway through his speech.

Finally, Demosthenes launched into his epilogue. Sensing the end was near, the audience straightened their backs under the burning sun.

"It is painful for children to be orphaned by a father. True, yet it is a beautiful thing to be the heir of a father's fame. And of this pain we shall find the deity to be the cause, to whom mortal creatures must yield, but of the glory and honour the source is found in the choice of those who willed to die nobly.

"As for myself, it has not been my concern how I might make a long speech, but how I might speak the truth. And now do you, having spent your grief and done your part as law and custom require, disperse to your homes."

A sigh rippled through the audience. Demosthenes stepped down from the platform. Soldiers marched about, conducting manoeuvres to honour their fallen comrades.

Philip's messenger awoke at the noise and promptly fell off his perch.

***

54.

Already drunk, the King of Macedonia could be heard through the doors of the vast banqueting hall. Putting his shoulders back, Alexander walked in accompanied by Hephaestion, Perdiccas and Leonnatus. Lagging behind, Cassander removed dirt from under his fingernails, while he scolded his page.

Inside, Ptolemy's hearty laughter reverberated through the hall. Quaffing wine, and snacking enthusiastically, his cheeriness was infectious. Hephaestion leaned towards his cousin.

"The man's irresistible," he whispered.

Alexander chuckled. "Don't let Cassie catch you speaking like that. You know he loves to twist everything."

"He's too busy telling off his page to hear. Meantime, it would be strategic to sit next to Ptolemy."

Cassander bowled up behind the group, stumbling over Perdiccas' long robe in the process. "What am I not supposed to be overhearing?"

Perdiccas tugged at his gown. "Get off! This took me all afternoon to select."

"Dressing up are we? Who is she – or he?"

Leonnatus rolled his eyes. "Shut up, Cassie! Let's find a seat."

"Good luck with that, the place is jampacked."

"We're heading for Ptolemy's corner," Hephaestion explained.

Cassander wrinkled his nose. "Bad choice."

"What do you mean?"

"Everyone knows he pays no attention to his grooming."

People were looking at the newcomers.

"How does *that* matter?" Leonnatus interrupted, controlling the urge to box Cassander's ears.

"He won't be able to recommend a manicurist."

"What, by Zeus' beard, has that to do with choosing a dinner group?"

"Everything. My page forgot to schedule me an appointment. Chaeronea's dirt is still under my fingernails. How am I going to find a pretty girl, let alone a wife, if I can't put my hands on her?"

"Tell her you fought at Chaeronea," suggested Perdiccas. "Women love heroes." He checked the hem of his robe. It was still intact.

The friends progressed through the crowd to Ptolemy's section, where the latter stood up and opened his arms.

"Alexander!" he boomed. "Heroes of Chaeronea, welcome to the old men's section."

Cassander's eyes widened. "Why doesn't anyone tell *him* to shut up?"

It was King Philip's turn. "My son, conqueror of Greece!"

"He's complimenting you," Hephaestion whispered. "Show your gratitude. Smile."

"Why?" asked Alexander. "You can hear the sarcasm in his voice. He's taunting me."

Philip waved his gold cup erratically around his head. "Come and join me, my boy. Slaves, bring another couch!"

Attalus paled. For his part, Alexander obeyed his father, and reclined on a couch next to him. Hephaestion stayed close to his cousin.

"It's a pity you're sober," said Philip. He beckoned to the servants. "Wine – bring wine for my beloved boy!" Accepting a gem-encrusted goblet, the prince noticed it was filled to the brim. Philip pushed the goblet towards his son's mouth. "Drink!"

Hephaestion put his mouth to Alexander's ear. "The wine is safe, cousin. I saw it being tasted when we came in."

The prince took a mouthful. His father clapped him on the back. It was then that General Attalus lifted his cup. "I propose a toast. To the King's wedding!"

A roar went up. Philip swayed on his couch.

"M-much o-obliged, G-General A-Attalus," he hiccupped.

"To Philip and my niece Eurydice," Attalus continued. "A true Macedonian, who is about to bear our sovereign a legitimate male heir."

"How dare you?" Alexander shouted.

"Attalus is only jealous," said Hephaestion. "Ignore him."

But Alexander was already moving towards the general with a drawn sword. "You stand in front of your future king, and dare to call a child not yet born, my replacement?"

"Calm down," Philip said, suddenly sober.

"And you," Alexander turned, waving his sword. "Publicly humiliating my mother and calling me illegitimate! Queen Olympias is mother of the only son fit to be your successor."

"You cocky little upstart! I set up your victory in Chaeronea, and this is how you repay me?"

Rising, Philip drew his sword and lurched forward. Tripping over his robe, he fell to the ground, between the couches.

Alexander opened his arms to the banqueters. "Fellow Macedonians, here is the man who was going to take you to Asia. Look at him! He cannot pass from one couch to the other."

Sheathing his sword, he walked out of the hall. Hephaestion hurried to catch up. Cassander heaved a melodramatic sigh and joined Leonnatus and Perdiccas as they scurried out. Ptolemy remained in the hall with the senior generals. No longer laughing, his face was grim.

***

55.

It was midnight. Guests, who had attended the royal feast, dispersed to their homes. Servants cleaned the banqueting hall. The wine-spattered floor mosaic, where Alexander had thrown his goblet, was scrubbed to perfection. Spatters on gilded marble columns were wiped off, and couches taken away to be re-upholstered.

In the corridors, light footsteps hurried across the tiles. Soon, Alexander was at his mother's door. "You summoned me?"

"We need to pack."

"It's the middle of the night."

"You tried to kill your father."

"I was dealing with Attalus."

"That's not what I heard."

"Attalus insulted you, Mother. I defended your honour. Father drew his sword."

"Then what?"

"His bad leg tripped him up. He fell."

"Which is fortunate for you. You will escort me to my brother's home in Epirus. You should go to King Glaukias afterwards."

"But, Macedonia waged war with him."

"Under Philip, who won, which is precisely why Glaukias will welcome you. Get your friends. We need to be gone before dawn."

***

In the first light of morning, Philip's generals assembled in the Great Hall. It was cold. Boys lit fires. Stewards served mulled wine. Servants handed out sardines and fresh bread.

Antipater accepted the breakfast. Scooping sardines from a gold saucer, with thin slices of cracker bread, he ate. Next, he drank a cup of wine. The heat, mixed with spices and fish, released nutrition into his body. Replete, he brushed his hands together to rid them of crumbs.

Parmenion did not touch the victuals. Attalus, still hung over from the previous night, continued to swill wine. One-eyed Antigonus and Amyntas chatted in low voices. They had already run two miles through the valleys around the palace, and were comparing times.

At the seventh hour on the sun dial, their king arrived.

"Where's Alexander?" he asked.

Parmenion straightened his posture and stepped forward. "He and his mother fled Pella last night."

"Why?"

"You attacked your son with your sword."

"I was drunk. Anyway, I didn't touch a hair on his head."

Amyntas cleared his throat. "Olympias is at the home of her brother."

"Alexander of Epirus?"

"Even so, my sovereign."

"Let her stay there, stupid woman! But, I want Alexander back."

Antigonus stepped forward. "My understanding is that Alexander is in Illyria."

"Illyria's a big place," said Philip. "Where, exactly?"

"King Glaukias' palace."

"That makes no sense. I defeated Glaukias in battle."

"Perhaps that's why the man feels obliged to show your son hospitality."

"Good point. Visit him."

Antigonus hesitated. "But your decree was to exile Alexander."

"I have no intention of permanently exiling the man fit to be your next king. Go to the court and ask for him. And take a gift."

With a short bow, Antigonus quickly left the room. General Antipater smoothed his beard. He had sent spies ahead of Alexander's party that morning.

***

56.

The trek took several days. One morning, the party of Macedonian exiles reached Epirus.

Cassander was eating a pomegranate on horseback. "I must say, this resembles Pella."

"The landscape is similar," Leonnatus agreed.

"I'll enjoy staying here," said Perdiccas. "There are streams in the meadows."

Cassander finished his piece of fruit. He wiped his hands on his tunic. "I'd like to catch a fat fish before lunch."

"My rod is with the baggage train," said Perdiccas.

Leonnatus looked about. "Where's Ptolemy when you need him?"

At the back of their party, Ptolemy caught sight of three cloaked men on horseback. Scouts had reported their whereabouts the previous night. Mentally calculating the distance to the palace, he galloped to the front. Several of the Companions had dismounted and were divesting themselves of their outer garments.

"What are you doing?" he asked.

"There's a stream up ahead," said Perdiccas.

"Join us for a swim," Cassander invited. "Leonnatus is getting our fishing rods."

"There's no time," Ptolemy replied. "We need to keep going."

"There's plenty of time!" Cassander exploded. "We're not expected at the palace until later this morning." He stamped his feet.

Taken aback, Perdiccas attempted to mollify him. "You're right," he soothed. "We still have time for a swim."

Leonnatus arrived, puffing, with several rods. "What's wrong, Ptolemy? You look tense."

"Nothing's wrong, Leo. Alexander doesn't want gaps between us, that's all. Let's tighten up a bit and ride closer together. We can always fish after lunch."

"Fair enough," said Leonnatus.

He handed the rods to Ptolemy and mounted his horse. The latter rode back to the baggage train and his veterans. One of them was engaged in picking a scab from his knuckles. He had been in a palace brawl before they left Pella.

"What's with the brats?" he asked.

Several veterans laughed.

"They thought it was time for fishing," Ptolemy explained.

"With Philip's men behind us?"

"They're Antipater's."

"I can see his son stamping the turf from here," one of the men observed.

"They're tired," said Ptolemy. "And they don't deserve exile."

"None of us do. I'm one of the Silver Shields."

"And I thank you for your service," said Ptolemy quickly.

"I shouldn't even be here," the man continued. "I belong to Philip's elite corps, for Zeus' sakes."

"I appreciate the risk you all take. It will not be forgotten."

The man appraised his young leader, who looked so much like Philip. "No, I expect not. It's a privilege to ride with you, General Ptolemy."

A servant from the baggage train ran up and took the rods away. They rode on.

***

At the palace, the Young Companions waited in the outer rooms while Alexander and his mother went into a reception chamber to meet their host.

There, King Alexander of Epirus embraced them. "What brings my beloved sister, and nephew to my home?"

"My husband exiled us."

"Both of you?"

"You needn't worry. Alexander won't be staying."

"My home is always open to my family."

Olympias stroked her son's cheek. "It's time for you to go, dearest."

"Stay, my nephew," the king persisted. "With your friends."

"Much as I would like to, Uncle, I must be going." Alexander faced his mother. "Although, I do wish I could leave Cassander here."

The king pricked up his ears. "Is General Antipater's son travelling with you?"

Olympias regarded her brother. "Why do you ask?"

"His emissaries visited me."

"When?"

"Last night. They left for Glaukias' court."

"*King* Glaukias?"

"The same."

"My son is trapped!" Olympias wailed.

Her brother took her hand. "Do not worry, dear sister. The general's only motive is to protect his boy."

"Uncle's right, Mother," said Alexander. "Antipater loves his son."

"So you think he's protecting Cassander?"

"And me. He was very kind when I was regent."

"I'm sure he is a friend," said his uncle. "However, to set your mother's heart at ease, I shall provide an armed escort and provisions for you, including fresh meat. Zeus be with you, my beloved nephew!"

***

57.

Snow capped the mountains and filled the valleys. It was a night outside for Alexander and his companions. Selecting terrain off the main road, they broke into groups, and made themselves comfortable under trees.

Ptolemy remained with the baggage train. After setting up the first watch, he chose a band of men to scout the area.

Leonnatus and Cassander picked a spot under a group of pines. Several hundred yards off the main road, their clearing was surrounded by dense thickets.

"I'm freezing, Leo."

"Be grateful we're dry. It's snowing."

Instructing the pages to build a fire, Leonnatus unpacked sheepskins. He threw one to Cassander, who was now perched on a rock.

Wrapping the warm animal skin around him, the latter gazed at the prince's retinue. A few hundred yards away, men were going through the same routine of finding somewhere to bunk down for the night.

"Why couldn't you choose to insult your father in the summer, Alexander?"

"Be quite, Cassie. He'll hear you."

"Why are you angry with me, Leo? You should be blaming the oaf who got us into this!"

"Blame isn't going to help. We need to stick together."

"Queen Olympias is tucked up in a warm bed in Epirus. Why can't we stay with her?"

"It could be dangerous, if King Philip finds out."

"What is more dangerous than freezing to death?"

"We've marched all night," said Leonnatus. "I'm tired and I miss my comfortable bed."

"Don't we all? But, I can take a hint. I'll be quiet."

Pages built a fire. Hephaestion spoke to their bodyguards, who checked to see if the flames could be seen from the main road. Only the jagged silhouettes of pines were visible against a night sky illuminated by the moon. There was no trace of humans. Not even their horses were visible from the road.

The bodyguards retraced their steps a short way. A thick blanket of new snow covered the broad highway. There were no imprints for the moon to reveal. Satisfied, they returned to camp.

Bodyguards roasted lamb skewers over pine logs. Wine supplies were broached. On Alexander's orders, everyone was allowed two cups.

Draining his third, Cassander tossed his cup towards his page. Lying on his sheepskin, he fell into a deep sleep. Muttering to himself, Leonnatus pushed his satchel under his head to make himself comfortable.

A few yards away, Alexander and Hephaestion were buried in the roots of a gigantic oak.

"This is like a real bed," enthused Hephaestion.

"I've done it before."

"It's cosy, cousin. A thick leafy canopy to keep you dry, and sheepskins with wood to seal in the warmth. We should tell the others."

"Cassie snores, and Leo talks in his sleep."

"Or perhaps, Antipater's son irritates you, cousin."

"One day, I swear I'll put that boy's head in a wall."

Alexander fell asleep. Hephaestion tucked his arms under his head. Through the thick leaves, he made out a single star in the heavens.

***

Morning stole across the mountains in a pink blush. Steam floated up from the horses' breath. Leonnatus and Cassander were standing by a giant oak, where sunlight glinted through the trees and onto the grass.

The latter pushed unruly locks from his eyes. Already, his hair was growing. He glanced in Alexander's direction and noticed him sleeping between the tree roots. "What do we have here, Leo?"

"It's our prince's way of sleeping in a forest."

"Why didn't you suggest it? I nearly froze to death last night."

Leonnatus shrugged. "I tried it once, but it rained. Roots hold water. I nearly drowned."

Picking up a tree branch, Cassander poked one of Alexander's bodyguards. Instantly, the man opened his eyes, seized the stick from the youth and broke it over one massive thigh.

"You savage! How dare you? I'm General Antipater's son."

Half asleep, Alexander twisted around. "That's what you get for provoking my men, Cassie."

"Sorry sir," said the bodyguard. "I thought you were one of Philip's soldiers. May I get you a Nestor's Cup?"

Cassander sat down with an injured look on his face. "And some of the prince's wine, while you're about it."

Stretching, Alexander rose. He folded his bedding into a neat bundle. Calling for Bucephalus, who was grazing close by, he leapt onto his back. "We have to be at King Glaukias' by midday."

Seeing Alexander ready to depart, Leonnatus motioned to his squires, who brought food and his horse. Grabbing a hunk of bread with cheese from one man, he tucked the provisions into his waistband, and mounted his steed.

Cassander took a wine cup, which Alexander's bodyguard offered him. He gulped it down. Grinning wickedly, he wiped his mouth.

"Many thanks, my fine waiter. One day I may hire you."

The man did not reply. Mounting his horse, Cassander settled in next to Leonnatus. Hephaestion was astride his roan stallion, waiting for his cousin.

Cassander gave a snort of derision. "By Zeus, that clown is boring, Leo."

"Don't let Hephaestion hear you."

"What can he do to me? We're all banished. My career is in tatters. Come to think of it, so is my cloak."

"Hephaestion is Alexander's right-hand man, Cassie. He'd kill for Alex."

"We're already dead men."

Urging his grey horse into the morning chill, Cassander took up the rear, where he spent most of the morning cracking jokes and sneering at the countryside.

***

58.

It was midday when Alexander's party reached the Illyrian court. His keen eyes detected riders to his left. Their cloaks made it impossible to distinguish their origins.

Hephaestion leaned across his horse. "Is there a problem, cousin?"

"My uncle said General Antipater sent emissaries here."

"Do you think we're being followed?"

"We *are* being followed. But, I don't know whether those men are Antipater's spies, bandits or even King Glaukias' scouts."

Hephaestion squinted in the glare of the morning sun. "I can't see anyone."

"Three riders, wearing cloaks?"

"Your eyes are better than mine. Do you want me to check, Alex?"

"There's no point. We're nearing the palace."

At the city's main entrance, wooden gates swung open on their bronze hinges. Alexander's party clattered down a central street and into the palace courtyard. Grooms bowed low before taking their horses to the royal stables.

King Glaukias received his visitors in the main reception area. "Welcome, Prince. Do not hesitate to ask, if you need anything."

"I require the identity of the cloaked riders, a mile from here."

"They are Antipater's emissaries."

"Acting for King Philip?"

"Acting for General Antipater. His son is with you."

"At least one of us has a father who cares," Cassander muttered at the back of the room.

"You are gracious to show us hospitality," said Alexander quickly.

"It is my pleasure."

"And unusual, considering your last meeting with Macedonia was on the battlefield."

"I am your father's vassal now."

"I understand, although I would like to end all conflict one day."

"How would you manage that, noble Prince?"

"By unifying the world under one king."

"That would take many wars."

"Many."

The host clapped his hands. Servants appeared. Alexander was taken to his room, next to the royal apartments, where he bathed, ate, and rested. The others walked to the guest wing, a short distance from their prince.

"My question," said Cassander to the others, "is why Dad didn't furnish us with provisions? My clothes are rags."

"I could have done with more wine," Perdiccas grumbled.

"I would have liked an extra blanket," Hephaestion added.

"I can smell incense," a different voice interrupted.

"I was wondering where you'd got to, Ptolemy," said Cassander. "Where have you been?"

"At the back, keeping close watch over the spies."

Perdiccas halted. "You *knew*?"

"How did you know they weren't assassins sent by King Philip?" Leonnatus ventured.

"I asked them."

Everyone stopped to stare at Ptolemy.

"You're brave," said Perdiccas at last.

"I also spotted Antipater's crests on their uniforms."

"Smart too," said Leonnatus. "By the way, I *can* smell incense. This is a civilised home."

Up ahead, several men approached them.

"I wonder who they are," said Perdiccas.

"Butlers," answered Ptolemy. "To take us to our rooms."

When the men reached the Young Companions, they bowed before escorting them to their apartments. Later, Cassander and Leonnatus took in an afternoon play, staged in their honour.

King Glaukias showed surprise to see fruit flying in one monologue. Cackling, coupled with a thick Macedonian accent at the back of the room, was enough to inform him that arresting the culprit was out of the question.

***

59.

In Pella, Parmenion, and other generals, including Attalus, Andromenes, and Amyntas, waited in the outer office of the palace. A fire crackled merrily in the centre of the room.

Andromenes nervously brushed dandruff off his shoulders. "Do you know why Philip has summoned us here?"

"Promotion," declared Attalus.

"Or the beginning of a purge," Amyntas countered.

"We are all loyal, to Philip," Parmenion said. "Don't worry, Andromenes."

"I'm not worried. I only wanted to prepare –"

King Philip entered the room. Unhooking his cloak, he threw it down on a chair. "I meant to be here earlier, but I had an appointment with Alexander's messenger."

Andromenes looked puzzled. "Isn't the prince in exile?"

Philip shot him a sharp look. "My son is at the court of King Glaukias. He will be back at Pella next week."

"And Olympias?" Andromenes asked.

"Her brother is providing a military escort to bring her back from Epirus."

The king made his way to the fireside.

"Parmenion was just saying how this group is composed of your most loyal generals," Amyntas said with a bright smile. "How may we be of service?"

"By taking part in my new campaign," Philip replied.

Andromenes scratched his beard. "But Greece is secured."

"All due to you, Philip," added Parmenion quickly.

The king sat on a stool by the fire to rub his aching leg.

"What's on our sovereign's mind?" asked Attalus. "Speak, dear friend."

"War. We go to Asia Minor next month."

Amyntas' mouth dropped open. "All of us?"

"What do you want us to do, Philip?" Parmenion asked.

"Liberate Greeks from Persian rule."

"How many men are we taking?" Attalus enquired.

Philip rubbed his right leg. The fire warmed his muscles, dispersing the dull ache. "Ten thousand. I need experienced generals. This will prepare us for the greater war in Persia."

Parmenion's eyes shone. "At last! How many years have we waited?"

While the others mumbled their assent, Philip's knee throbbed. He heaved a breath. "I have my daughter's wedding to attend in Aegae. After that, the Greek states will join us."

When the generals had departed, Philip continued to sit by the fire. The pain finally left his leg.

He rose from the stool and sent for Antipater. "I'm bringing back our sons, General."

"Shall I send out a delegation to greet them?"

Philip shot him a look. "You've sent quite enough delegations, General. What I would like you to do is keep an eye on Alexander."

"As you wish."

"Protect my boy, especially from his mother. If anything happens to me, Alexander is to be King of Macedonia."

Antipater remained impassive. "I understand."

"That will be all. And, thank you."

"I don't recall being of service."

"Of course you don't."

***

Olympias' carriage drew up outside her quarters in Pella. A guard opened the door. Alexander was waiting. He saluted his mother and helped her alight. Servants took her luggage inside, while the others followed with the guards.

In her apartment, Olympias took off her headscarf and draped it around her shoulders. A manservant brought wine in two gold cups. A taster sampled the beverage, after which it was poured out.

Olympias handed her son a drink. "Home at last, my darling."

"If you need anything, Mother, let me know."

"Philip wants Epirus in his right hand with your sister, Cleopatra's marriage. Perhaps he's afraid of me."

"He divorced you, Mother."

Olympias' lips curved as she sipped her wine. "I'm still powerful."

"We're back in Pella because I am the next monarch."

"Are you?"

"Who else is there?"

"Don't forget, your father's married again."

"Father's always getting married."

"This time, it's to General Attalus' niece."

"I overreacted at the banquet. General Attalus is ambitious which is not a crime."

"He's also Macedonian."

"I'm this country's future."

"Not if Philip lives for another twenty years."

Alexander paused. He fidgeted. "Mother, I'm tired."

"Will I see you at dinner?"

"I'll sup with Father."

The prince left without touching his drink.

***

It was the fifth hour of the afternoon. Alexander walked into the audience hall where Philip crushed him in a bear hug. "How strong you are!"

"And you, too, Father."

"Nonsense, I'm growing older by the day. My knee hurts and my spine curves over like an old man."

"Are you well enough to attend the wedding in Aegae?"

Philip's one seeing eye hooded. "Your sister is to be wedded to your maternal uncle, Alexander of Epirus. I will be representing the House of Philip. By the way, what do you think?"

"It's an excellent match."

"And will mollify your mother. She hasn't forgiven me for exiling her."

"Mother is very unforgiving."

Philip chuckled. "You know you are my heir, Alexander."

"I am here to serve you."

"Not just to serve. I would not have made an effort to get you back to Pella unless you were my successor."

"In twenty years, perhaps."

"I won't be around for another two decades. Come, let us prepare for your sister's wedding."

***

In Olympias' apartment, both she and Airlia spun wool together. Late afternoon rays spilled into the room in which the women worked. They chatted, occasionally breaking off to snack, or stroll about the balcony.

It was a perfect time of peace and relaxation. However, Airlia noticed an underlying tension in her friend. At sunset, she decided to broach a subject close to both their hearts.

"Are you concerned about Alexander's loyalty to his father, Olympias?"

"It's natural for a boy to revere his father."

"With Alexander, I suspect, it's love of a future throne, rather than of his parent."

"My son will be King of Macedonia."

"Do you truly believe that?"

Olympias picked up a piece of scarlet wool and wound it skilfully around her distaff.

"It's possible my husband may have brought us back to kill us himself," she laughed.

"It's no laughing matter."

Olympias pinched the wool. "To tell the truth Airlia, I worry all the time." She started spinning.

"If I were you, my dear, I would strike first."

***

60.

It was a perfect spring day. Clouds scudded across green rolling hills. Hephaestion ate breakfast with his cousin in the outer rooms of the palace.

"How is your mother, Alex?"

Alexander's brow was in knots. "More murderous than usual."

"Your mother's never killed anyone."

"Give her time. I saw her muttering an incantation over a statue of me this morning."

"What mother would not pray for her son?"

"She is a witch, who uses spells to get her way. What she fails to understand, is that we're back because Father needs me."

"Your father is married to a Macedonian, now. It could pose a problem for your future."

"That's what Mother says."

"She's right."

Alexander stared through the window, overlooking the hills. "There's a boar hunt this afternoon, Heph."

"If it's with King Philip, I would take some companions. You don't want to be on the stray end of a spear."

"Neither would he."

With a grim chuckle, Alexander pushed his plate aside, rose and marched out of the room. Hephaestion followed. Together, they headed for the stables.

Going straight to Bucephalus' stall, the prince led him outside. Stroking his thick glossy neck, he whispered to him. The warhorse's ears twitched as he shook his mane. Reddish glints from his glossy curls winked in the morning sunlight.

Hephaestion shook his head. "That stallion was made for giants, Alex."

"Beware of jealousy."

"It's fear. Bucephalus has grown several hands since I last saw him."

A groomsman brought Hephaestion his smaller roan stallion. The pair mounted their steeds and rode out at a leisurely pace towards the hills. They paused at a glade of trees.

"I have a confession to make, Heph. My parents' marriage ended years ago."

"King Philip has many wives. It must have been hard for your mother."

"Mother was Father's fourth wife! She knew Macedonian kings were polygamous."

"True. What then?"

"Father found Mother asleep with snakes, after the Dionysian rites."

"It's only natural. People worship snakes in Epirus."

"Father was repelled."

Hope sparked in Hephaestion's eyes. "I hear they have orgies, too."

Alexander laughed. Birds flew upwards from the trees, chirping noisily and chattering to each other. "The Dionysian rites start with a goat sacrifice, after which the main priest goes into a trance. There is drinking, Heph. And wild dancing."

"It sounds like a Macedonian feast."

Alexander patted Bucephalus. "I'll take you one day. There are women, too."

***

Cleopatra welcomed her mother with a kiss on the cheek. Olympias sat on the most comfortable couch, while Thracian maids served them refreshments.

An overweight grey cat drifted past. Noting the visitor, she yawned, stretched and deliberately raked the carpet with her claws.

Olympias looked about. Her daughter's room was smaller than hers, but tastefully decorated with new furniture. The flowers were fresh, as was the fruit in the gold bowl.

She picked at a stray thread from the couch on which she sat. "Is your future husband settled in?"

"Uncle Alexander arrived last night. He's upstairs in the guest room."

"Your brother approves of the marriage. So do I. It could be useful in the future." Cleopatra said nothing. Olympias fixed her with limpid blue eyes. "You would, I gather prefer someone younger?"

"No, Mother."

"Another man has your heart?"

"Uncle Alexander will be my husband."

"A lot can happen between now and the wedding night."

"I am privileged to leave for Epirus, the home of my loved and esteemed mother. I shall miss Pella."

"For me it was the opposite."

"You were in Epirus recently. What was it like?"

"I was in exile, my dear." Olympias helped herself to a fig. "This is delicious."

"It's from your homeland."

"That explains it." Olympias finished her fig and popped another into her mouth. She reached out and patted her daughter's knee. "Don't worry, my dear. Everything will work out. You have my blessing."

Olympias rose. She regarded the servants. They immediately averted their gaze. With a wave of her tail, the cat left for the patio.

Cleopatra accompanied her mother to the door. "Thank you for your blessing."

"You're welcome, dear. Be sure to say goodbye to your father."

After her mother left her apartment, the girl sat down on the nearest seat. A chill formed in the pit of her stomach.

***

Alexander and Hephaestion dismounted at the palace. Stable boys took their steeds away to be fed and watered. Famished, they visited the main kitchen, where they helped themselves to bread and cheese.

Chatting while they ate, they made their way to the prince's apartments. Outside the door, a messenger waited.

"Did my sister send you?" Alexander asked.

"Princess Cleopatra desires the company of her brother."

"Tell her I'll be along, shortly."

With a quick bow, the man hurried away. The boys entered the apartment where the prince hung up his riding cloak.

"Finally, Cleopatra is to be wed," said Hephaestion.

"You make her sound old."

"Any woman over twelve is old."

"My mother was thirteen when Father married her."

"That's different. Your mother's very pretty, Alex."

"It compensates for a soul as dark as night."

Hephaestion fidgeted. "I'd better be going. Your sister will want to see you."

"Have a glass of wine with me. All that bread and cheese has given me a thirst." A steward appeared from the main room and poured out two cups of white wine. "It's from Egypt," Alexander explained. "What do you think?"

Accepting a cup, Hephaestion took a sip. "It's different."

"One day we will visit the land of the Nile. I'll build a city there."

"You'll have to get rid of the Persians first."

Alexander raised his cup. "To liberating Egypt."

231

"To Egypt!" Hephaestion responded.

When he had finished the tasteless beverage, Alexander's cousin took his leave. Hurrying down the corridor, his first stop was at the dining hall. There, he asked a servant to pour him a cup of uncut Macedonian red. He spent several delightful moments, savouring the pleasure of a full-bodied wine.

Making a mental note to badger Alexander for an invitation to Olympias' Dionysian rites, he vacated the hall, and made his way across the gardens to his parents' home in the palace grounds.

***

Alexander was at his sister's door. Leaping up, Cleopatra embraced him.

"I like your perfume, Cleo."

"Uncle says it's from Egypt."

"He brought you a gift?"

Cleopatra blushed. "Several. You're here early, Alex."

"You summoned me. Never put off till tomorrow what can be accomplished today."

"Is that one of Aristotle's maxims?"

"My own."

Cleopatra indicated a chair, where a servant gave her brother a welcome drink of pomegranate juice.

"I wanted to ask about your time in Epirus, Alex. Is it a good place?"

"I escorted Mother there during our exile, but I spent most of my time at King Glaukias' court."

"As it turned out, there was nothing to fear from Father."

"Correct."

An awkward pause ensued. Cleopatra twisted her fingers, trying to think of how to steer the conversation round to her main goal.

"If you had been in Epirus on a family visit, Alex, what would you have liked to do?"

"The riding is good."

"I don't do much riding."

"It's a beautiful mountainous country, much like here. The palace is warm and habitable. I hear the food is very good, too. Unfortunately, I had to be on my way before dinner."

Cleopatra's face brightened. "Thank you, Alex. There is something else I wanted to ask. It's about the wedding."

"An excellent match. It will keep us bound together as a family."

"It's not that."

Cleopatra twisted her fingers again. Alexander rose and put his arm around her shoulder.

"Are you worried about the wedding night?" he asked softly.

"I saw Mother today."

The princess felt her brother's hand stiffen around her.

"What did she want?"

"To give me her blessing. And ... she told me to say goodbye to Father."

"That's appropriate."

"Brother, whatever happens, promise me that you will keep me and my husband safe."

"I don't know what you mean."

"Promise me by the footstool of Zeus, and on our ancestor Achilles, that you will protect us."

Alexander swallowed. "You have my word."

"Go now, dearest brother, and give Hephaestion my love."

Kissing his sister on the forehead, Alexander left her quarters. Putting his shoulders back, he walked with rapid steps towards his apartment. He needed a bath. Politics was always wearying, especially when it involved his family.

                                    ***

Stars dotted the night sky. Pausanias hurried across the pathways into the courtyard of the palace's east wing. At the royal apartments, he was announced by a guard to Olympias.

Stepping across the threshold, he caught his breath. In her
early thirties, the mother of Alexander was still a beautiful woman.

"Dear friend," she greeted her visitor, "I'm so glad you
could come."

"It is my pleasure, Your Majesty."

"Alas, I am no longer Queen."

"You are the mother of King Philip's son."

"Alexander is *my* son."

There was a hint of steel in the velvet tones. Pausanias shivered.

"You must be proud Cleopatra is about to wed," he
said, changing the subject.

"And to my brother, no less. Are you cold?" Without
waiting for an answer, Olympias barked an order. "Slave, light the
fire!" She turned a dazzling smile on her guest. "I forgot it is chilly at
night in Pella."

"You have been away far too long, my lady. I hope you
know you were sorely missed."

Olympias plucked a grape from its bunch and popped it between full red lips. "It is good to be home. By the way, do you think
Cleopatra's wedding to my brother is Philip's idea of an apology?"

"He's not a man given to them."

"Then it must be a strategy."

"The king is not known as Philip the Fox for nothing."
Silence fell. Pausanias shifted uneasily.

"You're right, my dear," Olympias said. "I understand
you are close to my husband."

"I was."

A steward poured out cups of date wine and served both guest and mistress.

"Rumour has it that King Philip humiliated you," Olympias said quietly.

"Worse than that."

"It can't be worse than exile," Olympias laughed.

"I was violated by Attalus' men."

The guest drained his cup, and banged it down louder than he intended.

"Did my husband defend your honour?"

"He's married to Attalus' niece. How could he defend my honour?"

"There is a way."

Dismissing her attendants, Olympias leaned forward. Overwhelmed by her beauty and charisma, Pausanias listened long into the night by the blazing fire.

***

61.

Heat rose with the morning sun. A procession of statues, representing the twelve gods of Olympus, made its way through a complex of buildings, and into the stadium of Aegae.

Behind its wall, Alexander waited with Hephaestion and the security guards. Pacing up and down, the prince tilted back his head.

"Is Father lost? The sun is high in the sky."

"He's getting ready, Alex. It's a big day for him."

"Bah! He wants to impress everyone by making us wait."

"Perhaps he wants to model himself on Apollo by appearing at the sun god's favourite hour of noon."

Alexander stopped pacing. "I hadn't thought of that. It's true my father wishes to be acknowledged as a god today."

A hail of nuts descended from the stands, accompanied by a cackle. Hephaestion shaded his eyes as he followed the direction of the flying macadamias. "Cassie's already bored."

Alexander swotted a fly. "I swear I'll box that boy's ears one day."

At that moment, Alexander of Epirus, clattered into the courtyard. He leapt down from his chariot to embrace the prince and Hephaestion.

"It's hot enough to bake bread!" he exclaimed. "Ready to celebrate?"

"We're waiting for Father," Alexander explained.

"King Philip should be here. I saw him an hour ago."

"Hephaestion thinks he wants to appear, like the sun god Apollo, at noon."

"That makes sense. Philip does want to be admitted to the Greek pantheon today."

Alexander looked over his uncle's shoulder at the carriage. "Where's my sister?"

"Your mother brought her to the stadium in the bride's coach."

"Cleopatra's not in the audience."

"And yet Olympias is here," Hephaestion pointed out.

"You know what young women are like," the older man laughed. "She's probably still getting ready."

The Epirite monarch's words were lost in the thunderous clatter of chariot wheels and panting steeds. King Philip had arrived. Wearing a white robe, embroidered with the Argead star, and crowned with a gold laurel diadem, he was the epitome of a god king.

"My two Alexanders! Are you both ready to see me acknowledged by the Greeks?"

"They do already, Father," his son replied frostily.

"Ah, but today I'm a god," Philip winked.

His bodyguards took their places. He waved them away. Flanked by his son and future son-in-law, Philip entered the stadium. Cheering from the audience greeted his appearance.

In the stands, Leonnatus noticed King Philip's garland hung over one eye. "Is he drunk already?"

Cassander roared with laughter. Perdiccas strained his eyes to study the king.

"Either that, or his bad leg is hurting," he said.

At the front of the stage, Olympias' lady-in-waiting, craned her neck around in the direction of the Young Companions. "I do wonder about your son's friends."

Olympias patted her knee. "At least they're making fun of my ex-husband, and not my son."

"They should have more respect."

At the bottom of the stairs, leading up to a stage built for the occasion, Philip turned to the two Alexanders.

"I'm ascending this stage as a divine monarch. This part is for me alone."

The pair hung back as Philip climbed a few steps up to the dais. A throne stood in solitary splendour, facing the crowd. Clad in white and completely alone, the King of Macedonia looked up to the heavens. A roar went up from the crowd.

"I have to admit, Leo," Cassander shouted above the din, "today our king *looks* like a god."

"I agree."

"Me, too," said Perdiccas.

Philip raised his arms to the heavens. Pandemonium broke out. The crowd went wild. Even the Greek ambassadors were impressed. Perdiccas, Cassander and Leonnatus stood, clapping and cheering with the rest. Suddenly, Pausanias ran forward.

High in the stands, Cassander squinted. "Has he spotted danger?"

A short distance away, Alexander looked on.

"I wish these people knew their place," he said irritably. "Father gives his men too many liberties. This is embarrassing. All of Greece is watching."

His uncle rubbed the bridge of his nose. "It is known that Pausanias is close to your father. You do know Attalus' men attacked him, don't you?"

"Is that what my mother told you?"

"What does it matter whether she or my spies told me? I do know your father did not defend his friend. He is married to Attalus' niece, after all."

"You have a point, Uncle. My father is part of Attalus' family, now. It would be unwise to side with Pausanias. However, they still seem close."

"Maybe they patched up their differences."

"Pausanias has to remember he is not special," Alexander said hotly. "He can't simply approach his monarch whenever he likes."

"I do believe he's about to kiss your father."

Pausanias embraced Philip. People in the crowd craned their necks forward. Greek diplomats whispered together. Suddenly, Philip gasped and toppled forward.

Leonnatus was on his feet. "The king has been stabbed!"

His voice rang out in the crowd as he leaped down the steps of the stadium. Alexander saw it. A red stain from his father's side covered the dais and dripped off the boards.

"Murderer!" he screamed. "Catch him!"

Philip's bodyguards galvanised into action. Cassander shoved his snacks into his pockets, unsheathed his dagger, and raced after Leonnatus. Perdiccas followed, accompanied by the other Companions. Forming a line on the stage where their monarch lay, they kept the crowd back.

Alexander ran to his father's side. Hephaestion materialised next to him, brandishing a spear. Bodyguards joined and blocked off the group.

Gurgling blood, Philip reached out to grab his son's chiton. "A-Alex, I have to t-tell you s-something –"

"Don't speak, Father. Save your energy. The doctor will be here soon."

"Your m-mother –"

Alexander's eyes scanned all sides of the grassy stadium. Olympias had vanished with her lady-in-waiting.

"She's safe, Father," said Alexander. "Let go."

But, Philip's fists were clenched over the garment. Trying to speak, his one eye rolled back in his head. Blood spattered over Alexander's tunic. Trying to cradle the dying man in his arms, the prince could only reach around his shoulders. Muscle spasms in his father's back kept jerking against him.

"We have to get him away from here, Hephaestion," he said, struggling with the thrashing body.

"Stay where you are, cousin. You're safe here."

Alexander looked up as he held the gasping king. Blood was now sprinkling his chest and face. "*Where* is the doctor?"

For a moment, it felt as though his father had laughed. Alexander looked down, but Philip's eye was glassy and unseeing. Several of the Macedonian king's bodyguards ran to catch the assassin.

Further away, Cassander shaded his eyes. "Leo, there's Pausanias! Men have a getaway horse for him by the oaks."

Leonnatus, started waving at the bodyguards, who were running in the opposite direction. "By the oak trees! He's getting away!"

Perdiccas caught up, halted and bumped into Leonnatus. Pausanias was almost at the getaway point.

Cassander looked about. "Where are our horses, Leo?"

"Tethered behind the stadium."

"This is a setup. There are no horses visible, except those by the trees."

"We have to get there before Pausanias does," said Leonnatus. "Come on Perdiccas!"

"Wait!" shouted Cassander, as the pair broke away. "I'm coming with you."

While the rest of the Companions stayed with Alexander, the trio raced away. Running at top speed, Pausanias suddenly tripped over a vine. Grasping a spear from a nearby guard, Leonnatus threw it at the assassin.

Striking the murderer in the back, it pinned him to the ground in a pool of blood. Perdiccas did the same. Catching up, Philip's guards plunged their long spears into the lifeless body.

Cassander clapped his forehead. "Idiots! Now nobody's going to know who assassinated our king."

"Shut up, Cassie!" screamed Leonnatus over his shoulder. "There could be others."

Cassander sheathed his dagger. "Don't worry, no others will show themselves. Pausanias was the sacrifice."

General Antipater strode to the group surrounding Philip. Several men bore the body away on a stretcher. Alexander was standing up, head bent as he wiped the front of his attire.

Putting a paternal arm around his shoulder, Antipater began talking to him. The prince's hand shook. The blood would not come off. A squire hurried forward with a clean chiton, so Alexander could change and his bloodied clothing be taken away.

Cassander and Leonnatus made their way back to the stadium. Perdiccas stayed behind to supervise the removal of Pausanias. As they neared the royal murder scene, Cassander noticed Alexander, in fresh attire, listening to his father.

"Dad must be helping," he observed.

Suddenly, shouting erupted. It started with Antipater and was picked up by what remained of the audience in the stadium.

"Alexander! Alexander! Alexander!"

With a sigh, Cassander took out a bag of mixed nuts from his robes. Tipping a few into one hand, he offered the rest to Leonnatus.

"We have a new king. By the way, where is Queen Olympias?"

***

62.

Rubbing his eyes, Cassander swung his plump body out of bed, and slid his feet into sheepskin slippers. Mornings in Aegae were cold. In his second family home, he was down the hall from where his father still slept. After an exhausting week, General Antipater was in no hurry to rise.

A maid brought the young master hot milk, flavoured with spices. Cassander's heart contracted at her beauty.

"Chloe, I pay more than Dad. You're welcome to join my staff."

"I was hired by your father," she smiled. "Drink your milk."

Fluffing up his pillow, the maidservant made Cassander's bed. He obeyed her, greedily absorbing a vision of her loveliness over the rim of his cup. On her way out of his chamber, the woman bumped into Leonnatus.

"I hope I wasn't disturbing anything," he said, lobbing a ball over her head.

Cassander dropped his cup to catch the ball. Milk splashed on the floor.

"What do you want, Leo?"

"You need to attend the king's funeral."

"Is Alexander dead?"

"That's not funny."

"I'm serious."

"He asked me to summon you."

"He could have sent a messenger."

"Aren't you pleased to see me?"

"I don't like being spied on."

Cassander picked up his empty cup and set it on a dresser.

"Look, Cassie, it's dangerous. Alexander and his mother are purging their enemies."

"Am I in danger?"

"Your father declared Alexander King of Macedonia, which was wise."

"I'm Alex's friend. Besides, I'm wasting away with grief."

"That's not in evidence, I'm afraid."

"What do you mean?"

"You're as healthy as Alex's horse."

"Are you saying I'm fat?"

"Bucephalus isn't fat."

"No, he's just enormous," Cassander chuckled. "You know, Alexander could be crushed in a fall, riding that monstrosity."

Suddenly, his eyes sparked. Buoyed with fresh hope, Cassander dressed quickly and followed his friend down the corridor to the stables. There, he selected a suitable steed for the ride to the funeral.

***

After lighting his father's pyre, Alexander backed away. Flames engulfed wooden logs and shot into the night sky. Leaping to the stars, they blocked out the moon.

"Goodbye, Father," he whispered.

A hundred yards away, the Young Companions watched. Alexander recognised their faces by firelight. All were sad. Even the plump features of Cassander looked wistful.

Tears streamed down the faces of Leonnatus and Perdiccas. Cleitus stood between them, his arms around their shoulders. Behind the trio, a silent Ptolemy was positioned next to Parmenion and Seleucus.

Hephaestion was a short distance away from Alexander. Ever ready to do his cousin's bidding, his face was pale in the torchlight.

The new king waited until the sun rose and the funeral pyre's flames were extinguished. Skilled men raked over the ashes. Then, they took King Philip's bones away, where they would be washed, wrapped and interred in a gold casket, ready for burial.

At the seventh hour of the day, Alexander retired to the palace at Aegae. His friends dispersed to their quarters. No one spoke.

***

<h1 style="text-align:center">63.</h1>

It was chilly in Pella. Autumn leaves swirled in eddies down the country lanes. At the home of Leonnatus, a tap at the front door heralded Perdiccas.

The butler announced his arrival, while a manservant took his cloak. When the visitor entered the living room, he saw Leonnatus chatting to Cassander by a fire. The latter was crunching a pear.

"I'm sorry to intrude, Leo," said Perdiccas. "I thought you were alone."

Cassander stopped eating. "More reports, have we, Perdie?"

"I only wanted to pay a visit."

Leonnatus beckoned his newest guest to sit by the hearth. "Warm yourself by the fire, Perdie. It's cold outside."

Avoiding Cassander, Perdiccas took a couch. He hesitated and cleared his throat. "I have sad news. Attalus' niece, King Philip's wife, Eurydice is dead, together with her children."

"I heard she took their lives, before killing herself," Leonnatus said.

"A tragic event," agreed Perdiccas.

"What are you simpletons talking about?" Cassander asked. "It's not suicide. Olympias killed Eurydice and her babes."

Perdiccas' face was grave. "That's only a rumour, and a dangerous one at that."

"I agree," said Leonnatus.

"Poppycock!" Cassander snorted. "Olympias was jealous of Eurydice."

"With good reason," Leonnatus replied. "Eurydice was of pure Macedonian blood. Any son of hers could potentially inherit the throne."

"Not with Philip dead, Leo," Cassander retorted.

"Alexander would still be in danger."

"What danger? Those children would have attained their majority in twenty years – plenty of time for Alexander and his heirs to be secure. Instead, that awful woman strangled Eurydice and burned those toddlers alive."

"They're *rumours*, Cassie," Perdiccas pointed out.

"Mark my words, friends, Alexander's mother deserves a violent death."

Cassander rose. Leonnatus looked surprised. "Where are you going?"

"For a walk."

"My cook is preparing suckling pig for dinner."

"How fitting, to be dining on defenceless baby pigs! I'm off to take the air."

The front door slammed shut.

***

It was a chilly afternoon, but warm in the sun. Alexander and Hephaestion sat in silence on a palace balcony. A wine jug and two gold cups rested on a table next to them. Servants hovered in attendance. After a while, Hephaestion rummaged about in his bag.

"I almost forgot," he said. "I know you're interested in botany."

He presented his cousin with dahlias. Their stripes of red and yellow caught the last rays of sun. At their ends, the bulbs were covered in wet cloth for replanting.

"Ah, yes – these remind me of Lysimachus. He used to give me botany lessons on the way to school."

"He wants some Persian specimens, too."

"Persia is a long way off."

"We're nearly there, cousin."

Alexander waved to a servant, who took the dahlias for planting in pots. Squinting in the late afternoon sun, he observed a figure in the distance.

"Do you see that man over there, walking in circles?"

Hephaestion shaded his eyes. "It's Cassander."

"It *does* look like our friend."

"Is that how you would describe him?"

"His father is in our camp – at least for now."

A fox darted out of the hibiscus bushes in the garden below. Birdsong diminished. The sound of scraping reverberated through the corridors, as couches were set up in the great banqueting hall of Pella.

Alexander was required to preside over every dinner. Unlike his extroverted father, he found the daily appointment a chore. Even now, his muscles tensed at the prospect.

Hephaestion reached for a wine jug. "Drink, cousin?"

"Anything to take my mind off."

Pouring two cups of red wine, Hephaestion pushed one across the table. He lifted the other. "To your reign."

"Did you know my mother executed Eurydice?"

"I do."

"And the children?"

"Yes."

"I'm angry."

"She's only protecting your claim to the throne."

"Now, do you believe my mother is murderous?"

"What are you saying, Alex?"

"I need to get out of Macedonia."

The sun dipped below the horizon. Alexander ordered blankets to be brought to keep them warm. Sipping his drink, he watched Cassander as the latter continued to spin frenetic circles.

Eventually, the exhausted son of Antipater walked to the house of Leonnatus where he was admitted inside. A shadow flickered in Alexander's eyes.

***

64.

Waves rolled in, each higher than the last. A storm was coming. Demosthenes reflected he did not need to practice speaking against Poseidon's noise any longer. Rich and successful, he was one of the greatest figures of the age. Barrister, orator and statesman, there was no one to rival his fame.

Sipping a cup of water, he scratched his beard. A letter, which had taken several days to write, sat on his desk. Outside, lightning crackled in jagged lines across the dark night sky.

A sharp knock at the door brought him out of his reverie. Pulling back the heavy oak, he welcomed a rain-drenched visitor. As the man stepped over his threshold, a roll of thunder juddered the roof tiles above.

"Pixodorus at your service, sir. I've come for the letter."

Demosthenes walked to his cedar desk. He picked up two sealed letters and handed them to his visitor. "Go to Asia. Deliver one to General Attalus. The other is a copy. Guard both with your life."

Pixodorus bowed. "My horse awaits, sir. We will leave immediately."

Demosthenes reached up to a shelf and took down a leather pouch. He dropped it into the man's hand. "To cover your expenses."

***

A solitary oil lamp flickered in the apartments of Olympias. Dismissing her servants, she settled down to wait.

Reading was one of her pleasures. Scanning her library, Olympias' hand hovered over the scrolls of Greek playwrights. Choosing Aeschylus' *Persians*, she sat by the fire.

Flames crackled pleasantly. Occasionally, branches snapped, releasing sparks. Outside, night owl's hooting preceded the soft flutter of wings, as it swooped from the eaves in search of prey.

At the tenth hour of the evening, Olympias' guard announced a visitor.

"I'm glad you could come, Isocrates."

"I am here to do your bidding, my lady."

Olympias ushered her guest out of the cold into her apartment, and made him sit by the fire. Taking a wine jug, which rested on the top of an oak cabinet, she poured the contents into a cup.

Isocrates looked about him. He noticed there were no servants. Shifting on his fleece-covered seat, he brushed aside any disturbing thoughts. It was rumoured the late king's divorced wife was a murderess, but he was too cold to care. Lifting his frozen hands over the flames, the man felt his blood stir in tingling pain. To his relief, he started to warm up.

Handing him the drink, Olympias took a chair opposite her guest. "I'm sending you to Asia."

"What is the task, Your Majesty?"

"To ingratiate yourself with Parmenion."

"Consider it done."

Olympias smoothed the creases of her dress and folded her hands in her lap. "That is not all. The task is one of some delicacy. It requires both tact and action."

"I'm listening."

***

65.

An Asian dawn always felt different to mornings in Greece. Attalus pulled his shawl around his broad shoulders. Out here, on his balcony, he wanted to watch the sun rise, which he never did at home. As the red and orange orb rose over the horizon, he felt a sharp wind whistle past his ears. It was time for breakfast.

A manservant entered the apartment with a Nestor's Cup. Attalus reclined on a dining couch. He was hungry and dug into his breakfast.

"What type of flour did Cookie put in?" he asked the servant.

"Macedonian, sir."

"It tastes of home."

Suddenly, a hooded stranger stood before the general.

"I'm sorry sir," a breathless guard ran in. "But this man did not wait to be announced."

The visitor pulled down the hood of his cloak to reveal his face. "I'm Pixodorus, from Athens, here at the bidding of the great Demosthenes."

"And it seems, too good to speak to an Asian guard."

"I can't converse in his tongue, General."

Attalus motioned to the guard to return to his post. "What is your wish, Pixodorus?"

"My master asked me to give you this letter."

Attalus recognised the seal. He took the package. "It smells of frankincense."

"Demosthenes is the uncrowned king of Athens. He can afford to gift you the expensive incense of kings."

"Your master is indeed a powerful man." Attalus opened the missive. His eyes roved over the contents. When he had finished reading, he fixed the messenger with a stare. "Did he give you two copies?"

The messenger produced the other letter. It was unopened. Satisfied, the general sent him to the guest quarters to rest after his journey.

***

It was the middle of the afternoon at the Asian fort. A cool breeze blew through the open windows of the waiting room. Taking off his broad-brimmed sun hat, Isocrates wiped the sweat from his face with a linen handkerchief.

Presently, he heard the sound of sandals. He straightened his back. Parmenion appeared with his bodyguards.

Recognising his guest, the general embraced him. "My dear Isocrates, what brings you to Asia?"

"Queen Olympias."

"It must be important. I'll call General Attalus."

"There is no need for that."

"What does the gracious lady wish me to do?"

Isocrates glanced at the bodyguards. "It's a state matter."

"Come to my office."

Parmenion led his guest out of the waiting room and down a corridor. Bodyguards accompanied the pair. On entering the office, Isocrates noticed that it overlooked an olive grove. Windows were open to let in the breezes. He took the seat offered to him.

Pouring white wine into two gold cups with his own hands, the general gave one to his guest. Saucers of dates, figs, and olives, sat on a ledge close to a bookshelf. From it, scrolls of battle strategies and maps peeked out.

Next to the spread, was a pile of napkins. The general often worked late, and preferred to have snacks on hand, rather than waiting for his cook to prepare meals. Parmenion drew up a side table and

251

placed the saucers and napkins on it. Isocrates fell to. After a while, he sat back, replete.

"I journeyed all night," he explained.

"Your message must be important."

"It is one of some urgency."

"I am happy to hear Olympias' wishes, but I cannot overrule King Alexander."

"They are of the same mind in this matter."

Wiping his mouth on a napkin, Isocrates delivered his message.

***

Evening glowed over the battlements. Inside his chambers, Attalus paced up and down. He read and re-read the letter. Summoning an attendant, he called for a member of his elite officers' core.

"I need you to take an urgent message to King Alexander."

"Do you have it, sir?"

"It will be ready this evening. Wait in the guards' quarters. You will leave for Macedonia tonight."

Dismissing the officer, he went out to his balcony. He reflected that the letter would be in his sovereign's possession within a few days.

***

It was raining in Pella. Aside from the sentinels on duty, the courtyards were empty. Alexander was in a rage. Surrounded by his generals, he stamped about the audience room in which they were gathered.

"Demosthenes dares ask Attalus to overthrow me!"

Ramrod straight, Hephaestion stood, saying nothing. In a distant corner of the chamber, Cassander shelled dried peas.

He popped several in his mouth. "Say what you like about Demosthenes, he's consistent."

"Hush Cassie," Leonnatus remonstrated. "Can't you see this is serious?"

"I can see Alexander is a serious *me-man*."

"What do you mean?"

"Have you noticed, Leo, it's all *me* and *I*? *My* ideas, *my* destiny, *my* teacher. By Zeus' beard, we all trained under Aristotle!"

"In case you haven't noticed, Alexander is our *king*."

"With no thought for others. Attalus revealed the Athenian conspiracy to our sovereign, hoping to demonstrate his loyalty. It won't do him any good."

Cassander threw a dried pea high into the air and caught it deftly in his mouth. Meanwhile, at the front of the room, Alexander kept up his red rage.

"I won't stand for this! It's bad enough that Attalus' niece Eurydice, replaced my mother. Her son was a threat to my throne before he was born. Now, Demosthenes invites this man to replace me as monarch of my own country?"

"I do wonder about Alexander's intelligence," whispered Cassander loudly to Leonnatus. "If Attalus wanted to replace him, he wouldn't have tipped him off."

"Keep quiet, Cassie."

Seleucus moved a few steps across the room to join them.

"For once I agree with your friend, Leo," he said in a lugubrious tone, his heavy-lidded eyes making him look both sleepy and dangerous.

"Why are you suddenly in my corner?" Cassander asked.

In answer, Seleucus held out his hand. Cassander shelled out dried peas. Craning back his thick neck, Seleucus tipped them into his mouth.

"Because you're right, Cassie. Alexander only thinks about himself."

***

Back in his home, Cassander unloosed his cape and handed it to an attendant. In the living room, he shuffled off his shoes, leaving them to be picked up by a comely maid. She bent down to put them away. With a smirk, he slipped on his embroidered slippers.

Humming to himself, the master of the house went outside to his garden and sat in a wooden seat. A table with wine and almonds was already set out. He drank a cup, laid back in the chair, folded his hands on his stomach and thought of his maid.

Sandals clattered down the marble steps into the garden. "There you are!"

Cassander jolted into wakefulness. "Pull up a chair, Leo. Have some wine."

Strong hands grabbed Cassander's shirt by the neck and pulled him to his feet. "You egoist, you nearly got yourself killed today."

"What are you doing? Guards! Help!"

Two burly men ran down the garden steps. Leonnatus let go.

"Don't touch him," Cassander ordered his men. "Bring a chair, and more wine with an extra cup. I only have enough for one. That's what happens when you're an egoist."

He smiled disarmingly and stood with his guest until everything arrived.

"Who is your housemaid, Cassie?" asked Leonnatus, settling into an ornate armchair.

"Which one?"

"I passed her on the way out here."

"Artemis."

"Slave?"

A wicked grin spliced Cassander's face. "Wouldn't you like to know?"

"Poor thing."

"I pay her well. I've never laid a hand on her. It's the truth. You need to stop judging others."

Cassander sat back and closed his eyes. It was a warm day. He listened to the comforting sound of a bumblebee. It always made its way past the garden in the second hour of the afternoon.

Leonnatus drained a cup of white wine. "King Alexander is our leader, Cassie. His destiny is inextricably tied up with yours and mine. He deserves respect, especially within earshot."

"Good point. More wine?"

"There's a purge going on. People are being killed for their partisanship."

"I didn't know you cared."

"We're the new generation, destined for greatness, which means you can't keep making subversive comments in front of royal henchmen."

The bumblebee drew closer. Cassander opened one eye. Resisting the urge to swot its fat form, he closed his eye again.

"Don't be hysterical, Leo. We won't die. Alex still has use for us. General Attalus, on the other hand, is a dead man."

*****

66.

It was evening in Asia. Cold blue stone battlements soared against a pale lemon sky. Inside his office, with a trusted adjutant, Parmenion discussed his predicament.

"You don't have a choice, sir," the adjutant said.

"But, Attalus is a general, like me. He's my brother-in-arms."

"Olympias is purging the court of anyone who opposes her. Look at what she did to Attalus' niece. It is even rumoured that she killed Philip."

"I serve only the King of Macedonia."

"When it comes to the throne, Alexander and his mother are of one accord. You need to do this, Parmenion, otherwise you could be under suspicion."

"I am the most experienced general in Greece. Alexander needs me for the conquest of Persia."

"Not if you defy his mother."

Parmenion chewed the inside of his nether lip. The setting sun glowed orange on his armour. Eventually, he looked up. His face was stone, his eyes hollows.

"Let Olympias and Alexander know it is done."

***

There was no rap on the door. No guard announced the men. Attalus gasped, as rough hands pulled him out of bed. A buffet across his face, broke his jaw. The general looked around for his sword. There were no weapons anywhere.

"Guards!" he called.

"We are your guards."

A sack went over his head. Twisting, Attalus was unable to get out of the grasp of a burly assailant. He relaxed his arms. So did his captor. With a jerk, the captive broke away. Ripping the sack off his head, he punched the nearest man and knocked him to the floor. Running outside into the passage, he saw twenty men in front of him.

"We're here to take you away," one of them said. "King Alexander has found you guilty of sedition."

***

Olympias hummed to herself. On her balcony, a bumblebee browsed her flowers. It was a warm day. The sun's embrace melted her worries.

Inside, Airlia sat spinning. She had brought with her a special dyed wool from Asia Minor. It would make a magnificent cloak for the cold evenings. The bee buzzed over to the next balcony, its tiny wings working frantically. Olympias re-entered her apartment.

Airlia looked up from her work. "Are you joining me, dear?"

Picking up a spindle, and the Asian wool, Olympias beckoned to an elderly woman. "I'll do mine outside. It's such a lovely day. Join me?"

Gathering up her work, Airlia rose and followed her hostess. The elderly servant hobbled in tow, carrying her mistress' spindle and wool. Outside, a breeze ruffled the women's draperies. On a table sat two cups of honey wine. It was quiet, and aside from the sentries below, there were no men about.

"It's time to celebrate," Airlia said, raising a cup. "To your victory, my dear."

***

Reviewing his correspondence, Alexander focussed intently on every piece set before him. Ensconced in a spacious office, he had plenty of room for his work. The royal secretary, Thersites sat in a corner, awaiting his commands, but the new king was intent on doing everything himself.

Hephaestion arrived with more reports. "Attalus was executed."

"Last week." Alexander riffed through the documents on his desk. "Today, we have trouble in Athens, Thessaly, and Thebes. There are even Thracian tribes to the north threatening war."

"Are you discussing it with the council?"

"I'm expecting everyone here shortly."

The silence was broken only by the rustle of papyri and parchment as Alexander inspected his correspondence.

At the tenth hour of the morning, a silver gong sounded in the outer court of the palace. The new sovereign cleared his desk of confidential reports. Beckoning to his secretary to tidy the rest, he rose and stretched.

Hephaestion opened a side door to the office to admit servants carrying food and drink. Soon, the clatter of footsteps heralded the Macedonian military elite. Talking loudly, they crossed the mosaic floor and filled the room. Servants offered the men stuffed larks, pastries, almonds, and strong wine from Illyria.

Once the council was convened, rumbles from the Macedonian military elite turned into plain talking. An unrolled map lay, pinned at its edges, in the centre of an oak table.

General Antipater analysed the situation.

"Macedonia has problems with its borders," he began.

"That's not surprising," Parmenion remarked.

"What do you mean?"

"Philip's dead. There's a power vacuum."

"That's nonsense, as Alexander is King," Cleitus interrupted.

"And head of the Hellenic League," Hephaestion added.

"He's young and untried." Parmenion faced Alexander. "I mean no offence. We know you are a great warrior. However, that is the view of the Greek states."

"No offence is taken," Alexander reassured him. "I know you to be a true friend."

"You have a point, General Parmenion," Seleucus said. "The Greeks are rebelling."

Alexander's brow furrowed. "They won't be for long."

"We must be careful," Antipater warned. "Macedonia was victorious at Chaeronea, but we are surrounded by enemies."

"You're not wrong General, but where to begin?" Perdiccas asked.

Alexander drew his dagger and stabbed the map. "At the beginning. We head south to our nearest neighbour."

"Then it's settled," Cassander yawned.

He tossed an almond towards the ceiling and caught it in his open mouth.

***

67.

On the morning after the meeting, Alexander donned his armour. Mounting Bucephalus, he joined three thousand Macedonian cavalry, and his Young Companions outside the gates of Pella. At the sound of the horn, they fell out.

Riding bareback on a new stallion, Cassander made quips, while crunching his morning bread and cheese. Leonnatus, who had already partaken of a Nestor's Cup with his officers, was content to listen to his friend while they trotted through the meadows.

Seleucus started out at the back with Ptolemy and the Silver Shields. Alexander had wisely assigned his father's crack unit to his half-brother on a permanent basis. Not only did he resemble the late ruler of Macedonia, but Ptolemy was a decade older than Alexander's generation.

Having an ideal leader, the middle-aged veterans remained loyal. For his part, Ptolemy had the easiest regiment to command. The men's experience, coupled with their fitness and ability, was unmatched by any division in the army.

As Commander of the Cavalry, Cleitus cantered along with Alexander. They chatted to each other, with Hephaestion joining in. Morning sun struck their faces as it rose over the mountains. Leonnatus lowered the broad rim of his felt hat over his eyes. Finishing his snack, Cassander adjusted his buttocks on his horse's back.

"You know Leo," he said, "I think I'm turning into a centaur."

"I'll regret asking this, but why do you think that might be?"

Seleucus ambled up behind them. "I gather he and his horse are one."

At the sound of his deep voice, Cassander jumped. "Stop doing that, Sel. I might mistake you for a Thracian, and then where would you be?"

"Don't worry about injuring me. I'm a good judge of reflexes."

Seleucus continued on his way to chat to other generals.

"Why does that sound like a threat, Leo?" asked Cassander.

"Perhaps, because you threatened him first."

Before Cassander could make a suitable retort, Hephaestion joined them. Sweat ran in rivulets down his face from under his sun-hat. "Cassie, we're looking for the pass."

"Between Ossa and Mount Olympus?"

"Exactly."

"Quarter of a mile away, to our right."

Hephaestion tipped his hat and galloped back to Alexander and Cleitus. Leonnatus was open-mouthed. "You know the route!"

"Even better, I know what Alexander is going to do next. You should have a snack." Cassander held out a piece of dried beef. "Trust me, you'll need your strength."

Leonnatus accepted the stick and started to gnaw its hard exterior. After a while, it softened so that he could chew it. The flavour was very good, and he felt his spirits lift.

***

By mid-afternoon they were in the pass, where hundreds of Thessalian soldiers were stationed. Leonnatus drew back on his stallion's reins.

"There was one thing you left out of your directions, Cassie."

"You're thirsty, after eating dried beef? Don't worry, there is a river to our right."

"Before or after the battle?"

Dusting off his palms, Cassander picked his teeth with a fingernail. He surveyed the bearded troops ranked in front of their army.

"Surely, you're not surprised, Leo. All passes are guarded."

Despite the presence of potential enemies, Alexander continued to ride along the passage between the mountains. A Thessalian captain galloped forward.

"Halt!" he cried.

The Macedonian king motioned his army to stop. Taking Hephaestion and Cleitus, he approached the captain on horseback. "I am King Alexander of Macedonia."

"Your Majesty must wait for permission to pass. Stay here."

Having given his directive, the man rode back to the line of troops.

Hephaestion leaned forward. "Does he jest, cousin?"

"I haven't time for this!"

Alexander swung Bucephalus around. Returning to his lines, he gathered several officers and generals together.

Ptolemy was the first to speak. "Do we attack?"

Alexander shook his head. "For now, start cutting steps into the mountainside."

Cassander tipped his hat back. "Which one?"

"Mount Ossa," replied Alexander. "To your left."

"But to what purpose?"

"To teach the Thessalians a lesson, Lord Cassander. Every division is to use thirty men each, starting with Ptolemy's Silver Shields. They will show the younger men how to work in relays."

***

Hours passed. Men toiled at cutting steps into the mountainside. When they were ready, Alexander's troops scaled the roughly hewn steps up the mountain, and made their way into a forest. Cleitus checked on the cavalry at intervals, ensuring they were all safe.

Cassander found more snacks in his saddlebag, which he passed to Leonnatus. Slashing at ivy and branches, Perdiccas kept his men close to him.

Meanwhile, at the rear, Ptolemy's Silver Shields watched for bandits. The men did not speak. Even Cassander was quiet.

***

It was close to evening at the pass. While his superiors discussed whether to allow the King of Macedonia and Greece through, Jason stirred his pot of lamb broth over a fire. Adding a handful of peas, followed by wheat and barley, he sang softly to himself.

Originally trained as a cook, his soup was the talk of his unit. Now he was in the Thessalian cavalry, not of a high rank, but still in the army and part of a privileged class.

Jason could now afford a home with land which he had bought last summer. He was even blessed with a wife. She was a pretty girl from the village where he had grown up. For a decade he had never made his intentions known, due to his low position in life. Now, Ariadne was his wife and mother to their three sons, and one spoiled, but angelic daughter! The man gave a beatific smile and looked towards the heavens. Life could not be better.

Lowering his eyes he saw, through the aromatic steam from his soup, an entire army.

***

Leonnatus took his sun hat off. A leafy canopy of tree branches arched overhead. Cassander was wearing his bronze helmet. They were still on the edge of the woods on a hilly incline.

Below them, through the nettles and bracken, the main divisions of Alexander's cavalry were lined up behind the Thracian army.

"This had better not take long, Leo. I can smell dinner."

Seleucus waved up to the pair from the forest floor. "Get down here!"

"Our great one has spoken, Leo."

"There's no need for haste. Alexander isn't advancing."

"He's going to negotiate first."

"Let's hope so, Cassie, for the sake of my empty stomach."

Seleucus waved more impatiently to the pair. "Get down here, both of you!"

"Come on, Leo, we should humour him."

"What for? We're the same rank."

"Let's think long term. I wouldn't be surprised if our Sel heads an empire one day."

Whipping away the nettles which stung his legs with his riding crop, Cassander picked his way down the wooded hill on horseback. Reluctantly, Leonnatus followed.

On the flat plain, things felt different. Tension was palpable. Even Cleitus had his hand on his sword. A cook for the Thessalian contingent took his stew off the fire and scuttled away to the safety of his men. Messengers hurried back and forth between the Macedonian army and the guardians of the pass.

Finally, a Thessalian delegation approached Alexander.

"It's the captain," Hephaestion said.

"And about time," Cleitus growled.

"I don't care who it is," said an irritated Alexander, "so long as there is an acknowledgement of my authority."

The man approached at an even pace. Movement rippled through the Macedonian cavalry. Men grasped their weapons more tightly. To their surprise, the Thessalian captain leapt off his horse, and bowed.

"King Alexander, we acknowledge you as our overlord of this pass and these lands."

Alexander's brow smoothed. He dismounted Bucephalus and spoke to the captain.

"Where do you want to set up camp, Cassie?" Leonnatus asked while they waited.

Cassander bit his nails. "Wait to see if we're staying, first." He inspected a piece of fingernail. "Knowing our king, it's a sure bet he'll keep going."

"He'll camp here. I'll wager dinner."

"You're on."

They waited in silence. Eventually, Alexander returned from talks with the Thessalians. He mounted Bucephalus. Motioning with one arm, he headed his army down the narrow pass.

Cassander threw Leonnatus a triumphant look. "You owe me dinner!"

***

68.

Riding in loose formation, the Young Companions were at the end of their journey. Yawning, Perdiccas picked up his waterskin and drank. He pointed. "I can see a town."

"It's Thermopylae," Cassander replied.

Reaching into his saddlebag, he too, took out a waterskin and drank. Then, he handed it to Leonnatus, who was riding next to him.

While he waited for his friend to finish drinking, Cassander watched the sun set. It was his favourite time of day. The sky glowed pink and orange. Birds twittered in the cool air as they searched for their last meal. A page ran up to Cassander. He spoke rapidly, before returning to join his peers.

Leonnatus handed the waterskin back and wiped his mouth. "Where is Alexander?"

"My page says he rode into Thermopylae with Hephaestion an hour ago."

Cassander repacked the waterskin in his saddlebag. He dismounted. Already, his staff were working. Leonnatus noticed his friend's tent was being pitched on high ground.

Pages banged wooden pegs into the earth and set the Argead banner in place. Its gold shield and bright colours resembled the Macedonian monarch's flag. Leonnatus also gave orders for his tent to be pitched.

Up ahead, the cavalrymen rested in groups. While they waited for their tents to be erected, the two young generals joined a group around the camp fire. Wine and food was passed around as weary soldiers relaxed.

Cassander's officers sought him out. He chatted with them, his witty remarks causing hearty laughter. Leonnatus noted the genuine affection the men held for his friend. Even after his tent was ready, Lord Cassander stayed up, talking and sharing his evening with them.

A full moon shone overhead. Those musically inclined, fetched their lyres and flutes. Songs sung in deep voices by the soldiers mingled pleasantly with lilting tenors from the young boys. Night turned into a new day and still they sang.

***

"Get up, Cassie!"

Pushing back his coverlet, the general squinted at the man blocking the morning sun.

"What time is it, Leo?"

"Time you were dressed."

Leonnatus threw him a robe. Cassander threw it back. "I can't wear that." He swung his legs out of bed. Putting his feet on the tent floor, he held his head in his hands.

"Are you hung over, Cassie?"

"No, Leo, I'm tired. We've marched all the way from Pella to Thermopylae for King Alexander."

"And now he orders us to be at the city hall. An assembly of the Amphictyonic League has been called. Get dressed, immediately."

***

Despite the impending assembly of the Amphictyonic League, Ptolemy was surrounded by his Silver Shields. It was pay day. Soldiers were lined up around the tents. Ptolemy personally supervised the process. He always ensured his men were paid on time and in full.

Seleucus waited for his friend. Dressed in ceremonial armour, his horse wore decorative trappings. Perdiccas joined him, also clad in his best armour.

After some time, Cassander emerged from his tent in the full regalia of an Argead lord. His robes were of the finest silk. A gold necklace hung from his neck, and diamond encrusted bracelets were fastened round his wrists. His hair was shoulder length and brushed to perfection.

Leonnatus followed him. By contrast, he was dressed as a soldier. He even wore a leather pectoral.

Seleucus smirked. "Greetings, mighty lords. Are you ready for the meeting?"

"It's whether Alexander is ready," Cassander snapped. "I don't see him."

Leonnatus steered Cassander towards their horses. Decked in bridles of gold and red, with smart blinkers of painted cedar, the handsome steeds awaited their riders.

After his men were paid, Ptolemy joined Seleucus. They brought up the rear, while Cassander, Leonnatus and Perdiccas rode ahead to join their sovereign. At the fringe of the encampment, they reached Alexander, who was waiting with Hephaestion.

Cassander's lips upturned with mischief.

"You know, Leo, I do sometimes wonder if we have two kings."

"Why do you think that?"

"Alexander is always refusing to marry. Maybe he already has an heir in mind."

"Our king has tried to wed. There have been several negotiations over the years. He knows Hephaestion can't inherit the throne."

"You know he can, Leo."

"So can you."

Cassander closed his eyes. "You don't know how long I have waited for you to say that." With a chuckle, he urged his steed ahead.

***

The hall was already full when the Macedonians arrived. Men from the surrounding Greek states were pressed up against each other. Many stood shoulder to shoulder.

Dismounting, Cassander tethered his horse a distance from the other visitors. He waited for Leonnatus. They entered the hall together. A wash of noise overwhelmed them. Almost immediately, Leonnatus was engaged in trying to push aside a large Attic shepherd chieftain who smelled of garlic.

The pair eventually reached the front. Cassander whistled to himself as he viewed the crowd. "Aside from Ptolemy's regiment, I've never seen so many old men gathered in one place."

Ptolemy was behind him with crossed arms. "I heard that."

"Eavesdropping, are we, son of Lagus, or is it Philip? I've just realised why you don't employ spies. Your ears cover large stretches of terrain."

"Have you paid your troops, yet, Lord Cassander?" asked Ptolemy. "Or did you spend the money on your finery?"

"My staff are paid every week."

"We're not talking about your pretty maids."

Alexander's head tilted towards Hephaestion. "Are those wolves already fighting? It's not even noon!"

"Ptolemy paid his troops, cousin."

"I've always liked him."

"It seems Cassander used his wealth on clothes and manicures."

"Ah well, he is due for a punch in the nose."

Meanwhile, Cassander pushed his face up close to Ptolemy. "My troops *and* household staff are paid every ten days. My finery, as you put it, is purchased within a budget. You could do with some grooming, Ptolemy. Your beard needs a trim and your armpits stink."

In a swift movement, Seleucus blocked Cassander. "King Alexander is about to take his seat."

On cue, their leader walked through the mass of tightly packed Greeks. At the front, a body of elders waited. Whispering ran through the hall.

"Is that Alexander?"

"He can't be older than my youngest son."

"Is this the great warrior of whom we're supposed to be afraid?"

"How short he is!"

At the front of the hall, Alexander stopped. He climbed the steps to where the men of the sacred league were seated. There, he addressed them.

"Men of Thermopylae, distinguished guests, and leaders of Greece, I thank you for inviting me to attend this morning's meeting. This league has a sacred commission, birthed from the original twelve tribes of Greece. First, in service of the goddess Demeter, it grew to serve that most noble seat of religion, namely the Temple of Delphi."

Appreciative murmurs ran through the crowd. Encouraged, the young king continued with his speech.

"It is my desire to pay homage to this league, and to follow the wishes of my father, the late King Philip of Macedonia. As you know, he was appointed the military leader of the League of Corinth which vowed to avenge the Persian wrongs done to Greece. I stand before you today as his successor, and the new King of Macedonia. It is my desire to have your fealty."

The room was silent. Distinguished leaders weighed the king's words. Alexander did not move. He waited for them to absorb the full impact of his speech. A few of the Greek elders put their heads together. Whispers gradually increased to low tones.

Finally, a statesman rose. "Your gracious words find favour with us. We salute Your Majesty, King Alexander as hegemon of the Amphictyonic League."

***

69.

During the afternoon, many of the Macedonian generals drifted to a communal tent. There, out of the noonday sun, they talked, played draughts and listened to music.

In a corner, Cassander lay on a couch with his lyre, which he strummed through the long hot hours. Leonnatus and Perdiccas eventually finished a lengthy game of draughts and joined him.

Cassander stopped playing. "Wasn't this morning easy for us?"

"Alexander knew how to handle our Greek friends," Perdiccas replied.

"There is nothing they could do against an army of our size," Leonnatus added.

"Everyone knows the league is a sacred band of old religious greybeards," laughed Cassander. "It's not worth much."

"On the contrary, it wields significant political power," said Leonnatus.

"I agree," said Perdiccas.

"That as it may be," said Cassander packing his lyre in its cover, "but I intend to have a bath and be rubbed down by a delicious girl. Then, I'll have a sumptuous dinner to which you are both invited."

"I could do with a massage," said Leonnatus.

He and Cassander snickered like schoolboys.

"Are you aware we leave for Corinth tonight?" Perdiccas asked.

"Then, I'd better be off for a nap," said Cassander. "You're both welcome to join me for a late supper."

Before Perdiccas had time to answer, Cassander was gone. Leonnatus, who preferred to stay with friends before a long march, remained in the communal tent.

***

Nighttime was cold in Corinth. Cassander had a hot bath, and a massage given to him by an elderly male attendant. Afterwards, he spent the evening chatting to Helen. He found her to be a good listener and felt at ease in her presence.

Eventually, she spoke. "Are you married, my lord?" Cassander baulked. "It's a simple question."

"It's the first time a servant has ever asked me one."

"My apologies. I hope I'm not to be beaten for my insolence."

"I consider you to be a friend."

"You just alluded to me as your servant."

"I don't beat my staff, or friends, except at draughts."

A guard entered the tent. "Perdiccas is here, sire. Shall I say you're sleeping?"

"Excellent idea! The man is a bore. Send him away. Now where were we, my pretty one?"

The tent flap raised. Perdiccas was standing in the entrance. Clad in a red robe, he held an alabaster jar.

"I'm here by your invitation for supper, Cassie. By the way, Athens is suing for peace."

"That's a first. Come in, come in. What took you so long?"

Helen's brows arched.

"That's not all," Perdiccas continued. "Alexander is now hegemon of the League of Corinth."

"It's getting to be a habit with our king. What do you have there, Perdie?"

"Perfumed oil from Egypt."

Perdiccas moved from the entrance into the main living area of the tent. He looked Helen up and down. She was a comely woman, not in the prime of youth, but still able to bear children. Cassander noticed her blush.

"Helen," he said quickly, "do us the honour of telling the wine steward to wait on us."

Bowing, she exited. Perdiccas handed his gift to his host and took a seat. After twisting the top off the unguent jar, Cassander inhaled its contents.

"Do you like it, Cassie?"

"It's worth a paean of praise."

Carefully setting the perfume on a shelf next to him, Cassander picked up his lyre. Running plump fingers across its strings, he began to sing.

Wine arrived, carried by an ancient, white-haired Greek. Perdiccas tasted it and found the vintage to be excellent. He settled back to enjoy the evening.

***

In the king's tent there was no music. Even Hephaestion was quiet. Alexander was reading a clay tablet. He frowned.

"What's the matter, Alex?"

"It's war."

"But the envoy was just here. You pardoned Athens."

"I'm not talking about Athens."

Alexander handed Hephaestion the clay tablet. His cousin handed it back. "I don't read bird signs."

"It's cuneiform."

"The letters look like bird's feet. What does it say?"

"Thrace is in revolt."

"That's not surprising."

"The Illyrians and Triballi, too."

"I recall your father received his leg injury from the Triballi."

"Actually, one of his infantrymen speared him by accident. However, the Triballi did attack and rob him. We need to put them in their place before going to Persia."

Music floated across the wind. Alexander cocked his ear. It was a familiar tune.

"Cassander's singing," Hephaestion explained.

"I remember the tune from Mieza. It's a song about a prince falling in love with his maid. Our friend is an excellent musician."

"You used to play, dear cousin, and much better than him."

"Until Father said it wasn't manly."

"That's because the visiting Greek ambassadors were making fun of you."

"He was jealous of my talent."

"He was trying to protect you, cousin."

"Father stopped me from playing. I was only a boy." Alexander put down the tablet. "The men need to train for mountain warfare. We leave for Thrace in the spring."

He turned on his heel abruptly, and left the tent.

***

70.

In spring the Macedonian troops were ready. Alexander set out north from Amphipolis. Leading eight thousand light infantry, twelve thousand heavy infantry and three thousand cavalry, he headed for Thrace.

Complaining that he had already lost half his body weight, Cassander insisted on snacking while he rode. Leonnatus stayed close, taking advantage of the refreshments. Perdiccas kept company with the king's favourites, while Ptolemy preferred the companionship of his Silver Shields. In the evenings, he and Seleucus dined together.

The march north was long. During the day, the army travelled. At night, the men camped in the woods off the main roads. In the morning, the soldiers were in good spirits. The air was cool and the banter jolly. Towards afternoon, they grew tired and travelled in silence.

On one such afternoon, Cassander was ambling along on his horse. The pace was comfortable, and he dozed.

"Do you know where we are going, Master?"

Cassander opened his eyes and saw no one. Looking down, he caught sight of Polymarchus on a pony. "Thrace. You'll become a man there."

"I don't want to fight, sir."

"You won't." Cassander winked. "But there are girls."

"I don't follow."

Perdiccas rode up. "We're nearly at the Agriani stronghold. King Alexander is stopping at his friend Langarus' home." He looked down at Polymarchus. "Don't worry, my son. There will be feasting, not fighting for a few nights."

***

King Langarus welcomed Alexander and his army. While the two kings spent most of their time together, strolling the vast castle hallways discussing battle strategies, the Macedonians embarked on their rest and recreation.

Leonnatus found a girlfriend and disappeared for a few days. Ptolemy took the opportunity to throw parties every night, which Perdiccas and Seleucus joined.

Relieved to be in civilisation once more, Cassander set up home. In the spacious apartments assigned to him by the gracious host, he read to Polymarchus, while Helen cooked for them.

Hephaestion took a much-needed break as a diplomat, and slept.

***

After a week with King Langarus, the Macedonian army set out for Mount Haemus. One morning, they neared the Shipka Pass. Alexander sent a scouting party ahead. The army continued to march. By the tenth hour of the morning, the enemy was in view.

Hephaestion pulled back on his horse's reins. "I see it."

"Tell the men to halt," ordered Alexander.

Across from the duo, Perdiccas stopped and removed his felt sun hat. Summoning a page, he exchanged it for his helmet.

Further behind, Cassander beckoned two of his squires. "Take my saddlebags to the luggage train."

"Yes sir," they chorused.

"Stay there with the women."

"Pardon me, sir," said one. "Aren't we supposed to fight?"

"Not this battle."

Up ahead, Alexander organised the troops. Archers moved to his right, while hypaspists took the left. The main phalanx of heavy infantry remained in the centre. Watching the proceedings, the generals waited.

Cassander pointed to the slopes ahead. "Leo, I see carts."

Shading his eyes from the sun, Leonnatus scanned the hills in front of them. "They're at the entrance to the pass. Are we dealing with farmers?"

Cassander gave a puff of exasperation. "Don't you see? The Thracians are going to roll them down the mountainside. We're going to be crushed!"

While the generals talked, Alexander gave instructions to the heavy infantry. Unit commanders spent some time getting them to all the men. He then turned his attention to the archers.

Ptolemy rode up to Cassander and Leonnatus.

"What is our king doing?" he asked.

"Organising," said Leonnatus. "He spoke to the infantry and archers. He'll address the hypaspists next, and then us."

"Figuring out how to escape the carts first would be an idea," muttered Cassander.

Pushing back his helmet, Ptolemy viewed the carts for several moments. "I'll inform my men."

Tapping his horse's sides with his heels, he returned to his troops. Alexander's army started to move. Inching forward in silence on the hot day, the men heard the rustling of the grass underfoot. Cicadas chirped. Butterflies winged their way across the scrub and trees which dotted the landscape.

Presently, rumbling filled the air. Horses reared on their hindquarters.

"Get down!" Cassander screamed.

"Stop panicking!" shouted Leonnatus. "Our men have their orders."

"To die? I don't even know why any of us follow this king. He's a madman."

Drowning out the conversation, wheeled carts rolled down the incline. Macedonian archers shifted to the right to avoid them. On the left, hypaspists did the same. Mounted on Bucephalus, Alexander made no move. At the back of the main army, Ptolemy waited.

Dozens of carts thundered down, towards the centre of the phalanx. The infantry moved out of the way to the left and right of the flying waggons. Those unable to avoid the immediate danger, dropped as one and covered themselves with their shields.

Cassander clapped. "Brilliant! Our king is a genius."

"There's one word for you, Cassie," said Leonnatus.

"I'm listening."

"I'll give you a clue. It's *not* loyalty."

The wheeled vehicles of destruction rolled harmlessly down the hillside and careened into the fields below. Macedonian infantry-men rose and dusted off their knees. Archers and hypaspists moved back into formation. Cheering broke out. The army started to advance.

Thracian tribesmen appeared over the mouth of the pass. Alexander's archers moved forward and released volleys of arrows at their front lines. Tribesmen fell by the hundreds.

As their archers neared the enemy, the Macedonians allowed the infantry to move forward with their sarissas. At close range, it was possible to impale men on the fifteen-foot spears with no risk to themselves. Line after line of Thracians were demolished. Finally, what was left of their military units turned and fled.

***

Alexander wrenched off his helmet. Sodden locks hung around his shoulders. He walked swiftly to his tent, all the while asking questions of a senior officer, who accompanied him. "How many are dead?"

"Fifteen hundred, sire."

"Are there any Thracian men alive?"

"There are."

"Round them up, with the women and children, for sale."

Alexander dismissed the officer. Entering his tent, he handed a servant his helmet, and sat down on a canvas-covered oak chair. Two attendants approached him. One set a gold foot bath at his feet, while the other lifted off the warrior's corselet and wiped him down. When the royal feet were clean and dried, the bowl with dirty water was taken away.

A new one was placed in front of Alexander, and the attendants poured water over his hair. Releasing it of blood and grime, the filthy water splashed into the new bowl. Lathering his thick locks with herbal soap, the men rinsed it again, dried their master's head with a towel, combed the unruly hair and tied it back. All, in a few moments.

Finally, the servants slipped a red robe over Alexander's head. Taking a cup of pomegranate wine, he rose and went to his desk where a map was spread across the dark oak.

Hephaestion entered the tent. "Are you going to sell the prisoners, cousin?"

"We need funds."

"And you need to eat." Hephaestion nodded towards the royal butler, who rose from his post and went to the army kitchen.

"I hope he knows what's on the menu."

"You eat lamb after fighting."

The king grunted as he quaffed his wine. His head was starting to thud. Being taken by surprise on the field of battle had sapped his strength.

"We must find King Syrmus of the Triballians," he said, rubbing his forehead.

***

71.

The Macedonian army caroused into the late hours of the evening. With Polymarchus tucked up in bed, and Helen engaged in her embroidery, Cassander appointed extra security over them, before departing his tent.

Once outside, wrapped in a fleece, he sat with his officers, drinking the uncut wine of Thrace.

"That's one lot of enemies out of the way, men!" he roared cheerfully.

"Unfortunately, not all of them, Cassie," said Perdiccas.

Nursing a cup of wine, the latter was seated on an oak log. Ptolemy joined him. Waited on by one of Cassander's girls, Leonnatus spent the evening, talking with her. Eventually, he convinced the lass to sit next to him, while his friend made his usual controversial remarks about King and country. Seleucus sat quietly by, taking in the revelry.

In the small hours of the morning, the fire died down. Ptolemy and Seleucus retired. Perdiccas stood and stretched his long limbs. Leaning forward, Cassander stoked the embers. Afterwards, he sat back and pulled his fleece tightly around his shoulders.

"Where to next, I wonder?" he ruminated.

"Danube," said Perdiccas.

Cassander lifted his wine cup and downed it. "I'm ready."

A short distance away, Leonnatus put his arm around the serving girl. Together, they walked to his tent. Cassander lay back on his elbows. Looking up at the stars, which hung like silver apples in the sky, he began to sing.

***

Alexander did not join his men that evening. Instead, he met with his scouts. Their leader relayed information about the surrounding territory which they had garnered over the afternoon.

"King Syrmus of the Triballians is in the River Lyginus," one of them said.

"*In* the river?" asked Alexander. "Are you sure?"

"He's o-on l-land, s-sire."

"Which is it? Is he in the river or on land?"

"Take your time and think," Hephaestion added coldly.

Several of the younger scouts shivered. Their leader spoke up. "Both, sire."

"You are contradicting yourself," said Alexander. "Speak up, and be clear."

"He's on an island of Peuke."

Hephaestion faced Alexander. "That's in the middle of the Danube."

"Then, we shall go there."

"It's an impregnable fortress, and the river is fast-flowing."

"Are you afraid?"

Hephaestion heaved a breath. "You need *ships*, cousin."

"I'll order them from Byzantium."

***

It was a hot spring day as Alexander's men trekked to the Danube. Leonnatus spent the morning riding alongside Perdiccas. In the afternoon, he joined Cassander, who was with Polymarchus, pouring water from a goatskin over his head and shoulders.

"How are you faring, Cassie?" he asked.

"Boiling."

Cassander handed the goatskin to Polymarchus. The boy drank and then poured the remainder over his head.

"Alexander thinks the Triballian monarch is hiding on Peuke," Leonnatus said.

"How are we going to get there? None of us swim."

"Ships are coming. Got any snacks, Cassie?"

Rummaging in his saddlebags, Cassander pulled out a bag of almonds. "Leo, is it my company you crave, or do you simply have a case of cupboard love?"

"Both." Leonnatus scoffed a handful of nuts.

Cassander offered him a goatskin of water. The latter gulped it down. "By the way, my hungry friend, what does Perdie say about our king's strategy?"

"Alexander has a plan to cross the river. I'll let you know the details when I find out."

Having finished refreshing himself, Leonnatus tipped his hat and rode down to Ptolemy.

Cassander turned to Polymarchus. "When you grow up, make sure your friends don't use you."

***

Leonnatus noticed the slow pace of the veterans as he neared the Silver Shields. Saluting Ptolemy, he fell in step with his horse's ambling gait. The general's demeanour was sombre.

"Anything the matter?"

"We can hear something, Leo."

"I don't see anything."

"Neither do we. I've halted the unit several times, but the sounds stop the moment we do."

"I'll drop to the back and check the land for you."

"There's no point. The only thing for it, is to move slowly and quietly. It will give us an opportunity to distinguish the sounds."

"And I thought your unit's pace was due to old age!" Leonnatus laughed. "Allow me to do you a favour, General. I'll drop back with a couple of men and scout the woods."

Several of the officers glared at Leonnatus.

"I'll accompany the whippersnapper," one of them offered.

"Me too," a grizzled, one-eyed veteran said.

"You have your men, Leo," said Ptolemy with a chuckle. "Go, but don't be long. Make sure my cavalry, closest to the woods, watch over you."

***

It was midday. The heat was soporific. Men nodded off as they rode. Cassander finished his goat waterskin and called for another. Ptolemy's troops strung out as they checked the rear. Suddenly, there was a clanking noise.

"Thracians!" Leonnatus roared.

Pandemonium broke out. The Silver Shields immediately wheeled their horses round to face the enemy. Perdiccas' troops were the first to join them.

At the front, Alexander was issuing orders. Hephaestion took over several cavalry units and galloped to the aid of Ptolemy.

Cassander, who was complaining of sunburn to Polymarchus, spotted Alexander's messengers heading towards him. After hearing their message, he started deploying his troops. All around, men yelled and brandished their swords.

"Time to ride with the baggage train, little one," said Cassander to Polymarchus.

"It's being attacked."

"In that case, fall back behind me, quickly."

"My mother is with the train, sir."

"Listen, Polymarchus, there's a group of acacia trees a mile away. Stay there until the battle ends. Don't worry about your mother. We'll protect her. Now, go!"

Whimpering, the boy did as he was told. Cassander adjusted his helmet, and tried to focus on the mayhem in front of him. Through the dust, he could see Triballi tribesmen battling the Silver Shields.

"Advance!" roared Ptolemy.

His soldiers had already pushed back several units. Perdiccas assisted in the protection of the baggage train. Filled with civilians, including women, children, engineers and household staff, many were screaming in fear.

Hordes of men with axes and pikes charged Alexander. Cassander's cavalry, which had already encircled the king, savagely repelled them. Leonnatus, whose men were now fighting in hand-to-hand combat, joined his friend's forces.

Cassander looked about. "Where, in Zeus' name, is the heavy infantry, Leo?"

"Behind us."

"They're supposed to be in front."

"They were, but we turned around. It's going to take time for them to get down here with their sarissas."

"Meantime, our men are about to be skewered for tonight's Thracian victory celebration. Look at those enemy pikes!"

To their surprise, the Macedonian infantry caught up, and started passing them. With Hephaestion, Alexander consolidated his position at the front line where he led his attack.

Leonnatus was ecstatic. "The enemy is retreating, because of Alexander!"

"They're retreating to the safety of a gorge," Cassander pointed out. "We won't be able to follow."

As the words left his mouth, the gorge swallowed the fleeing enemy. Alexander stopped. He wiped his brow and tilted his helmet up to see better.

"We can't beat these men," he said to Hephaestion.

"If we don't, they will be at our heels, cousin. The moment we turn round, they will attack us."

"I'm aware of that. We need a strategy."

Many of the generals were near their king.

"We could leave some units behind," Leonnatus suggested.

Alexander gave him a withering look.

"Or not," said Cassander under his breath.

Annoyed at their lack of imagination, Alexander rode Bucephalus away from his generals towards the light infantry.

Cassander leaned over his horse. "It was a good suggestion, Leo."

"Tell that to Alexander."

Seleucus came up to the pair. "Our sovereign always pursues the enemy, but you're both right. Leaving units here was a good suggestion."

Cassander grimaced. "I'm so glad you agree."

"Do you have a problem with me, Lord Cassander?"

"Not at all, *General* Seleucus."

With his nose in the air, Cassander trotted away. Scowling, Seleucus returned to his troops. Leonnatus ordered his own to wait, while Ptolemy pulled his Silver Shields back. Perdiccas kept several units around the baggage train. Meanwhile, Alexander spoke to the light infantry commanders.

Joining Polymarchus under an acacia tree, on the outskirts of the main army, Cassander provided lunch from a saddlebag. Sharing bread and cheese with the boy, he reflected that staying out of the afternoon heat was always a wise choice.

***

In charge of the main phalanx, Alexander waited behind the front line of unprotected archers and rock slingers. Hephaestion dug his heels into the sides of his horse and went up to him.

"Do you need anything, cousin?" he asked.

"Where is Philotas?"

"With his father, Parmenion."

"I want him on my left, with the generals Heraclites and Sopolis on the right."

"Consider it done."

Hephaestion wheeled his steed round and galloped away.

***

Stones fell into the gorge. Thracian pikes flew out. Signalling to the main unit to move in the direction of the attack, a group of sixty Macedonians clambered down the rocky sides of the abyss. There, they hid behind scrub and trees.

Scouts noted the narrow passes at the ends of the gorge. They reported their discovery to the commanders, who conferred with each other briefly. Next, several units split into groups and approached the chasm from different sides.

Alexander waited as the archers worked with rock slingers to fire a barrage of missiles at the enemy. Infuriated, the Thracians picked up the rocks thrown at them, and hurled them back. This went on for some time.

Afternoon sun blazed down on the Macedonian troops. Replete after his meal, Cassander dozed under the acacia tree. With nothing else to do, Polymarchus followed his example.

***

Noise in the gorge was building. Inside the rocky clefts, men engaged each other in hand-to-hand combat. On the plain, Macedonian soldiers controlled themselves, even as they itched to join their comrades. No one spoke.

Suddenly, Alexander's skirmishers ran down the inner sides of the deep ravine. Engaging briefly with the enemy, the attackers ran nimbly back up the rocks, and out into the open.

Shaking his master awake, Cassander's squire gave him his bronze helmet. The latter turned it around in his hands. "It has a fresh coat of polish."

"Are you pleased?"

"Now, not only my troops will see me, but the enemy as well."

"Have I done something wrong, sire?"

"Not at all. I like a good fight."

With a chuckle, Cassander crammed the helmet over his head. Mounting his horse, he rode out onto the plain.

A group of generals were watching the troops. Leonnatus beckoned Cassander to join them. The latter made his way over on horseback. He noticed that many were wearing their best armour.

"What are we doing, standing about in our finery?" he asked.

"Waiting," said Seleucus in a lugubrious tone.

"Alexander has to draw the enemy out first," said Leonnatus. He shaded his eyes with one hand. "By Ares, Cassie, your helmet shines like a beacon in the midday sun!"

"The work of an over-zealous squire. I pay my staff too well. On the bright side, my men will know where I am without me having to shout."

"They'll be shouting when you're dead from a Thracian axe throw." Leonnatus pulled a muddy cloth out of his saddlebag. "Here, tarnish it a bit."

Accepting the cloth, Cassander took off his helmet and rubbed it down. Meanwhile, assuming the entire Macedonian army was in flight, the Triballi followed the skirmishers out of the ravine.

Facing them, was a line of unarmoured archers. Delighted at the easy prey, wild tribesmen poured out of hiding and ran across the plain. Yelling as they ran, weapons raised, they made a deafening noise.

"Parmenion has joined our sovereign," noted Cassander, putting his helmet on. "Where's Philotas?"

"On Alexander's left," Leonnatus replied.

"Which means he's going to punch the Thracian right flank?"

"That's the idea."

Cassander whistled. "And I thought he was joined at his father's hip!"

"Heraclites and Sopolis are on our right."

"Posh sods, the pair of them."

"Sopolis is an aristocrat with his own cavalry units."

"I've heard of them both, but they weren't at Mieza. What's the use of bothering about nobodies?"

"It's important to know our army, Cassie."

"I've always concentrated on those most likely to assassinate me."

Apart from the skirmishers, Alexander's army continued to do nothing. Seleucus and Perdiccas took the opportunity to share lunch on horseback. Eating a loaf stuffed with cheese and coriander, Seleucus' thick brows hooded over his eyes.

"They're not in formation," he observed.

Perdiccas pulled his bread apart to get to the cheese. "And their front runners are on the left."

Now, the Thracians were nearing Philotas. Without hesitation, the young general charged their right flank. A corresponding attack by Heraclites and Sopolis into the Thracian left, crushed the advance, allowing the unarmoured archers to fall back.

Cassander lifted his right arm, signalling his troops to follow Alexander.

"Our turn!" he roared.

His men galvanised into action and moved forward. Suddenly, the momentum changed. With lightning speed, Alexander's central phalanx hit the Thracian centre. Lowering their sarissas, the Macedonian heavy infantry closed in. Cavalrymen maintained their positions, fighting off stray Thracians.

After a while, Cassander halted under a tree. Reaching into his saddlebag, he pulled out a container of figs. It was early afternoon, and he needed a snack. As usual, Alexander was in the thick of battle. However, the heavy infantry did the main work of defeating the foe. Impaling fierce tribesmen on their spears was effortless. At sunset, thousands of Triballi lay dead.

***

72.

It was late afternoon. The Macedonian army was resting while their dead burned on pyres. Most of the injured had their wounds dressed. Others were drinking while they waited for the victory dinner.

Hands clasped behind his back, Cassander walked along the stretch of his encampment, close to the river. Neither injured, nor wishing for anyone's company, he sought solitude.

Sitting on the banks of the fast-flowing river, he pushed his hair out of his eyes. It blew back in the cold wind. He tucked stray locks behind his ears and kicked out his short legs. It felt good to be by the water. He thought of Macedonia, with its rivers, and rustling thickets full of game.

"We need the mother of strategies to attack that island."

Cassander spun around to see Leonnatus looming above him. "I didn't hear you."

"It's the wind, Cassie."

"Join me. No talking. I'm thinking."

Leonnatus sat on the grass and dangled his legs over the bank. Neither man spoke. A few hundred yards away, Ptolemy emerged from his tent with Seleucus. He shaded his eyes.

"What are those two doing by the riverbank, Sel?"

"As it's Leo and Cassie, probably fishing."

"I need dinner. Let's pay them a visit."

"I'm with you."

Ptolemy strode over, trailing Seleucus behind him. When he reached the pair, he noticed they were merely sitting by the bank.

"You're not fishing," he said, surprised.

Leonnatus and Cassander looked up at the burly general.

"Join us," Leonnatus invited.

"Including Sel," added Cassander with a smirk.

Pursing his lips, Seleucus sat next to Leonnatus.

"We killed over three thousand today," said Ptolemy, positioning himself in the grass on the other side of Seleucus.

Cassander shuddered. Leonnatus placed a comforting hand on his friend's shoulder. "We're not speaking of war," he explained to the others. "Cassie's cleansing his soul."

"Fair enough," Ptolemy rejoined. "There has been enough killing for one day."

The men sat in silence until the first stars appeared in the heavens. Leonnatus closed his eyes and felt the wind on his face. Occasionally, Cassander heaved a great sigh.

At last, the day's battle receded from their thoughts. Seleucus' mind wandered to a girl he had recently captured. Daughter of a Celtic chieftain, he had been careful to treat her with respect. It occurred to him, as he watched the sun sink over the horizon, that she had been observing his physique during his morning exercises.

Cassander started to feel his old self emerging from the death and destruction of the day's fighting. A joke played on his mind. His lips curved as he ran through it silently. It would do for a banquet.

Picking his teeth with a grass stalk, Ptolemy suddenly thought of Thais. Of all the women he knew, his heart always returned to her. After this battle, there was a chance she would join the campaign from Macedonia with several of her companions. His heart leapt at the thought.

"Alexander is bringing ships from Byzantium," said a new voice.

Their reverie broken, the men lifted their eyes from gazing at the river to see Perdiccas looming above them. Without waiting to be invited, the newcomer took his place next to Cassander. His long legs reached the water, which glowed orange in the last rays of the dying sun.

"A good idea," said Leonnatus.

"It means we'll be waiting for a while," Seleucus rumbled.

"Our troops need rest," said Ptolemy. "We should have a party. The men need to take their minds off bloodshed."

"He's going to have difficulty," said Cassander, who was deep in thought.

Perdiccas turned sideways. "Alexander?"

"This current is so dangerous it could take out an entire navy."

The men looked down at the rapidly flowing water beneath their feet. One by one they vacated their seats on the bank.

"We could continue our evening at my tent," Ptolemy offered.

"I'm turning in early," said Seleucus.

Cassander brushed damp earth off his hands. "Lead the way, General. Come Leo, let's drink and forget."

***

King Alexander's tent encompassed an acre of ground. Men worked round the clock, hammering stakes into the sedge and furnishing his residence with tapestries and vessels of gold.

Hundreds of pigs and sheep were rounded up from neighbouring villages and slaughtered. A selection of the best wines from Greece were stacked on oak tables.

After several days, the army gathered on the banks of the Danube to watch ships sail into their camp from Byzantium. The vessels docked, and their crews feasted in the royal tent with Alexander's generals. Outside, Macedonian soldiers also celebrated the arrival of their makeshift navy.

In a week, dawn broke over the day of Alexander's battle at Peuke.

***

Ships were loaded with weapons and horses. Alexander supervised the proceedings. They waited until midnight before weighing anchor. Eventually, he climbed aboard his flagship with the Young Companions.

While the crew took their rowing positions, many high-ranking officers went below deck for supper before the battle ahead. In the meantime, many of the infantry used rafts to cross the river.

It was a warm night. Inside the hold of Alexander's flagship, Cassander fanned himself with his handkerchief. "It's hot in here."

"Be grateful we're not on those rafts," said Leonnatus.

"I'd be grateful for air."

"How about a walk on deck?"

"A brilliant suggestion, Leo! There is a reason we're friends."

Outside, the breeze refreshed Cassander. A steward brought pomegranate juice. He drank two cups. Resting plump arms on the polished cedar rails which surrounded the deck, the young Macedonian gazed at the river. A silver moon hung in the sky.

As their rowers pulled away from the shore, a white wake stretched behind them. Leonnatus strolled the wooden deck. He noticed Alexander standing on the prow with Hephaestion and two bodyguards. Next to the flagship were several others. Slicing through the water silently, they headed to the opposite shore.

Leonnatus joined his friend.

"The ships whisper through the river," Cassander said dreamily.

"Feeling poetic are you, Cassie? Who is she?"

Cassander's teeth flashed in the dark as he grinned. "Home."

"Home can be poetic."

The two stood together in silence. Stars filled the black night sky.

"This is what I want to do when I'm old, Leo. Gaze at the stars on a river in Macedonia."

"It's hard to imagine these boats are bound for battle."

"Trust you to spoil the evening."

"On the contrary, I hope you get your wish, Cassie."

Holding the rail against which they were propped, Leonnatus stretched back and crouched to release his hamstrings and lower back. Limbered up, he clattered down the stairs which led below deck.

Cassander continued to stare at the beauty of the night on the river. Eventually, silhouetted houses and the walls of a fortification swung into view.

***

Gasping in the shallows, foot soldiers disembarked from their rafts and tried to stand. Leather sandals squelched through the reeds as they waded to shore in the darkness.

While Alexander established battle positions with his generals, scouts reconnoitred the city, in search of weak points in its fortifications. The bulk of Cassander's troops disembarked close to the flagship. Ptolemy landed further down the river. Seleucus, Perdiccas and other generals all landed upriver, where the current was at its swiftest.

Leonnatus donned light armour while two of his officers gave him the latest campaign news. Already there were casualties in the tumultuous current upstream. He girded one side of his hips with a sword, and the other a dagger. Finally, he threw a blue woollen cape over the ensemble to hide any metallic shine.

Climbing upstairs to the deck, he spotted Cassander who was still there. The latter was now humming a soulful tune.

"Aren't you getting ready to disembark, Cassie?"

"My men draw strength from seeing me up here."

"You do realise the poetry is over? Put some armour on. You don't want a dressing down from our sovereign."

"Pshaw! Alexander's too busy with Parmenion to notice me. You should be worried about those idiots upstream – they're going to lose men before we even start."

"They have. My officers just told me."

"See?"

"We need to join King Alexander."

Pulling a face in the dark, Cassander followed his friend into the hold of the flagship. Over twenty senior officers and generals were grouped around a table. The atmosphere was stifling.

On catching sight of the pair, Parmenion's beard twitched. "It's good of you to join us."

Cassander bobbed his head. "For your wise words, General Parmenion," he replied politely, taking a seat at the back.

Lamplight flared over the wooden panels. Leonnatus was at the front, close to Alexander. The king was chewing his nether lip while he talked. "The scouts can't find any weak points in the city walls."

"That should tell you something," muttered Cassander.

"Give them time," Parmenion advised.

Cleitus nodded. "Agreed. There's bound to be a weak point."

"I say we attack at dawn," Alexander declared.

"Not in broad daylight, sire?" asked Philotas.

"We all saw your mighty exploits in the clear light of day against the Triballi," Alexander said, "but, I want to strike as the sun rises."

"If you mean to blind the enemy with the sun, we need to march around," said Parmenion.

"Seleucus and Perdiccas are landing upstream at the moment," Leonnatus pointed out.

"Precisely," Alexander agreed.

"A stupid decision," Cassander smirked.

"Do you want to share your comment with us?" asked Alexander.

To everyone's surprise, Cassander rose. He stood with his feet apart and clasped his belt. His confident stance compensated for his short stature.

"I saw our brave men battling the current upstream in their effort to civilise this region," he said.

Murmurs of approval rippled through the room. Alexander was impressed. "They are forming battle positions as we speak. We need to join them. All except Ptolemy. I want him to stay here with Philotas and note what happens on this side of the city wall."

Parmenion put a hand on his son's shoulder. "It's for the best."

"Leonnatus will come with me," said Alexander. "Now, let's all get some air."

***

73.

Dawn rose over the fortified citadel. As pink and orange picked out the battlements, Alexander moved forward on Bucephalus. The warhorse was well rested, and his muscles moved in sinewy undulations under his master.

"He's in prime condition, cousin," Hephaestion observed.

Alexander patted the strong neck, covered in a black curly mane. "My best friend is ready to fight with me."

"So am I."

"You and I are the same person, Hephaestion. There's no need to be jealous."

They continued to advance. Icy winds blew across the dew-laden grass. Leonnatus' cavalry regiments were part of Alexander's vanguard. Cassander absent-mindedly picked his nose. Seleucus and Perdiccas were in place by the walls with their men.

Peuke was on alert. Guards at the walls notified the city elders. In the castle's main conference hall, King Syrmus was already awake and consulting with his senior staff.

"The late King Philip's army is encamped at the foot of these walls," an adviser said.

"Macedonia is no longer ruled by Philip," Syrmus snapped.

"It is now led by his son," the adviser continued, "which means we have to review the enemy's potential battle strategy."

"Who is Alexander?" a general asked. "He has no war record. He isn't his father. How can we understand his potential strategy if we don't know him?"

Several generals murmured in agreement. King Syrmus raked his beard with stubby fingers. "I fled to Peuke, didn't I?"

"He caused havoc at the Battle of the Gorge," the adviser pointed out.

"Which means Alexander's a better fighter than his father," said Syrmus. "I once stole Philip's loot and injured him in the process."

"I thought the famous spear wound was caused by his own men."

"If that had been the case, Philip would have executed the man. No such thing happened."

One of the senior generals rose. "Macedonians and Greeks are outside these walls. But they are well built, and we are armed."

"I want to ensure Alexander does not breach them," said King Syrmus.

The adviser cleared his throat. His eyes shifted. "We are armed, it is true. The walls are strong, but I think our greatest strength is that Alexander does not wish to be here. It's a waste of his time."

King Syrmus threw up his arms. "What on earth are you talking about?"

"Alexander wants to conquer Persia, not the Danube. Let us remind him of that."

***

It was the tenth day. Macedonians scrambled up and down the battlements to no avail. Archers picked them off with ease. Those who were not despatched with arrows were killed with axes, thrown with pinpoint accuracy.

Others on the ramparts, poured cauldrons of boiling gravel onto Alexander's army. Heated stones trickled down the men's necks into their armour, scalding their backs. Screaming soldiers ran to the river to throw themselves in. As Macedonians did not swim, many were drowned in the swift current.

For his part, Philotas' arms were scratched from rose briars which curled up tall turrets. Try as he might, he could not gain the glory he had won at the Battle of the Gorge. Many of the soldiers had their wounds dressed in one of several army medical tents which were concealed in the nearby woods. Eventually, Philotas gave up and joined his comrades to have his wounds patched up by the army doctors.

Meanwhile, his father Parmenion, doggedly attacked the walls trying to breach a weak point. Perdiccas and Seleucus concentrated on the western tower for several hours, in their attempt to destroy the masonry. Ptolemy's troops stayed on the southern wall, close to the wood which protected the Macedonian medical tents.

Frustrated, Alexander threw his central phalanx repeatedly at the main gates. However, the Thracian resistance continued unabated.

Towards the middle of the day, Seleucus galloped over to Leonnatus. He pushed his helmet back. "Why are we unable to advance? We have thousands of heavy infantry."

"Peuke is replacing its men on those battlements every hour," said Leonnatus.

"Let me guess – axe hurlers, and sadists with cauldrons. For Zeus' sakes, they're pouring hot gravel down our backs!"

"There's an additional problem."

"The city gates?"

"They are protected with two sets of troops. King Alexander can't get inside."

"Let's hope we're alive at nightfall."

Seleucus pushed his helmet back into place and returned to his men. Battering the western tower was useless, but it was all his regiment could do.

***

Towards late afternoon, Alexander lifted off his helmet. Sweat was running down his head and face.

"We need siege machines, Hephaestion."

"You're right. We should have brought them with us."

"I won't make that mistake in Asia." Alexander gazed up at the battlements. "Our main problem isn't that we don't have them. Even if we wait, I can't see us taking these walls for several months."

"What do you suggest?"

"Conquering the Getae," said Alexander, nodding towards his heralds. "After all, our goal is Persia."

"But what about these people, cousin?"

"They're holed up like rats. It's unlikely they will want to bother Macedonia, while I'm campaigning in Asia. Especially, if I destroy the Getae."

***

Cassander wiped his forehead with a sodden handkerchief. Leonnatus galloped up to him.

"How are you feeling, Cassie?"

"Exhausted. I'm sure the heralds are dead. They should have called us in two hours ago."

"Alexander's angry at the lack of progress."

"He's always angry when he doesn't get his way. The fact is, we don't have siege engines."

"There's talk of using Ptolemy's Silver Shields. They usually turn the tide of battle."

"We need to stop. My men can't fight any longer. I want to bathe and play my lyre, in that order."

A red sun smacked into their eyes. Slowly and spectacularly, the fiery ball sank behind the city walls. Macedonian trumpet blasts rang out to signal the end of the day's fighting.

"You have your wish, Cassie. Alexander has notified his heralds. String your lyre. I'll be over for supper."

***

74.

Inside his tent, Seleucus slumped into a chair. His collarbone hurt. His muscles were fatigued and his skin was stiff with dried blood.

Several servants ministered to him. One brought a bowl filled with warm water and healing herbs. Another wiped him down, while a third stitched his most severe wounds with a fishbone needle and silk thread.

A wine steward poured uncut red wine from Macedonia into a cup, mixed in a white powder, and gave it to his master.

"Taste it first," Seleucus growled.

The man obeyed. While they waited, the final stitch was completed, and the thread cut and tied. The medic then attended to his patient's back. Bloodied pocks from heated gravel, dotted the general's neck and shoulders.

Eyeing his steward, who seemed to be suffering no ill effects from the wine, Seleucus stretched out one muscled arm and took the cup. The first sip was home. He relaxed. "I'd forgotten how good Macedonian wines were."

A guard opened the tent to admit Perdiccas. Dressed in ceremonial armour, the visitor had bathed, and aside from a scratch above his left eye, was unscathed.

"My apologies, Sel. I thought you were ready to receive visitors."

"Your medics are faster than mine, Perdie."

"I did not fight as valiantly as you today."

"Join me for a drink?"

"Maybe later. I'm doing the rounds. I'm here to let you know that Alexander is planning to fight the Getae."

Seleucus stirred. "But, Peuke hasn't fallen, yet."

"We march tomorrow."

With his parting words, Perdiccas left the tent.

***

Sipping his water, Cassander waited patiently for his pages to patch up his wounds. The tent flap opened. Leonnatus entered with a gold pitcher of Cretan wine.

"Are you badly hurt, Cassie? I have a great vintage, here."

"Only a few scratches. I'll drink after my lads finish stitching me up. You go ahead."

Sitting down, Leonnatus handed his jar to a servant, who poured the red wine into a gold cup and handed it to him.

"Alexander's leaving Peuke, Cassie."

"For where?"

"Land of the Getae."

"This *is* good news. We can't win here, you know."

"Peuke will take months, even with siege engines."

"And the ships are costing a fortune."

"They are sailing back to Byzantium, after the Getae campaign."

Cassander's pages finished the last stitch. His steward poured a cup of wine. Another servant brought a lyre, which he set next to his master's elbow. Dispensing with the need for a taster, Cassander took a sip. "Smashing vintage, Leo!"

Picking up his lyre, he began the evening's playing with enthusiasm.

***

The atmosphere in the royal tent was deadly. Hephaestion did not speak. Instead, he ate supper in silence. When he had finished, he selected a scroll of Homer's *Odyssey* and retired to a couch to read. After about an hour, he went to bed, and blew out the lamp.

302

For his part, Alexander's only words were directed to his staff. He sat at his desk and studied. No one visited him that night.

***

After they had sailed across the Danube, the Macedonians bade farewell to their ships. Without bothering to pitch camp, Alexander marched his army out towards the region where the Getae lived.

In the early hours of the morning, they reached a stream close to a hilly terrain. Several hundred yards away were trees. Halting his troops, Alexander sent scouts into the wooded area. After a short time they returned with reports that, while there was a village nearby, no one was patrolling the region.

Orders were given to pitch camp. Weary men fed their animals, and ate. By the fourth hour of the morning, most were in bed.

The sun was high in the sky when the majority of troops awoke. Guards, who had been posted around the camp, retired. Meanwhile, Alexander decided to rest the army for a day.

Most of the generals and senior staff ate breakfast together. Parmenion sat with his sons, Nicanor and Philotas. Cleitus gulped his milk and bread down, keen to return to his Greek woman from the night before.

"Do you think a rest day is wise?" Parmenion asked.

"The Getae tribesmen are two days' march away," said Alexander. "The farmers in the outlying villages don't know we're here."

"How can you be so sure?"

"I can't!" Alexander snapped. "But the scouts are sending reports."

"You have to take some things on faith," Philotas interjected.

"Correct," Alexander replied, glaring at his father.

***

75.

Next morning, whistling a merry tune, Cassander waited for the army to fall out. Following the Danube, they made their way to the tribe of the Getae. Green banks were dotted with leafy trees. Cicadas called out to one another, filling the men's ears with their song.

Dipping into his saddlebag Cassander drew out his lyre, which he strummed on horseback. Polymarchus rode with him, and together they sang throughout the spring day.

At sunset, Perdiccas was the first to notice an obstacle. "Our ships aren't going to get through here," he announced. "That means we can't sail to the Getae fort from the river."

"Our sovereign will be angry," said Seleucus.

"We'll get Hephaestion to tell him."

When he considered the time was right, Alexander halted the entire army. After his tent was pitched, he called a meeting of his generals, and they debated the problem of attacking the Getae. During the second hour of the next morning, they were still talking.

As usual, Parmenion was the first to offer a suggestion. "We need to get the ships up here in order to cross this treacherous river to fight the Getae."

Alexander shook his head. "The ships are of no use. They must be sent back to Byzantium."

"But how are we going to cross the river?" asked Parmenion.

"Bags," Alexander replied.

The tent was silent. Servants brought in refreshments.

"That's a good idea," said Cassander, accepting a toasted piece of sesame seed bread, smeared with sardines and garlic.

"I'm glad someone agrees," said Alexander. "Do you wish to explain?"

Cassander swallowed quickly. "Stuff animal hides with hay. Attach soldiers and float them across the water. Preferably at night, if you want to be unseen." He accepted another snack from a serving girl.

"Correct," said Alexander. "There's no need for further questions."

***

It was a moonless night. The banks of the river were filled with Macedonians, stuffing hay into animal hides. In some cases, several were tied to poles to allow more than one man to ride across the river. Others were made by individual foot soldiers for personal use. Rafts of logs were made for horses. Stuffed animal hides were attached to the sides as flotation devices, so they could cross quickly.

Leonnatus and Cassander decided to take a large raft together. Both wore knapsacks which carried their weapons and light armour.

"Hear the roar of that water, Leo!" Cassander exclaimed.

"Get on."

Once aboard, Cassander pulled out his lyre from his knapsack. "I wrote a tune this afternoon."

"I wouldn't play if I were you. What if the Getae hear?"

"The water will drown out any sound. Besides, I need to calm my nerves."

***

Once ashore, Alexander's soldiers dried off as best they could and waited for dawn. Cassander and Leonnatus hunkered down under a group of bushes.

Tightly packed together, with dry grass underneath, they took turns sleeping. At dawn, they both donned their armour.

305

"I've heard the Getae are wilder than the Triballi," said Leonnatus.

Cassander nodded towards a group of huts from which smoke snaked out of chimneys. "I can see them."

Beyond the village was a fortified township. Its turrets gleamed gold in the morning sunlight. Alexander's cavalry lined up outside the citadel. Men on horseback emerged from behind the walls. Cassander noticed they were struggling to get into formation.

"Why don't we concentrate on the villagers, Leo?"

"Because the king wants this city."

"These country bumpkins don't know how to fight. Look at them! They can't even make a straight line outside their walls."

"They're better fighters than the Triballi."

"According to Alexander."

"What's that supposed to mean, Cassie?"

"Our valiant monarch abandoned Peuke because he couldn't defeat the Triballi. Any farmhand could beat this bunch."

"Our king abandoned that city because a siege would take too long. We can't spend a year in some backwater when our goal is Persia."

"You don't see it, do you? Alexander lied to us. We couldn't take Peuke. What worries me is how many more lies are to come."

"What are you babbling about?"

"What is going to happen when we are stranded far from home? What lies is he going to tell us when Persia isn't enough?"

"Persia is the world."

"The world is bigger than Darius' empire. Alex has an insatiable desire to explore and conquer. In the meantime, this city is going to fall quickly and without a fight."

"So, the city falls instantly. That's good, isn't it?"

Cassander rubbed the bridge of his snub nose. "If you don't want to address the larger question of Alexander's duplicity, fine. This city will be full of marauding Macedonians before midday. I want good people for my estates, and so do you. Those villagers are our best bet."

"I'd rather obey my monarch and fill my pockets with gold."

"You'll be lucky to plunder anything by the time Alexander has had his share."

Kicking the sides of his stallion, Cassander turned to face the village. Despatching several officers to his crack units, he prepared for an attack.

***

As Cassander predicted, the main battle was uneventful. After the first Macedonian cavalry charge, the Getae fled, leaving their town to Alexander. Before midday, the Macedonians poured through its gates.

Focussing on the villagers, several Macedonian units, including Cassander's troops, descended on them. Preferring to keep casualties to a minimum, Cassander encircled a group of houses. He rounded up his senior officers and issued orders.

"Tell them to get their belongings. No killing. Keep the families together."

Frightened residents poured out of their homes and waited in lanes which ran between their huts. Soldiers rounded up the captives and escorted them safely to the baggage train.

Towards evening, Cassander ordered the huts to be burned. The fire was visible from both the Getae township and Macedonian tents which were pitched outside the city walls.

Standing in front of the settlement, it appeared as if Cassander was supervising the mass destruction of the villagers and their homes.

When it was over, and the huts were razed to the ground, he departed to his tent.

After his bath, he summoned Helen for a manicure. He watched as she buffed his fingernails with a small brush, and applied oil.

"You are very skilled, my dear," he complimented.

"I see you have more staff."

"Good people, don't you think?"

"They're frightened."

"This is war."

"You razed their homes to the ground."

"I got them out first."

"How very generous!"

Cassander withdrew a plump hand from Helen's ministrations and leaned forward. "Look, we are friends, so I will let you in on a secret. Alexander would have razed that village with everyone in it. It's what he does. Today, I ensured I reached the Getae settlement before Alexander, Perdiccas or – Zeus preserve us – Seleucus."

"How noble of you." Helen went to work on her master's feet.

Despite his annoyance, Cassander shut his eyes in bliss. "Your massage is delightful. I saved those villagers, you know. When we return to Macedonia, they shall have new, and much nicer homes."

Helen sighed. "People don't want that. They want to live in their own homes, on their own land."

Cassander opened his eyes. "What do you expect me to do?"

"Stay home."

"I'm King Alexander's subject."

"You're a rich man. You can make choices."

"That's where you're wrong, Helen. I have gold, but I'm not free. None of us are." Cassander regarded his nails. "Splendid! I'll have a nap. Wake me when the feast begins."

***

76.

Demosthenes leafed through his latest speech. It was designed to shock with its news. Temocles entered his study with fresh pomegranate juice, and a fish broth with roe and coriander.

The orator put down his speech. "How are you these days, my good man?"

"Er – well, Master."

"How is your family?"

"In good health, sir."

"Have you a son, yet?"

"Two."

"Excellent! Due to my statesmanship, they will not have to live in fear of King Alexander banging on their front door."

"Indeed, Master."

The steward bowed and left quickly. Having no curiosity about his master's achievements, he hurried down the corridor to the kitchen. Flipping an old cloak over his shoulders, he locked the main door and exited through a side entrance, which he bolted. Afterwards, he departed down a lane to his cottage on the estate.

Even though he cooked, his wife always prepared his own meals at home. It made for harmony. A matron needed to know she was valued.

***

Drunkenness was rife in the Getae citadel. While Alexander was relatively sober, most of his generals swilled uncut wine into the early hours. Beef, pork and fish, freshly caught from the Danube, were served on the conquered tribesmen's crockery.

Unlike his father, Philotas drank fast. As the evening wore on, he became belligerent. "I heard Lord Cassander, son of the mighty General Antipater, was merciful while everyone else was fighting."

Leonnatus gave a snort of laughter. Parmenion jabbed his son in the ribs. Seleucus raised one eyebrow, while Ptolemy pretended to be interested in the wine.

Alexander, who was chatting to Perdiccas, turned to his cousin. "Is that so, Hephaestion?"

"Cassie burned an entire Getae village to the ground. It's more than most of us did."

Satisfied, Alexander resumed his conversation. Some of the younger men started ribbing Philotas, while his father moved to block him from his king's view.

Ensconced in a corner, with two pretty serving girls, Cassander glowered.

***

A blazing sun was high over the Getae fort, when Hephaestion reached the foot of his cousin's bed. "Wake up, Alex."

Tousled red-blond tufts popped out of the bedclothes. "What time is it?"

"Noon."

"That's alright, then."

Alexander rolled over onto his side. In seconds, he was snoring. Voices in the living room floated down the corridor. The bedclothes erupted, and the head of the disturbed sleeper reappeared.

"Heph, who is making that racket?"

"I'm sorry, cousin. The generals are coming. There's trouble in Pelium."

Alexander rolled onto a pillow. "There's always trouble in Pelium. There's nothing *but* trouble in Father's so-called conquered territories."

"Philotas is here."

"I'm not getting up for him."

"Perdiccas and Ptolemy, are also here."

"An odd pairing."

"They arrived separately."

The noise increased. Parmenion, and other generals, joined the throng. Soon, the living room was full. Unable to sleep any longer, Alexander pushed back the covers. Hephaestion tensed.

"What's the matter, Heph?

"There's something in your bed."

A tail wagged. "It's Perdias." The dog whined and kissed his master. Alexander sat up and drew him close.

"Why is he here, cousin?"

"Mother sent him to me."

"How is Queen Olympias?" Hephaestion asked politely.

"The same – charging high rent for nine months in the womb." Alexander's brows crinkled. "Why can I hear Parmenion?"

"Cleitus, son of King Bardylis, and King Glaukias are stirring up trouble in Pelium."

"Glaukias is a friend. I stayed with him when Father exiled me."

"Things have changed."

"We need Pelium," said Alexander thoughtfully, as he scratched Perdias under the chin.

"We do, cousin."

"It's located on an important pass between Macedonia and Illyria."

"It is."

"And gives me easy access to Greece."

With a final pat on the head for Perdias, Alexander slid out of bed. His dresser moved forward from the shadows. Hephaestion took his leave.

***

77.

Clad in a red gown, Alexander crossed the carpet of the main living area. He calculated there were at least forty generals milling about. All were conversing in muted tones.

Standing behind an oak table Alexander viewed the gathering. "I have been informed there is a problem with Pelium."

"Revolt is a better word," Parmenion replied.

Alexander's eyes locked with those of his general. "Tell me more."

"Cleitus and Glaukias have formed a political alliance."

"Against Macedonia?"

"Naturally, against Macedonia."

"I want to be clear."

"We wouldn't be in your tent, if it were not so, my sovereign."

Cassander hurried past the guards and melted into the background. Irritation flickered in Alexander's eyes as he noted his tardy general's entrance.

"Political alliances are formed every day, Parmenion," he continued. "King Glaukias was a friend to me."

"Us," said Cassander.

Alexander pricked up his ears. "Does anyone have anything to say?"

Seleucus turned to Cassander. "Do you?"

The latter stepped forward. "King Glaukias was kind to us when we were exiled. I would be asking for clarification."

"Welcome to this meeting," said Alexander, his annoyance evaporating. "He was indeed a kind host to us in our time of need. There will be a reward for you when you return to your tent."

Cassander stepped back next to Seleucus.

"No thanks to snakes," he whispered.

"I'm not the one who is constantly disrespecting our monarch," growled Seleucus.

"Was Alexander the only one to go into exile? I distinctly remember the bunions on my feet."

"Hush, Cassie," said Leonnatus.

Alexander faced the gathering. "I see no alternative but to march on Pelium. Break camp and be ready by the second hour of the afternoon. You all may go."

***

Cassander hurried to his tent. His encampment was in a wooded area, outside the citadel. He wished to avoid potential marauders of the newly captured fort. Bandits were rife in the area and protecting his staff, with the women and children, was his priority.

A cape of gold thread and a copy of the *Iliad* lay on a table. Tossing the scroll aside, he picked up the cape to try it on. It was then he noticed the table was made of pure gold.

Helen was making breakfast. Cassander threw the cape across his shoulders and went to her side. Twirling about, he gave her a full view. "What do you think?"

Helen sniffed. "Showy."

"I'll make an impression at dinner."

Rolling her eyes, his housekeeper pushed past him. She laid a dark blue cloth over two oak tables. On one she placed pitchers of grape juice, water, and milk. Afterwards, she laid out linen napkins, and a finger bowl of water for rinsing the diner's hands.

On the second table, she placed several pottery dishes containing sauces and yoghurt. Plates of fried duck and oysters were added to complete the meal. Quaffing the grape juice, Cassander picked up a duck leg, which he devoured.

"Remind me to get you two homes when we return to Macedonia," he said.

He swirled his fingers in a gold water bowl and wiped them on a napkin. Throwing the cape on a chair, he left the tent to muster his troops.

***

Humming to himself, Cassander supervised the preparation of his men, before setting out with the army of twenty-three thousand for Pelium. Trotting on his steed, his saddlebags filled with snacks prepared by Helen, he was in high spirits.

During the second hour of the afternoon, Leonnatus drew up. He received a pastry, stuffed with shrimps and coriander.

"Who is your new cook, Cassie?"

"Helen packed my bags. I must say I make excellent staff choices."

The army travelled swiftly. After a few days, they were outside Pelium. Alexander sent scouts to gather information.

During the wait, Ptolemy and Seleucus shared a drink in the camp of the Silver Shields. Leonnatus ordered his servants to draw a bath.

Cassander slept in his tent, while Polymarchus read the *Iliad*. Helen ensured no one disturbed either of them.

***

The next day, the army stood outside Pelium. Perdiccas was on Alexander's right, with Hephaestion and Philotas. Parmenion held the left, while Ptolemy's Silver Shields were positioned some distance away from the main army. The waiting grew tedious, as messengers travelled back and forth.

Nudging the sides of his stallion, Ptolemy made his way to Perdiccas. "Any idea of why we're standing on parade?"

"A man called Cleitus, who is not to be confused with our good friend, is in charge of the citadel," Perdiccas said.

"Where's King Glaukias?"

"He's due, shortly."

Ptolemy's eyes scanned the hills. "There are men on those heights."

"That's because Alexander is getting ready to take them."

While the pair chatted, Leonnatus galloped up to Cassander. The latter rummaged through his saddlebags. "Helen made honey cakes."

"Listen up, Cassie. Alexander is going to attack the city and the heights. He wants you on the ridge."

"Where are you positioned?"

"On the plain. All the best, Cassie."

Cassander held out a cake, but Leonnatus shook his head and galloped back to the front.

Popping the sweetmeat in his mouth, Cassander looked up at the hills. Rain clouds were forming. Fortunately for him, Helen had packed a special waterproof jacket.

***

The battle lasted all morning. Cassander used his raincoat for an hour before the sun broke through the clouds.

By the day's end, the heights belonged to Alexander. Enemy soldiers, who were not cut down, scurried back into the city. Erecting barricades around the citadel, to ensure no one entered or escaped, Alexander's forces then laid siege to Pelium.

Back at the camp, Cassander bathed. Afterwards, a pretty girl massaged his feet and applied henna to his toes. At the ninth hour of the evening, Leonnatus burst in.

"Look who's here for dinner! Come in, Leo, the venison is very good."

"When did you get time to shoot deer?"

Polymarchus looked up from his homework. Cassander's eyes slid to Helen, who sat in a corner doing her embroidery.

"As you see, I have the best staff in the army."

"King Glaukias is here."

"Sit down, Leo. Have a glass of Mycenaen wine."

"You have Mycenaen wine?"

"I do."

"Cassie, aren't you worried that with Glaukias here, our army risks defeat?"

"I'm worried about you, Leo. You've refused my food twice in the same day."

Polymarchus, who was no longer doing his homework, rose and pushed a dining couch towards the visitor. Cassander clapped his hands. A wine steward appeared from behind a curtain with a carafe. He poured out two cups.

Accepting one, Leonnatus reclined on the couch offered him. "I suppose there's no harm in having dinner."

"I was starving after being on the ridge all day," said Cassander. "Don't worry, we won't lose."

The smell of venison filled the tent. The men ate and talked. After Leonnatus left, Cassander approached Helen.

"There's no need to keep your son up late."

"He's in service."

"I'm paying for his education. I'd rather he was awake for his lessons." Picking up a lamp, Cassander made his way to his bedroom. He stopped, as if remembering something. "Help yourself to the wine. Mycenae has excellent vines."

***

78.

Seleucus pulled on his gloves. It was chilly. Even the hardy Perdiccas wore two vests under his linen armour. They walked out of the breakfast tent together. Outside, they filled their lungs with fresh air.

"There's nothing like Illyria," Seleucus said. "King Glaukias arrived last night."

"My squire told me."

"How he got into the city with our blockade is a mystery."

Seleucus' eye caught a view of the plain before them. Thousands of Macedonian heavy infantry were training before the walls of Pelium.

Before he had time to ask the reason, Ptolemy rode up. "Are you two ready to watch the show?"

"I thought we were," said Seleucus, looking at a sea of sarissa-wielding infantry.

"Alexander's planning to take the city."

"With an infantry training session?" asked Perdiccas.

Before anyone had time to ask more questions, Ptolemy rode away.

***

Outside the city gates, the defenders of Pelium were arrayed in formation. All were watching the Macedonian army. Cassander and Leonnatus positioned themselves on a rocky outcrop.

Sarissas rose and fell like sheaves of wheat. Thousands of spear heads soared skywards, before descending into a horizontal attacking mode. They swept to the right, and then to the left, in complete silence. After several minutes, Alexander's phalanx moved forward.

317

Going through their paces, they displayed intricate manoeuvres, as if they were on parade. Horses and men turned and spun in perfect unison.

Cassander sighed. "It's beautiful!"

"You mean frightening," said Leonnatus.

"I wish Helen were here."

"You're fond of this woman."

"We have a friendship."

"You educate her son."

Cassander shrugged. "I'm good to my staff."

"You should marry her."

Instead of scoffing, Cassander weighed his friend's words.

"Perhaps I will."

***

Alexander gritted his teeth. The sarissa waving was reaching its peak. All around him, the enemy watched entranced. Suddenly, he gave the signal.

"Alalalalai!"

The Macedonian war cry battered enemy ears. Cavalry on the left, spun into a diamond shape and charged. Soldiers in the phalanx beat their spears against their shields. In seconds, Glaukias' men were running towards the fortress.

Cassander rocked back and forth on his steed with mirth. Leonnatus did not know if he was more fascinated with the fleeing enemy or tears flowing down the plump cheeks of his comrade.

In the distance, Alexander was talking to Hephaestion. "It seems we now have access to Thebes and Athens."

"A brilliant strategy, cousin."

Amusement glimmered in the king's eyes. "I recall it being your idea."

Winding Bucephalus' reins around his fist, Alexander turned his horse towards the tents. His sharp eyes detected the helmets of

Cassander and Leonnatus. On a steep incline, Ptolemy's Shields watched, he hoped with approval. His late father's veterans were a crusty bunch at the best of times.

Behind him, the clopping of Hephaestion's horse echoed in his ears all the way back to their tent.

***

79.

Two Macedonian officers, who were stationed at the fortress of Cadmei in Thebes, took the afternoon off. Strolling down the winding lanes of tree-lined boulevards, they chatted amiably in the warm sunshine.

Stopping at an intersection, which led to their individual homes, they visited their favourite snack shop. There, they bought freshly baked buns from an attractive woman, whom one of them thought he would marry someday. Giving her a wink, the would-be suitor picked up the buns and pushed a few coins towards her. Their fingers touched in the exchange. It was the best part of his day.

The friends shared their buns. Filled with goat's cheese and herbs, they were the perfect way to round off the afternoon. Knowing that soon they would part ways, the men dawdled, savouring their snack.

"Are you going to training tonight, Theseus?"

"Believe it or not, Aeschines, my mother has dinner on the table."

"Have you asked Andromache to marry you, yet? It's always good to have a wife to cook for you. While these buns are excellent, my wife says my girth has expanded overnight."

"I rather fancy the shop girl."

"You can't marry her."

"Why not?"

"We're Macedonian."

Suddenly, they heard a roar. Looking over their shoulders, they saw a crowd of people running towards them. Aeschines' hand automatically went to the hilt of his sword.

"Are we being invaded?" Theseus asked, finishing his roll and wiping his mouth with the back of his sleeve.

There was no answer. In seconds, the crowd descended on the men and tore them to pieces.

***

"Is it true Thebes is in revolt?"

Demosthenes looked up. It was late. His eyes were blurry, but he knew his wife, Cressida stood in the doorway. It was unlike her to meddle in his affairs. She had never disturbed him in his study before.

"It is," he replied.

"Is that why you're writing?"

"I'm preparing a speech. Are you going to come in?"

"It's not permitted for matrons."

"I'm inviting you."

Cressida stepped across the threshold. "I need you to tell me the truth."

"What do you mean?"

"I know you have enough to incite war against Macedonia."

"I'm writing a speech, not providing arms to Thebes."

"*Are* you going to incite war against Macedonia?"

Demosthenes picked up his pen and returned to writing. Disconcerted, his wife bowed her head and slipped out of the room.

***

Hephaestion was at the foot of his bed. Alexander raised his arm to shield his eyes from the burst of sunlight. Try as he might, he could not focus on anything but a dark silhouette of the man he knew better than anyone in the world.

He smiled and swung his legs out of bed. The blood rushed to his brain. He was not hungover. Hephaestion had probably made sure last night's wine was cut with water.

Yawning, Alexander stretched his arms to loosen up his shoulders. Any wounds from Peuke were healed. Perdias ran up to him and licked his hand. He patted his friend, who jumped up on the bed.

"What time is it, Hephaestion?"

"Morning."

"That's a curt answer. What's the matter?"

"Thebes."

"Are they at war with us already? We just cleared the pass."

"There has been a revolt. Macedonian city guards were killed."

"Is Athens involved?"

"If not, the city will be. You know what Demosthenes is like."

Alexander scratched his chin. "I need a shave."

***

Polymarchus was at the foot of Cassander's bed, squeezing his toes.

"By all the gods, what is it, child?"

"The next day."

Despite his annoyance, Cassander's mouth upturned. "I know that." He propped himself up in bed. A sunbeam smote him in the right eye. "For goodness' sakes put the tent flap down."

The boy hurried to obey him. Cassander yawned, and cracked his knuckles. In a few moments, Polymarchus brought him a tray with his breakfast.

"It's Thebes, sir."

"These rolls are good. Your mother's?"

"Yes, sir."

"I must ask her to marry me one day."

"Sir?"

"Never mind. What did you say about Thebes?"

"There's been a revolt."

"What do you expect? They're Greek. They are revolting."

The boy did not smile. "Macedonian officers were killed in Cadmei."

"I see."

Polymarchus was desperate. "The King is *shaving*."

Cassander dropped his roll. "Get my armour – now!"

***

Once dressed, Cassander went outside. Predictably the Macedonian generals were gathered in the royal tent area.

"Including the old gasbag, Parmenion," he muttered, bumping into the tall frame of Leonnatus.

"Hush, Cassie!"

"Morning, Leo. Alexander's still shaving, I see."

"A signal for us to be ready for battle. We mustn't allow the enemy to grasp our beards."

"Personally, I prefer being clean-shaven."

"Women like it, too. They say it makes me look younger."

"I didn't know you liked them, Leo."

"How could we have children without them?"

Cassander's brows arched. "Are you thinking of having children?"

"I have two already."

"Since when?"

"Five years ago. A boy and a girl with my favourite lady. We were sweethearts in Mieza."

"I didn't know you had a girlfriend."

"We kept it quiet. It comforts me to know that my family is safe in Macedonia."

"For now. No one likes us, and I'm not surprised. What are we doing, following this madman, Leo?"

"We're King Alexander's subjects."

"Helen told me I had a choice. I'm beginning to think she was right."

"Thebes is important."

"Who in Hades' name, gives a toss? A couple of officers were killed, so what? We shouldn't be there in the first place. Our home is Macedonia, not Thebes. Do you see Thebans parked at Pella, eating roast boar and swilling wine on our battlements?"

"I should hope not."

Alexander gave his razor back to his servant. With great ceremony, he washed his face and hands. Drying them on a red towel, he took his linen armour from his dresser and slipped it over his head.

A few hundred yards away, at the Silver Shields' encampment, Seleucus was astride his mount, next to Ptolemy. They shared a cup of pomegranate juice, mixed with honey.

"We'll be leaving shortly," said Seleucus.

Ptolemy held out a flat, warm pancake. "Bread?"

Accepting it, Seleucus rolled it up and ate in slow bites. "I notice you haven't shaved, yet."

"My beard is important propaganda."

"Ah, yes – Philip's veterans like to think he's still with them."

When they had finished, Ptolemy gave his cup to a page, who took it away to pack. The generals bid each other a courteous farewell and returned to their regiments.

Assembled in the cold morning, Alexander's army was ready. Heralds blew trumpets and the soldiers made their way to Thebes, behind their king.

***

General Chares walked up to Demosthenes in the assembly hall. "I hear our resident statesman has news for us."

"I do."

"It wouldn't be about our Macedonian barbarian, would it?"

"Everyone knows it's about King Alexander."

"I can't wait to hear the news."

Chares took his place with the men of Athens while Demosthenes mentally prepared himself. His fear of public speaking was always with him. As a youngster, he once choked in front of the mighty King Philip. Even now, though he had cured himself of stammering, there was always the possibility he would be unable to deliver.

Drinking a cup of water, the famous orator looked straight at his audience. He was ready. "Free men of Athens, we are gathered today because, like you, I have heard with joy of the revolt in Thebes against that most despicable of tyrants, King Alexander of Macedonia." Cheering broke out. Demosthenes paused.

"Tell us they've lynched the Macedonian guards!" a man called out.

"And the entire garrison is on fire!" added another.

"Where is Alexander?" a high-pitched youth called out.

"That is a very good question, and one I shall address," said the speaker.

The audience grew quiet.

"Let's hear it then," a grumpy statesman said at Chares' shoulder.

"King Alexander is dead."

The audience was in an uproar. Demosthenes stepped back from the podium. His shoulders relaxed. He had delivered.

***

80.

The march was relentless. Initially trained by King Philip to perform under the most gruelling conditions, the army kept up a fast pace on its trek down the length of Greece. Despite the speed at which Alexander travelled, thousands of Boetians had enough time to ready themselves and join his army when he reached their lands.

At one township, Ptolemy exchanged his officers' horses for new steeds. Noticing what he was doing, Leonnatus nudged his exhausted mount towards the intrepid buyer.

"Any chance of getting fresh steeds for my men, Ptolemy?"

"There's a farmer two houses down. Some of his stallions are in excellent condition."

Spotting Seleucus heading towards them, Leonnatus hurried to the house. A man of about fifty years old was standing outside his stables. Pulling out a reserve of silver coins from his saddlebag, the general managed to negotiate for thirty steeds and a pony.

Avoiding Seleucus, he ordered his squires to take the horses and pony to his men in exchange for their tired warhorses. He then paid a farmer to keep the animals in provender for a month.

When he had finished doing business, Leonnatus took the bridle of a magnificent black stallion, and sought out Cassander.

"Fancy a trade, Cassie?"

"I'm in no mood for riddles."

"He's exchanging our old horses for new ones," a child's voice explained.

Cassander looked down. Polymarchus was on a pony he did not recognise. His head snapped up. "Are you buying horses, Leo?"

"Exchanging them. We'll pick ours up on the way back. I've paid for a month's worth of lodging at a farm stable."

"I'm in!" Dismounting, Cassander patted his horse goodbye. As a squire took it away, he mounted a new one. "Polymarchus and I thank you."

"Yes, thank you, General!" the child echoed.

"I see you are teaching the boy manners," Leonnatus smiled. "You're most welcome, Cassie. You too, little one."

King Alexander rested his men for an hour. Then, they were off again.

***

Cressida was outside her husband's door. Demosthenes put down his stylus.

"Are you here to give me a lecture?" he asked.

"How do you know that King Alexander is dead?"

"He's been away too long."

"So, you really have no idea."

"It's an educated guess."

"What if he comes here?"

"It'll take months. We'll be prepared. I've already sent arms to Thebes."

"You are arms dealing? How did you make the Thebans believe you?"

"I'm only supplying arms. There's no charge. I told them I fought against Alexander and knew he was dead."

"You lied?"

"He's dead, Cressida. When Philip was assassinated, he left a callow youth to take his throne. Alexander is untried in battle. He's been absent from Macedonia for months."

Cressida entered her husband's office. Before he knew what was happening, she slapped him soundly on the right cheek.

***

81.

Two weeks after they set out, the Macedonian army halted outside Thebes. A low wall, where slaves and foreigners lived, ringed the city. Surrounding it, a double palisade and light fortifications housed Theban military units.

Cassander, Perdiccas and Seleucus arranged their military units in the formation required by their sovereign. General Parmenion spent most of the morning talking to Alexander and Hephaestion. Meanwhile, the army was at a standstill.

Leonnatus broke a sandal strap. He dismounted and took off his footwear. Making a mental note to speak to the army cobbler, he spotted Cassander riding towards him.

"Are we taking Thebes, Cassie?

"Alexander will make a decision, if Parmenion stops blathering. You have time to get new sandals. Thought you might like a snack."

Hoisting a pomegranate through the air to his friend, Cassander started peeling one for himself. They were ripe and easy to finish in a few bites.

Perdiccas rode over. "I've come to let you both know our esteemed sovereign may not attack Thebes. He does not wish our army to give the impression of being an invading horde."

Cassander turned to look at the thirty thousand infantry assembled in full view of the city. "It's a bit late for that, don't you think?"

Leonnatus handed his worn footwear to his page. "Get the strap fixed, boy."

"There are spares in the luggage, sir. I'll bring them for you to wear while you wait. By the way, our mighty king is moving the infantry."

As the lad ran off, Leonnatus mounted his horse. Cassander gazed thoughtfully after the disappearing boy. "You have a bright page there, Leo. I might buy him from you."

"He's not available."

Cassander's mouth slid into a mischievous grin. "I have a pretty wench from the last campaign on my staff." He turned to Perdiccas. "I've noticed *your* eyes roving over her, Perdie!"

The latter blushed. "I only came to tell you we're pitching camp." Kicking the sides of his steed, Perdiccas abruptly disappeared into the throng of men and horses.

Leonnatus faced Cassander. "Why did you have to embarrass him?"

"What do you mean? The girl is pretty. I want your page. It's a fair exchange. How about it?"

"Forget the girl! Perdiccas is a valuable general to Alexander."

"And a man to whom our sovereign might leave his future empire."

"Which is why you should stay on the right side of him."

Having finished his pomegranate, Cassander fossicked about in his shoulder bag and drew out two pears. He chucked one to his comrade in arms.

"I don't know about you, Leo, but my needs are modest. My ultimate goal is to die at home in my own bed."

Catching the pear, Leonnatus' eyes scanned the troop movements. His page was right. Alexander was moving the infantry out.

"We're heading towards Thebes, Cassie. There's bound to be a skirmish. That's your goal for now. Focus!"

Leonnatus' page returned with a pair of sandals. Without waiting, the youth slipped them onto his master's feet, so that he did not have to dismount.

"We are going to camp on the southern side of Cadmei's fortress, sir," he whispered.

Leonnatus was surprised. "Are you sure?"

"General Seleucus told me."

"That means our mighty leader is not spoiling for a fight, yet," Cassander remarked. "I have to get back to my men, but I'll trade you my pretty girl for that boy, Leo. Think about it."

With a cackle, Cassander tapped the sides of his horse and rode away. The page fixed imploring eyes on Leonnatus.

"Please don't sell me, sir."

"I'm your master. I can do what I want with you."

"Lord Cassander is strange."

"He's kind to his staff." The boy looked as though he was about to burst into tears. In a reflex movement, Leonnatus bent down and patted his head. "I was jesting. Don't worry, you're a page, not a slave. When you grow up, you will be an officer in my cavalry regiment."

Urging his steed to the front of his column, Leonnatus led his troops in the wake of Alexander's army to Cadmei.

***

On the way to the fortress, Alexander rode in front, while he chatted to Hephaestion. After a few minutes, Seleucus made his way to Ptolemy.

"Have you noticed thousands of Boetians have joined our ranks?" he asked. "Our sovereign now has an army big enough to crush Thebes."

"Alexander doesn't want war with Thebes, Sel."

"With thirty thousand infantry, three thousand cavalry, and our new friends?"

"When did you become an accountant?"

"I can add. We're fifty thousand strong."

"An impressive number."

"Equal to the entire population of Thebes."

Ptolemy's brow crinkled. The Macedonian garrison of Cadmei loomed in front of them. Soldiers began to set up camp.

"My tent will be near that small brook by a group of trees in the shade, Sel."

"Am I invited for a drink?"

"Since when do you have to ask?"

"Since you allowed Leo to take my horses."

"I was leasing them for the Silver Shields. You know my unit has men in their fifties."

"Seventies, although, I must admit, they're fitter than everyone else."

"I'm sorry, it was first come, first served. We only had a short break. I didn't expect Leo to approach me."

"Or else your alliances are shifting."

Ptolemy threw back his head and produced the belly laugh which endeared him to his soldiers.

"Come for lunch, Sel! If Alexander decides not to attack Thebes, I might even loan you a horse or two."

***

Dismounting Bucephalus, Alexander gave him to his most trusted squire. Then, he and Hephaestion made their way to the royal tent. In the evening, the Young Companions and older generals joined them. Parmenion and Cleitus mingled with Perdiccas and his officers.

Ptolemy and Seleucus arrived late. Clad in robes of silk, it was clear they had both visited the same barber. Their hair was cropped, and they were clean shaven. They took their place next to the senior generals and Perdiccas.

Standing at the back of the tent, Cassander was chatting up the help. Two heavily veiled maidens poured water into libation bowls. After performing their duties, they left quickly.

Chairs and fleece-covered stools were put out. Uncut wine was served and oil lamps lit. Fires were stoked in braziers, set around the tent at intervals to keep it warm. Handfuls of incense were scattered over the flames to ward off mosquitoes.

Alexander took his place on the royal couch, to signal that the festivities had begun. Leonnatus arrived, his hair dishevelled. Slipping into the back row of diners, he tried to look invisible.

Cassander's eyes sparkled. "My, my! What do we have here?"

"Do shut up, Cassie."

"My pretty girl was missing this afternoon. Why is your hair out of place before dinner and dancing, Leo? I have the proprietary right to know."

Ptolemy overheard the conversation. He lifted his gold goblet.

"Tell us all!" he roared from his corner.

Cassander ignored the intrusion. "It's clear *his* story is a prosaic one. That of too much drink."

"I was sleeping," Leonnatus explained.

"Well rested, are we?"

"One day, I'm going to join Alexander in smashing your head against a wall."

"Is that what he wants to do?"

"You must have heard him. It's no secret."

Cassander's eyes slitted. "I haven't."

"Are you surprised?"

"I am deeply concerned for my health. Alexander kills lions on his days off."

"With his bare hands. You should consider people's feelings before you speak, Cassie."

"Now, you sound like a woman." Cassander sipped his wine and looked about. "Speaking of which, there were girls here a while ago."

"Don't worry, there will be the usual ladies at the end of the evening."

"These were pure. Veiled young lasses from the hills."

"If they were veiled, how could you tell their age?"

"By their anatomical ripeness."

Leonnatus rolled his eyes. In the generals' corner, Alexander raised his goblet.

"To Macedonia!" he cried.

His men joined in the toast to their country. Platters of pheasant and fish arrived. Roast boar on a spit was carried into the tent. Servants set it up in the centre and cut slices for the guests.

Cassander stuffed himself with a variety of meats. When he had finished, he started on the desserts. Smoothing his hair into place, Leonnatus moved to where a young musician sang to the accompaniment of his lyre. Enjoying the music, the exhausted general drifted off.

His friend continued to feast. Afterwards, Cassander washed his hands in one of the fingerbowls. Cleaning his teeth with a fishbone toothpick, he observed the diners while his meal digested.

Alexander talked almost exclusively to Hephaestion. Parmenion and his son Philotas discussed a relative's upcoming wedding. Perdiccas was locked in an argument with Seleucus. His back turned to the generals, Ptolemy conversed with an elderly cavalry commander from the Silver Shields.

The sounds of the lyre attracted Cassander's ear. Picking up two wine cups, he joined Leonnatus. Gently shaking his friend's shoulder, he gave the sleepy diner a cup. The latter propped himself against a cushion. Together, the men cradled their drinks and chatted into the night, their minds on home.

***

82.

Behind the walls of Thebes, distinguished elders and generals sat around a large cedar table. Phoenix and Prothytes, leaders of the revolt against Macedonia, were in high spirits.

"Alexander is outside our walls," said Phoenix.

"I heard those uncouth Macedonians partying all night," an elder remarked.

"It's hard to believe they are here," another said.

"Maybe we should be wondering why any of us chose to believe that Athenian liar, Demosthenes," a general growled.

"Maybe, he really thought Alexander was dead," suggested Prothytes.

A senior cavalry officer snorted. "I note there isn't an Athenian ally in sight."

"Demosthenes sent arms," Phoenix said.

"But kept himself in the safety of his sprawling estate!" the Theban mayor blurted angrily.

Phoenix cleared his throat. "We need to address the issue of the army at our gates."

The mayor turned to him. "We're listening."

"As I see it, there are two options, siege or war. If we allow Alexander to lay siege to our city, he will eventually starve us into submission."

Prothytes nodded vigorously. "If we fight, we need to start early while there are still food supplies."

"I agree," said the general who had spoken earlier. "With food in our bellies, we are more likely to fight well and win."

***

It was a cold night. Cassander wrapped a fleece around him and headed for the guards' camp fire. On the way, he passed the generals.

Ptolemy and Seleucus were together, in the latter's tent, sharing stories. Bursts of laughter floated across the chilly night air. Nearby, the Silver Shields were partying with Seleucus' men. Many were dancing.

When he reached the fire, Cassander sat on an oak log. A man offered him warm goat's milk. Several soldiers were also seated on logs which were scattered across the grass. Others were sprawled on rugs laid out on the ground. Some had women. Everyone spoke in hushed voices while the fire crackled. Occasionally, sparks flew skywards, illuminating the darkness with orange and gold.

A twig snapped. Leonnatus loomed out of the shadows. He wore a sheepskin hat and carried a blanket.

"Can't sleep, either, Cassie?" he asked.

"My page forgot to warm my bed with a brazier."

"I hope it's not the one who forgot your manicurist after Chaeronea."

"His brother."

"I see there's still a lamp burning in Alexander's tent."

"You know him. He's probably reading the *Iliad*."

The same soldier, who waited on Cassander, handed Leonnatus a cup of milk. The latter accepted it, and joined his friend on the oak log.

"Do you think we'll be fighting tomorrow, Cassie?"

"Who knows the mind of Alexander?"

"That march tired me."

"Ptolemy's geriatric Silver Shields are still merrymaking, I see."

"They're a tough lot, who work hard and play even harder. I think it's a characteristic of that generation."

"Leo, do you remember the King of Illyria commanding men, in his eighties?"

"Perdiccas said it was like being pursued by his grand-dad on horseback!"

Explosions of laughter filled the night air. The pair watched soldiers throw branches on the fire. Sparks soared into the moonlit sky. Around them, the chill of the night created a strange stillness. Many of the men talked in low voices. Some returned to their tents with their women.

Lost in their own thoughts, Alexander's young generals cradled their milk cups and stared into the fire.

***

In the royal tent, Alexander dined with Hephaestion. Finishing his small portion of chicken and vegetables, the king asked for his plate to be removed by a servant. After finishing the main course, Hephaestion ordered dessert. By contrast, Alexander was pacing the carpet.

"I don't want to be harsh," he declared.

"But Thebes colluded with Athens in defying Macedonia, cousin."

"Thebes has always been independent."

"And a seat of culture and learning."

"Athens might not agree."

Dessert arrived. Hephaestion dug into his pastry, laced with honey and pistachio nuts. "What do you plan to do, cousin?"

"Make a fair request."

By the ninth hour of the evening, messengers were summoned. They were given their orders for the morning.

After their departure, servants made up the beds. Skilled hands warmed sheets with braziers. Extra fleeces were thrown atop woollen blankets. A servant filled up an oil lamp on the royal desk.

The pair hunted through a pile of scrolls for their favourite stories. While Hephaestion slipped between his sheets to read Euripides, Alexander studied the *Iliad* at his desk.

Outside, Ptolemy's laughter filled the night air.

***

At Thebes, the council buzzed with excitement. Phoenix opened the meeting. "Greetings on the second day of Macedonia's invasion."

Laughter greeted the opening remark.

"We heard he made contact," said an elder.

"Indeed, a messenger visited," Phoenix replied.

The assembly quietened.

"With terms?" the mayor asked.

"Demands."

A wave of angry sound washed over the gathering.

"Let me guess," the mayor said, his voice laced with sarcasm, "the tyrant of Greece wants Thebes to surrender."

"Not at all," Phoenix said.

An elder statesman rose. "Alexander must want something to be camped outside our walls with the largest army ever seen in Greece."

A young herald jumped to his feet. "He asks for Phoenix and Prothytes to be turned over to him."

"What was your reply, Phoenix?" Prothytes demanded.

"I have yet to deliver my message. It is why I called this assembly. What do you have to say, men of Thebes?"

A youngster, seated next to Phoenix, waved his arms. "That he surrender Parmenion and Philotas!"

Another stood on the bench he had been sitting on.

"Ask Macedonia to hand over the tyrant of Greece!" he yelled.

The roar from the audience was deafening. When the clamour had died down, Phoenix smiled.

"Alexander will have his answer. Despatch the messenger."

***

It was a dark night. Music floated across a breeze. Leonnatus stood at the entrance of Cassander's tent. The latter put down his lyre.

"From your face, Leo, I would say we're going into battle tomorrow."

"Our king has given no orders."

"I don't understand."

Drawing up a stool, Leonnatus rubbed his brow. "Neither does Perdiccas. Thebes insulted Alexander. Normally, we would be battering down the city gates by now."

"Our army has been preparing for three days, Leo. What can the matter be?"

"It's because this is Thebes."

"And Alexander is holding back?"

"He asked for terms. No king would do that unless he was trying to keep the peace."

An elderly steward poured Leonnatus a cup of local wine and set out a plate of fruit. Cassander ran his fingers across his lyre. "Let's drink and sing stories till dawn."

***

At Perdiccas' behest, fully armed soldiers from his unit slipped out of the tent where they had waited for several hours. Running to the southern end of the double palisade, they started battering it. After the first attack, they broke through.

***

Hephaestion was at the entrance to the royal tent. As usual, Alexander was reading before bed. He looked up from his scroll. "I wondered where you were."

"We have a problem, Alex."

“What’s the matter?”

“It’s Perdiccas, cousin.”

“What about him?”

“Some of his men attacked the southern palisade. They’re already through.”

Alexander was on his feet. “Throw the army at the enclosure!”

Hephaestion sent messengers to the generals and senior staff. The king ordered his armour. Throwing it over him, he called for Bucephalus. Choosing a spear and shield, he went out into the night.

Galloping to the southern enclosure, Alexander saw it was broken in one place. Confusion reigned. Men from both sides hacked and screamed at each other. Neither gave way.

Parmenion and Philotas threw their men behind Perdiccas’ skirmishers. The regiments of Leonnatus and Cassander focused on destroying more of the wooden palisade.

Hephaestion galloped up to Alexander, who was in position, but not moving. “Are you going to lead us in, cousin?”

“I must command the main attack.”

Tugging at Bucephalus’ reins, Alexander held him in position. Thebans poured out of the gates of Cadmei to face their enemy. Alexander launched a stinging advance which drove them back.

However, with their training in the gymnasium, the Thebans were fitter than the Macedonians. Combined with their desire to protect their families, they fought hard.

Several hours passed. Alexander replaced his exhausted troops at the palisade with fresh men. Meanwhile, the body count at the main entrance of the Electra Gate was mounting. Macedonians surged forward. Scrambling to get inside their city walls, Theban soldiers were cut down. The gate began to close, but stopped due to the body count.

Cassander was the first to see it. “They haven’t closed the gate, Leo.”

“What?”

"There're too many bodies choking the entrance. Tell Alexander the main gate of Thebes is open!"

Leonnatus galloped away. A crunch and cracking at the palisade signalled the end of the Theban defence. Perdiccas' men were inside the city. Bounding off the walls and into the streets, they started fighting civilians. Seeing his chance, Cassander and his bodyguards started to head in the direction of Perdiccas' units.

Suddenly, Alexander was confronted by a sweating Leonnatus. His arms, gashed by surface nicks, bled profusely. Bucephalus whinnied and reared up.

"The Electra Gate is open!" Leonnatus gasped.

Ptolemy rode up.

"Perdiccas is inside," he announced.

Pulling Bucephalus downwards, Alexander whipped out his sword. It flashed in the torchlight, which made it visible to the enemy on the battlements above.

"Advance!"

Hearing their king's voice, the Macedonian army pushed forward. News of Perdiccas' entry spread to the front. Soon, the Macedonian and Theban infantrymen were aware of the soldiers inside the city. Pandemonium reigned.

Blocked by soldiers, Cassander's bodyguards were unable to make a way for their master to reach the palisade. Giving up trying to move forward, the Argead lord settled back on his horse to watch the carnage.

He quickly discovered a source of amusement in the Theban cavalry. Disentangling itself from the walls, against which both men and beasts had been pushed, the entire unit fled into the night. Roaring with delight, Cassander slapped his stocky thighs.

The ominous tones of Seleucus were unmistakable. "Something amusing you at this dire moment, Lord Cassander?"

"It's like a play – not that you would know."

"Do you think me uncultured?"

"I think you will be emperor of a new world one day –
one in which we will take lessons from you." An easing of the troops
gave Cassander his opportunity. "Now, if you don't mind, I have a
city to plunder."

Leaving Seleucus to ponder his words, Cassander headed for
the broken palisade.

***

In the citadel, screams of men, women, and children filled the
air. Hours rolled by. Hephaestion galloped up to Alexander. "Shall I
tell them to stop?"

"What for?"

"Thebes is yours."

"It must be destroyed."

Hephaestion paused. "Your directions were to negotiate peace
with Greece before the invasion of Persia. Tonight was unexpected."

"Are you defying me?"

"I want to be clear about your instructions before re-
laying them to others."

"Thebes betrayed me. Its people revolted against Macedonia, causing me to interrupt my plans for Persia. I had to take an
entire army at unprecedented speed down the length of Greece. Did
they accept my terms? They asked for me to be handed over to them!"

"I understand, cousin."

"My father razed Olynthus to the ground, and my rea-
sons far outweigh his."

Hephaestion swallowed. "Am I to understand Thebes is to
be … razed?"

"I want no trace of the city by morning."

"And its citizens?"

"Men killed. Women and children sold into slavery.
Make an exception for the family of the poet, Pindar."

341

Unceasing wailing from Cassander's tent was heard across the camp. Household staff were at a standstill.

"Polymarchus, tell your mother to pipe down. If Alexander hears, I shall be executed."

"I thought he was only going to punch you in the nose, Master."

"On a good day," grumbled Cassander. "This isn't one of them. Now, for Zeus' sakes, if you don't want us all to die, gag your mother."

"What a solution! I'd hate to be the woman who birthed you."

"Don't be rude."

"Why don't you comfort my poor mother?"

"How?"

The boy took a linen handkerchief from inside his robe and stuffed it into Cassander's hand. "Console her. Dry her eyes. Pat her."

"Pat her? What do you think your mother is – a puppy?"

The boy pushed Cassander through the heavy curtain, which divided his quarters from Helen's accommodation. "In you go!"

"Excuse me, dear lady," said Cassander, "I heard distress –"

"I can't believe it! The most ancient of cities. The home of the great poet, Pindar!"

Overcome, Helen shook her head. She picked up a coverlet into which she had been crying. Stifled sobs filled the air. Taking a deep breath, Cassander assumed his most genial expression and walked up to his distraught housekeeper.

Bending down, he patted her on the shoulder. "There, there, wipe your eyes. The poet's house is fine. Alexander's orders. I know you don't think much of me, but I saved a hundred women and children."

Taking Polymarchus' handkerchief, Cassander placed it in Helen's palm. She dried her eyes.

"You're wrong," she said, blowing her nose. "Without you, we'd all be dead."

"Think nothing of it."

"Is that all you can say?"

"I'm not very good at this."

Cassander looked about and noticed a lyre. Smaller than his own, it still had the same number of strings. Picking it up, he closed his eyes. Licking his lips, he trailed his skilled fingers across the strings. Very softly, he began to sing. The sobbing stopped, so he continued. Relieved that normality was returned, his household staff went about their business.

Cassander pondered as he played. Women and children sold into slavery was the cost of war, but surely some of the other officers could have paid money to help a fellow human being. Thebans were Greek, after all.

Heaving an audible sigh, he sang more passionately. It was a poem by Pindar.

***

PART IV

83.

Sharp winds blew up from the Hellespont. Thirty-five thousand troops were packed into transport ships. Alexander had said farewell to his tearful mother a week ago at Pella. The Balkans and Greece were pacified. There was no need to delay further conquests. Troy beckoned.

Now, he and Hephaestion waited for the gangplank to be lowered from the royal flagship.

"Poseidon favours your voyage, cousin."

Alexander's eyes shone. "Troy awaits."

The gangplank was lowered. After everyone had climbed aboard, he gave the signal to leave port. Leading his navy into the jade green sea, the king stood on deck, and gazed at the horizon.

Gusts of wind ruffled his thick blond hair which the sun playfully lit with red tints. The vessels blew across the waves, far away from Greece. He did not look back.

***

Cassander quickly found his sea legs. At lunchtime, he paid a visit to the galley and ordered a large repast off the menu. By contrast, Leonnatus vomited freely into any empty bucket. Ptolemy ensured he and his Silver Shields travelled together, while Perdiccas' men addressed themselves to the task of drinking the moment they left port.

After several days, Asia loomed into view. Standing on deck, Alexander and Hephaestion looked out over Homer's wine-dark sea.

The king's eyes sparkled. "Can you see it, Heph?"

Hephaestion squinted. "That brown rim on the horizon?"

"It's land."

"How do you know?"

"Our captain told me."

Above, sails billowed. Before them, the sea was choppy. They were due to make landfall at Troy.

Behind the king's vessel, dipping freshly baked bread into a cup of goat's milk, Ptolemy breakfasted on the deck of his own warship. His shield sat propped against the rail.

Lysander, the navy's seer, joined him. Dressed in a long blue robe, he fitted in with his nautical surroundings. "It's a calm day, General. Most auspicious for a landing."

Finishing his breakfast, Ptolemy wiped his lips on a linen napkin. "Is Troy at peace, or at war with us?"

"All the world bows to Alexander of Greece, descendant of Achilles."

Ptolemy placed his napkin on the table. "I asked a question."

"Troy is at peace with us, sire."

"Now, that is what I like to hear! Have some bread, my good man. It's fresh."

Voices floated across the wind. Opposite them, on another trireme, Perdiccas leaned across the railing. Painted red, the ship boasted blue embroidered sails. It flew a green flag with his family insignia.

Leonnatus joined him on deck. He had rowed over one morning because Perdiccas stocked his galley, as he did his home, with the finest ingredients. His ships did not have provisions so much as cuisine, and his men were adept at turning local sea produce into a stunning assortment of delicious meals. Squinting at the ship sailing alongside theirs, several yards away, Perdiccas nodded his head.

"What do you think Ptolemy is doing with our seer, Leo?"

"Making up his mind."

For his part, after chatting to Lysander, Ptolemy propped his shield against the ship's railing and watched the headland loom into view.

Meanwhile, on his flagship, Alexander was becoming more excited. "Do you see it, Hephaestion? It's Troy!"

"A dream come true, cousin."

The men watched in silence as they drew closer to land. Winds buffeted them as their ships bounced in choppy waters. Eventually, the headland was in full view. Squires placed Alexander's ceremonial armour over his head and shoulders, and handed him a spear.

The flagship slid into shallow water and ground to a halt. Leaping off the bow first, Alexander waded to shore. A Gorgon's head glared out from his shield. On his helmet, white plumes rustled in the wind. Raising his right arm, he threw his weapon.

"I claim Asia as my right, won by the spear!"

Iron struck the shore. His spear stuck fast, its haft humming against the windy shoreline. Ensuring he was several seconds behind Alexander, Hephaestion was next to leap into the chilly sea.

Ptolemy's ship weighed anchor near his king. Throwing on his cuirass, he put an arm through his shield strap, and jumped into the water. When he reached the shore, he discovered Lysander puffing alongside him in waterlogged robes.

"Get back to the ship, noble seer. I'm only taking soldiers."

Relieved, Lysander obeyed, and Ptolemy continued up the beach with his men. Clanking weapons filled the morning air as the Macedonian army climbed the hill of Troy to its temple.

Meanwhile, Trojan guards sent messengers to inform their priests of the armed visitors. At the news, women fled the halls. Servants dropped their water jars, and acolytes ran to the surrounding fields.

Trying to stay calm, the high priest put on his ceremonial robes and went out to greet the foreigners. Awaiting Alexander, his knees knocked involuntarily under his garments. Soldiers gathered below the temple, but none climbed the hill or stairs. Instead, they waited.

Finally, a small party of men approached. Of these, its shortest member ascended the marble staircase. When Alexander stood before the high priest, the man could scarcely believe his eyes. Gold haired, ruddy and diminutive, the King of Macedonia appeared to be only a boy.

Bowing more deeply than he intended, to cover his amazement, the priest intoned a formal greeting. "Welcome to Troy, King Alexander. Welcome to Troy, descendant of the great hero, Achilles."

"May we see inside? I shall only bring my closest friends."

It was then the priest noticed the royal pilgrim's eyes. They flamed with mercurial light, both bright and dangerous. And that hair! Blond locks glinted with red fire. Hastily bowing his head again, the man led the way into the temple's interior. Alexander beckoned his party to follow him before hurrying in after his host.

***

In the Great Hall, King Darius listened to his Persian satraps without interest.

"*Who* is Alexander?" he finally asked.

Several courtiers tittered. Memnon of Rhodes, a prominent Greek commander in the service of Persia, stepped forward.

"Your Highness, if you permit me to explain, he is the new King of Macedonia, the late Philip's son."

"I have heard of Macedonia," said Darius. "A backwater of Greece, filled with ruffians and brigands, is it not?"

"King Philip unified Greece. His son is currently in Asia, with a large army."

"Twenty thousand men?"

"Thereabouts, Your Majesty."

"Of what consequence is that when I can put a million men in the field?"

"Because he is here, Great One."

"My spies reported him at Troy a few days ago. It is a place of pilgrimage for Greeks, is it not?"

"That's true."

"In my empire, pilgrims are free to go wherever they wish."

"Alexander is related to Achilles. His visit is war propaganda. His aim is conquest, not pilgrimage. He has left Troy, and is now progressing through your lands in Asia."

"What do you suggest we do?"

"Macedonia has an army which fights all year round, Your Majesty. For this, its soldiers need food. My recommendation is that the earth be scorched. Alexander will have no alternative but to turn back."

"And what do my satraps think?" asked Darius.

"It is outrageous that we should burn wheat for a Greek scoundrel," said Bessus, one of Darius' kinsmen. "We need to vanquish him on the field of battle, like real men."

"You have your answer, Memnon. Anything else?"

"If it is the will of King Darius, then so be it. If it is not, hear me out."

"I'm listening."

"Alexander is unstoppable. No one expected his father to turn Macedonia's army into a matchless fighting force. But, having achieved his goal, Philip conquered Greece at the Battle of Chaeronea. It is said Alexander at sixteen, was in the forefront of the main attack. Since his father's death, he has pacified Illyria and Thrace, razed Thebes to the ground for insurgence, and is now in Asia. This is not a man to be trifled with. He is undefeated in battle and will take more land. Your Majesty cannot afford to lose. I say burn the crops. Any price is worth it to rid your empire of this pest. Otherwise –"

"Otherwise what? I rule the largest empire on earth. This snivelling boy is to be repelled, I agree. However, it will be on the field of battle. The satraps will meet him. Now, I must attend to important affairs of state."

***

84.

It was late afternoon at the River Granicus. Troy was a distant memory as the Macedonian army now faced its Persian enemy across the river.

Parmenion kicked the flanks of his stallion and galloped to Alexander. "The light is fading."

"You're right, General. We need to attack now."

"We should attack in the morning."

"Why?"

"The Persians will send scouts. Once they find out the size of our infantry, they will flee under the cover of darkness. Then, we can cross unopposed."

"Do you think me a coward, Parmenion?"

"It will be dark soon. We can't fight in a river at night."

"Great deeds are achieved in battle."

"You risk losing the very men you need to secure further victories in Asia."

"This is our first confrontation against Persia, Parmenion. There are five commanders across the water. Hesitation sends the wrong signal."

"But the sun is due to set."

"We attack now. I will lead. Go back to your troops and stay there."

***

Cassander watched the king in discussion with Parmenion. Nudging his horse's flanks, he ambled up to Leonnatus.

"I know you read lips, Leo. What are those two talking about?"

"The light is fading."

351

"And will continue to do so while they jabber on!"

"Parmenion wants to wait until tomorrow."

"Let me guess – Alex doesn't."

Seleucus joined them.

"We're deploying troops," he growled from under hooded brows.

As he spoke, squadrons of Macedonian cavalry moved from right to left.

"Philotas is in command," observed Leonnatus.

Cassander chewed his nails. "Seven squadrons. My, my, aren't we in Alexander's favour?"

Archers and Agrianians joined the cavalry. A portly man on a horse jogged up to stand next to them.

Cassander shaded his eyes. "Who is that?"

"Amyntas," said Leonnatus.

"Socrates," corrected Seleucus.

Leonnatus frowned. He pointed to a man wearing a helmet festooned with red plumes. "*That* is Amyntas son of Arrhabeus."

"You're both right," said Cassander quickly. "The fatty in charge of the eighth squadron is Socrates."

Seleucus regarded Cassander's paunch. "I wouldn't say he was fat."

"Amyntas is nearby, wearing a red-plumed helmet," continued Cassander, ignoring the slight. "See, Leo?"

"That's what I meant – the one with red plumes!"

Seleucus looked over his shoulder. "There's Ptolemy. I must talk with him."

As Seleucus made his way towards the Silver Shields, Cassander and Leonnatus continued to watch.

"Nicanor is commanding the hypaspists," said Leonnatus.

"I see that licking Alexander's boots got him six regiments of Foot Companions."

"He's one of Parmenion's sons. What do you expect?"

"This is a meritocracy, Leo."

"Whatever you say, *Lord* Cassander."

Cassander shrugged and pushed back his helmet. "It looks as though Alexander has put Parmenion in control of the Foot Companions. Good choice!"

"Now, you approve of Parmenion?"

"I've always approved of him."

"But not his sons."

"They haven't earned the right to be in command of all these troops. Parmenion, however, is a great general with common sense. For instance, he's right about the fact we should fight in the morning. The sun is going to set."

"Your veering disturbs me, Cassander. A man's sons are part of him. I can see it's easy to go from being favoured to being on your personal hit list in a trice."

A wicked grin split Cassander's cheeks. "Does it make you uncomfortable, Leo?" He pulled on his horse's reins. "I must see where I'm to be stationed. Mark you, if it's next to Parmenion's sons, they can expect to receive a sharp jab in their eyes from my lance!"

Wheeling his steed around, Cassander sped back to his men.

***

On the opposite side of the Granicus, several Persian commanders, including Rheomethres, Spithridates, Arsites, Arsames, and the Greek mercenary commander, Memnon, waited. They had seen Alexander's soldiers move into battle formation, which now loosely mirrored their own.

"One of Philip's tactics," Memnon commented to a senior officer.

In the distance, the sun caught an intricately designed breastplate.

"Aren't those Alexander's plumes, sir?"

Memnon started. "Send word to Arsames! If we are to kill Alexander, we need to move the front line to the left."

When he received the news, Arsames agreed to the plan, and sent word to Arsites.

The anxious commander rubbed his hands. "It's best to cut off the head. If we kill Alexander, Darius will spare our lives."

More messengers were relayed to the remaining commanders and satraps.

***

Alexander watched with Hephaestion as the Persian cavalry moved into position along the opposite stretch of the riverbank.

"I see Memnon is on the left, Hephaestion."

"With the commander, Arsames."

"Is Arsites in charge of the Paphlagonian horsemen?"

"He is."

"And the Hycarnian cavalry next – interesting."

"Spithridates leads them, cousin."

"I can't see the centre. Who is positioned there?"

"The report does not say."

Alexander viewed the Persian right wing. He noted that Rheomethres was in charge of two thousand cavalry. Approximately, the same number of Bactrian horsemen joined another thousand Median cavalry.

Suddenly, he gave a mirthless snort of laughter. "They're moving!"

"I can't see anything."

Alexander pointed. Noting the Macedonian king's position, the Persians were now reinforcing their left wing with more cavalry.

"Look at the Greek mercenaries, Hephaestion, behind the horses. Who is in charge?"

The latter flicked through his report. "Omares, cousin. He's Persian but leads twenty thousand Greek mercenaries."

Cleitus galloped up with several elite officers. "This is your first major engagement in Persia, King Alexander. I promised your father that I would personally protect you on campaign."

"Your sister my beloved nanny. Now, on this historic occasion, you wish to lay down your life for mine. I am fortunate to have such loyalty in one family. You may ride with me, Cleitus."

More officers gathered around their king. Alexander dispensed orders in rapid sentences. Distinguished generals relayed their commands down the ranks.

As the Persians arranged and rearranged their troops, Alexander changed his plans. Parmenion, Perdiccas, Craterus, Coenus and Meleager, scrambled to place their soldiers at various vantage points.

Hephaestion continued to check the strategy, and supply his king with answers when required.

"How many infantry on the Persian side, Heph?"

"Five thousand."

"And cavalry?"

"Twenty thousand. Do you want to change your position, Alex?"

"I'm staying on the right to hit their left wing. Despite reinforcements, their cavalry's in the front line."

"Is that wise, cousin?"

"Persians don't know how to charge on horseback. It's the perfect place for a frontal attack."

"You know best." Hephaestion closed his report.

***

Parmenion shaded his eyes. His officers waited with him. One of them pointed. "Sir, Persian divisions are moving to the right. They directly face our king."

The general shook his head. "Why that boy insists on dressing up like a peacock is beyond me. He'll get himself killed before dusk!"

"Shall I take a message to him, sir?"

Shouts in the distance pulled their eyes to their right. It was too late. Alexander was already heading a charge across the river with two thousand cavalry.

"Stay and keep the others in check," said Parmenion. "Those are my orders."

Reining in his horse, which had become skittish, the general kept still and held his ground. Meanwhile, leading a few companions with mounted skirmishers and light cavalry, Alexander galloped towards the riverbank. Cutting across at an oblique angle, he calculated avoiding meeting his enemy as he crossed the river.

Seeing their opportunity, Arsames and Memnon rapidly advanced down to the river. Showers of spears flew at the front line. Men fell, but other units who were ranged behind the first soldiers, prevented the Macedonians from crossing. Soon, the rest of the Persian commanders joined in the fray.

While the Achaemenid cavalry resisted the Macedonian advance, men became entangled in the river bed. Cleitus separated from Alexander. His horse slipped on smooth rocks. To save both himself and his steed, he immediately dismounted.

More Persian units broke from the main lines. Only Rheomethres stayed with the bulk of his army.

"This is suicide," Cleitus panted, pulling his horse's bridle up the slippery bank.

War cries deafened his ears. Blood spilled into the river. Shields above him guarded his back, as he simultaneously cursed and encouraged his horse. Like the other animals, it was falling down, slipping back, scraping its knees and whinnying in fear and pain. Finally, Cleitus sheathed his sword while he pulled his steed upright.

A gap appeared in the sky as the soldier nearest to him, fell. Cleitus let go of his horse and drew his sword. Slipping, he sat down heavily. Mud squelched between his toes and buttocks.

Persian cavalry, rumbling down to the river in heavy chariots, toppled into the water. All around, men were entangled in leather reins and wooden spokes. Horses, who could free themselves, tried to recover their balance and climb up the bank. Cleitus looked up, ready to fight. Nearby, a Persian fell heavily into the river, covering him with a tidal wave of water. Roaring with annoyance, the Macedonian officer scrambled up the bank on all fours.

A black horse and its rider were trying to get out of the river. An arrow shot into the air and ripped through the man's jugular. Clutching at the arrowhead in his neck, he gurgled blood as he fell back. Trampling his master's head into the mud, the terrified stallion found a foothold and made his way to the top of the bank.

"I hope you don't do that to me," Cleitus muttered to his horse, which was now on his knees, straining to move.

He pulled at its bit and they both pushed ahead, up the bank. The struggle paid off. Cleitus' horse successfully made it over the top. Righting himself on his long legs, the stallion galloped away, leaving his rider to slide back down the muddy slope. Swearing oaths under his breath, Cleitus grasped reed stalks to pull himself upright. Gritting his teeth, he used them as leverage, but they slipped through his fingers.

Suddenly, two strong hands slid under his armpits and dragged him up the bank. A few steps away, he saw an infantryman holding his now khaki-coloured horse by the bridle. Barely breathing thanks to his helpers, Cleitus mounted his steed. With a war cry, he charged the enemy.

***

Darius' son-in-law, Mithridates galloped towards Alexander's position. Emerging from the Granicus River to a squadron of enemy cavalry bearing down on him, Alexander immediately picked up his spear. It promptly snapped.

Turning to a bodyguard, he stretched out one hand. "Quick, give me your spear!"

As the man obeyed, Cleitus suddenly broke through the chaos. Astride his mud-splattered horse, he narrowly missed a Persian chariot crashing into the river.

Mithridates was now a few metres in front of Alexander, who promptly punched his new spear into the man's eye. Screaming, the Persian fell off the back of his horse and onto a pile of corpses.

Seeing his fellow countryman fall, Rhoesaces, a Persian satrap commander, galloped to his aid. With a mighty blow, he struck Alexander on the head. A resounding crack was followed by part of a plume falling to the ground. The king reeled as half his helmet disintegrated. Seizing his opportunity for glory, the Persian commander, Spithridates, closed in.

Cleitus urged his horse towards his embattled sovereign. Oblivious to the danger behind him, Alexander ran Rhoesaces through with his spear.

Behind the Macedonian king, Spithridates lifted his arm to despatch the death blow. Tearing past at full gallop, Cleitus neatly lopped off the Persian's arm at the shoulder. Howling with pain, the man fell out of his saddle.

Reining in his horse, Cleitus stayed close to Alexander. He noticed several of the king's bodyguards were separated from their master. Some were not present. No doubt they had fallen to the Persians, or were drowned in the river.

***

With the death of Spithridates, the Persian units started to retreat. At the other end of the army, Parmenion observed panic taking hold of the enemy ranks. He watched as thousands of men, with chariots and horses, turn tail and flee the Granicus River. Only the Greek mercenaries were left. They had done nothing during the conflict, perhaps waiting for an opportunity which never presented itself.

Cassander was covered in cuts. Leonnatus' valet patched up his master. At the back of the field, Alexander was still encased in a crust of blood. Exhausted, he accepted a skin of water brought by a servant. Taking a towel embroidered with the royal insignia of Pella, he mopped his brow. Jogging his head towards an officer, he gave his orders.

"My divisions are to rest," he said.

"Which ones, sire?"

"Those I took across the river. The Greek mercenaries can be crushed by the infantry and cavalry from both sides. Wait for my order."

At that moment, one of the mercenaries ran from the centre of the field towards Alexander.

Cassander turned to Leonnatus. "This should be interesting."

"Your Majesty, King Alexander," the man said, "I am Diomedes."

"That's a Greek name. What do you want?"

"On behalf of the Greek divisions, I appeal to your clemency."

"You side with Persia and expect my mercy?"

"We did not fight you today, great Alexander."

"You were hired by King Darius, were you not?"

"W-we are G-Greek, Y-Your Majesty and are c-confident of your mercy. The d-divisions s-surrender to you, King Alexander."

"You lazy pack of traitors stood by while I was in mortal danger! There is no mercy for paid collaborators. Get out of my sight before I cut you down myself!"

Cassander howled with laughter, as the terrified messenger scurried back to his lines. Leonnatus' face showed the same scorn as that of Alexander.

Slowly and deliberately, the Macedonian infantry moved in with their long spears. Unable to escape, and completely surrounded, the Greek mercenaries were slaughtered to the man.

***

359

85.

News of the Granicus battle spread. Towns surrendered without a fight. Sardis capitulated first, then Ephesus. The latter was a place of culture and learning. Alexander instantly felt comfortable there and installed his army of occupation within its walls.

After ensuring his men were housed, he made his way to his own quarters. When the Macedonian king entered them, he was surprised. Marble floors with Persian carpets, and couches inlaid with gold and silk cushions denoted a Persian influence on this, most Greek of towns.

Hephaestion joined him. "That was another easy victory, cousin."

"We still have to secure these lands."

A wine steward poured the men a local vintage. They sipped their drinks without waiting for the taster. Guards admitted Parmenion and a nobleman by the name of Alcimachus. A close friend of the late King Philip, he was still employed by Alexander.

"Congratulations on a great victory, Your Majesty," he said.

Hephaestion smiled into his goblet and turned away.

"It was a good sign we have been welcomed to Ephesus," Parmenion agreed.

"Indeed," Alexander said pleasantly. "I am appointing you each a contingent of several thousand troops."

The senior general's brow wrinkled. "Are we fighting, sire?"

"I am sending you both out to ensure that Lydia, Aeolis and Ionia capitulate."

It was Alcimachus' turn to furrow his brow. "Are we journeying together?"

"If you like," Alexander replied. "But, I want Parmenion to branch out to the east, which includes Sardis. You are to go to the west, towards Teos and Cissus."

Alcimachus bowed his head. "We are honoured."

Parmenion shot him a sharp look from under bushy brows. Alexander picked up a handful of figs from a bowl.

"You are most welcome," he said, chewing nonchalantly, "and both have leave to go."

Bowing, the men departed. The oak door clicked shut.

"You got them out of the way quickly, Alex."

"It's important to keep our good friends busy."

"I could arrange for all of your father's men to be despatched to the far corners of your kingdom. Even the Silver Shields."

"We need the Silver Shields. They're our best fighters."

Alexander threw a fig into the air and caught it neatly between his teeth.

***

After dinner, Hephaestion excused himself to go to his office. There, he studied the latest spy reports and caught up with administration work.

Once he was alone, the Macedonian king settled down to read the *Iliad*. Annotated by Aristotle, it was his favourite copy of the book and he read into the night. At around the tenth hour, a guard at his door admitted Hephaestion.

Alexander put down his scroll. "Ah, what a welcome surprise. I was just thinking about you."

"I have good news, cousin."

Hephaestion handed Alexander a piece of parchment, which the latter scanned. "The Governor of Miletus, Hegistratus surrenders the city? This *is* good news."

"I thought you would be pleased." Hephaestion turned to leave.

"Stay."

"But you're reading."

"The *Iliad*. We both know it by heart."

"It's Aristotle's copy. You'll be learning from our teacher's notes."

Hephaestion bowed slightly and left. Despite their closeness, the man was always a model of decorum. Pleased, Alexander settled back to read. And realised he did not wish to be disturbed.

***

The court was filled with military commanders and well-known men of Ephesus. Warriors rubbed shoulders with philosophers. Teachers sat next to courtiers and shopkeepers.

Alexander entered the hall at the morning's ninth hour. His hair was washed and styled, his robes immaculate. A hush fell over the gathering.

"I wish to come straight to the point," he said. "Miletus has surrendered."

Immediately, the sound of whispering, followed by hearty cheers from the Macedonians, reverberated through the columned hall.

Cassander picked his nose. Leonnatus pulled a face. "Stop it! That's disgusting."

"I am disgusted."

"Why? Miletus has just surrendered. We have one less battle to fight."

"How am I to get gold without war?"

"We'll be given land."

"That's all I need – another house in the country."

Cassander resumed excavating the interior of his nasal passages. Leonnatus shook his head and returned his gaze to the front.

Alexander motioned the chancellor, who banged his staff several times on the marble floor.

When there was silence, the king spoke. "Parmenion and Alcimachus will administer my seal in the provinces. Any form of dictatorship is to be removed. Democracies are to be installed. Let the customs of these countries remain." There was a pause for effect. "I am also ordering the cancellation of all taxes in these lands, which includes those in Ephesus."

Cheering followed his announcement. Rising, Alexander permitted himself the smile of a benefactor. Afterwards, he swiftly vacated the hall.

***

86.

It was nearly the evening's ninth hour. Sentries clanked their weapons to show their alertness. Hearing footsteps, Alexander glanced at the water clock in his study. Presently, Hephaestion was admitted into the chamber, and stood before him.

"More good news, Heph?"

"I'm afraid not. Darius has mobilised his navy. There have been sightings in Rhodes."

"We also have ships."

"Not this many. Governor Hegistratus changed his mind. Now, he does not want to surrender Miletus."

"We need to go there, before that city becomes a fortress."

"I can send word to Admiral Nearchus if you wish. The navy can follow us. We'll need them to blockade the Persian ships."

"We need to recall Parmenion and Alcimachus."

"Now? It's the middle of the night."

"Send riders to relay the message. I need those two at Miletus. We move out at dawn."

Knowing it was useless to argue, Hephaestion departed the royal chamber for his office. There, he spent several hours ensuring all the army's senior personnel had their men ready to march in a few hours.

***

It was a cold morning. Leonnatus blew on his hands. Alexander had not yet arrived, and the army was waiting. He sent his valet to fetch his gloves, which he had forgotten in his haste to join the soldiers on parade.

Cassander was bundled up snugly in the appropriate gear required for a mountain march. Leonnatus strolled over to him.

"You look well prepared, Cassie."

"By Zeus, it's freezing! My nether regions are blocks of ice. I shall never beget children."

"You'll thaw. The sun hasn't come up, yet."

Leonnatus' valet ran up and handed him his fleece-lined leather gloves. Seleucus joined the pair.

"Who in Ares' name decided to march?" he growled.

"If you have to ask, you're sillier than you look," Cassander snickered.

"I shall forgive your rudeness, as one day King Alexander will crucify you."

"Not a chance, Sel! I shall outlive that tyrant of Greece."

Leonnatus rolled his eyes. He turned to Seleucus. "I was half asleep this morning when I came out here to stand on parade. I even forgot to dress properly. My valet just brought my gloves."

"I nearly beheaded the servant who woke me," Seleucus said, "until I realised Hephaestion was responsible."

"He woke everyone up in the city," Leonnatus chuckled.

Cassander patted his horse. "I'm surprised he wasn't in bed with our king."

Leonnatus and Seleucus glared at their friend.

"You really are most peculiar," said Seleucus. "Why make fun of Alexander, when you don't have a partner, yourself?"

"I prefer women."

"But they can't be soulmates."

Leonnatus laughed. "We've been trying to tell him that since childhood!"

"And it falls on deaf ears," said Cassander. "You see Sel, women fill my soul with poetic longing."

"That's all very well, but it's not the same thing as being soulmates," the irritated general objected. "Women are different from us."

Cassander closed his eyes and raised one arm, as if about to perform a song. "*For in other ways a woman is full of fear, defenseless, dreads the sight of cold steel –*"

Leonnatus turned to Seleucus. "He's quoting Euripides."

"I know. It's from his great play, *Medea*. It continues: *– but, when once she is wronged in the matter of love, no other soul can hold so many thoughts of blood.*"

With a mocking smile, Cassander applauded. "You know your poets, Sel! Which proves my point that men are fine for banter, and a wine-soaked sing-along. However, my sensitive soul craves unification with the right woman."

Seleucus' eyes widened. "You want to marry Medea? You must be a very lonely man. Medea was a murderess. She proved the fact that women do not have thoughts, only base passions. And to further your education, dear Cassie, Euripides was a dramatist, not a poet."

A trumpet blare shattered their eardrums as it announced the arrival of the Macedonian monarch. The Young Companions dispersed to their units.

Alexander noticed that only Cassander was positioned at the head of his division. He was singing, it was true, but the Macedonian king was more annoyed at the delay of the others. Waiting for several minutes while everyone organised themselves, he finally signalled his heralds, who sounded their trumpets to move out.

It was time to march on Miletus.

***

87.

Wave after wave of troops arrived at the citadel. Tents were pitched, and fires lit. Meat was spitted, and water boiled for bathing.

In the chilly dawn, Cassander's nose detected the sea nearby. Still on his horse, he closed his eyes and filled his lungs with salt laden air.

Leonnatus ambled up to him on his stallion. "Thinking of home?"

"Always." Cassander inclined his head. "Across the water, I perceive the isle of Lade."

"It's sixty stadia to Lade. If you can see that far, you must be a greater god than Alexander."

"Bah! Alexander's no god. I didn't see it, either. I perceive it. And all because I read Hephaestion's intelligence report this morning. Our navy is in Lade, and there isn't a Persian ship in sight."

"That *is* wonderful news."

"Isn't it? It would be good if you kept up with current events, Leo. One day you'll be caught out. Might find yourself headless and alone."

Kicking his steed in the flanks, Cassander trotted off to join his troops, who were awaiting further instructions from high command. His friend gritted his teeth.

"Is he irritating you?" asked a voice behind Leonnatus.

"I didn't see you there, Ptolemy. How are the Silver Shields? All about fifty years young, aren't they? Don't see them in battle much these days."

Ptolemy winced at Leonnatus' jibe, but laughed heartily. "It's true, they are old."

Seleucus rode up to them. "Your troops were here before us, Ptolemy."

"They cooked breakfast. Join us for lamb on the spit. What about you, Leo?"

"I prefer a Nestor's Cup first thing in the morning," Leonnatus sniffed.

"Suit yourself."

Waving a cheery salute, Ptolemy galloped away. Seleucus reflected for a moment before addressing Leonnatus.

"Don't be angry with Cassander. He's your friend."

"I'm not angry."

"I saw your expression from afar as he left you. Come with us and eat. Alexander still has to find out whether Hegistratus wants to concede the city to him or not. If we have to fight, we'll need a full stomach."

"Full stomachs make for sleep. I'll pass."

"Fair enough." Seleucus galloped away to join Ptolemy.

Perdiccas drew up, his horse snorting steam in the cold. "I wouldn't brush Seleucus off, if I were you, Leo."

"Why not? Unlike Ptolemy, I need nothing from him."

Perdiccas noticed an exhausted Parmenion approach Alexander. Bidding a hasty farewell to Leonnatus, he cantered over in time to hear the senior general's report.

"Miletus has surrendered, my sovereign."

"Intelligence reports say otherwise, Parmenion."

"My men need rest. We marched to Ephesus before we came here."

"Our navy is at Lade, General. We need to secure the forts along the coast."

"When do we leave?"

"Now."

A herald sounded a trumpet. Everyone rushed to pack. Alexander's troops were on the march again.

***

In two days the Macedonians secured the shore settlements opposite Lade. Townspeople greeted Alexander's army with food and water. His men secured the strategic points on the island itself, where the navy was stationed. The entire region now had outposts of Macedonian cavalry stationed along its shores.

At the end of the second day, Leonnatus rode over to Cassander. The men dismounted and sat on a grassy bank overlooking the water.

"You were right, Cassie. Our fleet arrived here before the Persian navy."

"You mean Hephaestion was right. Our head of intelligence is the most terrifying snoop. I wouldn't be surprised if we all wind up on the rack one day because of his due diligence."

Leonnatus decided to change the subject. "The townspeople are friendly, don't you think?"

"Friendship is fickle, Leo."

"I hope you aren't inferring something about our bond."

"We are not friends, only Alexander's Young Companions, united in our lust for war, women and gold."

Leonnatus picked up a stone and threw it in the water. "Whatever you say, Cassie."

"I do say, Leo. Most of us will end up killing our enemies, or one another."

"Hephaestion and Alexander wouldn't do that to each other."

"That's different. They're related, and everyone knows they're lovers."

"As is appropriate in Macedonia and Greece. I really do wonder about you, Cassie. It's good to have close friends. You should think about it."

"I hope you're not propositioning me, Leo."

"I've never fancied you. But you could talk to Seleucus."

"Zeus help us all! That man insulted me. I hope he didn't send you here as his pimp."

Cassander reached for his wineskin. About to raise it to his lips, he changed his mind and handed it to Leonnatus. They watched the sun set over the island behind their ships moored to the shore.

"You know what," said Cassander at last. "There doesn't seem to be room on Lade for anything but our fleet!"

***

88.

On the deck of his warship, the Persian admiral, Artaphernes saw land looming up ahead. Several vessels sailed alongside him. Another four hundred, were behind.

Gulls flew high above the sea, squawking in raucous unison. As Lade became more visible, the admiral took stock of the port. His chief officer waited for orders. Instead of issuing them, Artaphernes threw up his hands.

"We can't dock!" he exclaimed.

"We could ram the Greek ships, sir."

"They'd set fire to us."

"What do you propose?"

"We need to go to the mainland. To Mount Mycale, now."

***

Munching his cheese and coriander loaf, an archer looked over the ramparts of Miletus and choked. Another slapped his back.

"What's the matter, Erastus?"

"They've returned, Thales," gasped the first, looking for water with which to chase down his snack.

"Who?"

"The Macedonians – with Alexander."

Thales grasped his spear and looked over the ramparts. Meanwhile, Erastus took a goatskin of water and gulped the contents. The bread slipped down his throat and into his stomach. He felt better.

"You're right. We need to tell the others."

Soon, every guard and soldier stationed on the ramparts, was watching the arrival of the Greeks. Messengers were sent with the news to the Miletus governor, Hegistratus.

***

A senior courtier, Glaocippus, tugged his beard.

"I don't understand you, Hegistratus," he said. "I thought you surrendered to King Alexander."

"I changed my mind," the governor replied. "The Persian navy outnumbers his fleet three to one. It's better if we stay in Darius' camp. His protection means we can all live safely in Miletus."

"Alexander is back from Lade. Do you think we're safe now?"

"We will parley. I have sent that Macedonian boy a clever message. Watch great diplomacy at work, and learn!"

***

A messenger in fine robes, skilled in the art of speech, talked in Alexander's presence for some time.

"Get to the point, man," Seleucus growled.

Cassander snickered. Leonnatus tried to look impassive. Perdiccas' eyes were following a Greek serving girl. He reflected he had not seen a comely lass in some time. Hephaestion was listening carefully, as was Alexander.

"Your Majesty is most welcome to stay here in Miletus," the messenger concluded. "In fact, Governor Hegistratus welcomes you and your men."

Cassander burst out laughing. Hephaestion glanced at his cousin, whose face was like thunder.

"Under what star do you think we might be welcome?" Alexander asked, trying to control his voice.

"It is an open city, Your Highness, for both Greeks and Persians."

The king spoke in a calm tone. "I have a message for your governor."

"We welcome it."

"Prepare for a fight."

***

89.

The army was ready. Cassander was beside himself. Perched on his horse, he slapped his thighs as he recounted the messenger's visit. Leonnatus moved away at the third retelling of the episode.

Perdiccas heaved a deep sigh, looked to the heavens and made his appeal to all the gods on Mount Olympus to gag the storyteller. Laughing uproariously, Ptolemy nevertheless, took the earliest opportunity to return to his command of the Silver Shields.

With Parmenion on his left, and Hephaestion on his right, Alexander sat astride Bucephalus. They were all stationed behind infantry lines. Hephaestion's steed munched the grass underfoot. All was silent on the field, except for the sound of Cassander's mirth.

Irritated, Alexander turned to his cousin. "What is that idiot laughing about?"

"The messenger."

"He should be serious. We're about to engage the enemy."

"I don't think there's much anyone can do about Cassie's sense of humour."

"Mark my words, Hephaestion, I swear by my father Zeus I am going to put that man's head into a wall. He needs some sense knocked into it."

Alexander's heralds sounded their trumpets as his soldiers moved across the plain. From the bay, where Persian ships were moored, sailors could see the troops. Even Alexander's plumes were visible. Unable to do anything, the men on the vessels watched in silence.

Slowly, the Macedonian infantry advanced. High on the walls, morning rays of sunlight struck the men on the parapets.

An aggrieved guard shaded his eyes. "Blast!"

"What's the matter, Erastus?"

"The sun's in my eyes, Thales."

"Why do you think Alexander chose the morning to attack?"

A senior officer was pacing backwards and forwards. "If you have hats and visors, pull them down! Hold your positions. Wait for my signal."

"What if you're wearing a jolly helmet with no visor?" Erastus grumbled.

"Hush!" Thales counselled. "You don't want a telling off."

"I want to live. What if an enemy arrow takes me out?"

Adjusting their headgear as best they could, the men waited until Alexander's infantry was within range. When it was time, the senior officer on the ramparts gave the order.

"Now!"

At his command, a barrage of arrows and missiles flew at the enemy foot soldiers. Erastus crouched down.

"Are those javelin throwers behind us?" he asked. "I swear the idiot behind me nearly took off my ear."

From the plain below, Macedonians launched catapults and missiles.

"In Zeus' name, shoot!" his friend yelled.

"They're not dying," Erastus complained.

"That's because they're not looking up."

Overhearing his men, the senior officer peeked out from behind the protection of a buttress to see for himself. Keeping their shields locked over their heads, Alexander's men attacked the walls, rather than aiming at the city's defenders above them. This meant there was no need to bend their heads back, which would have exposed their throats and bodies. As a result, there were no casualties for the Macedonian king.

Undaunted, the senior officer on the city ramparts did not change his commands.

"Keep up the barrage," he ordered.

Below, the Macedonian army moved in battering rams. Rumbling across the plain, the monstrous engines of destruction trundled up to the walls. Due to covers of hides and bronze, all the men operating the rams stayed alive. Battering stonework and plaster, the machines inflicted damage on the fort, already weakened by the first assault.

Meanwhile, with nothing to do, the Macedonian generals looked on. Next to Perdiccas, Seleucus stood watching. Thoughtfully, he stroked one cheek. A Thracian lad of about fourteen had given him a close shave that morning. Wary of enemies tugging at his soldiers' beards, Alexander's orders were that they be clean-shaven.

After viewing the battle for some time from under heavy-lidded eyes, Seleucus, shook his head. "We're not getting far."

"The other side has the advantage," Perdiccas replied. "Missiles from a height are hard to avoid."

As the men spoke, more Macedonian infantry moved behind one of their battering rams to widen a breach in the walls.

Atop them, Erastus made his feelings clear. "Dear Baal, the dust is choking me!"

"Since when do you worship foreign gods?"

"Since our ones fled the scene, Thales. I have plaster in my lungs, and our walls are crumbling."

Meanwhile, on the plain below, Alexander kicked Bucephalus' flanks lightly with his heels. The siege engines were working, and he wanted to lead his victorious army into the city when its walls were breached. Parmenion and Cleitus followed.

Seizing the opportunity, Cassander rallied his soldiers: "Follow me, men. Fame and booty await!"

Hearing a commotion behind him, Alexander jerked his head about. "What's that buffoon doing now, Hephaestion?"

"Whipping up the fighting spirit. Say what you like about Cassie, he knows how to lead."

Seleucus rode up.

"We'll sup well tonight, Alexander," he said. "The castle walls are breached."

The king did not answer. He pushed back his helmet and squinted in the morning sun. Atop his gigantic horse, Alexander was able to see over most of his troops. Houses within the city peeked through apertures in the walls. But, while glimpses of the city were enticing, missiles rained down on his men from the ramparts.

Alexander beckoned to an officer. "Send word to Admiral Nearchus. I want our fleet to blockade the harbour at the back of the city. I don't want anyone getting away once we enter."

The man hurried off to relay the order to the admiral. Hephaestion jogged up to his cousin on horseback. "It might be a good idea to send another man in an hour, in case he doesn't survive."

"I can't keep sending messengers. The Persians can see us from the bay."

Throngs of infantry crowded round. Tiny breaches in the stone battlements widened. After several hours, the army penetrated the walls.

On the parapets, Erastus put down his bow. "I've run out of arrows, Thales."

"A new batch is coming."

Their senior officer loomed above them. "What are you two doing?"

"We have no arrows, sir," Erastus explained.

"There are stones next to you. What are you waiting for? Throw them!"

"We're archers, sir."

"THROW!"

***

<h1 align="center">90.</h1>

Fleet Admiral, Nearchus stood on the deck of his trireme, eating breakfast. He noticed a small boat heading for his vessel. The man rowing wore the armour of a Macedonian cavalryman.

Nearchus' bodyguards and several sailors approached the side of the ship at which the boat was aimed. Finishing his bread and cheese, the admiral downed a pomegranate juice. Brushing crumbs off his chiton, he gestured to his guards.

"It's a royal messenger. Bring him aboard."

Eventually, the man reached the side of the vessel. Sailors bent down and pulled him up onto the deck.

"Mighty Admiral, I have word from King Alexander," panted the visitor.

"Catch your breath. Have a drink."

Nearchus nodded in the direction of a waterskin. One of the sailors picked it up, unplugged the stopper, and handed it to the messenger.

He waved it away. "There's no time, sir. His Majesty commands the Meletian harbour to be blockaded."

"Two tranches lie at the rear end of the harbour," said Nearchus. "I gather we are to block the rear?"

"The Persian navy are obstructing the front, on the right of Alexander's army."

"Thought as much. Great numbers, and no strategy, those Persians."

Nearchus appointed an officer to show the messenger to a room where he could rest. Then, he relayed the royal order across the fleet. The navy split into two groups and set sail for the Meletian harbour.

Once there, the ships quickly docked in two harbours on the opposite side of Alexander's attacking army. Effectively cutting off escape routes, they waited for their king to enter the city.

***

Thales hung over the parapet. "Zeus above, Erastus! The Macedonians have broken in, and unlatched the gate from this side. We need to leave."

"But our position is on the ramparts."

"Do you want to die?"

"Our senior officer told us to hold."

Thales grasped his friend's upper arm and swung him around. Before them lay the corpse of their senior officer. Head upturned, he wore a permanent expression of surprise. From one temple, a trickle of blood ran down to his shoulder.

"I know a shortcut to the harbour," said Thales as he pushed Erastus forward.

Below, they heard the cries of men. Metal clashed on metal as invaders fought with the inhabitants of the garrisoned citadel. Erastus pointed.

"Aren't those Greek sails?" he asked.

"There is a place where enemy triremes are not parked. Come on!"

Pushing Erastus into mid-air, Thales jumped after him.

***

Rushing through the main gate, Alexander's men stormed the garrison. Seizing the men who had spent all morning hurling missiles at them, they butchered them on the spot.

Meanwhile, landing on a thatched roof, Erastus and Thales rolled off it quickly. Houses were burning. Torches hurtled through the air, causing hundreds of blazes.

378

Most of Alexander's troops concentrated their pent-up fury on enemy soldiers. Civilians, who lived close to the city gate, ran for their lives. Any who got in the way of the angry invaders were cut down.

Thales wrapped his officer's cape round his face to block out smoke. He encouraged his friend to do the same. They headed down a winding maze of streets. Ghastly screams of women and children rang in their ears.

The men finally found an empty doorway. In front of it, stood a pottery jar filled with water. Picking up an alabaster cup next to it, they took turns quenching their thirst. It was their first drink since dawn.

"The enemy is massacring everyone," said Erastus. "So much for the mercy of Alexander."

"He kills those who side with the Persians. A war of revenge, they call it."

Taking off his cape, Thales dipped the cup into the water and poured it over the fabric. Afterwards, Erastus did the same. Covering their faces with the cool cloth, they continued on their way.

After several more streets, it grew quiet. No one was about. Thales opened the door of a house. It was empty, and the men walked through, leaving by the back door. Erastus was surprised to see a group of Greek mercenaries piling into skiffs.

His friend beckoned him down the steps. "Some of us made this our escape plan. Get into a boat."

Erastus did not wait to be told twice. He scrambled into the first one in front of him. Thales followed and cast off.

***

All around, the city glowed red. The massacre was complete. Alexander gave orders to end the fighting, and retired to the city's main residence to rest.

In their living room, Hephaestion unwound the leather straps of his blood-caked sandals. "There is a rumour the surviving inhabitants fled to an island offshore."

"Which one?"

"It has no name, but it's rocky."

Taking a goblet of wine from a timid attendant, Hephaestion reflected that a drink had never tasted so good.

"We should attack at once."

"It's late, Alex. Our spies report about three hundred mercenaries on the island. They're not going anywhere."

Accepting more wine from the attendant, Hephaestion put it on a table next to him. He fixed Alexander with a bemused expression.

"Why are you looking at me like that, Heph?"

"Are you going to kill them?"

"Do you have to ask?"

"It might be better if you showed mercy. They are our countrymen."

"They sided with Persia. They're *paid*."

"The news of your mercy will travel. The Persians are going to lose. We need fighting men for the army. Why not enlist the best? They are paid for a reason."

Alexander pondered. "Very well, they can have my mercy, and the civilians, too."

***

91.

After the conquest of Miletus, the Persians sent a few ships to lure the Macedonians out to sea. Greek triremes routed them. Rather than continue trying, the Persians headed for Halicarnassus.

Hephaestion was busy in his administrative role. For Alexander's most trusted general, there was no let up. While the others feasted, or played board games, and Cassander became a virtuoso on his lyre, Hephaestion organised the affairs of a burgeoning kingdom, which threatened to one day become an empire.

Satraps were replaced. Boards of trusted men were appointed to collect wealth. There were always conditions. Some, Hephaestion expected, while others were those Alexander's unpredictable nature devised.

"They can stop paying taxes to Persia, Heph, but only on condition they join the League of Corinth. In that way we will ensure monetary support."

"What about religion?"

"They have their own gods."

"And customs?"

"They can keep their own."

"Isn't our goal to spread Greek culture?"

"We're Macedonian."

"I only mention it because it is the goal stressed in your speeches."

"Kings always make speeches."

"Halicarnassus is next on your schedule. When do we leave?"

"After we visit the city of Alinda in Caria. I will meet with Ada."

"Orontobates is the satrap of Caria."

"I'm well aware of the satrap's name."

"But Ada is of no value, cousin. She's a woman in exile."

"I shall make her Queen of Caria."

***

Ten days after Alexander's conversation with Hephaestion, they reached Alinda. On arrival, the city's cedar gates swung open. An envoy made his way towards the army.

Pulling on his horse's reins, Cassander turned to Leonnatus with whom he was riding. "I wonder what he's up to."

"To negotiate. It's not a huge fort, Cassie. I heard that it is run by a woman."

"Let's hope she's beautiful."

The envoy bowed before Alexander. "Queen Ada surrenders her city and bids you and your men welcome."

Alexander immediately summoned his high command. "We are to enter the city with respect. No pillaging. If I hear of one soldier misbehaving, his entire squadron will be punished."

Once inside the fort, Alexander dismissed his generals, and prepared to meet the queen. Swathed in silks and perfume, an attractive lady of about his mother's age, awaited him.

Bowing, she moved lightly across the marble floor. They exchanged greetings. After the formalities, she led him to her office. It was a small room, but well lit. Apple perfume wafted from a smouldering silver incense container. Indicating a seat, she called for wine and fruit.

Alexander looked around. "My office is similar to yours."

"Surely not! This is tiny, and you are a great king."

"I prefer an intimate space for my work. It creates focus."

"I wish my house was as grand as you deserve, Alexander. As you know, I was married to the King of Caria. We worshipped Greek gods."

"You wed your brother, Idrieus, as I recall. You both honoured Athena at Tegea."

"Unfortunately, my husband died, and I was banished by another brother, Pixadorus."

"My understanding is that when Pixadorus died, he was succeeded by his Persian son-in-law, Orontobates."

"Your Highness is well informed. Orontobates rules this region now."

"You seem sad, my lady."

"On the contrary, I am pleased to have gained a son. And one so young and handsome! Come, we must feed you. Do you like lamb?"

"It is my favourite dish."

Alexander looked directly at her. His face softened as he took both her hands in his.

"You shall be my mother," he said. "I will protect you and restore your lands to you."

"And I shall send special recipes to you, wherever you campaign."

"Then, it is settled."

Arm in arm, they made their way to the banqueting hall.

***

Hephaestion relaxed by the fire in a large room. Cassander and Leonnatus were playing a board game in one corner. Eventually, Alexander arrived. His face was flushed and his eyes shone.

"How was your interview, cousin?" Hephaestion asked.

"I have put Queen Ada in charge of the siege of Halicarnassus."

Cassander looked up from his game. "She'll be waiting a while. That fort is defended by Memnon and Orontobates. The latter is Darius' son-in-law and her mortal enemy."

Leonnatus studied the board, while his opponent was talking, in the hope of discovering a way out of the mess he was in.

Alexander threw himself on a couch next to Hephaestion. "We will take Halicarnassus. Its fall will give us Caria, a region which I will give her."

Leonnatus dropped a game piece in shock. Cassander laughed aloud. "Our great leader is in love with a woman! I'll personally come to the wedding. It'll be a treat just to see your face, Hephaestion."

"Her Highness has adopted me as her son," said Alexander. "Now leave us, you two."

Cassander pouted. "I want dinner."

"Oh do shut up, Cassie!" Leonnatus snapped. Taking his friend by the arm, he withdrew with a curt bow.

"You got us out of there in a hurry, Leo."

"If Alexander dismisses you, it's time to go. This is a big castle. We can order whatever we want, in any room."

"I wanted an answer from Alex. Are you afraid I'll make Hephaestion jealous with all that talk of Ada?"

Leonnatus stopped in the corridor. "Your rudeness will cost you your head one day, Cassie."

"It's only Alex."

"He's a king, aiming for the conquest of Persia."

"So are we all."

"Except that our friend will rule an empire." Leonnatus continued walking. "Although, I don't think being Emperor of Persia will be enough."

"What do you mean?"

"You don't know Alexander. He's ambitious – more so than us."

"We all want the world, Leo."

"You should show him more respect."

"Like Hephaestion?" Cassander sneered.

As they rounded the corridor, Leonnatus looked him in the eye. "That man will stay alive."

Alone at last, Hephaestion moved closer to Alexander. "Is it true you have already dined?"

"Ada wanted to personally serve me a special lamb dish."

"You've always liked lamb."

"I really am going to cede Caria to her."

Hephaestion laughed. "She must be a good cook!"

"Queen Ada does not prepare meals herself. And you must always address her as *Your Majesty*."

"Are you going to marry her?"

"No, but I am always pleased when an older lady turns out to be different from my own mother."

"Now, *that* I understand."

Hephaestion stirred the fire with a bronze poker and curled up on another couch. The formal feast was in a few hours. He could wait. Gluttony in a soldier was something of which Alexander did not approve. He closed his eyes.

92.

In a week, Alexander was leading his army out of Alinda to Halicarnassus. His personal cooks were armed with several of Queen Ada's recipes. She was tearful at the departure of her new son. Alexander also wept.

Cassander bit his lip to prevent himself from laughing. Leonnatus kneed him in the shins. Perdiccas was relieved to be on their way. No incidents had occurred in his military units because he had hardly slept. Seleucus had a bored look on his face. Ptolemy, as usual, brought up the rear with his Silver Shields.

Hephaestion cast his glance across the sea of cavalry and infantrymen as they fell out. By his calculations, on numbers alone, Halicarnassus would surely fall.

***

Drawing up to the city, Alexander's army pitched camp half a mile from the eastern gate of Mylasa. Shaped like a crescent moon, Halicarnassus was encircled by the natural protection of mountains, and boasted a well garrisoned fort and its own navy.

Perdiccas chose a position with a sea view. Ptolemy's Silver Shields were already organising lunch. Leonnatus scratched his well-trimmed beard. He turned to Cassander, who was yawning.

"Have you ever seen a city like this, Cassie?"

"I wonder how long the siege will take. The walls are thick."

"Memnon is Commander. Rumour has it he sent his family to Darius' court."

"Which means he is free to fight – and lose. Maybe, with any luck, the battle could be over in moments. After, we'll all have a rest."

"Are you tired?"

"Don't insult me, Leo. I'm not above putting a spear in your leg like I did on that hunt. At the moment, I simply want a sea view, like our friend, Perdie."

Leonnatus chuckled. "I remember spearing you. The boar was mine. You really shouldn't steal, Cassie. I'm going to pitch camp to the right. That should leave you with a nice view of Perdiccas' tents!"

"Good luck with your view of the fort."

With their parting shots, the two left each other to set up camp.

***

Seleucus was admitted to Alexander's tent, followed by two men.

"We have an important report for you, my sovereign," he announced.

"What is it, General?"

"The men will tell you themselves."

Seleucus stepped aside to allow the scouts to approach Alexander. They shook at the knees. "M-Mighty Ma-Majesty, w-we are r-reporting the o-occurrences of th-this m-morning in the h-harbour."

"So, you're stationed at the sea. That's an important job." Alexander smiled to set them at ease. "What's happening in the harbour?"

"The Persian fleet has docked, sire."

Alexander's mood changed. "Curse the Persians! A blockade means our ships can't deliver my siege equipment."

The men dared not answer. Seleucus cleared his throat. "Should we attack?"

"We should wait." The king composed himself and turned to the scouts. "Good work! My general will reward you with gold. You're both dismissed."

The men hurried out of the tent, followed by Seleucus. Hephaestion approached Alexander. "What do you plan to do?"

"Study the city walls."

***

It was a fine afternoon. A light sea breeze blew inland. Moving rapidly, three Macedonian divisions drew close to the walls of Halicarnassus. Grey blocks of moss-clad stone reared above the men's heads.

Alexander tilted his head. "They're high."

"And thick," said Hephaestion.

"There's always a weak spot."

"The gate is a weakness, but it will be defended. We should search elsewhere."

Suddenly, a hail of arrows descended on them. Skirmishers rushed out of the citadel, hurling javelins and rocks.

"Counter attack!" Alexander roared.

Two divisions of Macedonian infantry closed ranks and advanced on the enemy. But, the gates opened, and the skirmishers scampered inside to safety. Before the Macedonians could follow, the gates shut. Alexander's temptation to climb the walls was strong, but he restrained his instincts.

"Back to the camp," he ordered.

***

Several days later, the Companions stood in their leader's tent. Alexander was talking in his rapid manner. "I've checked the city from a vantage point. The walls are thick. There is no weakness at the gate. Do you wish to add anything, Hephaestion?"

"The gates are difficult to breach. They might be reinforced from inside."

"I agree," said Alexander.

Cassander snorted with suppressed laughter. Leonnatus glared at him. Fortunately, their king was stabbing at a piece of cured sheepskin, and did not notice either man. Sketched on the animal skin was a diagram of the city.

"We are going to the right of the citadel," he said. "The aim is to investigate the territory. We will also take our position west, outside Myndus Gate. Spies inform me the city will surrender if we attack tonight."

A murmur rippled through the gathering. Cassander spoke. "I'm glad you explained our excursion route, Alexander, because the long way round to that gate would endanger our lives."

Seleucus straightened his back. "We're bound to have success tonight."

The meeting ended. They filed out of the tent. Seleucus leaned towards Cassander. "Your favour with the gods astounds me, brother."

"How so, Sel?"

"Our monarch hasn't executed you, yet."

"Plain speech is the way of the Macedonian warrior. And my favour with the gods will extend to outliving you to enjoy a ripe old age." Cassander placed his helmet on his head and swaggered off into the night.

Leonnatus drew up alongside Seleucus. "You're talking to Cassie, I see."

Seleucus turned a glassy stare on him. "What of it?"

"I thought your alliance was with Alexander."

"I am one of his foremost generals."

"As am I, loyal to the sovereign, but also to my childhood friend."

"What are you saying?" Seleucus rumbled.

"It sounded to me as if you were threatening Cassie."

"Your peculiar friend spoke out of turn."

"The only peculiar thing about him is that he likes girls."

"He has survived up to this point because his father is Antipater." Seleucus mounted his horse. "Remember, the night is dark, Leo. Anything could happen."

The general joined the Companion cavalry behind the king. Leonnatus assumed a position as far from Seleucus as possible. At Alexander's signal, they moved out.

***

93.

Under the cover of darkness, concealed by the forest trees which ran outside the fort, the Macedonians reconnoitred the fortress. At midnight, they reached Myndus Gate in the west. There, they fell into formation and waited. An hour passed. Then two. Predictably, Cassander started making disparaging comments to anyone who would listen.

At three in the morning, Ptolemy rode over to Alexander. "How are you this evening, brother?"

"Cold, Ptolemy. Any ideas?"

"Why don't we give them a push? We could start digging to the left of the walls."

Alexander gave the order. His army divisions moved out of the way of the guarded watchtower. Tunnels were dug towards the walls in an attempt to take the town by force.

Seleucus rallied a group of his men. Specially selected for their nimbleness, they scaled the walls. Keeping their shields up with one arm, they protected their leader, who followed behind. It was a difficult climb. Every time a man was about to reach the top, he was picked off by archers or swordsmen.

Finally, one Macedonian deflected a death blow from an enemy with his shield clamped to his left arm. Knocking the man down, he threw his weapons over the battlements, and climbed in. Retrieving his spear, he held his ground against the defenders. His comrades followed him over the walls.

Seleucus, however, was trapped and forced to fight atop the wall. Below him, the Macedonians saw the stocky figure fighting in the moonlight.

Cassander could not resist. "I must say our friend dances well."

Alexander chose several hypaspists and Agrianians to scale the walls. With their assistance, Seleucus managed to get off the dangerous parapet and inside the town. Other Macedonians focused their efforts on the towers. One fell quickly. However, several divisions inside Halicarnassus ferociously fought off the Macedonians.

Cries towards his right, alerted Cassander, who was standing at the bottom of a fallen watchtower. The men who were fighting above him heard nothing. He pushed back his helmet to get a better view.

"What, by Zeus' beard, is that?" he asked a bodyguard.

"Reinforcements, sir. They've come from the sea."

"We need to tell the king."

Leaving the watchtower, Cassander galloped towards Alexander. The latter was preparing to engage in battle. Cassander pulled up to him, his steed bucking and snorting steam in the night air.

"What is it, Cassie? Are we being attacked?"

"From the sea. Somebody sneaked out of the city and called for backup."

Alexander made an impatient gesture towards his heralds. "Withdraw now!"

Horns sounded, signalling retreat. Roaring with annoyance, Seleucus climbed to a parapet. From there, he supervised his men as they slid down the battlements on ropes. Before the city's reinforcements could reach them, Alexander's men were off the walls. With blistering speed, they made their way back to Mylasa Gate and their camp.

***

Tearing his helmet off, Alexander handed it to a squire. Sodden locks fell in a tangled mass around his shoulders. Hephaestion removed his armour. Stacking their spears neatly against the wall, the pair sat on fleece-covered stools.

392

Servants brought gold basins, containing heated water and herbs. They placed them next to the stools. Boys with towels stood by.

Alexander kicked off his sandals. "It was a trap from beginning to finish. When I enter that city, not a man, woman, or child will stay alive."

"As you say, cousin. For now, you need to clean up."

Grumbling, Alexander stuck his feet into the water. Boiling heat burned his soles, but he did not feel it. After soaking them, he took them out, and the boys wiped his feet.

A noise outside preceded the entrance of visitors. Goading two men with his spear, a royal sentry entered the tent.

"Excuse me, Your Majesty, but there is good news," the guard announced.

Noticing the men's nervousness, Alexander tried to sound warm. "If that is the case, you can both have half the town's loot when I conquer it."

"The sh-ships have a-arrived, sire," one managed to say.

"With my siege equipment?"

"Yes, sire," the other replied.

"How did they avoid Darius' fleet?"

"By docking in an adjacent cove," the first said, managing to control his stammer. "The Persians have no idea they've landed."

"You will be rewarded! Three talents each."

Leaping up, Alexander donned the armour he had discarded. Not daring to hold him to his promise, the men bowed to their sovereign, and allowed themselves to be escorted out by the guard.

***

On the parapets Memnon, with his generals, watched the siege towers being erected on the plain below. "I thought we blockaded them, Ephialtes."

"Alexander still found a way to bring them in."

"What happened to the ambush on Myndus Gate?"

"The Macedonians got away."

"I heard they attacked in the middle of the night. An entire watch tower is being repaired. It could have gone very badly for us."

"Our garrison is well defended."

"Except that Alexander is alive and preparing to take the city with new weaponry! You know, these siege towers didn't exist in my father's day. Old battle strategies won't work any longer."

"He has to get near the walls first."

"Make sure he doesn't," Memnon ordered.

***

94.

Several divisions of Macedonians rode in a siege engine with an open floor. Protected under a shelter of wood and hide, the men clung to the sides of the contraption as it trundled out to Mylasa Gate, where archers and infantry defended the city.

Ephialtes watched in silent fury as arrows and javelins made no impression on the protected soldiers below. To increase his frustration, the men inside the siege engine filled up the trench around the walls with earth and stones.

Another general, Thrasybulus leaned over a parapet. "What are they doing, Ephy?"

"Filling in the trench. It will make it easy for their larger engines to get up close and batter the walls."

Before Thrasybulus had time to absorb the information, huge siege towers advanced. He noticed the Macedonians below shifted their focus from the trenches to digging under the stone citadel. "Ephy, those men are burrowing under our walls!"

Ephialtes conferred with his officers. Archers from the other gates were now positioned atop Mylasa Gate. Being confined meant there was less room. Eventually, the walls were at capacity and some of the defenders had no option but to fall back and wait.

*****

In the afternoon, sections of masonry and rock crumbled. Ephialtes bit his knuckles. Memnon turned to him. "Don't worry, we're holding."

"What do you mean? There are breaches in the masonry from those accursed Macedonian sappers. We should have killed them this morning!"

Memnon was calm. "We have thousands of troops."

"Let's just hope our mercenaries don't defect."

Memnon glanced sharply at his comrade. "They are backed by native troops. They're not going anywhere."

Macedonian infantry moved towards the breaches in the wall, attempting to secure a foothold. At mid-afternoon, scouts were sent out. One, soon returned.

"Are we making any headway?" Alexander asked.

"There is no progress, sire."

"Why?" The scout dithered as though he was afraid. "Speak up! I promise that you won't be harmed, but tell me the truth."

"Memnon is holding us off. It also – er – seems easy for him."

"Which means our troops need rest." Alexander turned to Hephaestion. "Send word to withdraw."

***

All night long, the sound of rocks being dragged into place reverberated around Mylasa Gate. As the breaches in the main wall were patched up with rubble, lime, and rock, stretches of curtain wall were also bolstered with a mixture of fresh earth and rocks.

Donning his armour, Memnon made his way to a chamber at the satrap's residence. It was a modest room, reserved for his senior officers, all of whom were waiting. He beckoned to a servant, who brought him a cup of cold water.

Draining it, Memnon turned to one of his most senior mercenaries. "Are the men prepared?"

"Your troops await you, sir."

Tightening his belt to keep his armour in place, Memnon went to the stables behind the house. Congregated in the cold night air, his men saluted him. Most of the soldiers carried weaponry, which included thick wooden sticks, in their saddlebags. Leaping on his horse, Memnon waved them out.

The main gates opened. A hinge creaked. Memnon winced, remembering he had ordered it repaired months ago. Fortunately, the sound of construction drowned out any noise. Moving stealthily across the plain, his men headed towards the siege towers. It was dark, and they could hear the Macedonian army carousing in the distance.

At Memnon's signal, his men opened their bags and took the wooden stakes out. The ends were black, having been bound in linen and dipped in pitch. The soldiers lit these ends, transforming the stakes into flaming torches.

***

Near their siege engines, Macedonian soldiers changed guard. Collecting their rations of salted fish, dates and wine, they settled down to eat. Some wisely kept a portion of their food aside. During the freezing hours of early morning, a snack was a good way to keep up energy.

One of the camp guards, closest to the northern siege engine, on the right of Alexander's camp, pricked up his ears. "Do you hear something, Leander?"

His colleague was engaged in pouring himself a cup of local white wine from Caria. "Idomeneus, we've just started our shift. I'm having a drink with my supper." He set down the wine pitcher, looked up and fell off his perch. "The towers are burning!"

Sharp cracking split their eardrums as a large section of wood crashed to the ground. Men ran to the northern siege engine.

Idomeneus pointed. "Look! The other is burning as well!"

The rest of the guards were now fully alert. All roared at the top of their lungs: "Help! Comrades! Attackers!"

Several hundred men, from Perdiccas' regiment were situated behind the guards. Most were resting, but on hearing the cries, rushed out to help their comrades.

Meanwhile, an officer on the lookout, alerted Memnon. "They're coming, sir!"

Memnon whirled his steed around. "Throw everything at the towers, men!"

Buckets of pitch, torches, and flaming arrows flew at both siege engines. In moments, the Macedonians clashed with the night attackers. Dousing the fires, they brutally and inexorably pushed Memnon's units back to the city.

The walls of Halicarnassus were now patched up, which prevented Perdiccas' forces from entry. The main gates swung open a short way, allowing Memnon and his skirmishers to run in, before slamming shut in the faces of the Macedonians.

***

Impatient for answers, Alexander faced the surviving guards who had been on duty, that night. Streaked with soot and blood, they waited for his questions.

"Are the towers still usable?" he asked.

"They're standing, sire," said Idomeneus.

"That's not what I asked!"

Leander stepped forward. His throat was dry. He swallowed hard, but no spittle was produced.

"We can't see the state of them at the moment," he croaked. "Neither tower has fallen. The fires have been doused. We need to check in the morning, in order to give you a detailed report."

"I see you speak the truth. An officer will give all of you new clothes and two talents each."

Trying to keep their joy from showing, the men bowed and left the tent.

***

A Persian adviser stood before Memnon. "We've lost a hundred-and seventy men. I will have to tell Darius."

"I will tell Darius," Memnon said.

"The Great King might query your motives in the tactics used against Alexander."

"Don't be ridiculous!" Memnon mopped the blood from a cut over his eyebrow. "I risked my life."

Meanwhile, Alexander received reports on the state of his siege engines, his enemy, and his wounded. As head of administration, Hephaestion collated the information.

"Alex, we can't fight for a few days," he announced at the end of the morning.

"How many of my men are dead?"

"None. Three hundred are wounded."

"There were bodies on the field."

"Memnon lost over a hundred and fifty, according to my count. However, the city opened its gates early. They took in the corpses before I arrived."

"He won't want to engage for a while. Let us break for a few days and be vigilant. He needs to bury his dead."

"Do we allow him to do so?"

"I don't see why not. It's always been my policy."

Hephaestion refrained from making any comment on the erratic nature of his cousin's policies, which seemed to veer according to his mood. Instead, he left the royal tent to continue with his work.

Outside, Cassander was talking to a group of Companions. "How many are dead, Hephaestion?"

"None, Cassie."

"I mean from the other side."

"Around a hundred and fifty."

"You're guessing because Memnon got to the field before you. Wake up, Heph! Lying about in bed all morning is costing us important information."

Cassander chuckled to himself and turned away to continue chatting to his group. Hephaestion did not react.

"I must do better," he vowed to himself. "Zeus bless Cassander."

Somehow, the prayer curdled in his stomach.

***

95.

Time weighed heavily on both sides. Fighting ceased, while Halicarnassus buried its troops with high honours, and compensated the grieving families with gold.

Alexander used the time to hold meetings on the latest intelligence. His soldiers took to resting and drinking, some more than usual. Known for their toughness, the accomplished men of Perdiccas' regiment were particularly devoted to the pastime of boasting about their deeds.

Speculating on the great riches which lay ahead, the glory and eternal fame, two of Perdiccas' men started to compare their accomplishments. They began drinking in the morning.

Night fell, and they were still sampling delicious wines from mainland Greece and Caria, locked in a competition that would not cease.

"I was the first to take slaves in the Balkans, Ajax. Guess how many? Ten!"

"I have a hundred now, Aegeus."

"This drinking bowl was from the treasure trove of Darius."

"Picked up from a soldier at Granicus?"

"Miletus."

"Ah well, mine's from Greece, after we sacked Thebes."

"You were at Thebes?"

"We razed it to the ground. You weren't there, but I must have killed a thousand men that night."

"Bah! You lie."

"I most certainly do not!"

"Prove it."

"I'll prove it right now, if you like. Suit up, Aegeus! We're attacking the walls of Halicarnassus."

"I'm game if you are."

Lurching to their feet, the men put their armour on. Cramming their helmets over their heads, they tottered out into the night.

***

At Halicarnassus, Captain Alcibiades yawned on the parapets. It had been a long day. He and his companion were ready to change guard.

Dinner, with a nice cup of red wine, and a bath, awaited him. He had also recently married the pretty daughter of a local farmer. Their evening activities as newlyweds were something he looked forward to with delight.

Hearing a noise, his companion craned his head over the battlements. "I see Macedonians, Captain."

"Impossible! They have a pact with us not to fight."

"They changed their minds."

The captain leaned over the walls. His stomach knotted. He could clearly see weaponry glinting in the moonlight.

"Sound the alarm. I'm going to investigate." Running down the steps of the watchtower, the captain reached the city exit by a side entrance. Rustling bushes alerted him to nearby intruders. "Halt! Who goes there?"

"Better men than you."

Out of the darkness, swords slashed at the captain, killing him instantly. Now, more guards within the city left their stations. Soon, a division gathered outside the walls.

Hearing the noise, Perdiccas' men, joined the fray to rescue their drunken comrades. Swords drawn, men on both sides fought frantically in the dark. Tens fell. Then, hundreds.

***

Throwing on his armour, Alexander grabbed a shield and sword, and called for Bucephalus. Hephaestion selected a smaller steed for manoeuvrability.

"Are you sure you want to risk losing your best war horse, Alex?"

"There's no time to select another. Come on!"

Outside the walls, confusion reigned. Perdiccas' soldiers launched themselves at the enemy units, which were now fighting outside the gates. Pushing them back towards the city, they demolished the first ring of curtain wall.

Alexander's forces encircled the enemy soldiers in a tight hug. Men fell on both sides. Finally, the units from Halicarnassus escaped the Macedonian slaughter. Fleeing into the city, they shut the gate on two of their divisions.

Corpses continued to pile up at the entrance before Alexander managed to take his men back to the safety of their camp. Infuriated, he called a war council.

***

Seleucus found himself next to Ptolemy. Leonnatus was perfectly coiffed and dressed. Cassander was in a corner, by himself.

Perdiccas stood to attention. His cloak fell over magnificent dress armour. He rested his right hand on the pommel of his sword. Noting Alexander was furious, he assumed a vacant expression.

"General, who, by the beard of Zeus, ordered your men to attack Halicarnassus at night?"

"I don't know, mighty sovereign."

"Do you expect me to believe that?"

"The men were drinking. You know how it is. They got into boasting about their deeds."

"Our troops do it all the time," Leonnatus interjected.

Alexander paced up and down. His lip quivered. "That's why we have discipline! There are hundreds, maybe even thousands dead!" He sat down with clenched fists.

Ptolemy moved forward. "Ask Memnon for a truce. He also needs to bury his dead."

Cassander laughed from the corner of the room. "One or two!"

Despite the remark, tension in the room eased. Alexander nodded. He threw Cassander a wry smile.

"Send a message to Memnon," he said.

***

Calling a war council, Memnon was the first to open the meeting. "King Alexander has suffered many losses. He requests a truce."

The Greek commanders were outraged. Thrasybulus stood up. "It serves him right. Who does he think he is, that little tyrant of Greece?"

Ephialtes pounded the table. "We should not even let him have his dead back!"

Memnon cleared his throat. "Let him have his dead back."

"Why?" asked Thrasybulus.

"We have dead, too. They need to be buried."

Ephialtes stared at Memnon as if he had lost his mind. "That may be the case, but what has Alexander ever done for you?"

"Alexander is not responsible for a drunken escapade."

Thrasybulus shook his head in anger. "Those hooligans cut down our men at night!"

"And we incurred devastating losses to the enemy," Memnon replied. "Victors should be merciful to the vanquished. I say we give him his dead back."

Many on the council joined Thrasybulus in their outrage. The discussion continued for several hours.

***

403

Finally, the dead on both sides were burned on sacred pyres. Weeks passed. Inside the garrison, Memnon plotted his battle strategy with Ephialtes and Thrasybulus.

"Alexander's army is at our gates and it's not yet dawn," Thrasybulus declared.

Ephialtes jumped to his feet, gesticulating wildly. "I'm not waiting for the city to be taken!"

"Calm down," Memnon said.

"But, we must act now."

"What is the battle plan?" asked Thrasybulus.

"I don't know about anyone else," Ephialtes replied, with an aggressive snort, "but I intend to take a group of two thousand troops and set fire to the siege engines."

"A good idea," Memnon replied. "I will assist from another gate."

Thrasybulus chewed his nether lip. "That leaves me to defend the city."

***

96.

While the generals discussed their strategy inside Halicarnassus, the Macedonian army waited outside. Perched on the walls above was a makeshift tower.

Seated on his favourite stallion, Cassander turned to Leonnatus and bobbed his head upwards. "What have we here?"

"They're going to fire on the infantry, Cassie."

"We'll have to keep our shields up."

"I'm going to warn my men."

"I've already prepared mine."

"Stop boasting, Cassie," a deep voice rumbled.

Cassander twisted around to see Seleucus. "I must say, you look particularly murderous this morning, Sel."

The thickset warrior's eyelids lifted. Ignoring him, Cassander turned round to address a senior officer in his cavalry regiment. Rattling off the amount of men to kill and be killed, he chattered at full tilt.

Seleucus moved past him. Checking the masonry repairs to the citadel, his eyes sought out the curtain wall which had been hastily – and in his view badly – patched up. Passing Perdiccas, who saluted him, he returned to his group.

Mylasa's gates swung open. Alexander sat up on Bucephalus. "They're coming – finally!"

Trumpets blared. A banner waved from the top of the battlements. Perdiccas squinted in the morning sun.

Leonnatus adjusted his helmet, making sure it was pressed down firmly over his scalp. "It's Ephialtes' colours, Perdie. An Athenian, who truly hates us!"

Perdiccas gripped his spear. "Where is Memnon?"

His question was lost in the tumult of blaring trumpets, as a thousand wild men charged out of the city. With loud cries, bearing torches and buckets of pitch, they tore at terrifying speed around the serried ranks of Alexander's infantry. Immediately, they set fire to the siege engines with a barrage of missiles, which included flaming arrows.

Meanwhile, with a frontal attack, Ephialtes prevented the Macedonian infantry from running to the aid of their countrymen. Seeing the fires, Alexander despatched his best fighters into the fray and ordered another group to deal with Ephialtes' men. During the entire time, arrows rained down from the city walls, causing hundreds of men and horses to fall.

Suddenly, the northern gate opened. Memnon flew out with his troops to hit the Macedonian army on the right.

Leonnatus whirled around in the blood and dust. "We're surrounded!"

Cassander neatly lopped off a passing Persian head. "Stay awake."

"We can't win, Cassie."

"Leo, I intend to stay alive. How about some help here?"

Heeding his friend's plea, Leonnatus closed ranks with Cassander to keep the Persians and Greek mercenaries at bay. Further away, Hephaestion galloped down the ranks to the back of the army, and up to Alexander.

Reining in his horse, he gasped for air. "What are you going to do, cousin? Our troops are suffering massive losses."

Alexander's brain fizzed. He calculated the approximate number of men on both sides, but could not find a way out of his predicament. Meanwhile, on his far right, Ptolemy's Silver Shields observed the battle with annoyance.

"We're not even trying," one of the veterans commented.

Ptolemy's ears pricked up. "What do you mean?"

"Alexander's soldiers are children. It's embarrassing to watch."

"That they are," another said fiercely, as he chewed a piece of dried beef.

"You two have a lot to say," remarked Ptolemy. "Do you have a plan?"

"We may be officially retired, but if you let us attack, we will make you proud."

Their words drifted over the regiment. Hundreds of men waved their weapons and cheered. Taken aback, Ptolemy rubbed his beard. The Silver Shields were reserves. But their monarch, positioned on the far left, was helpless.

"I will lead," he said.

***

Cassander looked up from the space he and the Companions had created around them. Due to their efforts, the enemy was giving them a wide berth.

He nudged his senior bodyguard and pointed with his bloodied sword. "Do I spot a sea of grey, yonder?"

"It's the Silver Shields, sir."

Bloodcurdling cries deafened the plain as Ptolemy's men charged to the right. Memnon's bodyguard dropped his lance.

"What's with you man?" his master roared. "Pick it up!"

"I-It's Philip, s-sir."

"Impossible! King Philip is *dead*."

The bodyguard lifted a trembling finger to indicate a bearded man at the head of two divisions. "Sir, who is that?"

Memnon squinted into the distance. His irritation evaporated. "Ptolemy – with Philip's men." Rallying his soldiers, Memnon faced the onslaught.

Meanwhile, the Silver Shields were engaged in a swift education of the younger warriors. Aged between fifty and seventy, the veterans collared those in their twenties. All around him, the general heard rebukes.

"Are you a man or woman?"

"Let go, you brutes!"

"Mouse, I think. Let's check under his kilt."

Manly laughter rang across the lines. Orders came quickly. "Lock shields!"

Macedonian warriors obeyed. Moving at high speed, they descended on the enemy. Giving no quarter, the old guard crushed Memnon's lines. Afterwards, they wheeled round the right flank, to slaughter Ephialtes' men.

Alexander turned to Hephaestion. "That's your answer – attack!"

Pushing forward with renewed energy, the Macedonians started to progress. In the thick of battle, the Silver Shields proved themselves lightning fast, strong and strategic. In half an hour, Ephialtes fell off his horse, slain by one of Philip's old guard.

Cassander squealed with glee. "Their leader's dead!" He pushed forward, with his men.

The other commanders rallied their troops. Filled with fire, the Macedonian army pushed Ephialtes' men back to the city walls.

So panicked were the citizens of Halicarnassus, that they closed the gates before all their fighters were safe within the city. Cries of their dying brothers outside, failed to move the men of the garrison to re-open the gates. When it was over, hundreds of corpses lay outside the walls.

"That was easy," Seleucus said to his bodyguards.

Behind him, Cassander fussed with a bandaged hand.

"I was right about you looking murderous this morning, Sel," he remarked.

Chortling to himself, he flicked the reins of his horse and breezed past his colleague. The Macedonian army returned to camp. It was sunset.

***

In his tent, an exhausted Alexander accepted wine flavoured with spices and honey. Hephaestion had already bathed and slipped into a comfortable robe.

"How many do you think we lost, cousin?" he asked.

"Hundreds. But, Memnon lost over a thousand."

"We might have killed more if Ptolemy's old men hadn't interfered."

Tilting his head back, Alexander loosened his neck muscles. "Ptolemy did the right thing. His veterans pushed us to fight hard."

"He won the day, cousin."

"We haven't won. Memnon's still alive."

***

In the war council chamber Memnon, Thrasybulus, and the satrap, Orontobates conferred over drinks.

"Most of the troops made it back into the city," said Memnon.

Orontobates turned to the Greek in surprise. "Your fellow Athenian is dead."

"We need to decide the next strategy."

"I am surprised you show no grief, Memnon. Doesn't this change things for you?"

"I am not crying, but then I am not a woman."

"Are you insinuating Persians are effeminate? It's a Greek joke, one as boring as it is untrue."

Memnon banged his goblet onto the table. "I know we've lost a thousand men! We can't afford to lose more."

"What do you intend to do?" asked Orontobates.

"Some people will stay in control of the garrison."

"And you?"

"Leave."

409

Fires broke out at the houses next to the walls of Halicarnassus. Armouries and artillery followed. Taking the path to his ships, Memnon departed for Chios.

At Alexander's base camp, the generals had retired for the evening. Strong winds blew up from the sea while the Macedonians soldiers ate and drank their uncut wine.

Leonnatus was asleep. Ptolemy celebrated with the Silver Shields, who were especially raucous. Cassander sat warming himself by an open fire with his cavalry officers. Seleucus joined him with his bodyguard.

"What do you think, Sel? For old men, our Silver Shields certainly know how to party."

"You'll be fifty someday, General Cassander."

The fire billowed and shot sparks into the night sky.

"I'm counting on reaching sixty."

"I wouldn't be that ambitious."

"Are you threatening me, Sel?"

"Not at all. One day I hope to enter into an alliance with you."

Seleucus stretched. Cassander observed the bulk of the man and wondered if he had done it on purpose. Then, he noticed the city was on fire.

***

A panicked scout made it past security, and into Alexander's tent. "There's fire in the citadel, sire!"

Leaping off his couch, the king ran outside. Drowsy with post battle fatigue, Hephaestion joined him. Soldiers congregated outside their tents, watching flames leaping up from the left side of Mylassa Gate.

Gusts of wind blew around the King of Macedonia, almost playfully knocking him sideways. He twisted his head about.

Hephaestion stifled a yawn. "What are you looking for, cousin?"

Suddenly, Alexander shot his arm to the right. "The fire's spreading. It's the wind. We attack now!"

***

Commotion at the end of the camp jolted Cassander, Leonnatus and Perdiccas out of their fascination with the flaming city.

A messenger stood in front of them. "King Alexander requires you to take the citizens of Halicarnassus captive."

Cassander groaned. "Can't we wait till they burn in their beds?"

"We would miss out on the booty," said Leonnatus.

"Correct," Perdiccas chimed in. "See you all inside Halicarnassus."

***

On board his ship, Memnon looked back at the city. He was safe. His wife and child would see him again. Sails billowed out in the breeze.

Sharing a bowl of dates with Orontobates, he smiled. "We picked the right evening."

"I'm not so sure."

"I set fire to specific areas to thwart Alexander, but the main city should be safe."

Chewing slowly, Orontobates indicated the shore with a nod of his head. "It's spread, my friend."

Memnon noticed a fire in the middle of the city. It was too late to go back. He shuddered and turned away. The island of Chios was up ahead.

***

PART V

97.

There was nothing in the town of Gordia, not even a shrine. Cassander pushed back his sunhat. "What a dump!"

"Keep quiet," said Leonnatus, who was riding next to him. "Alexander's directly in front."

"But why are we here after Halicarnassus? Surely Issus is our next stop."

"The Gordian knot."

"Leo, what *are* you babbling about?"

Ptolemy rode up behind them.

"There is a cart here with a knot which cannot be untied," he explained.

Cassander dismounted. "I want a bath and a masseuse to remove my aches and pains. Meanwhile, our king is running after knots on carts. Anyone would think Alexander was a farmer."

"There is a legend that whoever solves the riddle of the knot will rule Asia," said Leonnatus.

A wicked grin split Cassander's cheeks. "Now, *that* sounds more like Alex!"

The men entered a local tavern where the other generals were ordering drinks. They were all served a strange beer, the consistency of soup. Cassander looked about hopefully. Spotting the tavern owner, he approached him. Taking a ducat from a money pouch slung around his hips, he slid it across the counter.

"Do you have anything else, apart from beer?" he asked.

"My name is Attis, gentle sir. Locals usually drink beer, but for esteemed guests, we will open our best wine."

"Sounds good."

Cassander lifted off his cuirass and took a wooden chair. Discovering it had one short leg, he bent down. Shoving the blade of his dagger under the chair leg, he evened the balance.

"Hurry up, *Attis*," growled Seleucus. "I get moody when I'm kept waiting."

Staff swept the courtyard. Amphorae were placed on trestles under oak trees. When everything was ready, the taverner invited the soldiers outside.

"Let's go out under the trees, Cassie," said Leonnatus.

"Gladly, I was about to fall off this chair."

Cassander rose and followed his friend outside. He noticed Seleucus' soldiers were becoming drunk. One of them, in the desire to impress his superior, and thinking surly behaviour was appropriate, kicked over a stool. A lad carrying an amphora, promptly tripped over it. The pottery jar smashed on the floor, spilling expensive red wine.

"Stupid yokel!" the soldier shouted. "Why do you employ flat-footed staff, Attis?"

Alexander, who was already under a tree chatting with Hephaestion, looked up.

"Stop it!" he snapped. "You'll be reimbursed," he reassured the owner, who was now paler than the whitewashed houses of the surrounding streets.

Seleucus frowned at the uncouth soldier. "My comments are not an excuse for my men to lose their manners."

"B-but, sir," the man said, turning red with embarrassment, "the waiter should mop up, not get paid."

"I've a good mind to make *you* mop up," Alexander snarled.

"I'd be happy to give the order," said Seleucus, sitting down.

With a shaking hand, the taverner poured the latter a drink. Hephaestion looked across the road. He waved at a cart standing on an expanse of grass.

"What's that, Attis?" he asked, changing the subject.

"The Gordian knot."

The taverner wiped down the royal table and placed complimentary figs and grapes before the warriors.

Cassander helped himself to the fruit. "It's nothing but a cheap farm cart. By the way, these grapes are excellent."

In gratitude, he pushed two gold ducats in Attis' direction. Pocketing them, the taverner nodded towards a waiter, who brought more wine to the table.

"Legend has it that the man who can untie it will conquer Asia," Attis explained.

"That is why we're here," Alexander said. "I shall solve the problem."

"Cassander is right," Hephaestion whispered. "It's nothing but a labourer's cart, Alex."

Philotas, who was seated next to his father, belched. "Let's face it, this is a village. I thought there was a temple to Zeus here. I can't even see a shrine to Pan."

Parmenion nudged him in the ribs. Alexander banged down his goblet on the rough-hewn trestle.

"Lead the way, good sir," he addressed Attis. "Come, Hephaestion, let's leave these naysayers and write history, together."

Hephaestion and the soldiers, downed their beer. Pushing back their chairs, they accompanied Alexander and the taverner onto the street.

The Macedonian king walked around the roughly hewn vehicle. He noted the oversized back wheels. A yoke at the front of the cart was planted firmly in the ground to keep it upright. A knot of surprisingly small proportions bound the yoke and shaft together. There was no trace of the ends.

Alexander continued to circle the contraption slowly. His generals were unnerved. Soon, a crowd gathered. Some people shouted advice, but others jeered.

The tavern owner stepped back to allow Alexander and his officers space. A shopkeeper joined him.

"We thought you were a patriot, Attis."

"I am."

"You have Greek soldiers in your pub."

"They pay."

"Who is the lad with reddish-blond hair?"

"The King of Macedonia."

"He looks like a boy."

"His reputation is one of a fierce warrior."

"That's about to change. Woe to him for attempting this! He'll fail and news travels fast in Asia."

Carrying a goblet of the tavern's finest wine, Cassander sauntered outside. When he reached the cart, he jolted back. "By Zeus, even if I was sober, that's the most complex knot in the world."

"Oh do shut up," an irritated Leonnatus said.

Seleucus folded his arms. "For once, Cassander is right."

Ptolemy watched, surrounded by his Silver Shields.

"I hope we don't have to fight our way out of this," he whispered to an officer.

Anxiety now gripped the army. Perdiccas cast worried glances at the street which was jampacked with onlookers. Alexander continued his appraisal of the cart.

Hephaestion was at his shoulder. "There's still time to back away, Alex."

"Why?"

"You can't solve the riddle."

"I've already solved it."

Alexander drew his sword. The townspeople fell back. Marching up to the cart, he raised his arm. "It doesn't matter how the knot is undone!"

Swishing through the air at terrific speed, his blade slashed the knot before anyone saw it strike the rope.

***

It was late at the tavern's lodgings. Helen was asleep over her embroidery in the living room. Cassander returned when the moon was high in the sky. Quietly moving about the house, he slipped off his shoes and hung up his cape. Next, he stoked the embers of the fire which had been lit many hours ago.

Having bargained with Attis for rooms above the pub, Cassander knew he had made the right decision. Apart from Alexander, who was the town mayor's guest, the men were camped outside, in the cold, under trees.

Going to the kitchen, Cassander lifted off the pot covers. Bending forward, he inhaled fragrant spices.

"Rice!" he whispered.

He was aware the Persians and other Easterners placed great value on the grain of which the Greeks knew nothing. Picking up a plate and spoon, which sat on the bench, he carefully ladled some of the rice onto his dish.

Another pot contained aubergine with a mixture of herbs. Cassander placed a small portion next to his rice, and looked about for a meat dish. He found stew in a terracotta container, covered with a thick cloth to keep it warm. He dipped in his spoon and tasted the contents.

"Rabbit!"

Taking the food into his room, Cassander set it on a table. Yawning, he removed his outer clothes and draped them across the oak dresser. Unbuttoning his tunic, he let his girth expand with a sigh of relief.

Polymarchus was at his door. The boy rubbed sleep from his eyes. "Where have you been?"

"The King had to solve the riddle of the Gordian knot."

"Is that why we're here?"

"Yes."

"There's not much to see."

Cassander laughed. "You're right! Have you had dinner?"

"Ages ago."

"I'm having mine now. Go back to bed. We're on the road tomorrow."

"I hope it's more exciting than here."

"We're heading for Issus. Darius is there."

"The King of Persia? Are we fighting him?"

"It depends on whether our farmer, Alexander wants to untie any more knots."

The boy's face twisted. "You're funny!"

"I'm witty."

"Isn't that the same thing?"

"Wit is a dish best served cold."

"Can you tuck me in?"

"After supper."

When the boy left, Cassander removed his outer garments. He hunted for a robe in one of his many chests. When he found it, he threw it over his underwear. Shuffling off his shoes, he replaced them with warm socks from a pack of toiletries.

Taking his plate off the dresser, he sat down on the room's only chair. Eating slowly, Cassander savoured his meal. He had tasted rice once before on holiday at the late King Philip's court. The aubergine melted in his mouth and the rabbit was excellent.

When he finished, he washed his face and hands. Looking at himself in the mirror, Cassander noticed a line under one eyebrow. It was new. He touched it thoughtfully.

Taking a thick blanket from his bed, he fetched an oil lamp and padded to the living room in his socks. Placing the blanket over Helen's shoulders, he checked the fire again. Next, he went to Polymarchus.

The boy was already asleep. In the lamp light, his skin glowed golden. The young face was free of lines. Cassander stroked his forehead. He pulled the covers up to Polymarchus' chin and closed the door quietly behind him.

Going back to his room, he prepared for bed. It was known some of the generals said prayers before retiring. Alexander and Hephaestion were doubtless reading great works of literature.

Cassander slipped between the sheets. He stared at the ceiling. "Great Zeus, what are we doing?" He blew out the oil lamp.

***

98.

Issus was grey. The banks of the River Pius were dirty, and the village behind the Macedonians was small and low to the ground.

Perdiccas reflected, even the hills looked like dirt against the leaden sky. He heaved a breath and made a mental calculation. Thousands of cavalry were gathered on the opposite bank. It would take only moments to cross.

Cassander huddled under his waterproof cloak. Helen and Polymarchus were in a nearby village with the rest of the baggage train. Leonnatus tightened his cavalry ranks. Astride a black stallion, Seleucus brooded, while Ptolemy's Silver Shields watched from a distance.

Undeterred, Alexander rode up and down the lines, commending those who had fought bravely for him over the years. To the wild Thracians, who spoke broken Greek, he made it simple.

"Enemy! Kill! Booty!"

A great din answered him. The men's enthusiasm was infectious. By the time Alexander reached his own Macedonians, they were cheering out of sheer mass hysteria.

On the banks of the River Pius, Darius' army waited in silence. The Great King craned his head forward.

"Where is their leader?" he asked.

His general indicated a flaxen-haired man. "The man riding along their front lines, sir."

"Are you sure? Kings are supposed to be at the rear of their armies in chariots. That lad looks like a page."

"King Alexander is rallying his troops."

Darius grimaced. "He has no dignity."

On the other side of the river, Alexander was jubilant. Turning to Hephaestion, he tossed his head towards a row of archers, stacked in front of the infantry line.

"Look – mercenaries!"

Hephaestion was perplexed. "How do you know?"

"Darius planted archers in front of them. He doesn't think they can cope on their own."

"Now I see, cousin. It's where we attack."

Alexander grinned. "Soon."

Darius plucked his beard. Somebody should stop the young page and give the signal. He turned to his general, but it was too late. The Macedonian army was already launching its first attack at the archers. Panicked, the Persian bowmen let loose a volley.

Instead of piercing their enemy, the arrows hit each other. Raining like hail, they fell to the ground in a mass of wood and metal.

Alexander's men crossed the stream as one unit. Persian archers tried to flee, but in moments the Macedonian cavalry was on top of them. The inexperienced Persian infantry section broke ranks. Sounds of dying men and animals filled the air.

Having given the signal, Darius saw the Macedonian king riding towards his chariot. The heart of the Persian army was about to be pierced. Without waiting for his master's instructions, Darius' charioteer turned the horses around and galloped away.

"He's young," was all the Persian king could mumble. "He couldn't be more than eighteen."

"Alexander is twenty-three, Your Majesty."

"He looks like a boy. He has no beard – and those eyes …"

Darius shuddered as his chariot clattered away from the battlefield.

***

In the Macedonian royal tent, the generals gathered to celebrate their victory.

"He ran away!" The shock in Alexander's voice reverberated through the tent.

Ptolemy laughed as he quaffed a mug of Phoenician beer. "He was afraid of you."

"But, he's their *king*."

Cassander dismembered a pomegranate. "If Darius falls in battle, a million soldiers will be yours, Alex."

"Why do you think I directly attacked him?"

"In Darius' view, it made tactical sense to leave the field of battle," Hephaestion pointed out. "You would have surely killed him today, cousin."

A wine steward approached the group and poured drinks. At the half way mark of his cup, Alexander made a gesture. "That's enough."

Cassander held out his goblet. "To the brim, good man!"

Ignoring him, Alexander turned to Hephaestion. Perdiccas chatted to Cleitus and Parmenion. Leonnatus joined Cassander. The men spent the afternoon talking of home while sharing a fruit platter.

As the chill of evening set in, Ptolemy threw his cloak about him for warmth. Seleucus noticed his friend's carelessness about his appearance was still evident. The cloak was inside out.

"We have to go after the empire now," Ptolemy declared.

"Agreed," replied Seleucus.

"We shall conquer Darius' empire," Alexander added, "but not yet."

Perdiccas broke off a bunch of grapes. "Are you suggesting we stay here?"

"The Persian fleet is active in this region," said Alexander. "We need to capture the Phoenician coast."

Cassander crunched a pear and turned to Leonnatus. "Our monarch offers us wealth, Leo. The coast is rich. Its lands teem with cattle, and crops grow in abundance."

"Fruit, too," Hephaestion noted. "You should send some to Leonidas for old times' sake, Alex."

"I might," said Alexander, with a smile. "For now, I shall retire to read. We leave tomorrow."

Taking a handful of almonds, he left the meeting.

***

99.

Predictably, the Phoenician coast fell to Alexander. At Sidon, he replaced King Abdashtart with his own choice of Abdalonymos. Then, he marched on Tyre. Divided into two parts, Old Tyre was situated on the mainland, while New Tyre, with a secure fortress, was built on an island off the coast.

At Old Tyre, Cassander appropriated the first house. Made of stone, it benefitted from the sea breezes, and its view of the garden was unobstructed.

Ptolemy's Silver Shields occupied the main street, which overlooked the bay with its new city. After a great deal of fuss, and a heated argument with Seleucus, Perdiccas chose the largest house next door to Alexander and Hephaestion.

By contrast, Leonnatus peaceably selected a villa. Its green roof was the only one in the ancient city. It was also equidistant between the residences of his monarch and Cassander.

Later, the soldiers met for a bonfire on the beach, while senior staff congregated in their sovereign's outer courtyard. Although Alexander was conspicuously absent, it did not dampen the men's spirits, and they milled about, chatting. Most were hungry, after spending the day settling into their new homes.

"You've got quite a cottage there, Cassie," Philotas observed over snacks.

"It's *Lord* Cassander to you, my puppy."

"I'm the same age as you."

"If you were, you'd realise the selection of my house was based on experience. It is prime real estate, not simply a cottage. With an unobstructed view of the sea, it is worth as much as your villa. I deliberately chose its size because it keeps the heat in. Tyre is cold at night."

"Cosy for you and your family, huh, Lord Cassander?"

425

Taking a dagger from his waistband, Cassander pared his nails.

"I would be careful," he said. "General Parmenion can't protect you forever."

Swallowing, Philotas turned away and looked for someone else with whom to converse. Perdiccas and Cleitus joined them.

"You look piqued, young Cassander," Cleitus said, grabbing a goblet from a passing steward and handing it to him. "Drink up!"

"Where is Alexander, Cassie?" asked Perdiccas.

"Do I look like Hephaestion to you?" Cassander accepted the goblet which he downed. "Cleitus, you're a true friend. I hope Alexander appreciates your loyalty."

With that, he picked up several seafood snacks, stuffed them in his jacket pockets and left the meeting for his home. Meantime, Cleitus spotted movement from the corner of his eye.

"There's your answer, Perdiccas. Envoys are entering Alexander's gate. It's why he's not here. He must be waiting for them."

***

Three Tyrian envoys bowed before Alexander. They presented him with gifts of purple cloaks, gold, and olive oil. Hephaestion watched from the back of the room.

Alexander examined a cloak with a gold fringe. "These are fine gifts. Tyre is famous for its purple dye. What do you have to say?"

"We honour your visit, noble king. However, Tyre will not cede its territory."

"I understand. I simply wish to make a sacrifice at the temple on your island."

The envoys glanced at each other.

"We welcome the great Alexander to Tyre," one of them said.

"Excellent! I shall visit tomorrow morning." Alexander made a cordial gesture of dismissal and rose. "There's still time to join the men," he said to Hephaestion with a wink.

But, the envoys did not budge.

"Your Majesty, you're already in Tyre," one of them said.

Colour rose in the king's face. "What do you mean?"

"Your Majesty could worship in the ancient temple here, in Old Tyre."

"Get out!"

The visitors scurried away. Hephaestion made his way from the end of the room. "It was a clever idea, Alex. Worshipping at the island temple would give you New Tyre."

"I offered them peace, but now they can have the end of my sword."

"It could be months before you take the island, cousin."

Alexander paced the floor with rapid steps. "All Greece bows to me!"

"A prolonged siege could set back the Persian campaign."

"Without total domination we can't proceed. Leaving pockets of resistance in our wake is dangerous."

"Perhaps you could send envoys to ask for peace terms."

The king's temper slowly cooled. Taking a handful of nuts from a gold dish, he snacked quickly, before moving to a window. Outside, the sea crashed over the rocky shore. In the distance, New Tyre glimmered in the haze.

He turned to Hephaestion. "That's a good idea."

***

Telemachus and Aegisthus reached the island in a skiff, rowed by two soldiers. Shipping their oars, the rowers let the messengers off on a narrow strip of beach under the city walls.

Leaving the soldiers with their boat, the pair climbed up to the citadel. Soon, they arrived at the palace. After requesting an audience with the monarch, they were ushered into his throne room.

Azimilcus was surprised. "You represent King Alexander?"

Aegisthus stepped forward. "We do, Your Majesty."

"Why are you here?"

"Our sovereign thanks you for the gifts of purple cloth, gold, and oil."

"He must be a great man to have such good manners."

"He is, Your Majesty," Aegisthus said, warming to his work. "We are here to thank you on his behalf, and also to submit the terms of peace he extends to you and your island."

Courtiers around the two men murmured. Telemachus grew uneasy. Azimilcus snorted. "Peace?"

"They can't take the island, Your Highness," one of his advisers whispered.

"I know they can't." Azimilcus turned to the messengers. His face was stone. "I'll show you to what terms Tyre agrees."

Guards grasped the men, two on either side.

"We are envoys who come in peace," Aegisthus protested.

But, the King of Tyre only waved one bejewelled arm. "Away with them!"

Removing the visitors from the audience chamber, the guards dragged them outside. With difficulty, Telemachus twisted round to face one of them. "You're making a mistake."

"We'll see about that."

Before he could say anything more, a blade cut through his throat.

"I hate chatterboxes." The man wiped his knife across his kilt. "Now it's your turn."

Aegisthus managed to wiggle free. As he was about to run away, one of the men tripped him so that he fell into the mud. A sword in the ribs was the last thing he felt. One of the soldiers kicked the inert messenger.

"Pick up the bodies," the leader said. "Get rid of them."

Obeying him, the soldiers carried the dead messengers across their shoulders, and threw them off the city ramparts. Under the walls of the city, two Macedonians slid their oars into the water. They rowed for their lives.

***

100.

Perdiccas, whose soldiers had relayed the news, shifted his feet. Seleucus stood with his arms folded. Hephaestion watched from a corner.

Alexander's face was purple. "They did what?"

Perdiccas did not answer. Seleucus unfolded his arms.

"Clearly, they thought peace was out of the question," he remarked.

Overcome with rage, Alexander started pacing. "I didn't kill their envoys, but they have murdered mine and thrown the bodies off their walls! I don't understand it. They know who I am."

"Maybe they thought peace was a sign of weakness," Seleucus suggested.

"The ancient city of Tyre surrendered peacefully!" Alexander roared.

"Perhaps New Tyre's citizens feel invincible on their island," Perdiccas suggested.

Cassander arrived late, carrying a half-eaten apple. "Did you hear King Azimilcus threw our envoys off the wall?"

Seleucus turned around. "We covered that point. You're late again, Cassander."

"On the contrary, I'm here for the best part of the show."

Alexander glared at them. He turned to face Perdiccas. "Tell Admiral Nearchus to take our navy out there. They'll capitulate soon enough."

"But, it's not an ordinary island," Perdiccas demurred.

"I agree," said Seleucus. "The Tyrians will set fire to the ships. You can't afford to lose one trireme."

"The island is fortified, cousin," Hephaestion added. "High walls embrace the port. Any ships would be bombarded on all sides."

Alexander stopped pacing. He sat down. "Why didn't you say so?"

Perdiccas breathed more easily. "What would you like me to do?"

"Join the island to the mainland."

***

Men's shouts woke Ptolemy. Startled, he rolled out of his narrow bed. Getting up off the floor, he threw a robe over his naked body and went outside.

At first, all he saw was dust. Buildings to the left of him were crumbling. Checking the earth beneath his feet for one of Poseidon's shakes, Ptolemy found it to be solid. He grunted with relief.

Suddenly, he realised that Old Tyre was being demolished. Bleary-eyed, the general walked down to the shore. The position of the sun told him it was the sixth hour of the day.

To his right, hundreds of soldiers climbed up and down a wooden scaffolding. Some hammered rivets into place. Others carried wood and hide to cover the tower.

Up ahead, he saw Hephaestion supervising. The sleep deprived general picked his way over logs, hide, and canvas, until he finally reached him.

"Greetings, friend! Are you building a siege engine?"

"For use against the island, Ptolemy."

"But how is it going to float across?"

"It isn't."

The general darted a look at Hephaestion, who was not known for his sense of humour. "Explain yourself, dear friend."

"It will be rolled along the causeway to the island."

"There is only sea in front of us."

Hephaestion pointed to a pile of logs nearby. "We're building a mole, commonly known as a causeway, across the water."

"What is happening to Old Tyre? Are we at war?"

"Our sovereign needs stone."

"For the causeway?"

"You're catching on."

Ptolemy scratched his beard. It was a lot to take in before breakfast.

"My men are at your disposal, if you want more help, General Hephaestion."

"That's generous of you, but Perdiccas' units have been press-ganged into this morning's shift."

"We're still available."

Ptolemy walked back to his house. It was always diplomatic to offer assistance to Alexander's favourite when needed. People who did not had a nasty habit of disappearing in the middle of the night. Or worse.

***

Outside his house, Ptolemy bumped into the seer, Lysander.

"Did you know about this?" the general asked.

"I was dragged out of bed in the early hours to bless the building of a road. Where, or what for, I can't imagine."

"Alexander is joining the mainland to the island."

"Great Zeus! Maybe, I should have breakfasted, first."

"Have it with me."

Placing his arm around the priest's slender shoulders, Ptolemy led him to his humble stone dwelling.

***

101.

It was noon. The first relay of men left for lunch, and the next took over. Hephaestion exchanged his supervisor's position with Perdiccas. Afterwards, he made his way back to the royal quarters.

Wiping his feet on a mat outside a side entrance, he slipped off his shoes. Next, he entered the passage leading to his sovereign's private apartments. A guard immediately recognised him, and pushed the double doors open.

Alexander was in a corner, reading. "How is construction progressing?"

"The first tower is almost built." Hephaestion accepted a cup of wine from an attendant and helped himself to figs from a fruit bowl.

"And the causeway?"

"Poles are in place at the entrance to our harbour."

"We need men building this day and night."

"I've organised for relays of soldiers to work until the villagers arrive. We've drafted thousands to work unceasingly until it's finished."

"Good man." Alexander helped himself to the figs.

Together they crunched in silence. Afterwards, the king left to conduct an inspection of the causeway. Hephaestion lay on a couch. Without meaning to, he fell asleep.

***

Ptolemy awoke with a start. Grasping his dagger from under his pillow, he tucked it into his waistband. Slipping on his shoes, he cautiously opened the front door.

Orange flames by the shore illuminated the night. Hastily closing the door behind him, he hurried into the street. Lysander was already outside, watching.

"Where are the water boys?" Ptolemy shouted. "Why is no one doing anything?"

"Steady on, General," Lysander soothed. "It's not a fire. The men are working by torchlight."

Ptolemy sheathed his dagger. He noticed a nearby group of Silver Shields, who were chatting together in the flickering light. Straining his ears, he heard them above the noise.

"I'm glad they haven't called us up, Epictetus."

"We'd do the job in half the time, Gorgias."

"Don't let Alexander hear you."

Ptolemy chuckled at the thought of their monarch overhearing the men's cheeky banter. Suddenly, he saw a familiar flaxen head in the distance.

"That's right," said Lysander, as if reading his mind. "Alexander's supervising. Can you believe it?"

Deciding to investigate, Ptolemy made his way to where the workers were toiling. What he saw almost made him gasp. Alexander was moving up and down, spurring on the men, and commending them, as they sunk poles into water.

Spotting Ptolemy, he waved. "What do you think?" he asked.

"It's impressive."

But, Alexander was not listening. "Well done Jason," he encouraged a common soldier. "There is a bag of gold for you in the morning."

Ptolemy hid his surprise. He watched as Alexander exhorted the men, and rewarded those who worked hard.

"Never fear, good Ptolemy, we'll get the job done," he said at last.

"Rewarding the best is a noble action."

"And you, my brother, will receive six talents and a slave girl. Aethilla's father was a priest at Troy. I think you will find her of great value. She knows the *Iliad* by heart."

Ptolemy bowed his head. "As always, you are most generous, my sovereign. Your Silver Shields are ready, should you need their assistance."

"That's kind of you, but I don't need any help tonight."

Relieved, Ptolemy quickly departed. Drawing up to his home, he noticed Lysander still in the street, watching. Now, even more Silver Shields were standing about, making comments.

"Go back to bed, men," Ptolemy ordered. "I volunteered you all for duty. As it is, King Alexander has provided for a party."

Cheering from his soldiers accompanied their quick exit from the street.

"Is there a party?" Lysander asked.

"He gave me means for one. You're invited – at least to bless it."

The seer grinned in the orange glare of a thousand torches. "I see you got out of doing anything, General. Where are you going?"

"Bed. It's the middle of the night."

***

102.

With a sarcastic chuckle, Cassander bit into a piece of mulberry cake. It was a new morning. Men were heaving logs into place. Rubble from the demolished houses of Old Tyre provided the base for the causeway. They were still working in shallow water, but deeper was coming.

Leonnatus appeared at his side. Cassander finished his cake and brushed his hands. "Leo, have you seen what our god, the great Alexander has done?"

"Isn't it impressive?"

"Do you know what Callisthenes said? *The sea bowed to Alexander*. What a brown-noser!"

"Don't, Cassie! We're in earshot of our king."

"Oh, poop! One day I'll have his throne."

"I would keep silent about that."

"There's nothing he can do about it."

"Parmenion would disagree."

"That old man belongs to Philip's generation. I am Alex's companion."

"You're not much of a companion to him."

"Maybe it's because Alex's unstable nature is potentially dangerous, not only for me, but for all of us." Cassander called to Perdiccas who was passing by. "Wait!" Getting up, he ran after his friend, and was lost in the crowd of workers and dust.

Heaving a breath, Leonnatus set his face. His men were to help out on the second shift, and he wanted to ensure none drowned.

***

At dinner that night, Cassander laughed so much he fell off his dining couch.

"What is that fool doing?" Alexander growled.

"Perdiccas told a joke, cousin," said Hephaestion.

The king swigged his wine. He had already had too much. His eyes scanned the sea of generals in front of him.

"Perdiccas is funny," he slurred. "Tell us a joke, Perdiccas."

"Better him than me," Cassander puffed, climbing back onto his couch.

Ptolemy raised his goblet. "To King Alexander."

"To Alexander!" the generals chorused.

Pleased with the adulation, the king raised his goblet. Ptolemy gestured to a musician, who strummed a lyre.

"Sing, goddess, of the anger of Achilles, son of Peleus …"

On hearing the opening lines of the *Iliad*, Alexander's demeanour changed. A peace swept over him. He listened. Perdiccas breathed a sigh of relief. Jokes were not his speciality.

***

As the causeway advanced across the waters, New Tyre prepared for a siege. Women and children were bundled onto ships. Sailing away from the island in a mass evacuation, they found refuge with sympathetic allies in Carthage.

Meanwhile, weapons were sharpened as troops moved into strategic positions around the island city. Finally, the causeway reached deeper water. Men strained as poles were put in place, and rubble filled the seabed.

One sunny afternoon, Cassander and Leonnatus munched honey-and-fig pastries, while they watched from the shoreline.

"Any day now, Leo."

"What do you mean?"

As Leonnatus spoke, two skiffs moved up to either side of the causeway. He squinted at the craft. They did not look Macedonian. On nearing Alexander's workforce, men in the skiffs let fly a barrage of missiles. Screaming was heard from the shore as men fell.

"That." Cassander finished his snack and started to walk away.

"Where are you going?"

"To have a nap."

"Alexander needs us."

"And I need my strength to fight that fool's battle."

***

Retreating under a hail of missiles, Alexander and his troops returned to the shore.

"We need to wear full battle armour," Hephaestion gasped.

"We *are* wearing armour."

"Our workforce is mainly civilian, Alex. Hundreds are dead."

"Don't worry. We'll bury the dead and compensate their families. I also have an idea."

***

Days later, an excited Leonnatus arrived at Cassander's home in the middle of the afternoon. As the master of the house was asleep, a servant led the guest down a short passage to his bedroom.

Sentries at the chamber admitted Leonnatus, but left the door ajar so that they could monitor his actions.

Going to his friend, Leonnatus shook his shoulder. Being jolted awake was not on the list of Cassander's favourite ways to rise from a deep sleep.

"By Hades' beard, the next time you do that will be the last!" he exclaimed.

"Get up and come and see this."

"I sleep with a dagger under my pillow. I could have gouged your eyes out."

"Not likely. Your sentries are watching."

"To guard me, not you."

With much grumbling, Cassander dressed, and the pair went outside. Many generals were already there by the shore, close to the mole, where some had joined Alexander's team.

Large carts, made of canvas and hide, which protected workers within, were trundled by sweating soldiers across the sea road. At the end of the expanse, two siege towers were being constructed.

"Don't tell me we have to join Alexander in making that," Cassander groaned.

"Not yet, but isn't it clever?"

Cassander gave his friend a withering look. "We could be in Egypt, under palm trees, eating dates with nubile maidens. Instead, you bring me out in the noonday heat to observe a dusty road going nowhere, except to our death and destruction."

"We will reach Egypt. For now, we have to fight Tyre."

"No, we don't Leo. The great Alexander feels insulted, so we all have to pay. It's all about one man's greed and need for glory, and we're fool enough to follow him."

"What else are you going to do?"

"Outlive him. Build my own kingdom. Get married and have children."

Cassander left for his home. Leonnatus continued to watch the feat of engineering rising up from the waves. Men scaled the siege engines. Letting loose volleys of arrows, they retaliated against those on the battlements. Below, covered in protective awnings, men continued to build the pathway across the sea.

Leonnatus' face shone. It really was very clever.

***

103.

Hephaestion stood in the doorway of the royal study. Alexander was poring over battle strategies. He looked up.

"Enter!" he greeted cheerily.

Crossing the threshold, Hephaestion approached the map table behind which his cousin stood. He was pale and the muscles on his face were taut.

"Why so troubled, Heph?"

"One of our soldiers reported blood in his bread, cousin."

"His tooth probably fell out."

"He's not the only one. My spies also report that Tyrians are seeing visions of Apollo."

"That's a rumour."

"You know I don't deal in rumours, cousin."

"All your information is reliable. For that I am grateful. But these superstitious stories are a result of fear. Surely you know that."

"That as it may be, you need the men to be in fighting spirits."

"Another sacrifice, perhaps?"

"Increasing security might be more in order."

***

Towing ships filled with pitch, flammable materials and sulphur, the Phoenician triremes advanced towards both sides of the half-finished causeway. When they neared its end, they cut the ropes and released the vessels towards the towers. Skimming across the waters, the fireships collided with the jetty.

Exploding, the fireballs caught the siege engines, incinerating the troops on top of them. Hundreds of labourers close to the towers died. Survivors fled.

While war raged at sea, divisions of Tyrian warriors attacked stone carriers from Old Tyre. Without any form of protection, most of the workers were massacred. After they had done their job, the attackers departed before Alexander could retaliate.

***

Macedonian generals congregated in the stone hall of Old Tyre. Most had headaches. Pounding the table with his fist, Alexander was shouting. Hephaestion reflected his cousin's angry outbursts were becoming the norm.

"How is this possible? How have we been attacked on two fronts? Don't we have scouts? Lookouts?"

Parmenion was the only one brave enough to speak. "It was carefully planned."

"There are even raids from natives in the hills for my cedar! I need wood for the bridge." Alexander sat down. "It's one problem after another."

"There is only one solution," said Parmenion. "We continue."

"At least my senior general tries. What has happened to everyone else's tongues?"

Leonnatus stared into space. Cassander contemplated his boots. Even Seleucus did not dare say a word.

Hephaestion cleared his throat. His voice was calm, his enunciation clear. "It is difficult to arrive at a solution so soon after receiving the news. Perhaps if we reconvene before supper, our sovereign will be able to hear everyone's view and decide on the right course of action."

"A sensible idea," Alexander agreed. "Everyone is dismissed until evening. And I want solutions!"

                              ***

     Hephaestion waited as the generals filed out. Being the last in
the room, with an angry monarch, he was ever the consummate diplomat.
     "I know it's stressful, but there probably is nothing we
can do," he said.
     "What I object to, Heph, is the amount of gold I pour
into these men's coffers, and yet the hard decisions are always left up
to me. I have to figure out a way to get to New Tyre. I have to protect
everyone on the causeway. The only man who volunteers his help is
Ptolemy."
     "He is loyal, cousin."
     "And unlike the others, he craves no glory for him-
self."
     "He also leads the best fighting division."
     "You're right. The Silver Shields are tougher than any
of my young soldiers. Maybe they can come up with something."

                              ***

     Nervously stroking his beard, Ptolemy listened. The officer
before him, Eudoxes, was a trusted informer. No one suspected that
he was anything but another member of the Silver Shields, visiting
his general. Ptolemy's reputation for being open all hours was legendary.
     "Is that what Alexander said?" he asked.
     "I heard the monarch and his closest companion speak-
ing of you in glowing terms."
     The general dropped several gold coins into the spy's hand
and dismissed him. He sat still. A rustle in the adjoining chamber distracted him.
     Thais entered the room. "I waited for him to go."

"You look stunning."

Ptolemy meant it. Her simple long white dress, and gold earrings, showed off Thais' complexion and comely figure.

He caught her round the waist and kissed her tenderly. "It's good to see a Greek woman again."

"I would have thought the exotic slaves Alexander rewards you with, would have satisfied your appetite."

Ptolemy loosened his embrace. "I am older than Alexander. My priorities are different."

"Don't let him know that!"

Ptolemy laughed. "My girls aren't what they seem, dearest. The latest one is a priest's daughter who recites the *Iliad* all day." Swiftly kissing Thais, he led her to the bedroom.

***

104.

The council of generals buzzed with excitement. People had been brainstorming all afternoon. Cassander arrived, eating one of Helen's pastries.

"Any ideas, Leo?"

"Not a single one. How about you, Cassie?"

"I'm going to tell Alexander to march to Egypt. It's peaceful."

"My puppies," Seleucus interrupted, "I have a couple of thoughts that will cover your lack of contribution."

"Sel, the only dog here is –"

But Cassander did not have time to elucidate. Alexander walked into the chamber. He took his place behind a table and looked around.

"I agree with Parmenion," he said. "We continue. We will use sea power. I will visit Sidon to obtain more ships and stop the Arab tribes from stealing our wood."

"Where are we going to get ships at such short notice?" Perdiccas asked.

"We have a navy from Issus and the surrounding territories," the king replied.

"That won't be enough," Cleitus objected.

"You're right," Alexander agreed. "Hephaestion, find out if King Nicocreon of Cyprus wishes to aid our cause. Send him a message, now. We will be sure to have his answer when we reach Sidon."

The king left as quickly as he had arrived. Ptolemy caught Cassander's eye. "Off the hook. Time for a drink."

"Is it true that your lady, Thais, is back?"

"She will be serving drinks to my guests."

Cassander's eyes bulged. "It would be rude not to pay my respects."

"Come to my home as an honoured guest. For now, everyone's invited to a party."

Ptolemy placed his arm around Cassander's shoulders. His grip was tight. Making a mental note not to gawk at Thais, the latter made polite conversation. Others followed them out of the audience chamber. It was common knowledge the Silver Shields gave the best parties.

***

At Salamis in Cyprus, generals and advisers gathered in the west wing of the palace. The conversation was muted. King Nicocreon read the latest intelligence report. At the proper time, his sentries admitted a spy. The slightly built man, in a shimmering robe approached the throne.

Nicocreon put down his parchment scroll. "Any news?"

"Ships are passing this coast, Your Majesty."

"From where?"

"Macedonia and other parts of Greece." The informant hesitated. "King Alexander is in Sidon."

"He was laying siege to Tyre last time I heard."

"The Macedonian monarch is preparing for a naval attack on New Tyre. He's in Sidon amassing a fleet. His second in command, General Hephaestion, wants to know if we will contribute."

The king stroked his beard. He singled out his most experienced naval adviser. "What are the odds of victory?"

"With ships, it is always possible, but with Alexander's determination, victory is certain."

"Commit a hundred and twenty ships." Nicocreon winked at his adviser. "I don't want our blond god building any bridges across the sea to us!"

All week, ships arrived in Sidon's port. King Abdalonymos welcomed Alexander and his Companions, who watched in disbelief as Cypriot vessels docked along the shoreline.

A week later, as sunset swept the coast in a warm golden embrace, the Macedonian monarch realised he had his fleet. King Abdalonymos decided to celebrate the accomplishment with a formal dinner.

Hephaestion ran up the marble steps of the palace. His evening robe caught the sunlight. "You must have over two hundred ships, Alex."

"Bought any horses?"

"Several – none for Cassander."

"I should think not. His wealth matches his rudeness."

"No one has more!" Hephaestion laughed.

"I am picking out clothes for the celebration dinner. What robe should I wear?"

"The white gown with gold thread, given to you by Sidon's king. And perhaps, the purple cloak gifted by the Tyrian envoys."

"A strategic choice. You know Hephaestion, one day I will give you half the Persian empire."

"I wish only to be by your side, cousin."

"That is why I shall be so generous."

Swiftly, Alexander put a gold necklace, with a figure of Athena, around his neck. It was slightly crooked. Hephaestion went to his friend. Straightening the necklace, he stood back. "Athena never sat on so great a breast."

"It's a gift from Ada."

"Which proves women have their uses. Do you have a plan, cousin?"

"Byblos and Aradus pledged their allegiance, with eighty ships."

"Cyprus donated a hundred and twenty."

"That *is* good news."

"My latest reports say that other vessels from Macedonia will arrive in the next few days, as well as those from Lycia and Rhodes."

"Our win at Issus is finally paying off, Heph. Even those canny Cypriots, who wanted to see which side was winning before they committed vessels, sent ships."

"You will win New Tyre, cousin."

Alexander patted his necklace with its gold medallion of Athena. "I always win."

***

Dinner was held as the first stars came out. Alexander and his host, King Abdalonymos, with whom he had been on a lion hunt that week, were engrossed in conversation. Hephaestion was content to recline on a couch and listen. Perdiccas started drinking from the moment of his arrival and did not stop.

Having brought Polymarchus and Helen on the trip, Cassander stayed with them for most of the day. During the afternoon, he played games with the boy. When dusk fell, the trio had a light supper. Then, Cassander read to the child before bedtime. Afterwards, he chatted to Helen, until she took up her embroidery. On the eighth hour of the evening, he joined his colleagues at dinner.

Leonnatus welcomed his friend to a corner where there was an empty couch. The pair sat in relative privacy, eating and chatting, without being disturbed. Towards midnight, they both retired to their separate quarters.

***

105.

The next morning, after the celebratory dinner, the palace was quiet. Birds twittered in the empty courtyards. Servants swept and mopped floors. Flowers were cut and placed in bronze vases.

As dawn tinged the clouds pink, Hephaestion groaned. Alexander was shaking his shoulder. "Get up, we're going to Beqqa."

Morning sun struck Hephaestion's eyes. "Now?"

"Tell the Young Companions to get ready. I am dealing with the tribes today. They embargoed the wood needed for building my causeway at Tyre."

"Cousin, everyone's hung over."

"I'll wait for them in the main courtyard."

Hephaestion threw back the covers. Going to the washroom, he dunked a pail of cold water over his head and body. Afterwards, he dried himself off with a linen towel.

When he came out, Alexander handed him a list. "What's this?"

"We're only taking a few divisions to pacify the tribesmen. These are the warriors I want for our expedition."

Soon, Hephaestion was dressed and hurrying about, rounding up men. Cassander was on a palace balcony, eating breakfast with Helen and Polymarchus. Crunching his morning pastry, he listened to the news.

"Beqqa? But that's hundreds of miles away."

"Alexander wants you. We leave soon."

Stuffing the rest of the pastry into his mouth, Cassander's eyes ran over the parchment. "My soldiers are in bad shape this morning. Good luck with waking Perdiccas."

"He'll have to move, unless he wants to risk Alexander's wrath."

"Here!" Cassander slapped a bread pocket into Hephaestion's hand. "Pork and coriander. You'll need energy for the march."

***

Galloping with four divisions of his cavalry, Alexander's elite made their way to Beqqa. They rode all day. As the sun set, the trees were bathed in gold light. Wildflowers bloomed in the grass, and birds twittered in trees as they settled down to rest. Cassander chatted with Leonnatus.

"Look, Leo – poppies. Remind me to collect some on our way back."

"Their unripe seeds are supposed to be good for battle pain."

"It's the milk inside the seeds. Helen knows how to make potions."

A man carrying a knapsack jogged up behind the pair. His stallion was small and his armour consisted of only the bare essentials.

"Cretans carry gold vials full of poppy elixir," he said. "They use it for sacred rituals."

"Whose idea was it to bring Callisthenes?" asked Cassander.

The newcomer was put out. "My task is to follow King Alexander everywhere. I'm the record keeper of his victories."

Disdain crossed Cassander's face. "Nephew of Aristotle, I haven't forgotten your odes to our monarch's greatness."

Leonnatus looked askance. "Cassie, stop!"

"Thanks to you, Callisthenes," Cassander continued, "history will show these Arab raiders at Beqqa bowing to Alexander's might."

"That's true," Callisthenes responded.

"Minus the gruelling hours of fighting and loss of half our men?"

"Er –"

"You're nothing but a high-class brown-noser."

Cassander galloped off. Embarrassed, Leonnatus assumed a genial expression. "A vial would be a useful container for poppy extract, Callisthenes. Do you think it might be a good idea?"

"I would be honoured to make a potion for you."

They travelled together until the army arrived at a village. It was dark. Alexander's troops fanned out and surrounded the huts and palisades. Tribal campfires and torches burned in different parts of the settlement which was guarded by armed watchmen.

Dismounting his horse, Alexander crept up to the enclosure. Approaching from behind, he slew two guards in rapid succession. Macedonians grasped the torches around the settlement and threw them onto the huts. In moments, the villagers' homes were ablaze.

***

106.

Next morning, accompanied by his new fleet, Alexander and his troops made their way down the Sidonian coast, back to Old Tyre.

As they approached the city, his fleet faced Tyrian ships. After a brief standoff, Tyre's fleet was unable to successfully block the Macedonian king from returning to its waters. Instead, Tyre's naval captains resigned themselves to docking in their own harbours, leaving their enemy to take strategic positions on both sides of the causeway.

When dawn broke the next day, Hephaestion felt himself being shaken awake once again. Disoriented, he rubbed his eyes. "What is it, Alex?"

"We must build siege towers."

"Do we have enough wood?"

"Piles from Beqqa. Don't you remember?"

"The past few days are a blur. I do have a question."

"Go ahead."

"Where *are* we?"

Alexander tore open the drapes with a flourish. "Tyre. I'll let you get ready." The king slung a belt around his waist and was gone.

Casting his eyes to the ceiling, Hephaestion fell back onto the sheets.

***

Alexander spent the morning deploying ships around the island of New Tyre. The Phoenician part of his fleet sailed to blockade its southern Egyptian harbour, while Cypriots were sent to the northern Sidonian one.

Cassander and Leonnatus made their way down a street to Ptolemy's house. It was a fine morning. White clouds scudded across a light blue sky.

"I see Hephaestion is at the docks, Cassie."

"The price to pay for being close to Alexander – work and more work."

"Do you think Thais will join us this morning?"

"Be warned, she's off limits, Leo."

"She is a courtesan."

"She belongs to Ptolemy. Besides, Cleitus made a vow to protect her."

"I haven't seen that old devil in a while."

"He's no longer in Alexander's favour, having saved his life at Granicus."

Leonnatus was dismayed. "Our noble sovereign bears a grudge towards the man who saved his life?"

"If you save a man's life, he holds power over you."

"I never considered such a thing, Cassie."

"Now you know."

Cassander knocked on Ptolemy's door. Greeted by the host, they made their way to the living room. There, to their great pleasure, Thais welcomed her guests with decorum befitting a lady of the house.

In the meantime, neutralising any naval bullying from his enemy, Alexander ordered work on the causeway to recommence. Unfortunately, a storm blew up.

***

Workers huddled on the shores of Old Tyre. Rain fell in icy sheets. Rough seas crashed against the causeway. Pieces of the gigantic road broke up and were swept into the water.

Leonnatus and Cassander peered through the lattices of a window at Ptolemy's house.

"It's going to break up!" Cassander shrieked.

"Oh, shut up Cassie! Can't you offer a solution, instead of adding to the gloom?"

"We need *logs*, Leo."

"Nobody can do anything. Look at the workers trying to shelter themselves."

"You told me to offer a solution."

"If you're going to give advice, make it useful."

"We need to cut down trees."

"What, by Zeus' beard, for?"

"To throw into the ocean in a windward position. Don't you see, the causeway is crumbling?"

Thais nudged Ptolemy. His face appeared above their heads. "I understand what you mean, Lord Cassander. Breakers are needed to protect the sides of the causeway."

The irate Argead lord pulled his waterproof cloak around his shoulders. Without bothering to answer his host, he left the house.

"Go after him, Ptolemy," Thais urged.

Outside, gale force winds blew. Cassander pushed forward. Rain lashed his face. Gasping, he found himself blown back. Fighting the storm, he suddenly felt an iron grip on his right upper arm.

"Get back inside, Cassie!" roared Ptolemy. Steering his guest back into the house, he shut the door with difficulty.

"Why did you stop me? I was making progress."

"It's better to notify Alexander by messenger. I have one, who knows a shortcut through the alleys, which are sheltered from the wind."

Thais gave her bedraggled guest a dazzling smile. "My darling will see to it you are changed. Do join us at dinner, Lord Cassander."

Swallowing convulsively, the latter obeyed. He followed Ptolemy to a bedroom where, after many changes of clothing, he found something that suited both his flair and desire to impress.

***

107.

Once the breakers on both sides of the causeway were in place, it stabilised. The storm raged for days. Unexpectedly, one morning, the skies cleared. Uncut logs, which had absorbed the impact of the winds, were now integrated into the mole as bulwarks. The Macedonians continued their work.

As the sea road extended towards the island, Alexander moved siege engines into place and fired missiles at the city's defenders. Soon, the walls were cleared of Tyrian soldiers.

***

King Azimilcus rapped his fingers against a windowsill. "I thought we blew up the towers."

"We did, Your Highness."

"Why can I see a pair of monoliths from my window?"

"King Alexander – er – built them again."

"You know, in less than half a year that scoundrel has built four towers as large as mountains." Gazing out across the sight of the causeway stretching from the mainland towards the walls of New Tyre, Azimilcus stroked his beard. "Perhaps killing those envoys was not such a good idea."

***

Tyrian archers let fly a volley of flaming arrows at the sea road and nearby ships from Alexander's fleet. Vessels close to the walls on the south side of the island, were hit hardest.

Running across the bridge of his ship, a Macedonian captain, who was positioned nearest the battlements, was beside himself.

"Get down!" he roared.

An incoming hail of arrows struck four of his naval officers. More were shot at the triremes. Slain soldiers fell onto the decks.

"Turn the ship around!" the captain yelled.

His men obeyed. Other ships within Alexander's fleet retreated. Meanwhile, on the battlements of New Tyre, the victorious citizens built protective towers. From within them, Tyrian archers continued to rain down arrows and missiles on enemy vessels near their city.

***

It was the tenth hour of night. Hephaestion returned home after dinner with Perdiccas. As he passed the main street, he noticed Philotas was supervising the night shift of their causeway's construction. He had taken over from his father, Parmenion, who was probably at home getting ready to retire for the evening.

Stepping off the main road, Hephaestion entered a side entrance of the royal residence. A sentry stood to attention. Unclipping his cape, the general wiped his shoes on a tough brush mat. Yawning, he walked into the living room, where he caught his breath.

Alexander was readying for battle. His dresser, a man he had kept from his earliest youth, adjusted a buckle, around his waist. A breastplate, decorated with the gorgon, Medusa's head, glared from the king's chest. Sorting impatiently through several daggers, he settled on one of iron and gold.

Hephaestion stopped yawning. "Where are you going, cousin?"

"Out."

"Should I come?"

"You've worked hard all day. Besides, I need you on the causeway in the morning. Go to bed."

Clapping Hephaestion on the shoulder, Alexander went out. The door slammed shut.

***

Outside, the king walked quickly to a waiting ship, filled with soldiers, where he stepped aboard. A gust of wind blew the sails. His cape billowed behind him as the vessel slipped into the moonless sea.

At home, Hephaestion luxuriated in a hot bath. Grates close to the ceiling, let in air. Cicada song echoed through the stone bathroom. Snippets of conversation from sentries, and hoots of owls hunting in the olive groves floated through the grates.

The bather tilted his head back and closed his eyes. He thought he heard Cassander's singing. Hope, tinged with melancholic tones, floated on the evening breeze, down the street, and across the tree-filled garden. The exhausted general dozed.

***

108.

On board, Alexander's troops readied themselves. Men checked their weaponry as they prepared to make landfall. The king grasped his spear. A gust of wind pushed him to one side. He steadied his feet. Another gust of wind blew from the opposite direction.

"Give me safe passage, Poseidon, and I shall sacrifice a bull to you," he whispered.

Without warning, a squall of rain hit the ship, drenching everyone on board. A wave surged against the prow. Dropping their weapons, the men clung to the sides of the ship.

"Steady," Alexander encouraged them. "It's only rain."

Several waves crashed over the sides, filling the ship. The Macedonian leader noted his ankles were submerged.

"Nearly there!" he cried.

***

In Old Tyre, Cassander paused to refresh himself with a draught of wine. It passed over his lips and down his throat in one delicious wave of intoxicating flavour.

He resumed playing. Reclining on a couch, close to his favourite snacks, knowing that Helen and Polymarchus were safely asleep under his roof, filled him with happiness. Strumming his lyre, he opened his mouth.

A sudden gust of wind blew out the lamp.

***

Through his drowsiness, Hephaestion listened to Cassander's singing. His voice was sweet. Now and then there were pauses between verses. Perhaps it was the wind, or perhaps in Macedonian style, the bard was refreshing himself.

Outside, the wind picked up speed and knocked tree branches about. Raising himself in his bathtub, Hephaestion decided to end his ablutions. Wrapping a towel around him, he noticed there was no singing.

He made his way down the corridor to his room, and throwing off his towel, sank onto the bed. Trying to pull a blanket over him, he fell into a deep sleep.

***

"We have to turn back!" the captain yelled.

"I can see Tyre's walls," Alexander replied.

"We can't land, sire. The ship will be wrecked. Everyone on board will be drowned."

Clinging to the sides of the lurching vessel, Alexander felt a wave of desperation sweep over him. They were so close to the island. Poseidon knocked him back. Tumbling, he found himself tossed over the submerged boards. Sitting up, all he could see was blackness. Rain stung his face.

"Turn round!" he yelled. "Let's go home."

Straining on the oars, rowers battled the sea.

"We can't turn, Alexander," said the captain. "We'll be splintered by the waves."

"What do you advise?"

The captain let out a breath. It was the first time his sovereign had asked a question. "The men have to row us backwards. If it gets calmer close to Old Tyre, we'll turn."

"Do it."

The drenched king gathered his cape about him and went below deck.

***

In the early hours of the morning Alexander climbed the steps to his home. He heard singing. A light shone from Cassander's house. He saluted the guards who were surprised to see their king drenched to the bone.

Waking with a start, Hephaestion checked the moonlight streaming through his window. It was around the first hour of the morning. Faint singing floated into the room on the wind.

A noise in the pantry put him on alert. Casting about for a dagger, he remembered his weapons were in the front room. He took a breath to calm himself. The noise was probably more likely to be from a rat than an intruder. Besides, there were guards everywhere.

The bedroom latch turned. It was then Hephaestion realised he was naked. A towel lay next to him. He stood up and wrapped it around his loins. He could aways wrestle the burglar, he thought.

Alexander was in the doorway holding an oil lamp. "You're awake, Heph."

"You're soaked."

"Poseidon was unhappy with my efforts to take New Tyre."

Hephaestion was stunned. "You should always sacrifice first."

"I rather think Cassander's singing put the god out," Alexander chuckled.

"It's not a laughing matter, Alex. Cassie stopped for a while. Poseidon probably blew out his household lights, courtesy of your recklessness."

"The storm blew out all the street lamps on this side. My ship's captain could only see by the light of the moon as we docked."

"You must be more careful, cousin. A god's opposition can stop human plans."

Alexander removed his clothes. Taking a towel off a nearby shelf, he dried himself and threw a warm robe over his head. He blew out the lamp.

"No god is going to stop me. Goodnight, Hephaestion."

***

109.

Several Carthaginian ambassadors bowed before King Azimilcus. He was in the best of spirits. The sky was cerulean blue, Alexander had not yet reached the city, and now the Carthaginians were here to offer military aid to their ally.

"It's a pleasure to finally see you," the Tyrian monarch addressed the delegation. "You have good timing. As you can see, King Alexander has made progress with his sea bridge."

"We have seen it, Your Majesty," an ambassador replied.

"How many reinforcements can I expect?"

"While we can give refuge to the women and children you sent, our troops are already committed in wars of our own."

King Azimilcus sat still. Moments passed. Finally, he turned to his chief attendant. "Ensure these men are bathed and fed."

He rose. Aware of his stiff knees, he moved slowly off the dais.

***

Three hundred men, under the supervision of Hephaestion, worked around the clock, packing boulders and rocks around the narrow strip of beach adjacent to the walls of New Tyre. Shielded by covers of hide and metal, the Macedonians worked to build the road ever closer to the walls of the island city. Meanwhile, sweating profusely, burly Tyrian soldiers pushed a great metal creature towards the ramparts.

On the shores of Old Tyre, Cassander was eating a handful of roasted crickets. Polymarchus was at home, learning to write Greek, a useful skill which would benefit him in life.

Shading his eyes, the young general noticed a huge metal creature, with a wide mouth, being hauled into position on the island city's ramparts.

Up ahead, Hephaestion's and Perdiccas' men were helping to build the causeway. From the voices floating downwind, Cleitus and Parmenion sounded as though they were giving advice. Cassander snickered and reached for a cricket.

"May I have one?"

"I wondered how long it would be before you showed up, Leo."

Cassander held out a plump palm. Leonnatus helped himself.

"Salted crickets are my favourite snack, Cassie."

"I know," the latter sighed. "Do you realise I've been on a diet since we left Macedonia?"

"I'm afraid your stomach says otherwise."

"Wine makes up for my lack of nourishment."

Cassander belched. At that moment, the mouth of the metal creature on the Tyrian ramparts ejected a fireball onto the causeway. Crickets spilled into the sand. Leonnatus started choking on a leg. Cassander pummelled his back.

In a reflex motion, Parmenion and Cleitus drew their swords. Hephaestion and Perdiccas ducked behind a boulder as pandemonium broke out. Their workers fled the protective awnings, which were now on fire.

***

Hephaestion was breathless. "Cousin, the causeway is on fire!"

Alexander dropped the scroll he was reading. Together, they ran into the main street. Men were scurrying like ants down the causeway back to Old Tyre.

The king prodded the air. "What is *that*?"

In the distance, above the ramparts of the new city, a huge fireball shot from a metal dragon. Scorching canvas, and animal skin awnings, which covered the gigantic siege towers, it destroyed men and towers with aplomb.

"They have new weapons, Alex."

"How is this possible? Our spies said the Carthaginians couldn't help them."

"Tyrian engineers must be inventing new weapons."

"All I know, is that contraption has to be destroyed, immediately."

***

New siege towers were built. A wave of Macedonian troops headed across the causeway to protect them. Archers from below the walls, and across the waves, tried to pick off the men closest to the fire breathing apparatus.

"It's no use," Seleucus said one afternoon.

"We can't stop building," Perdiccas countered.

"How many men have you lost?"

"Seventy."

"Don't forget to count your infantrymen."

"Then it's hundreds."

"Maybe Cassie's right. We could be in Egypt by now. Intelligence reports say we could take that country from Persia without a fight."

"We can't stop."

"We can't get across the sea."

***

It was dark in Old Tyre. Helen locked the window lattices and drew the heavy curtains. They muffled the distant sound of

462

hammering which alternated with the roar of fire, and the sound of waves crashing against the bulwarks of the causeway.

Polymarchus lifted up his head from his homework and looked at Cassander. "How long do we have to stay here?"

"Until Tyre falls."

"When will that be?"

"I don't know. Now finish your homework."

"What if it's never?" Helen asked suddenly.

"Not possible," Cassander said.

"Why, my lord? Because Alexander never stops?"

"Precisely, Helen. Let that be a lesson to you, Polymarchus. Never give up and you will always win."

"We're going to die here," said Helen.

Her son began to wail.

"Hush, child," said Cassander. "We will leave one day, I promise."

He picked up his lyre and played a soothing tune. Helen sat down at her embroidery. Polymarchus stopped crying. Cicadas started singing outside. A bright moon rose above the hibiscus bushes of their small garden. Servants tidied up and went to bed. Still, Cassander played.

***

110.

Alexander was in another bad mood. And he was drinking. A turn of the sun dial indicated an hour of his rant had passed. No generals, except Parmenion, wanted to speak. Even Philotas was silent. Shouting had numbed them.

"I've spent half a year trying to get to that wretched island!" Alexander roared.

"And we're still building the causeway," Parmenion added.

"Why? Why aren't we there, yet?"

Cassander snickered at the back. "Sounds like something Polymarchus would say."

"It's the weapons," Leonnatus blurted to drown out the comment.

Alexander swept around. "What do you mean?"

It was then Leonnatus noticed his king was wearing a red cape. In the lamplight, he looked like an avenging demon.

"Er – the weapons. They have even constructed some type of mace with bits sticking out of it."

"How do you know this, Leo?"

"They lob them at our soldiers," growled a deep voice.

"Which means that at least Seleucus has some men trying to get into the city," said Alexander.

"My men are doing the same thing," added Perdiccas quickly.

"We are all attempting to take the city," said Ptolemy. "Even the Silver Shields volunteered."

"I know you stepped up from the beginning, Ptolemy. Everyone else had to be pressured into going across to the island. Why is it that I have to do everything myself?"

At this point no one spoke. They were too dumbstruck. Even Cassander's sarcasm froze in his throat. Hephaestion picked the moment to conclude the meeting.

"We are getting close," he said. "It will take another five days. Now, I think we could all break for the evening."

***

Outside, Cassander waited for Leonnatus. Seleucus acknowledged him as he headed home. No doubt there was a woman waiting for him. Next, a glum Parmenion trudged past, followed by his son. Cassander stiffened. There was something inherently repulsive about Philotas, but the latter did not notice him as he tried to catch up to his father.

Finally, Leonnatus appeared. The two walked out to the shore. Waves crashed in the darkness, their foaming heads defining the line between sand and sea.

Cassander waved pudgy hands as he talked. "What are we going to do, Leo?"

"Wait five days."

"We can't get across the causeway!"

"The siege engines have been rebuilt."

"I wish Alexander was dead."

"He's in a bad mood, that's all, Cassie."

"I don't care a jot for his unstable veering. This is *my* life. I want to get married."

"What's stopping you?"

"War!"

Leonnatus placed a hand on his friend's shoulder. "War provides brides."

Cassander stopped. A large breaker crashed behind him. "What are you talking about Leo? Who wants to raise children in this?"

Philotas loomed out of the darkness. He was walking on the shore by himself. The pair changed direction.

"Don't worry about him," said Leonnatus. "Even I couldn't hear you."

"What is that minister of Hades doing, following us?"

"He's just walking, probably taking a break from his father."

"Parmenion *is* an overbearing bore," Cassander admitted.

After the walk, they parted ways and returned to their respective homes.

***

111.

Over the next few days, Alexander's siege engines reached New Tyre. Descending from the multi-tiered platforms into the city, the angry invaders fought for every step of ground.

Hiding with his family in their home was all Demetrius could do. As a merchant, he earned his living from a successful string of shops which sold imported wares. His wife, Anath and children had not wanted to be evacuated to Carthage. It was too far.

Outside, he could hear shouts. It had been like this for months, with Alexander's towers growing closer. But, New Tyre had defeated the Babylonians. After thirteen years, men who were harder than this boy's band of thugs, were unable to breach the Tyrian walls.

Demetrius walked to the window. It was the middle of the afternoon, and he wanted to close its shutters. The familiar bark of a dog in the street echoed between the walls of the narrow lane. He leaned out and saw soldiers.

With a sinking stomach, he drew the shutters. "Anath, get our children to the courtyard. Stay under the eaves."

His wife did not ask questions. Taking their children to the courtyard, she hid. In the meantime, Demetrius drank a cup of cold water and waited. Presently, he heard it. The heavy trudge of boots up the stairs. Gruff voices. The cry of an indignant neighbour and the sound of scuffling.

They were outside his door. Demetrius readied himself to answer it, but never got the opportunity. The sound of a boot splintering wood brought down the entire front door. Burly men stood in the open space. Demetrius' voice failed him. The little speech he had prepared with its offer of wine, olive oil and all he had, including twenty gold ducats, dried in his throat.

A soldier struck him over his bald pate. "Get out!"

One of the men picked up the pouch of ducats. "What do we have here?"

Kicking him downstairs to the curbside, the Macedonians took turns to imprint their various boot sizes in Demetrius' posterior.

They tied his hands with leather straps. Terrified, the merchant barely felt the bands cut into his wrists. Fear knocked so hard against his ribs, he felt his heart would burst.

He looked about. It was sunset in an hour. Hundreds filled the narrow streets. Peering at the masses, he deduced rightly, that they were all men. An order was given. A trumpet blast deafened him in one ear.

Next thing he knew, Demetrius was marching down the street to the beach. It was golden hour. The sun was due to set in splendour along the shore.

***

Fires broke out across the city. Men were rounded up and crucified in a line across the beach. Women and children were separated to be sold into slavery.

Screams filled the evening air. Relieving pent-up feelings after the lengthy siege, the conquering troops went on a rampage, looting and slaughtering all in their way.

General Seleucus led some of the toughest men. Anger burned inside them as they pillaged the city. Anger with the wait, and with delayed glory, which they could have earned fighting in Persia. Anger with half a year's life wasted on a pitiful rock in the middle of the sea!

Not far behind him were Leonnatus and Cassander. Unknown to him, they were trying to contain some of the excesses of the troops.

Seleucus reached the shrine of Melqart. Kicking open the door, his blazing eyes rested on the sight of women and children cowering by the altar. Leonnatus and Cassander caught up with him.

Out of breath and sweating, Leonnatus pushed his helmet up. "Everyone who has taken refuge in a shrine is to be spared, Sel."

"I didn't attend the meeting."

"I'm serious, brother."

"It's from the king himself," said Cassander. He stood between the altar and Seleucus. "You'll be put to death, or worse."

His eyes travelled out the temple door, towards the shoreline. Seleucus' burning eyes pulled away from the civilians to the crucified men. With a grunt, he left abruptly.

Leonnatus' shoulders slumped. "I thought he was going to cut me down." He turned to the civilians. "You're safe. I will guard you. Cassander, go and make sure General Seleucus stays out of the temples."

"Why?"

"Because we care about the gods and these people."

"Some nark is bound to turn him in at the next sanctuary. He'll be crucified before the day's end."

"No one, except us, would dare stop him. You must go!"

Cassander made a dramatic sigh. "For once, King Alexander was going to add to my fun." He stopped on his way out. "As it is, he has spoiled my love of a sunset on the beach."

Despite his terror, one of the boys giggled. Winking at him, Cassander left. He was careful to close the door. Zeus could be certain the little one's father was hanging on a cross as the sun sank over the waves.

***

112.

Covered in gore and mud, Cassander entered the tent of Callisthenes. He sat down on a stool. The historian beckoned to a boy, who rushed forward with water, an empty basin, and towels. An adult male attendant poured wine for the visitor.

"No footbath for me." Cassander downed his wine.

The boy backed away quickly and retreated to the shadows. The historian leaned forward. "Is there anything I can help you with, General?"

"Details."

"Of the battle?" Callisthenes took out a clean sheet of parchment, laid it in front of him on his desk, and waited. "Is there something you would like me to add?"

"Tell me, were you a witness to the defeat of Tyre?"

"I saw some of the action, General Cassander."

"Up to what point?"

"When we reached the temple of Melqart, or Heracles, as we know him. Alexander spared all those who sheltered at the holy site. It was inspiring, so I came back to write. It normally takes me several hours to make a battle record. As you are aware, we must be on the mainland by morning."

"There's no need to explain. I'm not here to critique your practice. I wondered how you were going to spin the story of thousands crucified on the shore."

"Pardon me, I don't follow."

"Alexander had New Tyre's men crucified. Made quite a sight, all those tortured souls grumbling on their crosses in the setting sun. Hail to our great king!" Cassander picked out a splinter from his lower left leg. "Curse it! They should really make crucifixes out of something other than wood."

Getting up, he lifted the tent flap, and walked into the night.

***

Outside Callisthenes' tent, Ptolemy reined in his horse. "Adding yourself to history, Cassie?"

"Did you know our royal correspondent left as soon as we got to the Temple of Melqart?"

"Callisthenes writes. He doesn't fight."

"Nor does he have an appetite to watch justice being done, it seems. Wonder how he'll spin our great king's purge." Cassander lurched forward. "Ow! My leg's split."

"There's a surgeon's tent up ahead."

"I'll be dead by the time the doctor attends to me in one of those tents. Have you seen the queue?"

"There's one set aside, exclusively for generals. Go to your right. It's nearly empty. Seleucus was inside a few moments ago but there will be room for you."

"Oh, lumbering Sel, that's something to look forward to! Is he injured badly?"

"I have no idea. If you go now, you might find out."

Cassander hurried away on his bad leg. Ptolemy waited until he was out of sight. Then, he dismounted and led his horse to the historian's tent, where he tethered it to a pole.

***

Callisthenes pushed his parchment away and rose.

"General Ptolemy, what can I do for you?"

"Please sit. I know you're writing."

"Are all the generals visiting me tonight?"

"I'm not sure what you mean."

Ptolemy accepted a wine cup from the male attendant. He removed his cuirass. Twisting his neck, he checked his shoulder and back.

471

"Looking for splinters, General?"

"That's an odd question."

"I only ask because my last visitor was doing the same."

"I was stabbed. Tyre's bronze is famously sharp, Callisthenes. It always pays to check a wound made by a Tyrian. Sometimes it will go deeper than expected."

"Cadmus will attend to it, General. He studied medicine under Uncle Aristotle."

"I am honoured."

A youth of around fifteen years of age appeared. Baring his arm and back to the young doctor, Ptolemy chatted pleasantly. As usual, he elicited a cheery interaction. Cadmus brought implements. He smeared aloe vera over the cut and wrapped it with bandages.

Callisthenes sat back in his chair and regarded his guest.

"Cassander was here a few moments ago," he said.

Ptolemy drained his wine cup. "Was he?"

"He wanted me to add to the written account of the siege."

"Ah yes, Alexander's finest hour!" Ptolemy handed his empty cup back to the attendant who had served him. "A wonderful beverage. May I trouble you to have another?"

With a happy nod, the man ran to do his bidding.

"Frankly General, after what Cassander said, I'm having difficulty incorporating it into a paean of praise."

"Sparing all those men, and freeing the people from the temple?" Ptolemy placed his breastplate over his head. The attendant returned with his wine. He gulped it down. "I have seen mercy from Philip once or twice, but never anything like this. Even King Azimilcus was spared."

Giving the attendant and Cadmus a gold coin each, Ptolemy left the tent.

***

113.

Dawn broke across Old Tyre as the invading army prepared to leave. Ptolemy chatted to the king before joining his Silver Shields.

On his way back, he tipped his hat to Cassander. The latter was astride his horse, devouring apricots from a flax bag. Stopping to greet him, the older general exchanged pleasantries.

Seleucus trotted up to them on a new white stallion. Purchased from an Arab, its glossy coat shone to the envy of the surrounding officers. "It seems history owes different accounts of Tyre's conquest to the pair of you."

Cassander threw an apricot stone on the ground. He picked another from his bag. "We need some honest history, Sel. All we hear these days is how Zeus impregnated Olympias, making Alexander divine; how the sea bowed to him, and so forth. If Callisthenes isn't careful, one day the sky will come down to ring our king's head with a halo of light."

Ptolemy guffawed, and made an excuse to continue on his way back to his soldiers. Seleucus regarded Cassander for a moment.

"You were right, Cassie. Our king spared all those who took refuge in the gods' shrines."

"Noble of him, don't you think?"

"Thank you for saving my life. I was in war mode. You know how it is."

Cassander threw another fruit stone on the ground. "Always glad to help out, Sel. By the way, what has Ptolemy got to do with Callisthenes? Has he spun him a wonderful story of how Alexander plumbed the depths of the earth and rose to the heavens?"

Seleucus thought for a moment. "Our historian said you reported that two thousand men were crucified, but Ptolemy thinks it was more."

"I wouldn't be surprised. Alexander's mercy has limits, as we have all seen."

Heralds blew their trumpets. Without knowing it, they were on their way to Jerusalem.

***

It was midday. Bearded men, in white robes, emerged from the citadel. Alexander shifted on his horse and pulled back on the reins.

"They're unarmed," he noted. Motioning his party to stop, he dismounted.

Hephaestion controlled the alarm in his voice. "Cousin, your bodyguard!"

Ignoring him, Alexander walked to meet the delegation. Hephaestion nodded towards the royal bodyguards to indicate that they were to follow their sovereign.

Cassander peeled a pomegranate. "What have I always said? Our king is as deaf as a post."

As Alexander approached the priests, the men thought the clean-shaven Macedonian king looked more like a boy than a man. However, they concealed their surprise, and spoke courteously to him. Most had long beards, which Alexander found impressive. He asked questions about Jerusalem's city and beliefs. After a discussion, both sides realised they were intellectually minded.

As the sun rose higher in the sky, one of Alexander's bodyguards returned to the main party. He spoke to Leonnatus, Perdiccas and Ptolemy. Each, in turn dismounted and joined their king on foot. Then, the entire group entered the foreign citadel. The gates closed. Worry crossed the faces of the Macedonian generals.

Cassander munched his pomegranate. "Temple visit."

"How do you know?" asked Seleucus.

"Those men are Hebrew priests."

"Maybe so, but there are soldiers inside the town, Cassie."

"I doubt whether any of them is going to attack, especially during a visit encouraged by their holy men. It breaches the rules of hospitality."

Seleucus shook his head. His eyelids lowered. They waited for another movement of the sun in the sky. Some of the units dismounted, exercised, and then returned to their horses.

Cassander rummaged in his saddlebags for more fruit. Seleucus eventually took his horse to a nearby brook, where both man and beast drank. When he returned, Cassander pointed. "Look yonder, Sel. Alexander's on his way back, safe and sound."

"No priests, either."

The army waited. Ptolemy, Leonnatus and Perdiccas joined their units. Seleucus expected an excited comment in passing, but the generals were silent. Alexander mounted Bucephalus and led his army in the direction of Gaza.

In the late afternoon, they camped at a spring. Tents were pitched and sheep were slaughtered, while the generals gathered around a fire.

Seleucus sat next to Ptolemy. "This place could do with fewer mosquitoes."

"Indeed," replied Ptolemy, handing him a wine cup. "Insulation against their bites," he added with a grin.

Perdiccas, whose tent was already up, sprawled close to the fire with a full cup of Tyrian wine. "They have an unknown god."

"Those priests?" Seleucus asked.

"That city. The place is dedicated to Yahweh."

"Never heard of her."

"It's not a female goddess, Seleucus," Leonnatus explained.

"Easy mistake to make," said Cassander, joining them. "Ishtar has her mansions all over this region."

"I thought that it was a Hebrew name for her," Seleucus said.

"That's what we thought at first," replied Perdiccas.

"The god has no name or face," Leonnatus explained, "but is male – at least that's what we gathered."

Cassander was eating dates. "What was the temple like?"

"It was plain," Leonnatus replied. "There was gold, but no animals, or faces anywhere."

"How much gold?" asked Seleucus.

"Plenty!" Leonnatus and Perdiccas laughed.

While the men talked, Alexander rested in his tent with Hephaestion. It had been pitched first and he had no inclination to be sociable. Instead, he leaned forward, elbows on his knees, clasping his hands in front of him.

"They must have made you welcome," Hephaestion said pleasantly.

"It was a strange experience."

"As sacred as in Zeus' temple?"

Alexander lifted his head. The tent flap was open. A cool breeze blew in. "Their beliefs are different to ours."

"Do they worship Ishtar?"

Embers flickered through Alexander's eyes. "No."

Outside, the sheep were taken off their spits. The men grew rowdy with wine as they started to relax after their strange journey.

"What I want to know is why we didn't take the city," Seleucus said with irritation. "I was ready."

"Because its god had power," Leonnatus explained.

Perdiccas dipped a piece of bread into bean curd. "And mystery."

"That city's god is unknown," Ptolemy added. "Alexander thought it wise to avoid trouble. Gaza is going to be work enough." He turned to Cassander. "You would have liked it. Unlike us, the Jews believe that only men and women should be lovers. They marry for life, and to the exclusion of others."

"A people after my own heart!" Cassander enthused.

He downed his drink, rose, and inspected the nearest sheep. Juices were starting to ooze through the crisp exterior. Pages were waiting for it to cool down before they started cutting it up.

"The girls are pretty, too," Leonnatus remarked.

"I prefer mine Greek," said Perdiccas.

"So do I," Ptolemy agreed.

Seleucus raised his brows. "What barbarians those Jews are."

Cassander cut a piece of crisp skin off the barbecued sheep. He looked up to the heavens with dreamy eyes. "Oh, why didn't I go into that city!"

"You were too busy eating," Seleucus remarked.

Meanwhile, in the royal tent, Alexander was chatting to his cousin, who was trying to dull his senses to the roasting meat. "They have a book called the Torah, which they revere above any statue to a deity."

"That sounds civilised," said Hephaestion, hoping he was saying the right thing.

"They also have a very different idea about human relationships."

"More Persian – I mean eastern?"

"They are nothing like the Persians. They live simply, although I must say, they have many rules about what to eat and do. There were too many for the priests to explain."

"I don't understand why we didn't take the city, Alex. Its inhabitants sound uncouth beyond belief."

"Who is to say they are not right? The more I travel, the more I understand new things. I think one day we will discover that even Aristotle was not correct about the world in which we all live."

***

477

114.

"Tyre has fallen, Master Batis."

The Persian governor of Gaza crimsoned. "That's not possible!"

"Alexander conquered the city a few days ago."

"What happened?"

"Most of the men were killed. Women and children were sold into slavery."

"And the King of Tyre?"

"Alexander spared his life."

"Is he the only survivor? You seem healthy enough."

"Those who took refuge in the temple of Melqart, and other shrines around the city, were spared. The slaughter was terrible but Azimilcus and his family were pardoned by Alexander."

"I take it you are a religious man."

"Yes, sir."

"Stay the night, here in Gaza. I will provide an escort for your safety back to Tyre."

The man bowed and departed to his quarters. Batis stroked his beard. Walking to the main window, he contemplated the view of his hilltop citadel. The geography meant that no one could approach the city without being seen, and more importantly, its walls were impregnable.

After several minutes of contemplation, Batis called for his deputy. "I am informed that Tyre has fallen."

"That's the news, sir."

"The Babylonians tried for fourteen years and failed."

"King Alexander built a road across the water to New Tyre."

Batis laughed in disbelief. "A king who walks on water! What did he build a road with, I wonder?"

“Old Tyre.”

“What do you mean?”

“Alexander used the stone from its buildings to make a causeway, or as engineers dub it, a mole. He also used his navy.”

“But the Greek navy is small.”

“Alexander’s ships outnumbered the Tyrian fleet, sir.”

“Where was Persia’s navy?”

“Not at Tyre.”

Batis was silent for some moments. “We need soldiers and provisions.”

“Yes, sir.”

“The citadel must be stocked with food to last for six months. And hire those Arabs as mercenaries. They’re good fighters. And they like gold.”

“Consider it done.”

The deputy fidgeted.

“What is it?” asked Batis.

“King Alexander is on his way here. All the neighbouring towns have surrendered to him.”

“And you think we should?”

“He spares the towns which surrender. Those that do not are annihilated.”

“Alexander is not our sovereign. Gaza controls access to Egypt. How do you think King Darius will feel if we allow this upstart through?”

After his deputy scurried away, Batis sat back. Worry flickered through his eyes. He sat still for a long time.

***

It was September when Alexander’s troops started their trek to Gaza. Cooler than three months ago, the men found it easy and made steady progress down the coast.

Hephaestion, at the head of the navy, tracked the soldiers, supplying them with food and water. Ptolemy's Silver Shields kept to themselves as usual. Leonnatus and Seleucus joined forces to get provisions quickly to their men, and rest them as much as possible.

One morning, as Cassander jogged along on his steed, head bowed in thought, Perdiccas rode up.

"Everything alright, Cassie?"

"It's hot enough to bake bread."

"That's the Phoenician coastline for you."

"It's nearly the year's end, yet here we are, about to die of thirst."

"Not with mighty Hephaestion's supply ships."

Cassander reined in his horse. Pushing up his wide-brimmed hat, he looked Perdiccas in the eye. "You are aware, that after our seven-month siege at Tyre, there is another up ahead?"

"Gaza will fall quickly."

"Our scouts say differently."

Perdiccas was surprised. "Then you're better informed than my officers."

"That's because I breakfasted with Hephaestion when he docked this morning."

"Was King Alexander present?"

"The pair were discussing battle strategies. My point, dear Perdiccas, is that Gaza is the gateway to Egypt. It won't let us pass by without a fight."

"I see."

"Alexander is going to be the death of us one day. My only objection is his torture of us while we're still alive."

It was nearing noon. Up ahead, the turrets of a fortified city shimmered in the heat. Perdiccas wheeled his steed around in order to return to his men.

Leonnatus waved as he passed him. "How is Cassie?"

"Stay away from him."

"Bad mood?"

"Bad heart. His criticism of our monarch is unceasing."

"Oh, come on Perdie! We all grew up together. That's just the way he is."

"Remember, you're in Alexander's intimate circle. Be careful."

"Cassie's always been a jester. Why the sudden censorship?"

"You're a good man, Leo. If there ever comes a time, I'll back your promotion."

Perdiccas galloped back to his regiment. Leonnatus was about to urge his horse forward. It was his habit to wish Cassander well, before setting up camp in new territory.

Alexander was at the front of the column, giving orders. Suddenly, Leonnatus saw it. Cassander's impressions. Mocking the king. Pulling faces. The school humour, no longer innocent. Perhaps, it never was.

Leonnatus shook off his thoughts. But he did not approach Cassander.

***

Galloping around to Gaza's southern walls, the men pitched their camp at a distance from the citadel. Ptolemy moved his Silver Shields into battle position. In front, the phalanx and cavalry regiments lined up.

Alexander set to work on his strategy. Out of sight, soldiers started sapping operations, diligently burrowing tunnels to get in under the city walls.

Seleucus rode over to Cassander's tent. "You're wanted on the battlefield, Cassie."

"But, we just got here."

"Alexander says there's a weakness in a section of the southern walls."

"Our men have marched through the desert, Sel."

"I thought you should know."

"Why can't we rest, is what I want to know. The city's going to be here in the morning."

Seleucus took his leave and galloped back. Hephaestion accounted for the generals and senior officers. Afterwards, he rode up to his sovereign to give his report.

"Where's Cassie?" asked Alexander.

"Organising his crack troops," Seleucus called out.

"At least someone's thinking ahead," the king remarked.

He watched the siege engines. Their ponderous forms rolled with difficulty across the uneven plain. Hephaestion winced. Perdiccas fidgeted and wondered if he should say anything.

Cassander soon appeared, astride his horse. Still donning battle attire, he tied his loose cuirass into place.

"The engines are falling apart," he noted, tightening a shoulder strap.

"Where are your crack troops?" Perdiccas asked.

"My troops are exactly where they should be."

"Seleucus covered for you. Alexander wanted to know where you were."

"Tell him I was dallying with a maid."

"So, it's true."

"That I like women? I do. You should try it sometime."

Buckling his armour into place, Cassander made his way towards Seleucus.

"I'm glad you could make it, Cassie."

"Why we're here is a mystery to me, Sel. Apart from the siege engines, no one is going to get past those huge ramparts in one afternoon. Look at them!"

"Alexander wants us to be ready."

"He isn't. Have you noticed our engines are falling apart?"

At that moment, a loud snap reverberated through the still, hot air. The generals sat up on their horses as an engine lurched dangerously over a hillock. Suddenly, its canvas disintegrated. Men and wooden logs rolled to the ground. Several soldiers were crushed under the weight of the disintegrating tower.

"Keep going!" Alexander shouted.

His orders were relayed to the officers in charge of the engines. Cassander shook his head in disbelief. Another crack broke the still air. This time, the floor of the second engine gave way.

An entire contingent of men descended through the canvas and into the dust in a tangled heap. Soldiers died on direct impact with the hard ground. Others were killed with logs and falling debris.

Men on the ramparts of Gaza were wild with delight. Cheering at the enemy's misfortune, they banged their bronze weapons on their shields.

Hephaestion drew closer to Alexander in order to be heard. "You have to stop. The engines are unusable."

"But, we could take the city today."

Perdiccas was already at the royal elbow. "Hephaestion is right, Alexander. The engines must be repaired."

Far away on the king's left, Cassander laughed to himself. As the army retreated, he urged his horse back to the camp, where he dismounted. Giving his steed's reins to a waiting squire, he entered his tent.

A female slave greeted him with wine. Embroidered slippers sat next to a stool and a gold basin of water. She indicated the seat. Slipping off her master's sandals, she placed his feet in the basin.

"Who are you?" Cassander asked.

"Adama. I am one of your slaves captured from Tyre."

"Where is Helen?"

"With your son, Polymarchus."

"He's not my son. He's hers."

The woman blushed. "Forgive me, sir. Helen is training your Tyrian household staff and supervising the boy's homework."

"Makes sense." Cassander relaxed his sore feet in the warm water. "So long as she hasn't run away."

"It's not likely, sir," the woman said. "Helen said you are very kind." She kneaded Cassander's feet.

"You're good to me, Adama," he said.

"It pleases me that my lord is happy."

She took his feet out of the basin and briskly dried them with a towel. Before Adama could attend to them, Cassander took his embroidered slippers, and put them on his feet.

He stood up. "Take the evening off to see your family."

"Helen was right. You are kind."

"And you are a beautiful woman. I shall be boasting of my misdeeds with you to the generals."

"If you must sir, but –"

"Go on."

Adama thought rapidly. Her new master did not seem to be one who was easily angered, and she was curious. "Don't Greeks prefer boys?"

Cassander laughed until tears rolled down his face. "Go home, Adama." He dried his eyes with the hem of his robe. "When we get to Egypt, consider yourself a free woman."

***

484

115.

Seated outside by a campfire, Cassander munched his lamb shank. It was so tough, it almost broke his jaw. Perdiccas finished talking to an adjutant and joined him.

"Has Helen stopped cooking for you?"

"She's busy training my new staff."

"You have a gem there. Hold on to that one."

"What I want to know Perdie," said Cassander, "is where, in Zeus' name, is Leo?"

"Setting up camp. You know how long it takes."

"I do. It's why we always chat beforehand."

"Alexander may have summoned him. After all, he called you in this morning."

"He didn't."

"Did I hear wrong?"

"I said I breakfasted with Hephaestion. Alexander was there, but I wasn't summoned."

"But, why were you there, if you weren't sent for?"

"I ran out of provisions. Besides, Hephaestion does things with eggs you wouldn't believe. That one missed his calling as a housewife."

Cassander threw aside his bone. Stretching out by the fire, he yawned. Placing his hands on his stomach, he hummed a tune.

Catching sight of Leonnatus leaving the royal tent, Perdiccas moved his frame to block the scene. "Any roast meat left, Cassie?"

"Help yourself. There's an excellent wine from Tyre, too."

Cassander closed his eyes. Soon, he was snoring.

***

Ptolemy pushed his hat back. It was September, but the sun was already burning his fair Greek skin. He approached the king. "The men fixed the siege engines quickly, I see."

"They worked all night," Alexander explained.

Leonnatus emerged from the shade of a siege tower. "We'll be ready to move out shortly, sire."

"You've done a splendid job," Alexander congratulated him. "There's a gift in your tent."

"If she's anything like mine, she's gorgeous," Ptolemy whispered to Leonnatus. He turned to address his monarch. "Do you want the Silver Shields ready today?"

"You are always the first to offer me assistance, Ptolemy. There is another gift in your tent. I thought gold was appropriate."

In the pale morning light, the Macedonian generals gathered by the siege engines. A priest sprinkled water over a goat, in preparation of its sacrifice. Alexander ritually washed his hands.

Rushing over, Cassander made his appearance at the back of the group. "What's he doing?" he asked, pulling his outer tunic over his shirt.

"You're late," Seleucus noted.

"I was – er – sleeping."

At the back, out of Alexander's earshot, Ptolemy allowed himself a chuckle. Pressing his tunic into place with pudgy hands, Cassander peered over the generals' shoulders.

"What is Alexander doing?" he asked. "It's traditional for Macedonians to sacrifice a dog before battle."

"There are no dogs. He even sent Perdias back. We'll have to make do with a goat."

"My, my, how the mighty have fallen."

"Hush, Cassie!" Perdiccas remonstrated. "You don't want Hephaestion to hear you."

"Why? I'm not afraid of a purge, or disappearing in the night."

"What makes you so special?" Leonnatus growled.

"Talking to me now, are you?"

"You're always poking fun at our king. We're not at school, anymore."

"What's school got to do with it? I've always poked fun at Alex."

"He's King of Macedonia now, and soon to be Emperor of Persia."

"If he can't get a dog sacrificed, and siege engines to stay in one piece, we'll be lucky to get out of Gaza."

Leonnatus took a deep breath and focussed on the scene before them. Alexander lifted his hands to offer the animal to the gods.

A rush of wings interrupted the men's conversation. They looked up. A crow flew overhead. Dropping a lump of dirt onto Alexander's head, it flew off in the direction of the siege towers. Perching itself on an upper storey it cawed loudly.

Leonnatus paled. Ptolemy's grin evaporated. Dusting the dirt out of his hair, Alexander stopped what he was doing, and headed for his tent.

"Bring Aristander," he ordered an adjutant. "And have the goat released. It was the wrong sacrifice."

Entering his tent, he washed his hands in a gold bowl set up for such a purpose. Hephaestion, who had stayed behind, lifted his eyes from the list of supplies he was studying.

"Why are you frowning, Alex?"

"A crow dumped a clod of earth in my hair."

"That's a bad omen."

"I've sent for Aristander."

"Are you worried?"

"Let's see what he has to say, shall we?"

***

487

White linen robes fell to the seer's sandalled feet. His head was covered with a shawl of blue, and he carried a staff of religious authority.

"What do you think?" asked Alexander, after he had related the story.

Aristander bent his head. He knew they were about to launch an attack on Gaza. The siege engines were waiting, and the tent was filled with military men, all of whom were waiting for an interpretation of a cheeky crow's actions.

"The gods wish to speak to their son alone," said the seer.

Alexander immediately dismissed everyone, except Aristander. "What do the gods say?"

"The dumping of a clod in your hair means that you will suffer injury in the attack on Gaza. However, you will be the victor and look upon your enemies, as a lion after his kill."

"Good."

"That's not all."

"Does Zeus require a sacrifice?"

"Do not fight tomorrow. The men must stay in the camp."

"It is done."

***

116.

Inside the governor's conference room, Batis paced the floor. Surrounded by military officers, his stomach was in knots.

A general cleared his throat. "Alexander's army arrived last night."

"I can see it from here," Batis snapped.

One of the commanders of the Arab regiments stood up to speak. He was a slim man, with a pointed beard, and dark hooded eyes.

"The enemy doesn't seem to be doing anything, Governor," he said in a deep voice.

"What do you mean, Bur-Anat?" was the reply. "Alexander has brought enormous siege engines to Gaza!"

"They are battered from his war at Tyre. Today, as you can see, there is no one on the scaffolding."

The men in the room craned their heads towards the open windows. Batis stopped pacing. "That's true."

"King Alexander's soldiers are not preparing for battle."

"How do you know?"

"My scouts told me this morning."

"The Macedonians must know our city can't be breached," the general who had first spoken, pointed out.

A buzz of conversation filled the room. Batis nodded to Bur-Anat. "Friend, now is the time to attack."

***

A contingent of Macedonian soldiers was eating breakfast by the siege engines. It was a slow morning and their king was still hunkered down, on the instructions of his soothsayer. There was nothing to do except wait.

Commander Aias chewed on dried meat from his pack. His men were waiting for breakfast to be brought from the main camp. It was already an hour late, and they wanted to be working on the assembly of more siege engines.

A senior officer looked up. "Do you have any bread, Commander?"

"The boys will bring it shortly, Castor. Drink your milk. We still have the engines to repair. I want the floors fixed as soon as possible. You can start on that pile of canvas."

"For that, I need bread. No one can be expected to work on an empty stomach."

A veteran soldier spat in the dust. "I wish I'd stayed with the Silver Shields. There's more action in their camp than out here. And the conversation's better, too."

"Be careful, old man," Castor retorted. "Or I'll douse your grey hair in milk."

"The name's Brontes – or *sir*, to you."

Aias dropped his dried meat. "The gates just opened."

"Are they mad?" exclaimed Brontes.

Castor drained his milk. "Mad or not, old man, grab your spear and defend yourself!"

***

Four regiments of Arab mercenaries charged out of Gaza's gates. At lightning speed, under the command of Bur-Anat, they headed directly for the siege engines.

The Macedonians braced themselves for the attack. In minutes, the Arabs were on them. Despite their battle experience, despite their weaponry, and the fact they had warning, the Macedonians were slaughtered.

Afterwards, having demolished the enemy contingent, Bur-Anat's men set the giant towers ablaze.

***

Alexander was reading the *Iliad*, while Hephaestion attended to administration work. As the army was short of fresh meat, and the hills around Gaza contained game, he despatched several units on a hunting expedition.

It was a peaceful morning until the noise started. Hearing shouts, Hephaestion stepped out of the royal tent. Fiery flames shot into the bright blue morning of a Gaza sky. Startled, he took a step back. Then, he found his voice.

"Fire!"

Throwing aside his scroll, Alexander leapt up. Donning his armour, he rushed out to join Hephaestion. Other officers gathered round.

"Heph, go and put on your armour." Alexander turned to the officers. "Get the Companion cavalry and hypaspists, now!"

Waiting while watching flames streak across the sky, seemed to take forever, but presently, the men Alexander had ordered, were congregated in formation.

Soon, he was leading the regiments towards the siege engines. Attacking furiously from the front, he repelled the Arabs back to the city walls.

***

After the skirmish, Alexander rode back to the camp. Two Arab regiments suddenly emerged from the city gates. Cassander was resting on his spear. Still waiting for his heart to return to normal, he was incredulous. "Do they want more?"

491

Pulling a splinter from his leg, where an arrow had broken off, Seleucus squinted into the distance. "It's like something from a bad dream."

Leonnatus galloped back to the camp where the king was still standing outside his tent. "More Arabs are heading straight for us."

Alexander gestured to his squire. "A fresh horse," he ordered.

"You need to stay behind us," Leonnatus advised him. "We'll cover you."

Ignoring the advice, Alexander rode onto the plain. Watching the advancing contingents, he assessed the situation. "They're moving slowly, Leo. It's only a messenger party."

"With soldiers?"

A man was riding out in front, headed straight for the Macedonian king.

"Watch out Alex, you could be dead by nightfall!" Cassander laughed.

Seleucus turned to him. "It's fortunate for you that he's too far away to hear."

"I am but a court jester. My words are of no importance."

"And yet, you might have a point, Cassie. Remember Aristander's prophecy? Our sovereign should be careful."

"A soothsayer's nonsense!"

Seleucus shook his head. "There is no hope for you."

"I have a future and a hope, Sel. One day I shall be King of Macedonia."

"Only Macedonia?"

"I'm a homebody at heart. The empire Alexander carves out of Mother Earth will go to ambitious men like you."

"You may yet be of use, Lord Cassander," Seleucus said with a smile.

A hundred yards away from the banter, Leonnatus stayed close to his king. "Should I rally the men?"

"Stand down, Leo." Alexander stepped forward as the Arab regiments pulled up before him.

Further back, Seleucus moved away from Cassander to consult with Perdiccas. "There's a curve in the enemy ranks."

"The Arabs look as though they're hemming in our monarch," Perdiccas added.

Cassander found a pomegranate in his satchel. "Alexander has already isolated himself by moving forward." He crunched his fruit. "I suppose he is our brightest star, destined to always be at the forefront of things."

A worried Ptolemy rode up. "I sense a trap."

"I'll put our archers on alert," Perdiccas said.

"Good man," Ptolemy replied. "The rest of us should move."

By now, the Arab on horseback had dismounted. Flinging himself in the dust, he prostrated himself before the Macedonian king. The royal bodyguards moved forward.

"Stand back!" Alexander commanded.

"Pardon me, Your Majesty," the supplicant begged. "My name is Bur-Anat. I am an Arab mercenary commander. These are my troops. We were press-ganged into the service of the Governor of Gaza. We ask for mercy. Please forgive us, illustrious king."

"You are forgiven. Rise and be received."

Bur-Anat rose as he was commanded. Several yards back, Hephaestion caught the gleam of bronze. "Stop!"

It was too late. Bur-Anat's unsheathed sword slashed at Alexander's neck. Dodging the blow, the king moved to one side, but an archer's arrow struck him from behind, embedding itself in his right shoulder.

Hephaestion's men rushed forward and hacked the Arab archer to pieces. Perdiccas and Leonnatus followed suit. Soon, Alexander's men beat off their enemies, forcing them to retreat to the city gates.

Afterwards, on their return to camp, Seleucus picked up the dead Arab's bow. "Our king should really have seen that coming. Who surrenders with two units of men?"

Cassander wiped his brow. The heat was stifling. "Gives one hope for the future of assassinations, doesn't it?"

Concern flitted across Leonnatus' face. He pushed past them and headed for the royal tent.

***

Batis was overjoyed. He grasped Bur-Anat by his thin shoulders. "Well done, Commander!"

"I only nicked Alexander's neck."

"But your archer shot him in the shoulder."

Triumph sliced Bur-Anat's face into a smile. "He did."

"Five talents of gold are in your chambers. I have also taken the liberty of reimbursing your soldiers with a talent each."

"You are most generous."

"You are the hero of Gaza."

Batis motioned to an attendant who carried a piece of silk draped over his arm. Taking it, the governor flicked the material outwards. It shimmered with rainbow colours. Surrounding courtiers exclaimed at the beauty of the garment.

Slipping the garment over the Arab leader's head, Batis embraced him. "Now that you are wearing the robe of honour, come, sup at my table."

So saying, he led the way to the dining hall.

***

Leonnatus waited at the royal tent for the sentry to announce him. After some moments, Hephaestion arrived.

"How is King Alexander, General?"

"Resting, Leo."

"The Arabs were repelled back to the city."

"Thank you for letting us know."

"I trust that my king, and your dear friend, will recover soon."

"He will." Hephaestion's stare was stony.

Inclining his head, Leonnatus took his leave and made his way back to his tent. Cassander was standing at its entrance. "What can I do for you, General?"

"So formal, Leo! What happened to our friendship?"

"We're still friends. Come in. I need to change."

Cassander followed Leonnatus inside. "You badly hurt?"

"Only the usual cuts and bruises."

"That's a nasty one above your left eye. I have an excellent physician. He could boil you a potion."

"It's just a scratch. Where were you in the Arab skirmish, Cassander? I didn't see you."

"Fighting on the left."

"Ah! I was on the right."

"By the time we finished, those Arabs were at the gates of Gaza, begging to be let in!" With a short laugh, Cassander lay on a couch. A serving boy handed him wine. "Taste it first," he commanded the lad.

"It has been tasted." Leonnatus took the cup from the boy and drained it. "Pour our visitor another."

Cassander accepted the second cup. He wriggled into the couch for comfort and crossed his ankles. "I fear for your safety Leo, now you don't talk to me. You can't trust Alexander's sycophants. By the way, I am more than happy to get you a potion. It's better than wine for killing battle pain."

Leonnatus tried to smile. "I'm fine. I need to see Perdie, now."

***

Perdiccas was dining on poached salmon and shellfish. When Leonnatus entered his tent, he was ushered to a couch. A variety of dishes was set up so quickly, the guest had no time to refuse.

"You fought well today," Leonnatus complimented his host.

"And you, too. Our sovereign is still alive." Perdiccas raised his goblet. "To King Alexander!"

Leonnatus picked up a cup from the side table, next to his dining couch. "To Alexander! May he win Gaza as he did Tyre."

"An excellent toast. By the way, I saw Cassander at your tent."

"He offered me a potion."

"He is a skilled herbalist. Do you remember him in Aristotle's medical classes? He and the old man were always hunched together over those wooden tables, studying herbs and mushrooms."

Leonnatus chuckled, remembering the japes they had engaged in with frog's legs and sheep's eyes. "Part of me was worried Cassander's potion would be the last thing I ever tasted!"

"You should make your alliances clear. Alexander trusts you, but you cannot be friends with Cassander at the same time."

Leonnatus pondered for a moment. "I am loyal to all my friends."

Perdiccas, who was already tucking into the next course, barely heard him.

***

Hephaestion sat by Alexander's bed. "How are you feeling, cousin?"

"Happy."

"That's an odd thing to say."

"Don't you see? Aristander said I would be injured."

"He was right."

"He also said I would conquer Gaza. Now the injury is out of the way, we can take the city."

Hephaestion nodded towards a young female attendant. The woman was a Thracian doctor and never far away from Alexander. "Put another poultice on your master's shoulder," he commanded sharply.

"Not yet, mighty one. The herbs are slow acting. It will be ready for a change tomorrow morning."

"She's right," Alexander said. "Many thanks for your care, cousin."

Hephaestion rose to leave. "You are closer to me than a brother. Now get better soon."

He closed the door quietly behind him. The woman let out a sigh of relief. To her, Alexander's henchman was the most dangerous man in Greece.

***

117.

Ptolemy scratched his head. He wondered if being in a retired men's regiment meant he received news last. In front of him, mounds of earth stretched around the citadel. And they were rising.

He decided to consult with one of his Silver Shields. "Is Alexander building a mountain?"

"He is walling in Gaza, sir."

Leonnatus and Cassander arrived on horseback. The latter was peeling a banana. He stuffed the whole fruit in his mouth with relish.

"Maybe, he plans to suffocate the enemy," he offered indistinctly.

Perdiccas pulled up. "Our king is building mounds around the walls so he can attack from above." He frowned at Leonnatus. "It's nice to know where your loyalties lie."

"The last time I checked, we were all friends," Leonnatus retorted.

"Agreed!" Cassander said merrily.

Ptolemy was puzzled. "I thought siege engines attacked from above, Perdie."

Seleucus arrived on a magnificent white stallion. "Not always."

"Nice horse, Sel," said Cassander. "I thought you'd be helping to bury Gaza."

"My men are ready to do battle, which is more than I can say for yours."

"Mine need rest." Cassander threw away his banana skin. "Don't slip! It would be awful if your white charger turned brown with dust. Come, Leo, let's leave Alexander to bury the city. There's wine in my tent, and I've learned some new songs."

The pair galloped off.

***

Men worked day and night. Mounds of earth rose around Gaza. Soaring higher than the walls, the answer to everyone's questions became clear. As Alexander rolled out his military machine, archers and missile throwers took their positions atop the earthen bulwarks.

Inside the city, Batis spent long hours at his office. One morning his wife visited him. Due to the siege, her maids complained that they did not have supplies with which to clean the house. When she entered her husband's office, Batis' wife was struck by two things – the light, and her husband's agitated state.

"You are going to wear out the carpet," she said.

"Where are the reinforcements? They are supposed to be here. This Macedonian upstart is building mud walls to eclipse ours!"

"King Darius will send men. Don't worry, the tyrant of Greece can't enter Gaza."

Batis sat down. "It's unlike you to make a visit to my place of work. What's the reason?"

His wife presented him with a list of items they required. Leaving as quickly as possible, she made her way back to their home. It was not proper for a woman to invade the workplace of men. Still, there were standards which she intended to meet. Complaints about cleanliness brought shame to the household, and to her personally, as the lady of the house.

Batis reviewed the list. He put it aside and walked to his window. All he could see was earth piling up around his ears.

***

After several weeks, the earthworks were as high as Gaza's city walls. Alexander moved his heavy artillery into place. One morning, the city was not only encircled with mud, but with Macedonians and Greeks.

Inside his office, with his generals, Batis paced up and down. "You told me he would use siege towers."

"With respect, Governor, he did," one replied.

"They collapsed!"

"Which is the reason for the earthworks," an adviser ventured.

Thuds against the building marked the first wave of fireballs. The meeting ended. Everyone filed out to defend the city with their men as best they could. Batis resigned himself to wait.

***

Outside, Alexander's troops fired into the city from the earthworks. Storming several sections of the walls, they soon breached them.

Ptolemy's brigade supervised the younger men. Perdiccas, Alexander, Parmenion and Philotas had already chosen various sections of the city as theirs.

Dust flew up around Cassander's ears. Blinded, he started to choke. A grip on one shoulder preceded a wet cloth around his face.

"Thank you, kind stranger," he wheezed.

"Fall back, Cassie. Let your men do the work."

"Leo?"

"I have to get back to Alexander. Think about Helen and her son. You must reach Egypt alive."

Unable to do much more than breathe into the cloth, Cassander squinted. Through a dusty film across his eyes, he could see he was already on the upper wall. It was one short step inside. His men were waiting.

"Forward!" he cried, waving his sword.

As Cassander's men poured into the city, he realised his mistake. He was not going to die. That he knew. No Gazan was defending the city properly. But, as he wiped his eyes with his friend's cloth, he took in the scene. His heart sank. It was worse than Tyre.

Houses were already burning. With ruthless efficiency, every man in the city was being put to the sword. Women and children were rounded up to be sold into slavery.

Taking a deep breath, Cassander walked through a heap of rubble towards a group of civilians. Even if he saved only one child, he would be able to sleep that night.

***

It was over. Buildings blazed. Women wailed and children screamed. Many Greeks were still pillaging. Most had stopped.

Alexander faced Batis and a Gazan interpreter. The Persian governor's cheeks above his black beard were white. A trickle of blood ran down from one temple. The Macedonian king's wounded shoulder began to throb.

"I have conquered Gaza," he stated. Batis' back was rigid. He did not say a word. Alexander turned to the interpreter. "Does he understand me?"

The man was careful to bow low. "He does, Your Majesty."

"Let me be clear. I am the conqueror of Gaza. Governor Batis is vanquished. He must surrender to me."

The interpreter relayed the message. If Batis comprehended, he gave no sign.

"It is possible he only recognises King Darius," Perdiccas offered.

"I defeated Darius in battle!" Alexander screamed. "All Asia bows before me." He faced the interpreter. "Tell him that," he said in a calmer tone.

There was still no sign of obeisance from Batis. The man stood as immovable as stone.

"You good-for-nothing dog," Alexander snarled.

Beckoning to two of his officers, he commanded them to tie the governor down. There was still no sound from him. He did not cry out or beg for mercy. Infuriated, Alexander barked orders to his soldiers. They hesitated, but the savage commands increased in their heat and volume.

Stabbing the governor's ankles, they threaded a rope through the bleeding punctures. Then, they tied both ends to Alexander's chariot.

Leaping into the carriage, Alexander flicked the reins. Dragging the governor in the dust around the walls of Gaza was a delight to his angry soul, long after the insurgent was dead.

***

118.

It was a black night. Inside the castle at Gaza, Cassander sat in his room, nursing his drink by the fire. His attendants were dozing. A lenient employer, he did not reprimand them.

Seleucus stood at the cedar door. "May I come in?"

"Make yourself at home. Helen's gone to bed. Wine?"

Rousing themselves, the attendants bustled about. Seleucus was led to a fine couch, embroidered in gold thread. Phoenician wine was soon at his elbow, with dates and an assortment of meats.

"I must say, Lord Cassander, this citadel is well appointed."

"If you forget the wind whistling down the corridors. However, the fact Polymarchus understood his homework tonight, means more to me than where I sleep."

"I didn't see you at supper."

"Did Alexander ask for me?"

"He sat by himself. I don't think he noticed anyone."

"I'm still recovering from his disgusting act."

"Our sovereign was imitating Achilles at Troy. You must remember the passage in the *Iliad* where he drags Hector's corpse around the walls of Troy."

"Precisely – corpse. Batis was alive!"

"He would not kneel to our king."

"So what? The Gazan governor served Darius. Alexander is not King of Persia yet."

"Still, Batis should have acknowledged that Gaza had fallen."

"Alexander could have killed him first. My ears are still ringing with that poor devil's screams." Cassander shook himself. Downing his wine, he held it out for a refill. "I'll take the one from

503

Mycenae," he said to a yawning wine steward. "What about you, Sel? Care to join me in a victory celebration?"

"That's what I'm here for."

***

Alexander's haggard face was at the door. "How are you, Hephaestion?"

"The accommodation is sumptuous. Are you staying, cousin?"

"I'll sleep alone tonight."

"Would you like me to read you a passage from the *Iliad*? I could come to your chamber for a bit."

"I know that book by heart. Achilles is my ancestor."

"Today you demonstrated actions worthy of him."

Alexander bade goodnight and walked back to his room at the end of the corridor. Feeling a draft, he pulled his cape close. Nothing, he reflected dismally, warmed the ice around his heart.

Hephaestion returned to the book he was reading. It was a play by Euripides. Everyone, he reflected, had had their fill of Homer for one day.

***

Gathering in the cold of dawn, the Macedonians and Greeks waited for the signal to fall out. Cassander drew on a pair of woollen gloves Helen had given him at breakfast. The present cheered him. His nerves were still frayed from the Gazan governor's demise.

Leonnatus stayed close to Alexander, but there was a friendly wave from him. Rolling his eyes, Cassander waved back.

Trying to lighten the mood, Ptolemy was boisterous. Laughing and joking with the Silver Shields, there was no one who gave off more joy than the older general. His men loved him. Being the image

504

of King Philip, meant his troops felt as if their late king was still with them.

Seleucus passed Cassander. "Nice gloves."

"My ride – I mean my slave – gave them to me."

Seleucus laughed. "You can't fool me! They're from Helen. You treat your women well. In return, they take care of you."

"True, I'm even giving Adama her freedom in Egypt."

"And Helen?"

Cassander pursed his lips. "She is my family now. But Adama does not need to be lugged around Persia with us."

"Are you thinking she will find a husband in Egypt?"

"I hope so. It's a peaceful country. Adama does give wonderful foot massages, though."

"No doubt."

"You must have one."

"I thought such an offer would be for Leonnatus?"

"He's had several. I'm buttering you up, now."

"What is your agenda?"

"I know you will be in charge of a great empire after Alex dies."

"And you may yet be of use to me. I shall enjoy a foot massage very much, Lord Cassander."

Seleucus tipped his wide-brimmed Macedonian hat and galloped off to join his men. Cassander twisted his frame around. Behind his men was the baggage train. Adama and Helen would be with them. He also had new staff, including a hundred children and their mothers from Gaza.

Facing forward, he patted his horse's neck. The stallion was making the most of the grass tufts beneath his hooves. Finally, the army moved forward on yet another long march, this time towards Egypt.

***

PART VI

119.

In the distance, a solitary chariot moved towards Alexander's army. Gaining momentum, it became visible through the mirage created by the heat. Its rider flicked his horses with a whip as they galloped across the sands.

At the rear of the army, Ptolemy continued to chat to Seleucus. Not noticing the advancing chariot, they continued to ride at a normal pace. Perdiccas was at the front, with Alexander's group, where Leonnatus and Cassander were already pulling back on their reins.

Hephaestion shaded his eyes. "Is that charioteer going to attack us by himself?"

"He's a messenger," said Alexander.

Cassander peeled an orange. He popped a section into his mouth. "But of who, or whom? It's a mystery."

Leonnatus leaned over. "Shush, Cassie! This is serious."

"Well, I can't see anyone else, Leo."

Alexander turned around on Bucephalus to face the pair. "Neither can I," he said, with a half-smile. "You really should listen to Cassander, Leo."

A hot gust of wind blew Alexander's words across the army. A ripple of mirth from the men followed. Ptolemy and Seleucus suddenly noticed the charioteer. Spurring their horses, they rode to the front.

"Do you need backup, Alexander?" Ptolemy asked.

"It's a trap," Seleucus warned. "There's bound to be an army behind the sand dunes."

To their surprise, the messenger slowed to a halt. He got out of his chariot and waited.

Alexander turned his head abruptly to his left and right. "I sense more chariots."

"Our mighty leader smells expensive cedar a mile off!" Perdiccas jested.

As the Macedonians laughed, a group of chariots appeared on the horizon. They joined the first one. Perdiccas' felt his throat go dry.

"Send a messenger to them," Alexander commanded.

Waving to an adjutant, Hephaestion barked orders. "You heard our sovereign! Find out if we have friends or foes."

Obeying him, the man tore across the desert on horseback. Alexander's entire army came to a standstill. Tension flooded the atmosphere as they waited. Cassander finished his orange. With a weary sigh, he put his hand on his sword.

"So much for Egypt being a peaceful land," he muttered.

Meanwhile, in the distance, the Macedonian adjutant, closed in on the strangers. Four men walked across the white sand to greet him. To his surprise, they bore gifts of gold and silver.

"These are for your king. We welcome Alexander-the-Great to Egypt."

***

With their chariot escort, the Macedonian army entered Pelusium. While his troops waited, Alexander rode into the palace. The grand building was situated in the middle of a sleepy township.

Stray dogs lay in the sun, too weary to bark. Under date palms, children played desultory games. Occasionally, one would spin a top, which would clatter into the dust after it stopped rotating, not to be picked up again. Shops sold wares, but no one made an attempt to interest the soldiers. Some shopkeepers stared at them. Others simply dozed.

Inside the courtyard of the royal residence, horses were unhitched from their carriages and taken away by stable boys. Preferring to keep Bucephalus as close to him as possible, in case he needed to make a getaway, the Macedonian king tethered him to a post in the courtyard.

When the Macedonian party arrived in the reception hall, hundreds of courtiers fell on their faces. A slim man, in long robes and a curled beard, rose from an ornate chair to greet the strangers.

"What are they doing?" Alexander asked the man.

"I am Merzaces, the Persian satrap. Your subjects are prostrating themselves before their new King of Egypt."

"While their respect impresses me, I am not crowned yet."

"Memphis is where Egyptian kings are coronated. I can arrange for Pharaoh's fleet to take Your Majesty there, if you wish."

"I do wish it."

"Then, it will be done." The Persian satrap prostrated himself.

***

Outside, Cassander emptied a waterskin over his head. "I do wish Alexander would hurry up."

"Let's hope he's safe," Perdiccas said.

Cassander snorted. "Of course, he's safe. This place is not exactly bristling with armed attackers."

"I wouldn't be too sure," growled Seleucus.

"It could be a trap," Leonnatus pointed out.

Just then, Alexander appeared.

"We were about to come and get you," said Parmenion.

"How was the reception, cousin?" Hephaestion asked.

"If you need us for battle, we're ready," Philotas offered.

Cassander rolled his eyes. Alexander noticed. He looked from Philotas to Parmenion.

"We're going to Memphis, where I shall be crowned Pharaoh," he said.

Leonnatus nudged Cassander. "It's happened. He's finally caught you out."

A wicked grin split Cassander's face. "It's not me he's caught out."

***

120.

During the river trip to Memphis, the shore was lined with cheering Egyptians. It was November, which was the Egyptian season of *Akhet*, when the Nile was in flood.

At the harbour, it was impossible for the army to disembark due to the crowds. The flotilla of boats bearing the foreigners bobbed helplessly on their moorings in the water. Alexander did not improve matters by striding about on deck, waving to his new subjects. Eventually, native police intervened. The crowds were pushed back, and the army disembarked.

At the palace, the guard was doubled. Even the lowest ranked soldier in the Macedonian army found it impossible to walk the streets without being mobbed. After a week, the city settled down enough for the authorities to go ahead with a scheduled welcome parade.

Insisting he sacrifice to the Apis bull, which the Persian king, Cambyses had killed, Alexander secured respect, as well as adulation. After several more days, the seers of Amun considered it safe enough to proceed with the coronation.

On the fourteenth day of a chilly November morning, Alexander stood in the temple, bare-chested, wearing a pleated kilt and sandals. Ptolemy surrounded the temple with his crack troops. Inside, the king's bodyguards kept in the shadows.

Accompanied by several priests, Hephaestion and Perdiccas, Alexander walked past the first pylon. The air was heavily incensed, and the chanting of the holy men was hypnotic.

A priest, wearing a falcon's mask, representing Horus, appeared out of the gloom. Hephaestion fell back. The man took one of Alexander's hands and led him to a stone chapel. A second priest, impersonating Atum, god of creation and the sun, appeared. Taking Alexander's other hand, he and the first priest left the chapel for a hall. There, Alexander was to undergo the initial rites of transformation from mortal to divine king. Handing their charge over to another group of holy men to be purified, the two priests departed.

***

Outside, Cassander fanned himself. "It's hot, Leo!"

"It's Egypt."

"Why these people insist on doing things in temperatures which would cook my breakfast, is beyond me."

"You didn't have to come."

"My leader is being crowned. I must be here."

"I'm going to talk to Perdiccas."

"Go ahead, abandon me, for the King's pets."

"If you wish to complain all morning, that's your prerogative."

"I do have a complaint, Leonnatus. I've always been a friend. You, however, are only available to others when it's politically expedient."

"That's not fair."

"It's *true!*"

Cassander's words, pitched at scream level, reverberated through the temple courts. Ptolemy, who was waiting for Alexander inside the sanctuary, pricked up his ears.

"What was that?" he asked a senior officer.

"It sounded like Lord Cassander, sir."

"Check the streets. Make sure there are no mobs on the rampage."

***

Deep within the temple, Alexander was at a pool's edge. Four priests stood at its corners. One wore a mask representing an ibis' head, another looked like a dog. The Macedonian knew them from his reading, prior to the coronation, as Thoth god of wisdom and Seth, god of chaos.

He thought he heard a scream but brushed it off. It was a strange environment, and he was bound to be under stress.

"Go to the centre of the pool, Your Majesty," a whisper sounded in his ear. As he obeyed, Alexander noticed two falcon-headed men. Taking a breath, he closed his eyes. When he opened them, he saw more priests wearing animal-headed masks.

How many deities can there be?

Straining his eyes in the cloudy gloom, Alexander stepped into the water. It was pleasantly warm. He relaxed.

After solemn incantations, the masked priests lifted up a gold ewer each. The vessels had long spouts, which extended to the centre of the pool. In one motion, they poured the contents over Alexander. No longer ordinary water, the liquid represented divine life, itself.

When they had finished, the priests representing Thoth, Seth, Dunawy, and Horus of Behdet, led Alexander to the *House of the King* which consisted of two pavilions in a large hall.

"One is *Per-neser*, the House of the Flame," a falcon-headed priest whispered. "I'm Dunawy, by the way. You're not seeing double, Your Highness. There are two hawk deities here."

Alexander thought he heard a trace of amusement in the man's voice.

"What is the House of the Flame?" he asked the priest.

"It is an old shrine from the north, Your Highness."

"And the other?"

"That is the Great House or *Per-wer*."

"Pharaoh?"

"That's what it means."

The other falcon-headed mask bobbed into view. "Stop talking!" he hissed at his colleague. "By the way, I'm Horus of Behdet, Your Majesty. We will go to the first house now. There are several deities, namely Nekhbet, Buto, Neith, Isis, Nephthys, Horus, Seth –"

"Do pipe down," said the first falcon.

"But, he should know," said the second.

"There are too many deities to remember."

Trying to keep a straight face, Alexander accompanied them into the first house.

***

A unit of soldiers exploded from behind the walls of the temple. Sixteen cavalrymen dashed into the street.

"What now?" groaned Cassander.

"They probably heard you," said Seleucus, behind him.

One of the horsemen galloped up to them. He dismounted. "Mighty Lord Cassander, are you alright?"

"Apart from having backstabbing friends in high places, seeking to go higher, I'm fine."

He glared in Leonnatus' direction, but the general was engaged in a deep conversation with Perdiccas.

"Very good, sir," said the cavalry officer. "General Ptolemy sent me to quell a disturbance. Is there any trouble here?"

"None," answered Seleucus on his comrade's behalf.

The man remounted his horse. With a gesture to the other officers, he galloped back into the temple, followed by his unit.

Parmenion leaned towards his sons, Nicanor and Philotas, both of whom were watching. "Why is it wherever we go, Lord Cassander stirs up trouble?"

"He's an idiot," scoffed Philotas.

"On the contrary, he's a fine general," Nicanor said.

His father looked at him. His brother sniggered. Nicanor quailed and set his eyes firmly on the cobblestones.

A cool breeze wafted the conversation across the street to where Cassander was standing. The latter gave no indication he had heard but his eyes darkened with black fury.

Inside the temple, Alexander met the god Amun's daughter, a snake goddess in the southern chapel. Shrieking, she ran to embrace him. Fortunately, one of the quarrelling falcons had managed to brief the unsuspecting Macedonian. Even so, Alexander flinched. Her cries were deafening.

Next, a priest wearing a leopard skin and wig, plaited and curled on one side, approached.

"I am Inmutef," he said in a low voice. "I'm here to crown you."

Immediately, the first crown in a series, was placed on Alexander's head. If only Hephaestion were here! They had both dreamed of this coronation, in the world's most ancient land, since boyhood.

Then, white and red crowns of Upper and Lower Egypt, were passed over him separately. Next, they were amalgamated into the *pasekhemty,* or Double Crown. Alexander knew it by its Greek name of the *pschent*. In this form, they were both placed on his head. Now he was Pharaoh!

There were others. Ra's unwieldy *atef* crown, with multiple parts, reminiscent of the menorah, which Alexander had seen in the Jewish temple of the god with no name. Then, there was the *ibes* crown, with its two enormous plumes, which intrigued him. He wanted to ask questions, but kept still. There were more to come, so many, he lost count.

Afterwards, Alexander was taken to another shrine where his favourite, the blue war headdress or *khepresh* appeared. Representative of the many domains of the sun, he was crowned with it, and blessed by the priests, while kneeling on a cushion.

Amun touched the nape of his neck and intoned the new king's five-fold pharaonic title. He was then taken to a chamber where he was presented with two sceptres. One was a crook, with which to shepherd his people, while the other was a flail, to bring them into line.

Finally, Alexander was brought into a throne room. He had seen the gold of his father, and those of many nations since. However, the beauty of the gilded throne, with its winged deities, picked out in semi-precious jewels, was breathtaking.

Seated on it, Alexander was coronated with the Double Crown of Egypt once more. In full regalia, he was led outside to the courts to be presented to the priests, who bowed to him. In a change of tradition, Alexander retired to the temple, where he divested himself of his garments.

Taking his horse from the courtyard, he joined Hephaestion and Ptolemy. Guarded by the Silver Shields, he made his way back to the palace in time for dinner.

*****

<h1 style="text-align:center">121.</h1>

After his coronation, the new King of Egypt settled into his residence in the palace of Memphis. Sprawling for several miles, it included royal offices, workshops, the Ministry of Foreign Affairs, administrative buildings, kitchens and the harem.

Army personnel were quartered in the outlying buildings of the palace. Now a man of leisure, Ptolemy sent messengers with gifts across the sea to summon Thais. Afterwards, he threw a party, which the generals, and many soldiers, attended.

Meanwhile, Leonnatus, Cleitus, and Philotas set about finding Egyptian girlfriends. Parmenion and his cronies investigated the library for scholarly works. Seleucus took up the study of cuneiform. For his part, Perdiccas found the most comfortable bed in his new home, where he diligently slept twelve hours a day.

Determined to enjoy his break from endless campaigning, Cassander adopted Egyptian garb. He increased the wages of his household staff, who in turn, cooked him the best local dishes. Taking Polymarchus under their wing, they introduced him to their families, where the boy played with children of his own age.

Helen started weaving with noblewomen of the neighbourhood. Spending many days on the rooftop at her loom, she learned their customs, and how to speak their northern Egyptian dialect.

For his part, Cassander visited the surrounding vineyards, which he learned were connected to his property, rather than to that of the palace. He was even shown his own wine, stored in granite cellars.

Most intriguingly for Cassander, his servants gave him a tour of the garden. To his surprise, he saw ponds where he could fish in the privacy of his own home. Quick to capitalise on the opportunity, he spent many a happy afternoon, dressed in white linen, fishing like a native nobleman.

It was on one such afternoon, that Leonnatus discovered him, seated on a chair behind an acacia tree, by the water. Plants from Egypt stood in tidy rows around the pool's edge, where blue and white tiles bordered a mosaic of fish.

Under a portico, two attendants sat in the shade surrounded by ornate chairs, panniers, and a table set with refreshments.

Helen was enjoying playing *senet*, an Egyptian board game, with Polymarchus. She glanced up at the visitor. Her son waved, before they both returned to the serious business of trying to defeat one another.

Dressed in fine robes, Cassander was on his cedar chair, an ebony rod in one hand, fishing for perch.

"It's hard to recognise you, Cassie."

"Have a seat, Leo. It's good fishing."

A servant hurried from underneath a portico, with a rod. Another picked up a chair and pannier, and placed them next to Cassander.

Leonnatus sat down. "What bait are we using?"

Cassander pulled a gold-lidded bucket from one side and pushed it towards him. His friend removed the lid. Inside the bucket was a porous pottery jar filled with meat scraps. It was the same shape as the vessels which kept water cool on every street corner.

Selecting a piece of liver, Leonnatus baited his hook. It was pleasant watching the fish dart in and out of crystal-clear water. Helen clapped her hands as she won another pawn from her son. He retaliated by taking several of her pieces, while laughing with childish joy.

Leonnatus noticed that the pond, although filled with aquatic life, also contained decorated mosaic tiles. There was even a portrait of a king at the bottom, hiding under algae.

He leaned forward. "Darius?"

"An ancient king, Leo. He was an Egyptian by the name of Thutmose-the-Great."

"How do you know?"

Cassander bobbed his head in the direction of his servants. "My staff say his name is written on the sides of the pond. He was Egypt's greatest conqueror – but we won't tell Alex."

"Speaking of which –"

Cassander groaned. "I knew it. You're here because of him. At least, have some wine." He beckoned to an attendant.

A cup was in Leonnatus' empty hand before he could protest. With the other, he balanced his rod. A perch was nibbling the bait cautiously. "I'm sorry, Cassie. I volunteered to tell you –"

"We're not at war, are we? I'd hate to lose all this."

"Alexander wishes to visit an oasis after his coronation."

"An oasis doesn't sound too bad. What's the catch?"

"The last foreign army that attempted the journey did not return."

Cassander dropped his rod. "They all died?"

"I didn't say that. Only, that they did not return."

"Leo, when people don't return from the desert, they're presumed dead!"

"They might have reached the oasis of Siwa and lived there."

"Siwa borders another country – a most unfriendly one."

"Libya."

"Which has always been Egypt's enemy!"

"Some pharaohs were Libyan."

Pushing back his stool, Cassander rose. His small frame was puffed up and his arms flailed about. "Now I remember! It has an oracle."

Helen was looking at the pair. Polymarchus could not decide whether to cry or be alarmed.

"It does, Cassie. That's why –"

"Don't tell me, Leo – I know all about King Alexander and his blasted soothsayers! He's more self-obsessed than a pretty girl looking into her mirror. What does he want to know? Whether he is the son of Philip, or Zeus?"

"That's precisely what he wants to know," said Leonnatus.

Helen cleared her throat. "Your Lordship, may I ask you to lower your voice?"

"You may ask," said Cassander, "but I will not!"

His face became the colour of ripe pomegranate as he stomped about, shouting at the skies. Finally, he sat down on his stool again and picked up his rod.

"I am going to fish," he announced. "Anyone who isn't, please leave."

Helen, Leonnatus, and the attendants vanished. Unlike the others, Polymarchus got up slowly from his board game. He sat next to Cassander on the stool vacated by Leonnatus.

Picking up the abandoned fishing rod, he attached a piece of meat to its hook. With a sudden and complex wrist action, he flicked the line out into the middle of the pool.

Cassander was surprised. "That's quite a flourish you have there."

"Thanks, Dad."

"You're welcome, son."

Polymarchus grinned. He drew his stool closer to Cassander. In silence, the pair sat together and fished until the sun set over the trees. Acacia, persea and hibiscus bushes glimmered. Vines glowed orange and gold.

At twilight, servants appeared. Picking up the panniers full of fish, they made their way to a grill which was set up at the back of the garden. The weary fishermen rose and wandered over to where dinner was being prepared. A cook stood at the grill made of bricks, topped with a bronze plate, under which acacia logs burned. Adding a range of meats with the fresh fish, the man deftly sliced garlic, scattered spices, and squeezed lime juice over the food.

Helen and Leonnatus, seated on couches, their backs resting against embroidered cushions, ate freshly baked bread, stuffed with cheese and coriander. Cassander and Polymarchus took their seats, as if nothing had happened.

Cooking smells rose into the night air, and wafted into the homes of the generals who lived nearby. Eventually, the combination of grilling food, limes, and garlic, grew too strong to resist. Seleucus, Ptolemy, and Cleitus joined the dinner. Philotas and his father brought desserts. Others brought only their stomachs.

Disciplined as ever, Alexander stayed in his palace rooms with Hephaestion, planning a route to Siwa in the most significant move of his career.

***

122.

It was morning. Cassander was pleasantly surprised to find his head was clear. Humming to himself, he swung his legs out of bed and shuffled on embroidered slippers.

An attendant brought him a gold basin in which he washed his face and hands. Next, the man handed his master a linen towel. Drying himself, Cassander went to the bathroom to brush his teeth.

Once he was ready, he emerged to choose his clothes for the day. His dresser stood in front of several riding outfits. "What attire does His Lordship require for the trip?"

Taken aback, Cassander was about to make an acerbic reply. Then, he remembered. Alexander!

"Er – is the Siwa trip today?" he asked.

"The others went to the palace an hour ago to breakfast with His Majesty. No one's left for Siwa yet."

"Why didn't you wake me? Why didn't someone tell me?"

"We thought you knew, sire."

Leonnatus entered the chamber. "Ready, Cassie?"

"I want breakfast."

"It's ready. Several of our friends' horses are still in their stables, so you have plenty of time."

An annoyed Cassander pushed past his friend and went to the dining room. He ate a bowl of cooked beans with bread. It was the simple fare of Egyptian people, and he relished the flavours of beans, spices, and herbs. He also knew it would fill his stomach until lunchtime.

His leather satchel lay on a nearby chair. Taking a few pieces of fruit from a bowl, he picked up his bag and stuffed them into it.

Leonnatus entered the room. Cassander looked up. "Where's Helen?"

"On the front porch, waiting for you."

With an impatient breath, Cassander flung the satchel over his head and across one shoulder. He went outside and ordered his horse from a servant. Helen was chatting with two of his squires. One was holding his sunhat which he seized.

"Both of you get your horses and go to King Alexander's main courtyard," he snapped.

The men departed quickly. Leonnatus appeared on the porch, where he politely inclined his head in Helen's direction.

"I'll wait for you there, too, Cassie," he said.

Leaving Cassander to say his farewells, Leonnatus made his way to the palace.

***

Arriving at the royal residence on horseback, Cassander noticed that only a few of the Companions were present. None were his friends. Philotas, Craterus and Meleager milled about, chatting and laughing. Hephaestion waited with Alexander for Bucephalus.

Servants and baggage handlers made up the bulk of the expedition numbers. There were no women. Irritated at the thought he might have been able to stay at home, Cassander dismounted. Presently, his squires joined him.

Leonnatus clattered down a staircase into the courtyard with a cup of pomegranate juice. He was joined by Perdiccas, who wished him well, before repairing to his residence at the back of the palace. Taking his stallion from a squire, Leonnatus went up to Cassander. He offered him his cup.

Cassander accepted the drink. "Is Perdie living in the palace grounds?"

"He has diplomatic work to do."

Leonnatus mounted his horse. Downing the juice, Cassander did the same. Ptolemy appeared late from his supervision of the baggage handlers. He hoisted himself quickly across the back of a black stallion. The party trotted out of the courtyard behind Alexander and the other men.

Adjusting his sunhat, Cassander realised he felt well. The first part of the journey was easy. In a few minutes, they reached the river boats assigned to take them from Memphis to the north. Many of the generals, with military units, were already aboard.

Cassander was surprised. "Are we all going to Siwa, Leo?"

"We're visiting Lake Merotis first."

"Siwa would be easier to get to from Memphis."

"But not safer."

"Since when has Alexander done anything safe?"

"The army of the Persian king, Cambyses, was lost in the Western Desert. Those men probably started their journey from the palace."

"I thought a foreign army like ours went missing, Leo. Now you tell me it was none other than Cambyses who lost his army?"

"Lower your voice."

"If the Persian king couldn't get across, what are we doing?"

"That's why we are travelling by a known desert route. Now, please board. Everyone is staring."

Grumpily acquiescing to his friend's request, Cassander walked onto the boat. The upper deck was less crowded. He visited his quarters, which were small, but well-appointed, with Nubian maidens to serve him refreshments.

Afterwards, Cassander went on deck. It was pleasant cruising. He and the men spent the day watching the verdant lands of the north slip past the bows of their boat.

***

When they reached the harbour at the mouth of the Nile, Alexander's party disembarked. They headed towards the Macedonian fleet, which was moored further up the coast. Riding for two days, they stopped frequently to rest themselves and their horses.

On the third day at dawn, the men breakfasted by the sea. Cassander was deep in thought. "How far do you think we've ridden, Ptolemy?"

"About fourteen turns of the sun dial."

"That's over three hundred and fifty thousand cubits."

"Thereabouts. Why do you ask?"

"Alexander's consulting with his seer."

Looking up, Ptolemy noticed Alexander pacing the shore with Aristander. Ptolemy rose and hurried towards the king, with Seleucus in tow. Leonnatus downed the remainder of his goat's milk and followed. With a smirk, Cassander tagged along. When they reached Alexander, they found him immersed in drawing on the sand with a stick.

"What are you doing?" Ptolemy asked.

The king raised his stick. His eyes were bright. "See the island of Pharos, brother?"

Together with the others, Ptolemy's eyes followed the direction in which the king was pointing.

"Is that what it's called?" he asked.

"It looks like a pile of rocks," muttered Cassander.

"This is the natural basin for a harbour," Alexander continued.

"I see what you mean," said Ptolemy.

"And the perfect place for a sea port!"

"If you say so," said Cassander in a low voice.

"Hush, Cassie," Leonnatus remonstrated.

As usual, Alexander did not hear. He was too busy sketching his vision of the city. "With a full view of the harbour, there will be temples, and palaces here. Behind, I see the township, with houses and shops for its citizens. A major crossroads will unite them all."

He continued to draw. An Egyptian attendant approached, carrying a linen bag. Alexander took it, drew his dagger, and made a hole underneath. Crumbs spilled out as he paced up and down, tracing the buildings he had drawn in the sand.

"This city shall be called Alexandria. May she be prosperous for all time."

"Most impressive!" said Ptolemy.

The army picked up on the general's tone. Enthusiastic cries and cheering broke out. Artists sketched the moment on papyrus, while scribes copied the layout of streets. A flock of crows circled. Suddenly, they descended. Pecking at the delicious crumbs, they commented loudly to each other as they hopped about.

In an agitated state, the king consulted with his seer. "This is a bad sign."

"How so, Your Majesty?"

"The birds are eating the grain, Aristander! Surely, it means this place will be impoverished."

"On the contrary – this is a sign that Alexandria will be prosperous. Her granaries will feed the world, just as your bread feeds these birds."

Relief washed over Alexander. He handed the bag to a nearby squire.

"Artists, bring me the drawings when you've finished," he ordered. "Scribes, you have until sunrise to complete your first drafts. All work requires my royal stamp of approval."

With his usual rapid steps, he returned to his tent on the shore.

***

123.

It was time to leave for Siwa. The king selected a few men. Most of the morning was spent in waiting. Jade green waves gently lapped the white sands of the new seaport of Alexandria. Meleager, Craterus, and Leonnatus sat on rocks close to the shore, and chatted.

Cassander removed his hat. He shook his locks out to feel the wind blowing through his hair. He closed his eyes and sighed with pleasure. *This reminds me of home.*

Philotas walked over. "I'm surprised to find you with us, Lord Cassander."

"The surprise is mutual."

"Alexander is only taking a few trusted friends to Siwa."

"I disagree. You're not a friend, Philotas."

"The same could be said about you."

"I've been with Alex since he was a child. I know him. You, on the other hand, have never left the knee of your father, General Parmenion."

"I'm fighting like everyone else. Anyway, what are you talking about? You're General Antipater's son."

"Who is in Macedonia, minding his own business. In contrast, yours accompanies you on every campaign." Cassander turned away to view the sea.

Philotas stood awkwardly in silence for a few moments. "I only came over to make your acquaintance. It's a long journey." He walked back to the others.

Leonnatus rose abruptly from the rock, on which he had been sitting, and joined his friend. "I see you are important enough to attract one of Alexander's favourites, Cassie."

"Bah! Philotas will be dead before we get to Persia."

"You're not planning to poison him, are you?"

A strange ripple crossed Cassander's lips. "So, you remember my facility with potions!"

"How can I forget? Aristotle thought you were gifted."

"That as it may be, I won't be Philotas' executioner."

"I hope there is one. I can't stand the man."

Cassander tilted his head towards Hephaestion. "There's no need to worry."

"Don't be ridiculous, Cassie!"

"I'm serious. Parmenion and his sons wish to set up a dynasty. Do you think our noble sovereign is going to stand for that?"

"And you think Hephaestion will do the job?"

"He always does Alexander's dirty work."

"And I thought the purpose of this pilgrimage was to find out the future from an oracle."

"Let's just say this trip to Siwa will determine our future." Cassander frowned at the sea.

Leonnatus saw they were ready to depart. He tugged his friend's sleeve. They made their way from the shore to where their steeds waited. A few Egyptian porters strapped their belongings to pack animals. Ptolemy was overseeing the process. Arguing with the guides on the nature of the route, he flailed his arms about and roared.

Ignoring Cassander, Philotas joined Meleager and Craterus. Alexander scratched his jaw. He nudged Hephaestion.

"Cassander didn't fall for the bait," he chuckled.

"To test him with Philotas?"

"I wonder about Cassie's loyalty."

"You needn't. He's an honest man." Hephaestion's forehead furrowed. "Unlike Parmenion's brat."

The party moved forward into the wide expanse of desert.

***

124.

Riding down the coastal road was pleasant. Alexander and Hephaestion were at the front with Ptolemy and their guides. Philotas made an awkward trio with Meleager and Craterus. Trying to keep up with their bawdy banter was impossible.

Enjoying the sea breeze, Leonnatus found he could think, as he jogged alongside Cassander. While everyone chatted to pass time, his friend was quiet. Occasionally, the latter dug into his satchel for a snack, which he shared.

After ten days, the town of Amunia, loomed up ahead. The party slowed to a halt. Before they could decide on what to do, the gates opened, and an emissary walked out. He was followed by several men, and the town mayor.

Cassander leaned across his horse to Leonnatus.

"It looks as if we have a bed for the night," he whispered.

"Let's hope they have women, too," rejoined Leonnatus.

Overhearing them, Philotas grinned at the pair. He was met with stony faces.

"The welcome committee seems friendly enough," Ptolemy remarked to Alexander.

After a cordial interaction with the townsmen of Amunia, the new King of Egypt entered the gates. Inside, the visitors' horses were taken away to be watered and fed. The guides accompanying Alexander were ushered to servants' quarters, while the generals were shown to their own rooms within the main living area. They were simple, but airy and clean.

In his room, Alexander stripped off. "This is a good, quiet spot, Heph."

Hephaestion's eyes sought out every corner for potential spies. "A bit rustic, isn't it?"

Alexander went to the bathroom, where he found a bronze pail full of water. A cup sat next to it with soap and sea sponges. Taking the cup, he poured water over his head. Next, he lathered up the sponges, and scrubbed himself thoroughly.

Afterwards, he dried himself off with a towel and re-entered the main room. Taking a fresh robe from his pack, he flung it over him. Hephaestion was still in his dusty robes.

"Wash!" Alexander commanded. "We have an audience with the town chief."

***

Having appraised his room, Cassander walked into the corridor. A tall man, wearing a pale blue robe and linen headdress, rose from his position on a stool.

"May I help you, sir?"

Cassander slipped a gold piece into the man's hand. "I'd like a bath."

Presently, a wooden tub was brought to his room, where he reclined in its spacious interior. Several maidens poured warm perfumed water over his head and shoulders. Flower petals were strewn over bubbling suds, while a harpist launched into a song of welcome. Although he could not understand the language, Cassander sang along, feeling the best he had in days.

The other generals made do with their facilities. When it was time, servants called on the party to take them to the audience hall, where the chief of the town greeted them. Making gifts of horses and chariots, he signed a peace agreement with Alexander. Afterwards, they feasted until late in the evening.

In the morning, the King of Egypt departed, promising to collect his gifts on the way back to Alexandria. It was a cool, fine day as his party turned inland. Leonnatus soon noticed there were no more sea breezes. Instead, the hot sun beat down. Their guides were undaunted. Chatting together in their own dialect, they were perfectly comfortable with their surroundings.

After several hours, the Macedonians began to realise the desert had no end. Ptolemy decided to address his concern to Alexander. "We should stop, brother."

"There's no shade anywhere."

"We need to rest."

"But, Ptolemy, the guides are perfectly happy to continue. They must know when to halt."

"They're used to this heat. We aren't."

The party stopped. Quickly, Cassander pulled out two linen head scarfs from his satchel. He wrapped his head with one piece of linen, so it fell about his shoulders. When he had finished, he went to Leonnatus.

"What's this, Cassie?"

"Take your sun hat off."

Reluctantly, Leonnatus did as he was told. Cassander deftly wrapped his friend's head with a piece of linen. He stood back. Leonnatus touched the folds.

"It feels light," he remarked.

"It will trap the breezes when we ride."

After the lunch stop, Alexander was keen to be on his way. They rode for several more hours until sunset. The guides found a rock shelf under which they encamped. Taking acacia twigs from panniers, they built a fire. As was their custom, the Macedonians broached the wine supplies.

"Don't drink too much, Leo," Cassander said in a low voice.

"Are you my wife, now?"

"I was privy to some information during my bath."

"You had a bath?"

"With pretty maidens."

Leonnatus' eyes bulged. "I only had cold water from a bucket."

"You pay for what you get. Now, listen carefully. The sun robs us of liquid."

"That's why I'm replenishing my fluids."

"Wine will rob you of the water in your body. Those ladies told me a thing or two about how to survive out here."

Philotas was already drunk. His head popped up from behind Meleager and Craterus.

"Did you bathe with maidens or scientists?" he slurred.

"Neither," said Cassander. He drew closer to Leonnatus. "Drink as much water as you can tonight."

He left his friend to sit by the fire with the guides.

***

<h1 style="text-align:center">125.</h1>

The sun beat down for three more days. The Macedonians ran out of water. It did not occur to them to cease drinking wine at night. Hung over and thirsty, the party continued through the burning sands. Free of any headaches, Cassander looked for a solution. Scanning the horizon, he sighed. And noticed something.

Urging his tired stallion forward, he drew up alongside Ptolemy. "Tell the men to get all our containers out of the saddlebags."

"Why?"

"Rain is on its way."

Tilting back his broad-brimmed hat, Ptolemy's surprise was obvious.

"You're suffering from sunstroke, Cassie!" Philotas jeered.

Cassander balled one fist, but kept his voice calm as he addressed Ptolemy.

"You'd be wise to advise it," he said.

"Alright, but only for you, Lord Cassander."

The party halted and Ptolemy organised all the pots and utensils for the expedition to be brought out. Just as they finished putting out the last pot, a squall of rain hit the party. Drenching the sands within minutes, the rain was accompanied by lightning. Thunder boomed overhead.

"Get off your horses," Alexander ordered.

"Hold the containers!" Ptolemy yelled.

Cassander held out an open waterskin. The wind howled around his shoulders, whipping his linen headgear. Through a series of loops around his head, it stayed on.

"Do the same as me, Leo," he advised.

Leonnatus drew extra cloth from his headdress around his face and wedged it into the folds. Strong winds blew around his ears. He bent his head and shut his eyes. Rain fell in stinging icy sheets. Streams of water rushed across the dry dunes and flooded the landscape.

Alexander held onto his faithful horse and prayed to Zeus.

***

After the rainstorm, the sun came out, and the desert was as hot as before. At the campfire that night, Cassander kept up his regimen of water with only two cups of wine. Leonnatus followed his example.

Philotas drank as if he had never seen wine before. Alexander told stories, mainly from the *Iliad*, while Hephaestion and Ptolemy listened. Meleager and Craterus entertained themselves with bawdy jokes.

Moving to where the guides sat, Cassander offered them fruit. He struck up a conversation, in which he tried to elicit information on the remaining distance to Siwa and the upcoming terrain.

Later, he watched the stars. Huge as pomegranates, they hung so close he felt he could reach out his hand and pluck them out of the night sky. A twig fire burned steadily through the hours of darkness, casting flickering orange light across the rocks under which they camped.

After a fitful sleep, the Macedonians started out again. And hit trouble.

***

126.

It was hotter than usual. Even the guides were lost. Sands glimmered with the promise of water. But when the men drew close, they found only more sand, stretching away to the horizon.

At the front of the party, Alexander appeared to be progressing in a straight line. Too tired to talk, the rest followed. By noon, they were exhausted. The sun beat down in relentless waves. Neither Cassander's, nor Leonnatus' headgear, provided sufficient relief.

Eventually, they found a rocky escarpment, under which there was some shade. Alexander squatted next to Hephaestion.

"Do you think we're getting closer to Siwa, Heph, or further away?"

"Alex, even the guides don't know."

"They're useless. I should execute the lot of them."

"They speak the language of Siwa. We need those men."

Meleager and Craterus drank from the same waterskin. They exchanged a few words and fell silent. Philotas sat with his back against the rock. His head hung down. Its wide overhang sheltered him, but there was no relief from the heat.

Ptolemy sat apart from the others. His eyes scanned the sky. "Great Zeus, we have a destiny," he whispered in prayer. "Help us."

Cassander mopped his face. "I need another bath, Leo."

"You must tell me how you managed it in that place."

Philotas perked up. "Yes, do!"

Ignoring him, Cassander drank more water. He handed Leonnatus a juicy pomegranate.

"Did I hear you had a bath?" Alexander asked.

"Indeed, he did," said Leonnatus. "With women."

Meleager and Craterus inched forward.

"Tell us more," said Meleager.

"We're about to perish of heat out here," said Alexander. "Take our minds off death."

Cassander rubbed his snub nose. "There's no secret. I pay."

"You're wise," said Ptolemy. "Your last memory will be of being pampered by young ladies in perfumed water. Not even mighty Pharaoh has that."

"True," said Alexander, laughing.

"And might I say, well done," Craterus added.

Suddenly, Ptolemy saw it. He was on his feet, pointing at the sky. "Birds!"

"That means Siwa's near," Cassander said, scrambling to his feet.

Rising, the others tilted their necks back to watch the birds. They were heading in a different direction to that of the party.

"We veered left," Alexander said. "We need to get back to the road by following them."

Mounting his horse, he cantered in the direction of the birds. Everyone followed.

"Here it is," said Hephaestion, when they reached a faint line.

"Some of it must have been covered by the sand," Craterus remarked.

Jabbering with excitement, the guides bobbed their heads.

"This is it," said Alexander.

With confidence, the party rode ahead.

***

127.

It was mid-afternoon when they reached the outskirts of Siwa. Up ahead, a pool beckoned. The Macedonians threw off their dusty robes and dived in. Beneath them, through transparent waters, uneven rocks resembled coral.

Blue and green flickered through Alexander's eyes as he stood on the edge of the pool. Hephaestion ducked his head under.

"It's fresh water," he announced, "bubbling up from a spring."

"That is why it is called the Spring of the Sun," one of the guides explained.

"What did I tell you, Alex?" said Hephaestion. "These men are useful, after all."

Ptolemy settled at the rim and kicked his feet. Cassander stripped off and plopped into the water. He gasped. Like most Macedonians, he could not swim, and the water was deep.

"Paddle!" Meleager and Craterus chorused.

"Yes, paddle Fatty," Philotas chimed in.

Ptolemy's eyebrows raised. A shadow crossed Alexander's face. Leaning over the edge of the wall surrounding the spring, Leonnatus reached out his hand. Cassander grasped it, and pulled himself to the edge, where he could hold on to the wall.

"There are steps over here, Cassie. You can climb out."

"I'm fine. It's refreshing. Did you hear that pillock, Philotas?"

"No," Leonnatus lied.

Cassander's eyes narrowed as he watched Parmenion's son dive and splash about. The rascal could even swim.

After an hour, the Companions climbed out of the pool. Taking fresh clothes out of their packs, they changed. Feeling clean for

538

the first time since setting out, they snacked on goat's cheese, bread and dates.

Eventually, the party headed down the road to the township of Siwa. The sun was shining brightly in a clear blue sky. Trees lined the route. Up ahead, a startling patch of green palms, surrounded by water, greeted their eyes. In its centre stood a compact citadel of white-washed mudbrick. There were no people in the streets.

Hephaestion shaded his eyes. "They know we're coming."

Alexander and his men proceeded with caution. Tethering their horses under an awning by a closed shop, the visitors made their way through the long narrow streets between the houses.

Up ahead, perched on a hill, a stone sanctuary beckoned. In solemn silence, the fair-haired young king approached. Suddenly, at the sanctuary door, priests greeted him in Greek. One of them held a papyrus scroll.

"Welcome, Son of Zeus."

Stunned that his question had already been answered, Alexander thanked the priest, took the scroll, and listened to a brief prayer. He ended his visit by bowing his head for a blessing.

Leaving the dark sanctuary, lit only by oil lamps where the gold statue of Amun lived, Alexander emerged into the daylight a new man. Exultation lifted his heart. Smiling, he grasped Hephaestion's arm. They made their way to where the others waited.

***

Leaving Egypt, Alexander went on to conquer Persia. At thirty-two, he was master of the known world. At thirty-three he was dead.

No one knows the cause. His successors warred for forty years over the empire he created. After his death, Seleucus formed the great Seleucid empire. Ptolemy became Pharaoh of Egypt, married Thais, and began the great Ptolemaic dynasty.

Cassander became King of Macedonia, but not before Alexander fulfilled his promise to put his head into a wall.

However, that is another story.

***

Epilogue

Standing at a wooden rail, Alexander felt high above the earth, but close enough to see it.

"What a wonderful place!" he exclaimed.

Holding a goblet of wine, Hephaestion moved to the rail. He checked the forest below.

"Are you going back to your funeral, Alex?"

"I want to see what happened."

"Leave this, cousin. We have a different life now."

"They fought over my empire, Hephaestion."

"Does it matter? It's gone now, and we're here."

"I thought we would be on Mount Olympus with all the gods."

Hephaestion sipped his wine. "The Greek gods were a demanding lot. It's best to be free of them."

Alexander followed his cousin inside, where he threw himself on a couch. "I *am* very glad you are here, Heph. Your death before mine broke me."

"Poison will do that."

The sight of a bearded man the pair had grown accustomed to, entered the room. "Are you still grumbling, Alexander?"

"Not at all, Lord. This place is wonderful."

"Time moves differently here. You will find you have been bemoaning your death for thousands of earth years."

Hephaestion chuckled. "And I have been listening all that time."

Alexander looked into the bearded man's eyes. "Lord, I wonder if it was all for nothing."

"You have a legacy." With that, the man vanished.

"I wanted to ask Him where the other Companions were," the Macedonian king sighed.

"You already know," Hephaestion pointed out.

With an involuntary shudder Alexander reached for a goblet. The drink was pleasant. Looking into it he saw gold as if it was air, and yet somehow, liquid. Suddenly, he was struck with a revelation.

"It was the wine, wasn't it?"

***

Biography

Sharon Janet Hague is a lawyer and writer with an interest in ancient Egypt. Holding a master's degree in Egyptology from the University of Manchester, she pens articles for various publications.
For more on the author, you may visit her website at:
https://sharonjanethague.com

***